I0589608

WHAT WAKES THE HEART

Karen A. Wyle

Oblique Angles Press
Published in the United States of America
ISBN 9780998060460

Cover design by Kelly Martin of KAM Design

Author photograph by Holy Smoke Photography
Title page art adapted from Shutterstock image
by Karen A. Wyle

Dedication

To my brilliant and indomitable mother.

Chapter 1

St. Louis, MO
June 1883

SUSANNAH was greatly tempted to skip down
the road like a child as she approached the imposing
front steps of William Simmons Normal School. That
urge had never come over her any of the other times
she'd walked there, all the days of the weeks and
months she had studied so hard to obtain her teacher's
certificate. But only last Saturday, she had lined up with
the other sixteen girls in her class, looked President
Brecker in the eye almost like an equal, and accepted
the precious document along with his congratulations.

And as she turned to go, he had tapped her arm and
said quietly, with a smile that said they were friends
sharing a secret, "Come see me on Monday afternoon,
Susannah. I may have some good news for you."

When she told Pa, he'd beamed at her and said, "Only
the beginning of the good things in store for you, I'm
certain." And Ma had smiled for the first time in days,
some of the lines in her forehead smoothing away.

With all things coming together as she'd planned, a
weight of worry — no, fear, fear of failing, fear of
disappointing Ma and Pa and herself — had lifted, and her
very feet felt lighter for it.

But she kept to a ladylike pace, walking steadily and
with her spine as straight as Ma's had once been. She was

glad of it when she saw the trim, dapper figure of Charles

Elliott approaching. He tipped his newly brushed hat and said, in his usual cultured tones, "Good afternoon, Miss Shepard. I hope I find you well? You certainly appear to be in good health and spirits."

She hoped she didn't blush at the personal nature of the observation. She could not deny that the idea of his scrutiny, and its apparent result, brought her some pleasure. "I am very well, thank you, and hope you are the same. Please don't think me rude, but I have an appointment and mustn't delay."

He gave a slight but graceful bow and tipped his hat once more. "I wish you a most fruitful appointment, Miss Shepard. Until next we meet."

He went on his way and she hers, allowing the encounter to bring a smile to her lips, until she reached the school building and mounted the steps one more time. It need not be the last time — she might visit, as other alumnae had done during her time there, to encourage the girls and tell the professors all they had accomplished since graduation.

The walls of the hallway bore student attempts, and more successful teacher efforts, to reproduce famous paintings, including several Vermeer works showing women engaged in various artistic pursuits. She paused in front of *The Music Lesson* to remove her bonnet and smooth her hair.

President Brecker's office awaited her at the end of the hall. She had seen it so often, but had she ever entered it? She had never been called there to be scolded or warned, like some of the others. Indeed, though she had tried not to let it inspire improper pride, the president had lately made a point of encouraging her, even praising her diligence and her suitability for the teaching profession.

What good news might be waiting behind that door?

She knocked, her breath coming short as she strained to hear any word from within. Almost at once, the door opened, and there he stood, smiling broadly, his gold tooth glinting. "Susannah, my dear! Come in and sit down. You may hang your bonnet on the peg."

The suggestion further buoyed her spirits. Clearly Mr. Brecker had not invited her simply for a short social call, but had matters to discuss that would take some time. She would like nothing better than to follow his instructions, but he had hardly left room for her to enter. She searched for the words to say as much, but in a moment he stepped back enough for her to get by. Once she had hung up her bonnet as instructed, he waved her toward the chair at one side of his desk, then walked around behind her toward his own. Something brushed her hair as he went by. His waistcoat? But it had been buttoned snugly around his midriff.

Mr. Brecker sat down, the springs in his chair squeaking under him, and leaned toward her. "As I told you on Saturday, I have some news that should be welcome — though not surprising, for such an able scholar as yourself." He paused, looking at her intently, and cleared his throat before he went on. "You may recall that my own sister is in charge of an excellent school in this very city, a school much prized by parents, to the point where they are happy to pay the fees necessary to maintain its quality and keep its facilities in good condition. There is rarely a vacancy among its staff, for none leave without pressing need, but it just so happens that one of the instructors is shortly to be married and will be departing."

He paused again. Was he waiting for her to express

interest? Her interest must be obvious. But she asked, as he appeared to wish, "How is this instructor to be replaced?"

He studied her, for what purpose she could not guess. "While the final decision will of course be my sister's, she is naturally inclined to rely on my judgment. If I recommend you to her, I am confident your acceptance — and your future — will be assured."

He would hardly have called her here and given her this news if he did not mean her to have the post. But he had not yet said as much. What remained for her to do or to say? "Indeed, sir, I would be very happy and grateful if you see fit to recommend me."

He leaned back in his chair, pushed it a little ways back from the desk, and licked his lips. "Come here, my dear."

She wrinkled her forehead, an action which suddenly reminded her of the lines in her mother's face. "Sir, I am not sure what you mean."

He stood up, passed behind her again, and shut the door. Then he came back and stood next to her chair, holding out his hand. "Your gratitude is to your credit. Gratitude is a virtue we teachers prize, when we have done well by our pupils." As she sat looking up at him, he leaned down and picked up her right hand, pulling her upward. His hand felt warm and surprisingly soft. "I know you must be anxious to express it."

Once before, or it might have been twice, Susannah had noticed men in the streets following her with their eyes, looking at her with something between need and greed, something ugly. It had made her walk faster to leave them behind. Mr. Brecker's eyes held that look now. He pulled harder on her hand.

Susannah rose out of her chair — and moved away,

tugging her hand free of his grasp. "Mr. Brecker, I would of course be grateful for any assistance you give me, so long as it is based on my merits. When would it be possible for me to meet your sister?"

He seized her hand again and pulled hard, so that her bosom pressed against his broad chest. "My dear, your maidenly reserve does you credit. But you must trust me to do what is best for you, to guide you." He slid two fingers into her hair and drew out a strand. "So fine a color. I have always favored dark hair. And yours, my dear, shines like a blackbird's wing. And your eyes are as green as the fields of heaven."

She could feel the blood blazing in her cheeks as she shoved herself free. She must say something, but what could she possibly say? Had she misunderstood? But what could he possibly mean, but what it seemed?

She looked back at him, hoping to see confusion, or even hurt. But it was anger that narrowed his eyes and tightened his mouth.

Susannah backed away until she could feel the doorknob in her hands. Then she spun around, grabbed her bonnet with one shaking hand, yanked open the door, and ran down the hall, like a child running from some dread thing.

She had wanted to skip, on her way to the school. It felt like a memory from a dream. Now, she found herself dragging her feet as she walked toward home.

In the moments it took for her to step onto the porch and open the front door, her parents had come to their feet, standing close together, their faces just beginning to light with expectation. Whatever the look on her own face, it was enough to extinguish that light. Her father cocked his head, puzzled and concerned; her mother, quicker to assume misfortune, went pale.

Susannah walked to the kitchen table, not looking left or right, and fell into a chair. She hid her face in her hands and then felt her father's strong, wiry hands resting on her shoulders. "Tell us what happened, my girl."

She waited to hear her mother sit down before she let her hands fall to her lap and told the tale, looking down at the table. She looked up when she heard her mother hiss, and felt Pa's hands clutching tighter. "That son of a bitch," he said in a low, savage growl. "I'll go over there and take him apart."

Susannah couldn't remember her father ever threatening violence, let alone taking violent action. She had no way to weigh the chance of it, except that some instinct told her that threats so rarely uttered had more real intent behind them. Ma seemed to agree. She shot out of her chair and ran around the table, grabbing Pa's arm. "Philip, you can't! People listen to him. He can ruin the paper with a word, and get you arrested as well!"

Pa let go of Susannah's shoulders and let Ma lead him to a chair, while Susannah pondered just how bleak things had become. "Even if Pa does nothing — Mr. Brecker was angry when I refused him. And a man who would act like that . . . he'll be spiteful enough to ruin my prospects, at least. If he doesn't outright slander me in some way, he'll at least make sure I can't get a teaching job anywhere in this county or the next."

She closed her eyes as she gathered the strength to go on. "Pa, I can help you with the paper now. It was good of you not to ask it of me when I was busy with school, but now . . . ."

She expected anything but the taut silence that greeted her surrender. She opened her eyes and searched

Pa's face. She knew that look. It meant something had been kept from her, to spare her, or to spare Pa from putting trouble into words. Meeting her eyes, he forced a smile. "You'd be a great help, at that. We'll talk about it later." And he went out the back door to the porch, feeling for his pipe in his waistcoat pocket.

Ma sat down, more heavily than Susannah was used to seeing. Susannah swallowed and asked, "What wasn't Pa telling me?"

Ma shifted about in her chair. "Pa gets tired sooner than he used to. If . . . if your big brother had lived, he'd likely be taking over much of the work."

And her younger brother Ned was too restless and wild to be an ideal replacement. But something wasn't adding up. "Then why was he . . . e*vasive* about my helping?"

Ma didn't answer.

"What else is going on? Please! I'll have to know eventually." She moved her chair closer to Ma and clasped both Ma's hands in both of hers.

Ma finally sat up, straightening her spine, and said dully, "If it was just the work getting to him, of course he'd want you to help, as much as he'd rather you had the future you've wanted. But . . . the paper hasn't been doing well lately. There's been so much competition in the news business. . . . Trying to outlast the other papers drained our reserves. If things don't improve, we'll need more money coming in from somewhere."

Susannah hadn't yet cried, but she could feel the tears coming. "You were, you both were, counting on Mr. Brecker offering me something with good pay."

Ma's eyes grew shiny as well. "And now, I don't know what's next. Ned may have to leave school, not that he'll mind that so much, and apprentice himself somewhere. The butcher we use has been saying he could use someone. Pa will be asking around for someone else who might. Or he could try another town." Her eyes had dried, but the worry showed in them.

If Susannah knew Ned, what he'd want would be far from St. Louis, hacking through wilderness or breaking wild horses. Right this minute, he was probably out in the woods setting traps for squirrels or rabbits, or pretending he was finding his way through untracked wilderness out West. Which was far from holding a job and meeting an employer's obligations. But he'd try, if the family's need pressed hard enough. Ned alone far from home, sure he could handle things, would be easy prey for anyone seeking to take advantage of his ignorance. It was a frightening prospect for a mother. Or a sister.

But something Ma had just said was trying to come back to her as an idea. What was it?

Try another town.

Mr. Brecker's spite might reach to the next county, but the world didn't end there, nor even at the state line. There would be other teaching jobs — more all the time, as people pushed ever westward. And the school's reputation —

No. If she mentioned the school, anyone thinking of hiring her would write to its president.

But she could try. She could list her attainments, at least.

What would Ma and Pa say? Pa would hate to see her leave. Ma wouldn't like it much better, but she would understand the need.

And what about Charles Elliott? Should the thought of him even give her pause, when they had barely spoken other than in company? It made no sense, with the cold fact of her family's situation confronting her, to let her girlish daydreams interfere with her duty.

The idea might come to nothing. But Susanna could place an ad, at least, and see what happened.

Chapter 2

Cowbird Creek, NE

JOSHUA and Clara walked in their front door arm in arm, with Joshua leaning on Clara a little more than the reverse. It had been a long day for their medical practice, made more intense at the end by the fear — thankfully not realized — that they would have to amputate a young girl's hand. The walk home had been barely long enough to let Joshua's heart slow and his breath grow even.

As they walked in, Alice jumped off her grandma's lap, the seven-year-old embodiment of energy and impatience, and ran to hug them around the knees. Joshua had just time enough to brace himself and keep from staggering. He reached down to loosen Alice's hands, then hoisted her into his arms. "Good evening, lambkin! Have you been keeping your grandma company?"

Clara's mother smiled up at him wearily — understandable, given the hour and the strain of keeping up with Alice all day. "She has, and minded me well the whole time."

Joshua suspected that report erred on the side of generosity, but if Alice had been particularly difficult, Mrs. Brook would probably have hinted at such.

Clara's mother said her goodbyes and left to walk home. Alice waved goodbye to her energetically enough that Joshua had to tighten his grip on her, and gave Joshua a smacking kiss on the cheek before wriggling to be let down again. He had a guess as to what she wanted next, and he was right — she ran out of the room and ran back in with a book. It was one he and Clara had bought for her birthday, *The Vagabonds and Other Poems*. She stopped in front of him and bounced on her toes, waving it back and forth. "Read with me!"

Not *read to me*, not any more. Could anyone but a parent know that bittersweet pang of mingled pride and loss? A teacher, perhaps, one who cared deeply about his or her pupils. Which led to another thought he needed to discuss with Clara.

In the meantime, he sat in the big rocking chair by the fire, a lamp on the little table on the other side, and patted his lap. Alice clambered up, just managing not to whap him on the nose with the book, and nestled comfortably against him. He made sure she was settled and opened the book to one of their favorites of the poems, laying it across both their laps. "'The Vagabonds.' We are two travelers, Roger and I. Roger's my dog . . . ."

Alice insisted on reading one line in four on the first page, but soon subsided into comfortable listening. As Jacob had expected, it only took two pages for Alice's dark head to fall forward and a little to the side. Her back against his chest moved in the slowed rhythm of her breathing, and he could barely hear her soft little snores. Clara had been sitting across from them; she got up and slid the book away without waking the sleeper, leaving Joshua to rise and carry Alice to the little room they had added onto the back of the house. The blankets were folded at the foot of the bed, to make the next operation easier. As Joshua lowered Alice onto the bed, Clara raised the blankets and tucked the child in, her hand lingering on Alice's shoulder. Joshua fetched Alice's rag doll from
the foot of the bed and laid it on the pillow, where Alice

could see it if she woke up in the night.

They walked softly out of the room and repaired to the sitting room. Joshua hesitated near the sideboard where they kept the bottle of whiskey, rarely touched these days except to offer to company. Clara came to his side and put an arm around him. "Are you troubled? I might have a guess as to why."

He steered them from the sideboard to the settee, staying close to Clara so she could maintain the embrace as they sat down. "You saw how eager she was for us to read together. And how little we managed of it."

Clara leaned her head on his shoulder. The warm burden of it eased his spirit, as she must have known it would. She took in his words and replied, "She ran to you to be with you as much as for the book's sake, or more."

"I know. But she ran for the book, directly afterward. She's reading remarkably well for her age. And the number of questions she asks, and the range of them, makes clear how bright she is. I would delight in undertaking her education, as I expect you would, but unless our practice fails to an extent that would make it hard to care for her, I foresee no time when we will have the leisure to teach her properly."

He knew, and knew Clara knew, that he could manage without her expert assistance as a nurse if he had no choice. But they both knew, as well, the greater toll the work would take on him if he did so — especially if, God forbid, a case arose where the lack of her aid affected the outcome. On those days where they both bided at home until called for, they could devote that time to teaching Alice, or attempt it. But the lack of a predictable routine, and the inevitable random interruptions, would much reduce the value of such efforts.

Clara sat up and turned toward him. "Why does

Cowbird Creek not have a school? I half expected it would, even when I moved here."

Had the thought occurred to Joshua before he had a child of his own? Perhaps when he saw a child in his practice, one whose mother despaired of restraining the son or daughter's constant questions and explorations. What he did not recall noting, at any time, was an answer to his next question. "Who in town would make a good teacher? A poor teacher who suppressed the children's curiosity instead of making use of it – or a teacher who used such harsh discipline that the pupils associated learning with pain and confinement rather than excitement or pleasure — would surely be worse than no teacher at all."

Clara cocked her head and raised an eyebrow, rather like a teacher expecting more of her student. "You may recall, perhaps, that it is possible for people to come to Cowbird Creek from elsewhere. You might even think you have observed the fact, and benefited thereby."

At that, of course, he had to interrupt their discussion to kiss her. But before he could follow the kiss with anything more, a memory intruded. He had been waiting at the counter of the general store, a few days since, and passing the time by glancing through the copy of the *Omaha Daily Bee* that lay on the counter. He had flipped past the page full of advertisements, idly noting the variety of inquiries and offers.

He pulled away slightly and said, breathless, "Please be so good as to remind me, later or tomorrow, to work on an advertisement we could place, to seek a suitable teacher for a school in Cowbird Creek."

Clara smiled, stood, and took his hand to lead him to their bedroom.

* * * * *

St. Louis, MO

Susannah had not thought to rehearse what response she would make to friends and acquaintances who congratulated her on her teacher's certificate. That achievement felt hollow, this morning, but she did her best to smile and thank them without revealing as much. Then there were those she knew slightly, or not at all, who looked at her oddly, with coldness or a smirk that suggested knowledge of some unfavorable secret. Unless she was imagining it, as she fervently hoped.

She could not, of course, place an ad in Pa's paper — not if she meant to keep her efforts from her parents until, or unless, they bore fruit. But she felt the worst sort of traitor as she opened the door to the offices of the St. Louis Post-Dispatch and heard its cheery little bell announce her presence.

The clerk at the counter looked up and smiled at her. If he knew who she was, he gave no sign of it. But his look lingered in a way she would hardly have noticed a week ago. She lifted her chin and handed him the fair copy of her much-rewritten advertisement. No one reading it would know, she trusted, the hours it had taken to produce it, writing and crumpling one draft after another, some of the ink smeared with the tears she had shed.

The clerk read through the copy, muttering the words as he did so. "Teacher, holder of a certificate . . . language, geography, history, mathematics, morals deportment . . . mature and responsible . . . Available to travel . . . . Very good, miss. But you should say how those interested are to respond to you."

Of course. As the daughter of a newspaper man, she should have thought of that. She must guard against emotional distraction and the errors into which it could lead her. It meant more words and a greater cost, but there was no help for it.

She tightened her lips and fought the urge to turn tail and run out of the office. Had she even brought enough coin? She fished out her coin purse and counted. Before she could finish, the clerk drew her attention by clearing his throat. His offhand professional manner had been replaced by some sort of uncertainty, and he moved as if, behind the counter, he was shifting his weight from foot to foot. "I shouldn't . . . that is . . . before I take your ad, you might want to see this." He pushed a copy of a different newspaper across the counter, folded to the pages of ads, and tapped one section of it before pulling back his hand.

Teacher desired for new school, under construction. Small friendly town. Must be able to teach all branches of modern education. Pupils up to age 15. Reply by ad or telegram to Dr. J. Gibbs, Cowbird Creek.

There was no mention of references — but that might come later.

She could reply with an ad, and might owe the helpful clerk that return favor. But in how many papers had "Dr. Gibbs" placed this ad? It would ensure he saw the response, and most promptly, if she used a telegram instead. So she gave the clerk a grateful smile, retrieved her copy, and left to find a peaceful place to write her reply.

A reply that would make its way to Cowbird Creek, wherever that might be.

* * * * *

Cowbird Creek

Karol Marek, known to people in Cowbird Creek as

Carl, decided that hauling sacks of flour for almost an hour was long enough for a break. He could stretch his back, at least. And the miller was deep in talk with two customers, their wagons already loaded, and wasn't likely to argue about it.

Stretching felt so good that the relief was all he thought about until he was through. Then, as he was about to get back to work, some of the miller's conversation caught Karol's ear. What was that about a school? A new school just being built?

His first thought was that he might be able to pick up some of the construction work, before and after mill hours. He and his father were the only ones bringing in money, and Bronka was growing out of her skirts and shoes.

Which led to his second thought, and it should have been the first. Bronka had always loved to read, even as a little girl. Not only storybooks, but books about history, about other countries, anything she could find in their grandfather's library. She had been so grateful when he gave her a Polish translation of collected Shakespeare plays, fresh from the bookshop; and so afraid when it seemed the book might be too heavy for them to bring. Karol and his father had left their spare pairs of shoes behind, to make room.

Could Bronka go to this school? Would it be allowed — a girl, and a foreigner?

One of the customers talking to the miller was the doctor, who had a little girl of his own. Karol moved closer and listened harder. Dr. Gibbs was saying something about the school board, inviting the miller to join it. He would hardly be on the school board if his own daughter was kept out.

"Mayor Pomfrey has agreed to join us . . . ."

The doctor, the mayor, the miller . . . . Dr. Gibbs might not be rich — he dressed plain enough, except for his boots — but all of them were among the higher class in Cowbird Creek. Would the children of workers like Karol and his father be welcome?

Too, there was the question of Bronka's English. It had got better, of course, in the five years since they arrived in America, but she spent most of her time at home with their mother, speaking nothing but Polish, and so she could not speak English as well as Karol could. On the other hand, going to school would give her the chance to get better.

He would talk to Mama about it when he got home. And now he'd better get back to hauling sacks.

Mama bustled about the kitchen, getting supper ready for Karol and his father. She and Bronka had eaten before either of the men arrived. Bronka had taken herself off somewhere, which made it a good time to tell his parents — in Polish, of course — about the school, and ask what they thought.

Papa stroked his beard as he listened, forgetting to eat. "Our Bronka would love to go to school. But we shouldn't tell her about it until we're sure she could go."

"Eat, eat!" Mama hated to let food get cold, now that he and Papa had saved up enough to buy her a proper stove. "What does the girl need school for? I never had time for such a thing."

Papa took a big bite, chewed it up, swallowed, and smiled fondly at her. "You wed me when you were fourteen, and had been telling your family for years before that you would marry me some day. But Bronka is not so much like either of us. She reminds me of your father, with all his books."

A picture popped into Karol's head of Bronka holding her big Shakespeare book, sitting in the easy chair and smoking their grandfather's pipe. He choked back a laugh. Mama narrowed her eyes at him and said stubbornly, "She can worry about school when I've taught her everything she'll need to know to take proper care of a husband and a house."

"*School?*" Bronka burst into the room, waving the dishcloth she must have been mending. "There's going to be a *school*? And girls can go to it? Oh, what a wonderful place we've come to!"

Karol put up his hands as if to hold back her eagerness. "They haven't finished building it. They may not even have a teacher yet."

Bronka ran around to where Papa sat and caught hold of his arm. "Please, please let me go to school! I'll wait as patiently as ever you could ask, if I can only go when it opens." She let go and spun around to face Mama. "And I'll be so much help to you, before and after school, you won't be sorry!"

Mama got that look that told Karol more than she realized about what it was like to be a parent — the worry and the love. "You're already much help, *córeczka*. I just hope this school could be all you expect. So little in life turns out the way we expect it to."

Papa grinned. "Marriage, for example, is much more annoying than anyone told Mama ahead of time."

Mama reached over and swatted his knee.

It had been a clear day after two rainy ones, and some light lingered. Karol had not eaten so much for supper that he needed to walk it off, but walking might quiet his mind. He should be able to get to the creek before sunset, and the water might wash away some of his worry.

As he got close, dots of yellow caught his eye, and his heart sped up for the few seconds it took to remember. The bright yellow globe flowers he had known as a boy, playing by the stream near the village, didn't grow here. A few more strides showed him the evening primrose, open to the fading light, not curled tight as the globe flowers would have been.

There were days when America and Cowbird Creek felt almost like home. But not today.

* * * * *

Joshua set the latest letter down on the counter where Clara was updating their inventory of medicines. Once he had her attention, he said, "It appears we have a teacher."

Clara looked up and studied him. "Do you still have doubts? I have tolerably few."

Did he, in fact? Clara had, for the most part, dispelled the one that had most troubled him. He sat down, put his hat on his lap, stuck out his legs, and said, "Her lack of references still makes me uneasy. But you're quite right that at this distance, we have little way to assess such, be they the most fulsome of encomiums or outright slander or anything between."

Now came her smile. "And if I know the man I was so astute as to marry, his ideas of how a teacher should comport herself and what priorities she should bring to her post will not necessarily be the most common. How did you persuade the other school board members to overlook her lack of references?"

Joshua grimaced. "My initial attempts were met with enough opposition that I ceased arguing with them and let their impatience work for me. We've had no other applicants in all the time the ads have been running. Apparently, trained teachers from cities and larger towns have little appetite for the challenges to be faced in the first school in an unknown place."

He knew he must sound discouraged, from Clara's putting her hand over his and applying a reassuring pressure. She said in a quiet, soothing tone, "I found Miss Shepard's letters well written. She has a good vocabulary, but did not unnecessarily flaunt it. And she answered your questions in what I would call a forthright manner."

Joshua suppressed a smile. That would naturally be a quality of which Clara approved. He did wonder, however, how Miss Shepard would respond if he asked her why she had no references to show — or at least, had not made a point of providing any.

Perhaps, as they came to know her better, he would ask, and she would answer, that question.

Chapter 3

SUSANNAH looked out at the late summer landscape, concealed a yawn of fatigue behind her hand, and gave thanks for how smoothly her travels had gone. Pa had at first insisted that he would accompany her, but Ma had drawn him aside, speaking to him with the high pitch of worry in her voice, and he had reluctantly conceded. Ma must have been reminding him how much he was needed at the paper as he struggled to keep it afloat. Susannah herself had opposed Pa's next suggestion, that Ned escort her instead. They would be paying for his travel not only to Cowbird Creek but home again, at a time when every penny was precious. And what mischief might befall him on the journey home, with no sister to look after, and no doubt feeling very satisfied with himself after discharging his duty?

Her parents had instead assuaged their anxiety by flooding her with advice. And indeed, she was fortunate that they had, years before, traveled by train. She had not known how little she knew when it came to train travel. Which was, come to think of it, a principle she needed to ponder, as applicable to everything from teaching, to the subjects she would teach, to arriving in a new town and dealing with strangers.

To start with, she would be unpleasantly hungry by now but for Ma's warning that not all routes included dining cars, and that dining in such cars could be expensive; also, that when the train pulled into a station, there might not be enough time for all the travelers to make it through the lines for vendors selling sandwiches and the like. Beef jerky, increasingly stale bread, and dried fruit might not please the palate, but they had sustained her well enough through the long and uncomfortable journey. And now, as the light outside the train, when it showed through the smoke from the engine, took on the gold of late afternoon, she had not too much longer to wait before she arrived.

Pa had warned her to keep her valuables in her traveling case rather than her trunk, in case some inattentive — or drunk — porter unloaded it at the wrong station. At least she was wearing the best dress and shoes that could hold up to traveling. She couldn't know whether whichever member of the school board met her train would care about her attire, but at least she would not have poor dress as an additional reason to be self-conscious. Or nervous.

She had enough to be nervous about without that detail — though being nervous might be a pleasant change from being homesick. Except that somehow, she seemed to be enduring both feelings at once.

She leaned back against the seat and closed her eyes, hoping she might be able to nap. Surely the chugging of the engine, the clicking of the railway ties, could lull her to sleep. That steady rhythm . . .

. . . reminded her of watching a steamboat recede down the Mississippi River, its big red paddle wheel going round and round, churning the water into a wide wake, while up on the deck carefree people in white linen and straw hats listened to the music of a brass band, the sun winking off its instruments . . . .

She fished for her handkerchief, wiped her eyes, and almost jumped to hear a knock at the entrance to the car. Hastily she picked up her book, abandoned on her lap, and called up a smile as a well-dressed gentleman peeked in. He hesitated, looking at her intently, before saying, "I beg your pardon. The travelers in the car I occupied previously are filling it with enough smoke that I began to find it hard to read. May I intrude?"

Susannah gestured to the bench across from her. "Of course! And it's a pleasure to meet a fellow reader. What are you reading?"

The man reached into the small satchel he was carrying and produced a new-looking copy of Finney's *Sermons on Gospel Themes*. "I find train travel lends itself to contemplative reading matter."

Susannah could not help but find it faintly disappointing that the gentleman had not chosen something purely literary. It might have been something she'd read, and if not, she could have asked him how well he liked it and whether he would recommend it. She smiled politely and returned to her novel, *Hoosier Schoolmaster*, which she hoped would provide useful (if vicarious) experience as well as entertainment.

She soon forgot her companion, and indeed her surroundings, in the story, though in shifting on the bench to relieve an aching hip, she happened to notice him withdraw a pipe from his waistcoat pocket and then hastily shove it back out of sight. She wondered briefly at the sensitivity that would send a smoker out of a smoke-filled car, but the thought did not occupy her long.

She had reached a rather exciting scene when she noticed a change in the sound of the engine, and then the slowing motion of the view out the window. They must be approaching Cowbird Creek's station. Suddenly, she found it as difficult to breathe as if she were in the smoke-filled car the gentleman had fled.

The small railroad depot at which they were arriving looked as if a simple wooden structure had been updated to resemble a standard design, as a less expensive alternative to new construction. The roof, newer than the building itself, had the steep pitch of the Victorian style, and some white gingerbread trim had been nailed to the tops of the dark red walls. As the squeal of brakes filled her ears and the train came to a stop, her companion stood up and gestured toward the upper shelf on which her case lay. "May I fetch your belongings down for you?"

The offer was more civil than she had been, declining conversation to bury herself in her book. "Thank you very much. That would be most helpful." She expected that he would hand the case to her as soon as he retrieved it, but instead, he gestured for her to precede him out of the car and trotted along behind.

Looking ahead to the platform, she saw a man in perhaps his early forties with brown wavy hair, a neatly trimmed beard, a clean frock coat, and well-polished boots. He caught her eye, smiled in a friendly way, and bowed. That must be Dr. Joshua Gibbs, town doctor, who had placed the ad she had seen. Susannah carefully descended the iron stairs and turned back to thank her fellow passenger and take her case — but in an instant, he had pushed past her, almost knocking her off the bottom stair, and was walking briskly toward the back of the train.

Susannah gasped, which delayed by precious seconds her ability to cry out — but when she could, she outright yelled. "STOP THAT MAN! Please! He took my case!"

Dr. Gibbs, and a portly man who appeared to be

with him, looked around to follow her pointing finger. The fact that her hand was shaking may have made their task more difficult. But a younger man, muscular, who had been helping the porters unload people's trunks, looked up at her shout. He spotted the thief, who was moving more quickly than anyone else on the platform, and ran after him. Susannah watched with her hands clasped tight, still on the bottom step until the conductor sounded the warning whistle. Dr. Gibbs came forward to take her hand and help her down, an attention she would have considered quite unnecessary if she had not been trembling.

Both the thief and the young man disappeared into the crowd. Dr. Gibbs waited with her in considerate silence, but the heavier man chose instead to say heartily, "Welcome to Cowbird Creek, Miss Shepard! As the mayor of this fine municipality, I came here today to welcome you, and to convey the gratitude of all its inhabitants for your willingness to assist us in educating our young people."

Susannah tore her eyes away from the crowd on the platform and managed a smile, though she was glad she couldn't see herself and judge its success. "That is very kind of you, Mr. — Mr. Mayor. I am grateful in my turn for the trust you have placed in me, and I promise to do my utmost to justify it."

But now she had little attention to spare for pleasantries, as the young man walked back, panting a little, with her precious case in his left hand. Susannah reached for it, but Dr. Gibbs was there before her, taking it and saying earnestly to the young man, "I greatly appreciate your assistance, Carl. I would have been most sorry to greet our new schoolteacher while presiding helplessly over the loss of her possessions. Miss Susannah

Shepard, may I make known to you Carl Marek, who works at our local mill and also helped to build your new schoolhouse."

Mr. Marek had a broad face, wheat-blond hair, and short beard, and the most unusual eyes, bright blue and slanted a little upward at the outer corners. His expression had brightened at hearing who she was, or what she was doing in town, and then gone stormy at hearing himself described, before he wiped away the look and stood expressionless. Did he think she would despise him for being a laborer? She put out her hand to shake his. "Thank you so very much, Mr. Marek, for rescuing my case. I thought myself very wise to keep my most valuable belongings close at hand, but clearly I failed to take proper care of them."

Mr. Marek hesitated before he took her hand and shook it firmly. His palm was calloused and tough, his grasp strong. "You're welcome, miss. I was glad to help, and that I managed to catch up with the — the fellow." Susannah wondered what more colorful term he had almost used. She was also curious about the trace of an accent in his speech, as it did not sound like the German intonations with which she was more familiar.

Dr. Gibbs asked him, "Am I correct that the thief managed to escape you? I do not in the least fault you for failing to apprehend him — you kept your focus on the purpose of your intervention, and I am sure Miss Shepard is glad of it."

"Indeed I am," Susannah hurried to say. "I would not have wanted you injured in any struggle that might have resulted, and I am sure such a wretch is capable of anything." She abruptly remembered her trunk, sitting unattended somewhere on the platform. "Do you know where the larger luggage has been unloaded? My trunk is dark green with brass fittings, and has my name on the labels."

"I'll go see about it." Mr. Marek strode off, his long legs making quick work of the distance to the spot where, she now saw, a great heap of trunks had been deposited.

Dr. Gibbs looked toward the pile and said, "If you'll excuse me, Miss Shepard, Mayor, I'll go bring the wagon closer to the trunks. Miss Shepard, would you be so good as to inform Mr. Marek that I'm doing so? He'll know the area I mean."

Susannah looked after Dr. Gibbs as he too walked off, somewhat at a loss. The mayor offered his arm. "May I escort you on this errand?"

She took his arm, and they proceeded at a sedate pace to where Mr. Marek was pulling her trunk out from under two others. Now that she was less flustered, she began to notice her surroundings once again, and what struck her was the air all around her. Even with the lingering smoky odor of the train, it was sweet and unpolluted, as if she were strolling through the rarefied neighborhood of Lafayette Square or the green acres of Forest Park.

As they approached the pile of luggage, Mr. Marek finished extracting her trunk, managing to hold it in his arms until he could place it on the platform. It had taken her father and her brother to load the trunk onto the train, and they had had to stop and set it down once between the wagon and the platform. It must be marvelous to have all that strength at one's command. Her arms felt all the weaker by comparison. Mr. Marek carried the trunk from the platform to a nearby patch of ground and slid it into the back of a wagon. Dr. Gibbs sat on the seat, holding the reins. The mayor, puffing alongside, stopped to catch his breath before saying, "You'll be at Miss Wheeler's boarding house, I understand. A most respectable establishment. I hope you'll come to tea with my wife and I, Miss Shepard, once you've settled in."

"How kind. Thank you very much." She refrained from shaking her head at the man's grammar, and reflected ruefully that if the invitation ever materialized, she would have the choice of wearing the same outfit on that occasion or dressing more simply. It had been foolish to assume that a town this size would have little in the way of occasions requiring a display of fashion.

Mr. Marek still stood nearby. The mayor glanced at the younger man before walking away with his brow furrowed, clearly wondering whether Mr. Marek planned on somehow imposing himself. Susannah had no such fear, but did wonder if he had something to say — perhaps about the school? It was possible, though it seemed unlikely, that he had a child of his own.

Mr. Marek pulled himself up to his full height, cleared his throat, and said stiffly, "I hope I may ask a question of some importance to me before you go your way."

She had been right, after all, and felt not a little smug at having guessed. The feeling lasted only until he asked, "Are you prepared, as a teacher, for pupils whose English is not good?"

In all her study and preparation and imagining, this simple possibility had never crossed her mind. That shortcoming must have been obvious, for the man took a step backward, his expressive face showing both disappointment and disapproval.

Joshua looked down at them. "Carl, could you — " He had probably meant to ask Carl to help Susannah into the wagon, but instead hesitated before sliding over on the seat and stretching his arm out and down. Dumbly, she took his hand in her right, grabbed the seat in her left, and pulled upward. Her skirt caught on some rough spot or protuberance, but fortune smiled on her to the extent that the fabric failed to rip.

Carl tipped his hat, still silent, and walked away. Joshua covered the awkward moment, whose cause he had probably not overheard, with a description of the boarding house to which she was headed. "Miss Wheeler has put in modern plumbing, with the necessary down the hall from your room and a bath with hot and cold running water on the next floor down. Her meals, as I hope you'll find for yourself when you arrive, are excellent — I've had the privilege of eating at her table — and she accepts only genteel boarders. But please don't be afraid to let me know if anything about the arrangement poses any problem."

The plumbing was a welcome surprise. Hotels and many of the wealthier residents of St. Louis had that luxury, as had her college, but her family had only looked forward to such a feature as a goal, a goal currently receding.

Was there any chance the schoolhouse would be similarly equipped? Surely not . . . . She could have asked Mr. Marek about it, since he'd been helping to build it. But she had missed that chance, and from his demeanor as he left, she could not be certain of having another.

Dr. Gibbs was quite right about the food at the boarding house. It was good, and there was plenty of it. Though she had to fight homesickness that threatened to steal her appetite, as she sat down at a table full of strangers.

At least she had no need to come up with topics of conversation, or even to listen much to talk about people and events of which she knew nothing. The other boarders were full of questions about her — where she came from, how much bigger it might be than Cowbird Creek, how she had come to be a schoolteacher, what she planned to teach.

She met with some surprise at the list of subjects. "Geography makes sense," offered the only man at the table, a dinner guest with an easygoing manner and yellow teeth, "for youngsters who may end up going west, or move back east, or wonder where their grandpappies came from. And figuring, they'll need that almost no matter what they do, if'n they don't want folks to cheat 'em. But ain't their parents good enough to teach 'em morals? And what in tarnation is rhetoric?"

She did her best to explain that "rhetoric" was just a name for knowing how to state a position clearly and defend it, which citizens in a democracy should surely be able to do. She added, and emphasized, that her teaching on morals wasn't meant to replace that of parents, but to reinforce it. There was no need, in casual conversation with people she was just getting to know, to enter onto the thorny path of what a teacher might do when parents held, and would seek to perpetuate, the sort of views that the state of Nebraska thought undesirable.

Of course, several of her fellow boarders wanted to know how well she liked Cowbird Creek. She was able to say, honestly, that everyone she had met had been most kind and helpful (declining to mention the thief, who most likely had nothing to do with the town), and that she had had little time to explore and learn about the place, but looked forward to doing so.

What she most looked forward to exploring, of course, was the school itself.

Dr. Gibbs had offered to show it to her, but what if

she found it wanting in some way? It would be better to make that discovery without the presence of one of the men presumably responsible for its design and construction. So after breakfast on her first morning in town, she assembled the maps and charts she planned to display and set forth, having asked Miss Wheeler for directions. She took only one wrong turn on the way. In a town this size, one could not get nearly as lost as one could at home.

She had known the schoolhouse would be small, but knowing and seeing were far from the same. The building could have fit three times over on the first floor of the primary school she had once attended. It was whitewashed and still smelled of sawn wood, the bricks of the front path unworn. There was a belfry, but no bell.

She took a deep breath and mounted the two steps to the front door, only then realizing that she had no key. She tried the knob, and it turned.

The door opened right into the classroom, with no anteroom or hallway. There were, naturally, rows of double desks, with an aisle down the center of the room to divide boys from girls. The aisle became wider halfway between the front and back of the room to accommodate a cast iron stove. The building's insulation must not be up to the task of keeping in enough heat to fill the room were the stove at one end.

She moved forward to examine the big desk at the front of the room, placed to one side of a wall-mounted blackboard atop a platform about ten inches high. The height would let her survey the room, and it was not so great that children standing in front of her would have to look up very far. But she would have to be careful not to trip when she went to and from the desk.

She dropped her maps and charts on the desk to free her hands. Upon closer inspection, the desk didn't look new, but the top had been polished and a new blotter placed on it. The jar of ink at the corner of the desk felt full and had no drips on the outside. Opening the drawers, she saw that the largest was filled with slates and the soapstone pencils for them. She would have expected that most pupils, at least those old enough to have come to school before, would have their own — but of course, if they had lived in Cowbird Creek all their lives, they had had no such opportunity, unless their parents had used slates in their instruction.

Looking around the room brought home to her that a small schoolroom meant less available wall space. With two windows on one wall — with glass, she was relieved to note — and two wall cabinets on the wall opposite, she would have to choose carefully what to display. The map of the continents and countries should take priority over the map of the United States, with which her pupils might be more familiar. The large blank area on the African continent, often called the Heart of Africa, might stir some young imaginations. She could probably do without the grammar poster, finding books with the same information or drawing up her own materials. As for natural science . . . would it be frivolous to choose the most beautifully illustrated charts, as a reasonable way to increase the children's interest? There was little reason to do otherwise. And during difficult days, she might benefit from allowing her eyes to linger on that spot of beauty.

Looking around one more time, she noticed a door in one corner. Would she be fortunate enough to find a water closet? Investigating, she found instead a large chamber pot, along with a cracked desk top which had presumably arrived in that condition, and which for some reason no one had thrown away. The necessary must be somewhere outside. She opened the back door for the first time and saw it, of sturdy construction from the look of it, set to one side of a pleasant grassy yard with a tree she could still imagine climbing.

She closed the door, returned to the desk, and had just found a pot of paste in a shallower drawer when footsteps, and the creak of the door, drew her attention. Dr. Gibbs stood in the doorway, his hands clasped behind his back, smiling but, she thought, a little nervous as well. "I hope you've found everything to your liking. If anything you require is missing, please let me know, and I'll do my best to supply it before you welcome your pupils."

"Thank you. I've just begun looking at everything, but I'm already impressed with the supplies. I'll be sure to tell you if I lack anything essential."

Dr. Gibbs moved to the wall cabinets and opened one. "All the McGuffey readers are here, in what the board has estimated will be sufficient quantity for this year's students, as well as a selection of literature for the older ones. From our correspondence, I know you are prepared to teach other subjects without relying on a text, but please let me or one of the other board members know if there are additional books you find you need. As I told you, we have a library in town, a fairly good one given our size, and I'm sure the librarian, Mrs. Grant, will be happy to help you find whatever you deem suitable. She's been away visiting family, but is scheduled to return on Monday. That will be your first school day, will it not?"

Susannah nodded, trying to ignore the butterflies in her stomach at the thought.

"Then when you dismiss school on Monday, I'd be happy to introduce you, unless someone's injury or sudden illness requires my attention."

She had brought as many books as would fit in her

trunk, which was not a great many. The library would be a blessing, and the librarian might even become a friend. "Thank you for your consideration and generosity."

"And here is the back door, with the wood pile only three yards away so that whichever pupil you assign to filling the stove will not have to spend too much time in the cold."

How many of those building new schoolhouses gave thought to so many details? "I greatly appreciate your forethought, in this and other matters."

Dr. Gibbs smiled and said, "I'll leave you to get acquainted with your domain." He gave a little bow, turned, and left.

Susannah put aside any lingering thoughts of their discussion, retrieved the pot of paste, and set herself to finding the best locations for the map and charts.

Chapter 4

ALICE had barely managed to hold still long enough to get into her blue and white check first-day dress. She had been dressing herself for almost two years, except for needing help with buttons, but this morning, her constant wriggling and gesturing and jumping up and down greatly complicated the process. Joshua finally resorted to informing her that if she weren't dressed and ready by the time he and Clara needed to leave to open their practice, she would have to spend the day with her grandmother instead of going to school. He regretted the tactic at once, as she burst into heartbroken tears. By the time they had soothed her and got her dressed, there was no time for a proper breakfast, and they had to pull together a meal she could eat while walking to the schoolhouse. Joshua's conscience had been uneasy about choosing the site for the school at the shortest practical distance from their house, but now, carrying a squirming bundle of excited child in his arms as she showered him with crumbs, he gave thanks for his past practicality.

Fortunately, there were a few other children already waiting. As he set Alice down not far away from them, he knelt down on one knee and held her hands, looking in her eyes. "You must sit calmly unless Miss Shepard has set you to some task that involves moving about. You must listen to her, without chatting with your schoolmates, and follow her instructions. I would be sorry to hear that your conduct fell below what she has a right to expect."

Alice, fidgets banished, nodded solemnly and then threw herself into his arms. He hugged her tight, kissed the top of her head, and let her go. Clara intercepted her and squatted down to kiss her cheek.

They stood hand in hand, watching Alice scamper up to the children, and made their way to their office. They said nothing at first, Joshua dwelling despite himself on all the ways the day could go wrong. After a few minutes, Clara squeezed his hand and said, "We have prepared her for this new part of her life. And Miss Shepard will be patient with her, and kind. Or so I believe."

That last betrayed Clara's own concern, and she must have known it. He lifted their joined hands and kissed hers, not caring who saw. "You wrote to her about Alice, I recall."

"I did, despite your scruples about taking advantage of your role. I can't regret it. One bad experience could affect the entire course of her schooling, or at least require much effort on our part to restore her enthusiasm."

They had reached the office. The blacksmith, a frequent patient, waited outside. Joshua said quietly as he reached for the door, "If necessary, we are capable of that effort. But we may as well expect a better outcome, and have reason to do so."

* * * * *

Bronka's chatter from the kitchen roused Karol well before dawn — though he might have been able to keep sleeping if he'd been less uneasy. He ignored it as long as he could before he gave up and got out of bed.

He had asked Bronka whether she would rather have him escort her to the school — though he would have to leave her there before it opened and head to the mill — or have their mother go with her instead. She laughed at him. "Of course I'll go with you, silly! You won't tell me not to talk so much, or complain that I should be staying home instead and learning to cook everything Mama's mama did. You understand."

He understood how much she wanted to learn, and how happy she was to be going to school at last. But he also understood what she might be facing, one of the oldest pupils and yet knowing so little of what the others already knew, and most likely not a one of them speaking anything but English. Or if they did, it would probably be German. And her teacher had no idea how to help such a student, unless she had learned since he spoke to her.

He had always taken care of Bronka as much as he could, ever since she was born alive and healthy – Mama's miracle, after the two babies she lost. Coming to America, struggling to help support the family, shouldn't have changed that. He should have practiced English with Bronka more often. He should have found her English books to read, and coaxed her to read with him. But it was too late for wishing.

They reached the school, and Karol led Bronka to the stone bench he himself had set in the grassy yard where the younger children could run about and play at dinnertime. It was chilly for September, but Mama had loaned Bronka her thick winter coat, much warmer than Bronka needed. He wished he could stay until more pupils arrived. Or until the teacher did. She was such a little thing, maybe shorter than Bronka, and finer-boned. She might need help with something.

But he could hardly risk losing his work at the mill. He chucked Bronka under the chin. "You'll be fine. I'll be counting on you to tell me all about it when I get home."

Bronka beamed at him. "Of course I'll be fine. You said the teacher seemed nice, didn't you?"

Karol just nodded. He had said that, and bit his tongue not to say what else he thought. "I'll see you tonight."

He waited until he reached the corner before he looked back. Bronka was sitting very straight, looking at the steps to the school as one might look toward the gates of Heaven.

* * * * *

Susannah entered the schoolhouse through the back door. Doing so would allow her to greet her students all at once, with her best foot forward, fully composed, displaying as much confidence as she could muster. She stopped at her desk to place her lesson plans in a drawer.

Dr. Gibbs had given her a list of the children she could expect — not, apparently, all the children who could have attended — and their ages. She chose the rows of desks closest to her own for the youngest children, putting a copy of the first McGuffey reader on each desk along with a slate and pencil. Those pupils who could already read it easily would trade it for one of the more advanced ones. She put slates and pencils on all the other desks, stood still for at least a minute to gather her courage, and opened the front door.

A small cluster of children — though several of the girls, and one well-dressed boy, were old enough that the word *children* hardly applied — turned from where they were standing and talking, or scrambled up from where they were sitting on the bench or steps or ground, and moved toward her, coming to a halt on and around the bottom step. She found herself, at the same time, startled at how few there were and at how many. A few of the children made their manners to her, the boys bowing and the girls curtsying. Those must be the children of parents more accustomed to school etiquette. The other children stared at them or attempted to imitate them.

When almost all the whispers and murmurs had died away, she stood up as tall as she could, acutely aware that the oldest pupils were taller, and said, "Welcome to Cowbird Creek's first school! I hope you are as excited as I am to be part of this special moment in town history." A few children clapped or cheered; others simply stood waiting.

She cleared her throat and said, "Come in, please, and if you have brought jackets — " She paused, noticing that one of the taller girls wore what looked like a winter coat. " — or coats, hang them on the pegs just inside the door on the right-hand wall." She pointed, in case any of them found it challenging to tell left from right. "Those of you ages six, or younger, up through age nine, take a seat at one of the desks at the front rows — that is, the ones closer to the stove. Those ages ten to twelve, choose seats in the next rows, and those ages thirteen and older, in the rows at the back. Girls on the left side of the room, and boys on the right. In you go!" She stepped aside to let them stream into the school. The tall girl with the coat surged forward so energetically that she almost ran into the children in front of her before she caught herself.

As the pupils started sorting themselves into seats, she made her way to the front and wrote her name in large script on the blackboard. A moment after, she wondered whether including her first name might tempt one of the bolder pupils to challenge her by addressing her improperly — but it would be worse to erase it.

She turned around to see two boys of eleven or twelve

shoving each other, each apparently determined to sit nearest the aisle where he could make eyes at a girl with a round face and curly brown hair. She grabbed her ruler and rapped on the desk. "Take your seats at once, please. If you aren't certain where to sit, I will assign you a place." She gave them both what she hoped was a suitably stern look. They looked down, then turned toward each other and, in a quick flurry of hand gestures, settled the matter by the time-honored method of "rock, paper, scissors."

She settled herself behind her desk, which inspired more of the children to take their own seats. Once all had done so and (at least for the moment) were quietly attending to her, she led them in a simplified version of the "Our Father," writing each line on the blackboard as she did so. When they had all finished in something close to unison, she stood up again and said, "All those seated in the first rows, please stand."

A few, including one bright-eyed girl with dark hair, popped up eagerly, but some moved more slowly, looking alarmed, and one little boy, to her dismay, shrank down in his seat and started to cry. In what was probably an undignified hurry, Susannah rounded her desk to crouch down in front of the crying boy. Reaching out to pat his hand, she said in as reassuring a manner as she could, "There, now. It's all right." He sniffed, wiped his eyes and nose on his sleeve, and turned his face away.

She would have liked to do more to soothe him, but that would have to wait. She stood again, moved in front of her raised platform, and said, "Let me explain how we will be doing things. After this, if I ask some number of you to stand, I'll usually go on to tell those children to step forward and line up in front of my desk. If I ask only one or two of you to stand, that will be so you can read aloud from a book, or go up to the blackboard and write something or solve an arithmetic problem. Do you all understand?"

The little boy took a final sniff, but at least looked back up at her. She returned to her desk, stood behind it, and said, "Now, those I mentioned, come line up as I've described. Then I'd like all of you to tell me your names, how old you are, and what you learned, at home or in any other town, before you came here today." She tried to look as authoritative as possible as the children made their somewhat chaotic way forward. Once they were in something close to a straight line, she pointed to the child farthest to her right, nearest the windows. "You first, please. And everyone else, wait quietly until it's your turn."

The recitals went smoothly, if of varying clarity and length. The boy who had cried was now able to tell her cheerfully that his name was Petey. Only two of these children had failed to follow her directions as to where to sit, and belonged further back. Rather than take the time for reshuffling, she told them to stay where they were until tomorrow.

The little girl who had stood up so promptly, a seven-year-old named Alice — hadn't Susannah received a letter from Mrs. Gibbs about her? — might well be advanced enough for the second reader. Petey had never, to all appearances, so much as opened a book. Susannah sent the children back to their desk and instructed them to read as much of their McGuffey Readers as they could, then called the next oldest group forward to answer similar questions. That group proved easier to manage, old enough not to be obviously afraid of her and young enough not to challenge her authority.

She wrote a series of arithmetic problems on the blackboard and told them to copy them onto their slates and solve them. Then it was time for the relatively few oldest pupils.

It would be easier to start with one of the girls, but she was not here to be timid. The tallest boy's clothing suggested a town origin and a wealthy one; his confident address confirmed it. When she moved on to the next boy and asked him the same preliminary questions, he grinned at her and said, "I'm Amos Johnson, and my folks say I'm eleven. Can't rightly remember being born, to tell you if they got it right."

Amos would be a challenge. But no, it was too soon to make judgments of that kind. "And your schooling up to now?"

"I can read well enough. Better than our horse or our donkey, and that's good enough for me!" He laughed at his own wit and went on, "I'm better at figuring, but Ma wants me to get better yet. I like hearing Pa's stories about the War of Independence and the War of the Rebellion, and I reckon I'd like to know more about how it all happened."

"Thank you, Amos. I'll bring a book tomorrow to begin filling in the gaps in the stories you've heard. In a few minutes, I'll set you some mathematics problems, so I can better assess your skill at — figuring." She moved on to the last boy in the group. He proved to be as slow of tongue as Amos was quick. He would test her skill, if not her control of the classroom as Amos was likely to do.

Susannah turned with relief to the remaining girl — the one who had seemed so eager to come into the school earlier. The girl had blonde hair and blue eyes, and reminded Susannah of someone she couldn't quite bring to mind. "And your name and age?"

The girl curtsied. When she stood up again and spoke, her accent made clear that she had come from some other country, and had not entirely mastered the language of her new one. "Miss Teacher, my name is —" What came next was a sequence of syllables that reminded Susannah of water over stones in a creek. At Susannah's obvious puzzlement, she blushed and said more slowly, "Bron-is-swa-va. But I am most often called Bronka. Oh, and I am fifteen years."

"And your education, Bronka?"

"I was not allowed to attend school, back in Poland. But my grandfather let me read his books, and borrow them. I read whenever I can. And I started doing the shopping for the family when I am twelve years, so I have done many figuring."

"Thank you, Bronka. I'll bring a book so I can see how well you read. For now, you may all sit down."

As Susannah approached her desk again, it came to her just whom Bronka resembled. It was Mr. Marek, who had chased after the thief and rescued her case, and then had asked her about her experience teaching those whose English was poor. They must be family. If anything could make it more important that she do her best for this girl, it would be the debt she owed Mr. Marek.

Susannah sat down, pulled out a spare slate, and quickly wrote down a series of arithmetic problems from easiest to most difficult. Then she opened the cabinet holding books, those Dr. Gibbs had provided and the ones she had brought from her trunk to add to that collection.

Not Shakespeare, of course. The Bard's language was difficult enough for those who began learning English in their cradles. Even Dickens might be too challenging. . . She chose *Little Women* and called Amos and Bronka back up.

Amos took the slate with a smirk, which could have

meant confidence or just the attempt to look confident. He had, at least, brought his own pencil, and sat back down and set to work without further banter. Susannah watched to make sure he had started, then handed the book to Bronka, who reached out and took it with what Susannah would have to call reverence. Perhaps, if Susannah could allow it without loss of authority, this girl could become something of a companion, another with whom she could share the joys of literature.

Susannah flipped the book open to the start of the first chapter. "Start here, please, and read aloud."

Bronka took an audible deep breath and started reading. "Plah-ying . . . peel-greems . . . Hree-stmaas . . . won't be . . . Hree-stmaas . . . Weet-ah-oo-t . . . ." With each syllable, it became clearer that she had no idea what she was reading. Behind Bronka, pupils who should have been busy with their McGuffey readers or their arithmetic were gawking, or poking each other, or even whispering. Susannah swept her gaze around the room, meeting as many eyes as she could, her stern expression sending most — but not quite all — of the pupils back to their assignments.

Bronka finally, mercifully, stopped trying to read, her fair complexion blotched with red. "I am most sorry, Miss Teacher, but my English is not enough good."

Susannah gently retrieved the book. "That's all right, Bronka. I should have given you something easier." She took the book back to the cabinet, put it in, and pondered the selections. Best to start with one of the McGuffey readers, the Sixth — no, the Fifth . . . or the Fourth. She started to close the cabinet and then, her heart sinking, grabbed the reader for the first form and slid it underneath the other.

She returned to Bronka, who looked up as she approached with an almost desperate hope in her eyes. Susannah handed her the Fourth Reader, open to the first set of full sentences. "From here, please. Take your time."

Bronka's performance was a little better — but only a little, not good enough to suggest that she could actually understand all she was reading as she read it. Not that the text made that easy, stringing together words more for the vowels they shared than for any meaning in them.

The boy sharing Amos's desk (what was his name?) snickered, then yelped as Amos apparently chastised him in some manner Susannah could not see. Good for Amos. Susannah glared at the boy and said, "And how many languages do you speak? Perhaps you can share one of them with your fellow students?"

The boy flushed and looked away. Susannah silently retrieved the book and opened the First Reader, flipping through the introduction for teachers and the pages for printed and written alphabet to the first lesson. She handed it to Bronka, her heart sore to see that the girl had gone pale and had tears in her eyes.

Bronka, her voice shaking, started to read. "The dog. The dog ran." She turned the page. "The cat. The mat. Is the cat on the mat? The cat is on the mat." If Bronka had been six years old, born in Cowbird Creek, Susannah would have said she read rather well.

Susannah reached out to close the book. "All right, then. We'll start there. There will be reading time every day, and you can make your way through this book and then go on to the next. Now and then, I'll ask you questions about what you've read —" She stopped herself before she could add, *to make sure you understand it.*

"Thank you, Miss Teacher," Bronka whispered,

looking down at the book, and walked slowly back to her desk, her hand with the book hanging low at her side.

Chapter 5

FOR THE REST of that school day, Susannah had little time to brood. She spent much of the time moving from one group to another, checking and reviewing their arithmetic, listening to them read, giving them history and morals lessons. The history, she did her best to deliver as exciting or thought-provoking tales; morals she approached by asking questions and then, as often as not, asking the children to examine their answers. The children's growing interest and the questions they asked made her feel more wide awake than usual. It gave her a glow of satisfaction that almost let her forget how poorly she had dealt with Bronka's needs.

She had scheduled dinnertime for an hour, assuming that would be long enough for the pupils who lived close enough to go home for dinner to reach home and return, while those who lived farther out went outdoors to eat the dinners they had brought, play, and socialize. After reviewing and adjusting her plans for the afternoon, Susannah borrowed a desk near the window to watch the children while she ate her cold ham and buttered bread. There were few times when being petite had advantages, but it did make sitting in a pupil-sized desk more comfortable.

Amos, she saw, was whittling. He had not got far in shaping the wood, but the curves suggested a female figure in the making. Susannah looked away. If the figure progressed to the point of indecency, that would be the time to intervene. The younger girls had been huddled together a moment before and had now scattered in what was probably a game of hide-and-seek, Alice calling out suggestions as to where the others should look. Meanwhile, a line of boys played snap-the-whip, one of the smaller boys flying off the end across her field of view and laughing with all his might.

They looked so carefree, out there enjoying the warm September day and their interlude of freedom. As she swallowed the last bite of ham, she resolved not to extinguish those buoyant spirits, even as she instilled in the children the discipline and work ethic it was part of her duty to teach.

When she called the room to order again, several of the children who had gone home were missing, straggling in up to twenty minutes later. This soon, she could not be certain whether they needed more time than she had allowed, or were testing her discipline. Time would tell.

Dismissing the pupils in late afternoon, she couldn't help noticing that Bronka left with a slow, dragging step, very different from the bouncing impatience with which she had entered. Susannah sighed and gathered up her lesson plans and the notes she had made during the day. About to leave, she looked up startled when the door opened. She'd forgotten Dr. Gibbs' offer to introduce her to the librarian. And he was holding the little girl Alice in his arms. Catching Susannah's eye, he beamed and said, "Yes, this is our daughter. I hope she gave you a minimum of trouble? This will have been the longest she has needed to sit still, by a considerable margin."

"She did very well." Susannah forbore to mention that Alice had done her share of squirming, along with the other young children. For whatever reason, probably having to do with the family schedule, Alice had stayed at school during the dinner hour, and Susannah had been glad to send her outside to run about.

Dr. Gibbs gave Alice a kiss on the head and said, "I'm glad to hear it. Are you ready to meet our Mrs. Grant?

Thank goodness his concerns about Alice's first day had not made him forget! "Yes, indeed. I find I have a question to ask her. Although I can start with a question for you, if you permit."

Dr. Gibbs cocked his head. "I hope you won't mind my saying that something seems to have perturbed you. What unexpected challenge has the day presented?"

Susannah smiled ruefully. "As you divine, something did arise — and I even had a warning I failed to heed, or at least to act on. Do you know what sort of name — that is, from what country of origin — Bronka might be? Or, what was it, Broni-swa-va?"

Dr. Gibbs freed a hand to stroke his beard. "It sounds Slavic. But I believe your impulse to consult our librarian was a good one. Let us do so."

Camelia Grant had come to Cowbird Creek with her husband, now deceased, when he accepted a position with the town's one bank. Rather than return to her family back east, she had remained in the home her husband's employment and her family's resources had allowed them to build, one of the town's more impressive structures. She had donated to the library the more popular and less valuable volumes from her private book collection, and when the previous librarian left town, she accepted that post.

Given this background, Susannah expected a lady with elevated manners, even a little standoffish. She was pleasantly surprised, and relieved, to see the librarian welcome Dr. Gibbs with a hearty, "And here you are again, Joshua! And little Alice, of course. Come for something meatier than fairy tales? Ready to start her on the Greeks, or some rousing tales of heroic charges into battle?"

Dr. Gibbs chuckled, setting Alice down and giving her a gentle push in the direction of a shelf with intricately colored covers. "Today, I come to gratify your curiosity and enlarge your social circle. May I introduce to you Miss Susannah Shepard, who has made it possible for Cowbird Creek at last to open a school?"

Mrs. Grant thrust out her hand for Susannah to shake. "Delightful! My dear, you can have no idea how some of us have been anticipating your arrival. Has the school opened yet?"

Susannah shook hands and said, "I am very happy to make your acquaintance, and look forward to making the acquaintance of your shelves. Yes, the school opened its doors just this morning. And — I would have been eager to meet you in any case, but I am hoping you might be able to assist me with a question of some urgency."

Mrs. Grant pulled out a wooden chair from a corner and waved her toward it. "Sit down and tell me what you need! And you must call me Camelia. It'll save time and confusion if you start there, instead of waiting until we actually know each other." She pulled out what must be her own usual seat from behind the nearby desk and plopped down before Susannah had managed to do so.

Susannah hoped she was managing to hide her mortification and regret as she described her exchange with Bronka. Before she could even ask about the name, Mrs. Grant — Camelia — interrupted with, "Hmm — might be a Polish name. Short for Broniswava, I believe.

By the way, that's spelled B-r-o-n-i-s-l-a-*w*-a — the Poles pronounce 'l' like our 'w,' at least some of the time, and 'w' like our 'v.'"

"Oh, thank you! I very much wanted to know where Bronka might come from. Do you by any chance . . . ."

But the librarian had already jumped up from her chair and was squatting in front of a small bookcase. "I keep all my foreign language books here. Not too many of them so far, but I'm hoping more of our immigrants will bring their books in future. And I keep in touch with other librarians to learn what's available where. Let me see . . . here it is!" She pulled out a thick volume and opened it. "If your Bronka likes poetry, or even if she doesn't yet, this would be perfect for her. It contains the work of three famous Polish poets, patriots all, commonly called the Three Bards. And their poems have a sort of revolutionary character that rather bridges the gap between an immigrant's past and present, wouldn't you say?"

Susannah stood up and peered over Camelia's shoulder. What she could see struck her as an unlikely stream of consonants, interrupted with more "y"s than the more usual vowels. Her inspection was interrupted by Camelia's shutting the book with a bang and holding it up. "Here, take it. Mind the weight!"

Susannah took the book, which was indeed heavy, and began stammering her thanks, but Camelia was still rummaging through the other books on the shelf. "Let me just make sure I don't have the history book I heard about somewhere, published in Polish just last year . . . no, but I'll start tracking it down." She stood up, grunting a little. "Just as well I haven't had much call for books in other tongues just yet. Those lower shelves aren't kind to my bones. Enjoy your youth, Susannah! No aching bones for you, I'd wager. What are you, twenty?"

Susannah straightened her spine. "Twenty-one, actually."

Camelia grinned. "Excuse me! Twenty-one, of course."

Susannah had almost forgotten Dr. Gibbs' presence, but now he came up holding two books, Alice scampering at his side. "I overheard your discussion of the Polish poets, and it inspired me to find some poetry Alice might enjoy. We'd like to check these books out, if you'd be so kind."

"Terrific! Just let me write the titles down . . . and your Polish poetry, Susannah, if you'll let me call you that."

"Of course. And thank you so much."

"My pleasure! I'll let you know when I get hold of that history book. Alice, you come back and read me some of those poems, will you?"

Alice nodded her head energetically. Dr. Gibbs turned to Susannah and asked, "May I carry that book along with ours? It's not such a long way to Miss Wheeler's establishment, but long enough for you to be carrying a book near half as heavy as you are."

Susannah reminded herself not to bristle at jests about her size, tiresome as they had become once she realized she had no more growth to expect. "That would be most kind of you. Shall we go?"

Dr. Gibbs held the door for her, armful of books notwithstanding. Camelia waved, putting her arm and shoulder into the gesture, and finally, Susannah was on her way home. Or to as much of a home as she would have for who knew how long.

* * * * *

Karol walked home from the mill as fast as he could walk without attracting stares. What had Bronka's first day of school been like? Visions of all going as well as Bronka expected took turns with dread of all going as poorly as he feared.

He burst through the front door and found Mama stirring a pot of stew. She turned, smiled her welcome, and bent to sniff the stew, saying ,"Almost ready!"

He kissed her on the cheek before asking, "Where's Bronka?"

"Where should she be? Feeding the chickens. Go tell her it'll soon be suppertime."

He went out back to the chicken coop. Bronka was sprinkling grain and scraps, talking softly to the hens. Karol frowned. Bronka only did that when something troubled her.

He saw her notice his footsteps, but she didn't turn around. He walked up to her and put a hand on her shoulder. "Bronuisa, it's time to eat."

She reached up to pat his hand, still without turning. "I'll be right there."

Karol and Mama had already sat down when Bronka came in, drops of water on her face as if she had washed it at the pump. He hesitated to ask her about school with Mama there. If the day had gone poorly, Mama would start in on how a girl didn't need schooling, especially a girl Bronka's age, almost ready to marry. He tried not to bolt his food down, a task made easier by how slowly Bronka picked at her own.

He helped Bronka with the dishes to make the job go faster, and then followed her to the family bedroom. She sat on the side of the bed and looked down at her hands, folded in her lap. He sat down next to her. "Tell me what happened at school today."

Bronka bit her lip. "The teacher was kind. She saw that I could not read English well, and gave me a book to help me."

"What book?"

Bronka reached under her pillow and pulled out a book with a dull gold cover and black binding. The title read, *Eclectic First Reader*. He took it from her and opened it, turning a few pages. The chart of letters might have been useful if it had included English pronunciations. As for the text . . . he read aloud, his voice getting rougher with each word: "The dog? The dog ran? The cat? *Co do diabla!!*"

He slammed the book shut. Bronka shrank away. "Don't be angry! I couldn't read the other books. And this one gets better."

Karol breathed deep until he could say, almost calmly, "I'm not angry at you, my sunshine. You can go back and tell her you can read all this, and then she'll give you something worth your time."

Bronka shook her head. "I am to read all this, and the next, all the way until the ones for pupils my age. It will help my English."

He gave her a hug. "Of course it will. And you and I will start speaking English more." He added, in English, "You can read a little before you go to bed. Good night, little sister. God keep you until the morning."

He went back out to the yard and, in spite of the low light, chopped wood until his arms were sore, swearing as he worked.

* * * * *

Susannah was getting dressed before breakfast when someone knocked on her door. She opened it partway to find Miss Wheeler looking ill at ease. "You have a caller, Miss Shepard. I've put him in the sitting room. It's rather early for anyone to call, but I imagine he hoped to find you before you left for the school."

Susannah hurried to fasten her last buttons. "Can you tell me who it is?"

"A young man, wearing working clothes. He seems rather . . . impatient."

In her short time in Cowbird Creek, Susannah had been introduced to only one man who would wear work clothes. And she had, without dwelling on the fact, looked forward to seeing him again at some point. But not after yesterday. "I'll be right down."

Carl Marek was pacing back and forth in the sitting room, almost bumping into furniture on each pass. He whirled around as she entered, glaring at her and brandishing a book. She stepped backward despite herself as she recognized the McGuffey reader.

"This, you give my sister? This is what she gets on her first day of school, after dreaming of school her entire life? *This!*"

Susannah sank into the nearby easy chair, hoping it might influence him to sit also. "Mr. Marek, I did try —"

His big hand clutched the book so tightly she feared he would damage the cover. "The dog! The dog ran! For a girl fifteen years old! Do you know what Bronka brought with her to this country, instead of linens for when she gets married or clothes to look pretty in? She brought Shakespeare!"

Susannah gaped at him. "But — she couldn't even read *Little Women* when I asked her."

Mr. Marek rolled his eyes. "In Polish, she reads Shakespeare! She has been reading in it every night before she goes to sleep! But now, of course, she will need to practice how to read 'dog' and 'cat.' And in front of the others, you gave her this!" He threw the book down on the chair in which she had hoped he would sit.

Another trip back and forth across the room, and then he stopped and said, his voice hard and bitter, "You will have to give her back this book yourself. I have to get to the mill. My sister must not go without her book about Cat and Dog. What a shame that would be! She might have to read Shakespeare instead!"

And with that, he stomped out the door and slammed it behind him.

Susannah sat in the easy chair, shaking all over. She greatly wished to cry, but she was due at the table for breakfast, if there was still time, and then needed to appear at school, composed and ready. The first step was to stand up. She did so, first gripping and then releasing the arm of the chair, and gave herself one minute to achieve some degree of composure.

So when Miss Wheeler opened the door, concern on her face, Susannah burst into tears.

Miss Wheeler hurried over and put her arms around her. Susannah struggled not to cry harder at this reminder of home and mothering. The older woman tsked and hushed and muttered "there, there," while Susannah got herself under control. Miss Wheeler let go and pulled a handkerchief out of her skirt pocket, dried Susannah's cheeks, inspected her, and finally declared, "You'll do. Hurry to breakfast, child."

After crying in front of her hostess, Susannah could hardly protest the name of child, even to herself. She followed close behind as Miss Wheeler led her to the dining room. Just before they entered, Miss Wheeler said under her breath, "I'm sorry to have allowed an *unreliable* young man to disturb you on these premises. You may be sure I won't be admitting him again."

Susannah, taking her seat, reflected dismally that it was unlikely Miss Wheeler would be called upon to take the trouble of refusing Carl Marek admittance.

Chapter 6

IN THE RUSH to get to the schoolhouse on time, Susannah almost forgot the McGuffey Reader and the book of Polish poetry. In fact, she had to dash back into the boardinghouse to retrieve them. By the time she approached the school building, she could see on her way to the back door that most, if not all, of the pupils were gathered out front. She put the reader on Bronka's desk, slid the big volume of poetry into one of the deeper desk drawers, took one deep breath, and opened the school.

Bronka trudged in, saw the McGuffey Reader on her desk, and blinked in puzzlement. She looked up at Susannah, and back at the book. A blush rose in her cheeks, and she bit her lip and looked down. If Susannah had needed confirmation that Bronka neither knew of her brother's visit to the boarding house ahead of time, nor was glad to know it now, she had confirmation enough.

Susannah directed her first efforts of the morning to the younger children, hearing them read and correcting their figuring, giving them a lesson in geography. As she made ready to call up Bronka's group, she saw that Bronka was conscientiously reading the primer, though she laid it on her desk before coming forward with the others.

Susannah wrote a series of arithmetic problems on the board, told the students to copy them down and work on them, and then retrieved the volume of poetry from the drawer. "Bronka, when you finish that reader, I have something for you to read before the next one. I obtained it from our local library, and am in the process of trying to find a history book that might also be of interest."

Bronka looked at Susannah with eyes wide, and then closed them to blink away tears. "Thank you, Miss Teacher. So much. I am most grateful."

"It's no more than my job, just as you are far more than your present knowledge of written English. All of you may go back to your seats."

They did so. Bronka, as soon as she sat down, worked diligently at her arithmetic, but from time to time, one hand crept over and caressed the cover of the book of poetry.

* * * * *

Karol was about ready to go back in from his fifteen-minute dinner break when he spied a woman approaching. If he had seen her before, he hadn't taken note of her in any way. She might be twenty years or more older than he, with reddish-brown hair and a brisk walk that covered plenty of ground at every stride. She walked right up to him and asked, "Bronka's big brother?"

Karol blinked and said, "Yes. My name is Carl Marek." Something about the way she looked him right in the eye made him wonder if he could have gotten away with introducing himself as Karol.

The woman stuck out her hand. "It's my lucky day, then! I'm Mrs. Camelia Grant, town librarian. I haven't yet met your sister, though I look forward to it, but I did have occasion to discuss her recently with someone who wishes her well."

Karol glanced toward the mill and back. "I must get back to work. I want to hear about this talk you had, but it will have to be another time."

She smiled, obviously not taking offense. "Of course, of course! Could you come by the library after work? It's about halfway between here and the town square, half a block west of that really tall hickory tree. Can you find it?"

"I can find it. I'll come after work." He would find it, no matter how many people he had to ask.

Five hours later, his stomach rumbling, he headed the opposite direction from home and finally reached the library. It was a building the size of a small house in town, with fresh green paint and steps bordered by large bushes. Only now, as he knocked, did it occur to him that the librarian might have preferred to be home having supper at this time of day.

The librarian — Mrs. Grant — opened the door with an energetic yank. "Oh, excellent! I was so hoping you'd make it. Come in! I've had some good news since we spoke last."

She waved him to a chair that barely fit him and opened a big ledger on her desk. "I thought you should know the work that Susannah Shepard, our new teacher, has put in to try to find something good for Bronka — or should I call her Bronislawa?"

By the time Karol hauled his jaw back into place, she was rattling on. "Yes, Miss Shepard came to see me after school ended yesterday —"

Karol clenched his fists in his lap. "Did you, then, tell the teacher to hand Bronka that book for little children?"

Mrs. Grant lowered her head and looked at him sternly, whether for interrupting her or for what he had said he couldn't be sure. "I spoke to her after she felt it necessary to resort to that choice. She was far from happy about it, and came straight here to ask me about any Polish books I might have available."

He stared at her. "*Polish* books?"

"Well, she did have to ask me what sort of name Bronislawa was, but once I told her, yes. She was so happy to see that I already had something suitable! I imagine she's given the book of poetry — well, lent it, naturally — to Bronka at school today."

"And all this happened yesterday?"

"Yes. I said so, didn't I?"

Karol stifled a groan. Miss Shepard had done these things yesterday, and this morning, he had accused her, shouted at her —

He remembered, now, the stiff way she had stood, the way she had stared at him. It would be bad enough if he had offended her, but the truth he must face was worse. He'd frightened her.

If only he could go back in time, rescue her from himself, and knock himself down as he deserved.

But here he was, keeping Miss Grant waiting. "I'm sorry, I must go. Thank you for telling me this."

She chuckled. "But I haven't told you the latest news! Miss Shepard and I talked about a history book, Polish history, that I'd heard about somewhere, but I couldn't think where. So I sent a telegram to the Polish Roman Catholic Union in Chicago, and they found me a library with some Polish books, and I sent a telegram to *them* asking where I could order this book or whether I could do an interlibrary loan. I'm sure I'll be able to get hold of it." Her expression shifted toward what he'd have to call sly. "You can tell Miss Shepard about it, if you should happen to speak to her."

He nodded dumbly and got up. She stopped him with

one last word. "But if you were thinking of going to Miss Wheeler's, you might want to wait for morning. It's rather late for a call."

He could have groaned again. Given the scene he'd made, he doubted he would be allowed across Miss Wheeler's threshold. He would have to make his apologies at the school.

* * * * *

Susannah made sure she had more time to prepare the next morning, arriving at the schoolhouse a full fifteen minutes before the school day began. She had just put down her notebook and started cleaning the slates from the previous day's arithmetic problems when a knock came — at the back door. She opened the door to find, of all people, Carl Marek, holding his hat in his hands.

Before she could speak, or do anything else, he blurted out, "I'm very sorry. I wasn't just rude — I was cruel. I hope you can think of some way for me to make it up to you, because I can think of nothing."

Susannah stepped back. "Come in, please. And I don't understand. You had good reason to be upset. You warned me, at the train station, to be prepared for pupils whose English was poor, and I failed to pay sufficient heed. I should have had some better plan, one that would have spared Bronka's feelings and given her a better path forward."

Mr. Marek shook his head. "I had much more warning than you, and did almost nothing. I started learning English before we even left Poland, and I should have made sure Bronka did the same. And once we came and settled in, I should have made Bronka talk to me in English, whether or not our parents helped."

Susannah's shoulders relaxed for what felt like the first time in months. "Let us forgive each other, and ourselves, and start afresh. And I'll do all I can to make things easier for your sister."

Mr. Marek put out his hand. "Shall we shake on it? Is that something women do in this country? Mrs. Grant did."

It was to Camelia, then, that Susannah owed this new accord between Bronka's brother and herself. "Some of us do, and I would be glad to." She suited the action to the word. His handshake was firm, but he didn't jolt her arm up and down as she had half thought he would do, given how tall and brawny he was, and how strong his arms appeared.

"Oh, and Mrs. Grant gave me a message for you. She has found out more about how to get the history book. She didn't say which book. Do you know?"

"No, she didn't say — probably because the name was in Polish. But it was published in 1883, I think."

Mr. Marek's face brightened. "That could be a new book by —" What followed was a string of syllables she could never have repeated, let alone remembered. "We will both be very glad to be able to read it."

Susannah suddenly remembered the time. "I must go and let the children in."

"Of course. Thank you for accepting my apology." He turned to go, then turned back. "And if it would be proper, I would be happy for you to call me Carl." He smiled, the first time she had seen him smile since the train station, and she saw he had a single dimple. "It will be easier for you to say than the book title."

Susannah laughed, which felt wonderful, and said, "I will do that, and thank you. If you like, you may call me Susannah."

He smiled again. "Sus-ann-ah. That is not so easy to

say. But I would be honored."

Mr. Marek — Carl — put his hat on, tipped it in a goodbye salute, and let himself out the back door. Susannah composed herself and headed to the front.

When Susannah returned to the boarding house after school, Miss Wheeler came up to her with an expression somewhere between puzzled and pleased. "I had a most unexpected visitor today. Indeed, I almost refused to let him in. Can you guess who it was?"

Susannah nodded, then realized she should answer. "Was it Carl Marek?"

"It was indeed. And so soft-spoken, I hardly recognized him. He apologized very prettily, and several times. He told me he'd apologized to you as well — is that true?"

"Yes he did." What else needed saying? "I'm convinced he was sincere. And he had reason to be upset with me."

Miss Wheeler brushed her hands together as if dislodging dust. "Well, that's all behind us now. Do you expect the young man to come calling again, in a more civil manner?"

An excellent question, for which Susannah had no answer.

* * * * *

Even though he ran half the way to the mill, Karol still came panting in a few minutes later than the owner had the right to expect. Mr. Grint, taking his morning smoke in the yard, twitched an eyebrow at him. "You know, Carl, this might be the first time you've ever been late. Care to tell me what kept you? Though I can hardly complain, with you working here as long as you have and never been late before."

He had had enough of apologies for one morning, but he forced one out. "I'm sorry, sir. I had to correct a mistake, and wanted to do so as soon as I could."

The miller peered at him and stroked his chin. "Hard to say on such a chilly morning, and with you running here, most like, but would you be blushing, young feller? Did that mistake of yours involve a young lady? Didn't know as there were any Catholic gals the right age, but I don't keep up on everyone who comes to town."

Because, of course, no good Protestant girl would look twice at a Catholic man — even though there were plenty of Catholics in the state by now, especially farther north. Karol turned away and muttered, "I'd best get to work." He went inside without another word.

As he dumped grain into the receiving hopper and went down to the basement to make sure it was flowing properly down the chute, he brooded over Grint's comment. Why shouldn't a Methodist, or Lutheran or whatever type of Protestant girl lived or moved to town, be willing to convert, or at least to raise her children as Catholic? Weren't they all Christians? And he would bet some Protestants, if they knew enough, would envy the ceremony, the beauty, and the history of a Catholic service — at least, the services back in the old country. The only Catholic church within a reasonable distance of Cowbird Creek could barely afford candles and incense, and had yet to manage stained glass.

In his mind's eye, he could picture a pretty girl kneeling at the altar rail, closing her eyes to receive communion, the bliss of the moment written on her face . . . .

If that girl bore more than a little resemblance to Susannah Shepard, schoolteacher, it made no real difference. It was just a fantasy. Any girl would do.

Chapter 7

IN THE SHORT time between President Brecker's outrageous conduct and Susannah's departure for Cowbird Creek, her feelings had been in such tumult — such an ever-shifting swirl of shame, anger, confusion, and apprehension — that she had seen none of her friends from the college. How could she explain to the girls who looked up to Brecker, just as she had, what he had shown himself to be? Or if she refrained, from fear of their incredulity, how could she justify her abrupt change of course?

She regretted that now. No one else could understand so well the challenges she faced, and how her present and future differed from what she had planned.

But at least she could write to those few who had been her true friends and confidantes. She would start with Louisa, the one she had known the longest. Louisa, always encouraging, never petty — the kindest of their circle, if not necessarily the most profound thinker among them.

Dear Louisa,

By now you will have heard of my new position. I am almost as surprised by it as you must be! — but the school board and townspeople here have been most obliging, and done their best to make me feel at home.

That was as true as such language ever was.

I suspect the average attainments of my youngest pupils are less than will be the case for those you encounter, but there are a few who are every bit as well prepared as the children in St. Louis are likely to be.

One such pupil, at least — Dr. Gibbs' daughter Alice. And with a certain amount of generous overstatement, she could include the oldest boy in the school.

Several of the others are notably bright and eager, like tinder ready for the match. I find it particularly fulfilling to provide the spark for which they have been waiting, whether their families knew it or no.

Susannah put down her pen. She had not realized, until she wrote those words, how fervently she meant them. She had been too focused on her difficulties, and her insecurities at confronting them, to tally her blessings as she ought.

To be sure, I have had a few challenges to surmount. Some of the children tended to be tardy until I began starting the school day by reading a story, chosen for its likely interest to the offenders. Another and more upsetting difficulty I encountered allows me to pass on the wisdom I learned only by erring. Do not assume that all your pupils will be native speakers of English! It is, of course, impractical to learn every language that families in our growing country may speak at home, but you may at least locate the resources that will allow you to help those pupils more effectively. I was fortunate that Cowbird Creek possesses not only a surprisingly well stocked library, but a well-educated and very energetic librarian.

In sum, then, my dear friend, you need not worry that I am disappointed or unhappy. Rather, I give thanks for having been directed onto an unexpected, yet unexpectedly rewarding path.

Please let me hear from you, when convenient, and tell me your news, and that all is well with you, as it truly is with me.

Yours faithfully,

Susannah

She read over the letter and frowned. There was no

way to avoid naming her current location, not if she wanted a return letter. But she would have liked to ask Louisa, as a confidential favor, to keep the name of Cowbird Creek to herself. Unfortunately, Louisa was the reverse of secretive by nature, and any such request would require the very explanation Susannah had decided not to give. She sighed, folded the letter, and addressed an envelope. Just writing the name of her home town revived her homesickness to the point that she had to wipe a tear off the paper before it could soak in and spread to smear the ink.

Susannah had written her parents almost as soon as she reached Cowbird Creek. She had intended to write again after receiving their reply. When none came, she did her best not to wonder when it might, or to count the days. It had not been so very long. They were busy with their own affairs. They had not forgotten her.

But it was a great relief to stop at the general store after school on Saturday and find an envelope addressed in her mother's pretty hand.

Dearest Susannah,

I apologize for how long it has taken for me to write you. Before I explain, I hasten to say that all is well, that we are all well — now. I own that I suffered from some indisposition, beginning shortly before your letter arrived. It was nothing very serious, but my head rather ached, and I was too tired to attend to many of my duties. Indeed, I spent some days abed.

Susannah's breath came short. She forced herself to breathe more deeply, and read once more the reassurance of her mother's present health before going on.

Your father was all that was kind, spending as much time as he could spare caring for me and doing as many of the household chores as he could fathom. He did make me promise I would not take him to task for poor performance! Your brother also assisted, spending more time indoors than he is wont, and without complaint, at least any expressed in my hearing.

I have exercised great self-control, since I was able to leave my bed, in resuming my usual activities only gradually, and resting often, so as not to relapse into illness. I must boast that I have succeeded in that effort.

Pa read me your letter several times while I could not easily read it for myself, and we have often shared with each other our hopes that all is going as you hoped. Your brother, also, speaks of you often, and admits that not until you left did he realize how much you helped him, nor in how many ways, nor how much he valued your company. I believe your absence has taught him a profitable lesson. He still plans to go a-venturing, though the details of those plans vary from week to week, or even day to day. In the meantime, he has assisted Pa at the paper on several occasions.

It is not only in our little family circle that you are missed and remembered. Almost every errand I run includes someone asking how you're doing and whether your position is all you'd hoped. I was startled, and more than a little affronted, when Mr. Brecker, who misbehaved so badly, had the nerve to come up to me at the greengrocer's and say how much he hoped you were thriving, and where was it you had gone again? Of course, I was no more than civil, made the most general of replies, and did NOT answer his question.

Susannah dropped the letter on the dressing table and put her head in her hands. Ma might not have answered, but after all the people Ma or Louisa might have told about Cowbird Creek, it was all too likely that someone else at the greengrocer's had been happy to oblige him with that information.

It was no use fretting, or wondering what the scoundrel intended to do when he found out where she'd gone. She left the letter on the table, rather than pick it up in a hand gone less than steady, and bent over it to keep reading.

Another inquiry came from a more congenial source. Charles Elliott came to tea at the Wellingtons' house where I was also invited, and drew me aside to say how sorry he was that he'd had no chance to bid you farewell. He asked whether I thought you'd consider it too forward if he were to write to you. I told him I couldn't say, but would ask. How would you feel about him doing so? I don't know whether he expects you to return to St. Louis at some time, so you could further your acquaintance with him in person, or whether he simply wants to preserve some connection with you, even at a distance.

Charles Elliott! She had hardly given him a thought since stepping off the train. Her imagination was not so creative as to fit his almost aristocratic style and manner, his secure place in society and excellent prospects, within the same frame as Cowbird Creek's narrow streets and the humble storefronts lining them, its jovial farmers with their uneducated speech, her pupils with such uneven attainments and capacities . . . .

She put aside the matter of Mr. Elliott and his request, reading the last precious paragraph, and then reading it over again.

We look forward very much to your report of your new community, your living situation, and of course the commencement of your career. I know you are sensible enough to find in all these every blessing they contain, and not to repine for any alternatives you may have expected in the past. We pray for you nightly, and know you keep us in your prayers as well.

Your loving parents

Susannah kissed the paper on a spot with no writing and laid it on her dressing table, stroking it as if her mother could feel the caress.

She could wait until the morrow to decide what to do about allowing Mr. Elliott to write to her. But she would rather not have the question lingering as she settled herself for rest, and then into the Sabbath Day. She shifted her weight to sit more comfortably in her chair and did her best to organize her thoughts.

She had first to ask how such letters would affect her as she went about the life and duties she had chosen. Would they revive any lingering regrets, reinforce any dissatisfaction to which the events of any particular day might give rise? Or would they provide a salutary reminder of ambitions and dreams she need not, necessarily, abandon for all time?

Really, that was all that mattered, for the present. She need not, indeed could not, decide what her side of the correspondence would entail until she received a letter from Mr. Elliott and saw how he envisioned it.

She pulled out a fresh piece of paper and picked up her pen.

Dearest Ma,

Thank you so much for your letter, and for beginning with reassurance as to the duration and nature of the illness you went on to describe. Please, continue to guard your health with the prudence you have already brought to the period of your recovery. And please convey to Pa my gratitude and admiration for the role he played in that recovery. And the same to Ned, in such measure as he has deserved it.

I have been welcomed most warmly by the school board, and the inhabitants, of Cowbird Creek. Dr. Gibbs, in particular, has been most thoughtful in his oversight of the school's construction and in equipping it. I am also fortunate to have met the town librarian, a singular woman with remarkable energy, dedicated to preserving and enlarging the library collection. My students naturally pose a range of challenges, some of which I have met more successfully than others, but I try to face my errors, to correct them to the greatest extent that is in my power, and to pray for guidance in improving my performance.

She paused, holding the pen over the inkwell to preserve her paper from any stray drops. When no last-minute doubts appeared, she wrote:

I am willing to enter into a correspondence with Mr. Elliott, if he remains interested in doing so. I have not, of course, formed any expectations of any sort from his suggesting such correspondence. Indeed, who knows whether, when I am next able to come home for a visit, he will even remain a resident of St. Louis.

Please let me know whether you continue to regain your health, and any other news of you, our neighbors, and St. Louis you care to send.

Your ever loving daughter, Susannah

Susannah received a letter from Charles Elliott only a week after sending her permission for him to write. She carried the letter up to her room, feeling rather as if she had plucked a chocolate from a box of candy and carried it away to eat in secret.

She had never seen his handwriting before, but it was just as she would have expected, the letters in neat lines and of similar size, slanted enough to be elegant, but with no vulgar flourishes.

Dear Miss Shepard,

Thank you for permitting me to write to you. I hope that you are flourishing in your new surroundings, and that the denizens of Cowbird Creek — have you discovered what a cowbird is? — appreciate the gift of your presence.

I don't know whether William Simmons Normal School's curriculum assumed that you would be teaching in environs similar to its own. Did your classes prepare you in any way for a more rustic student body? I would imagine their parents might pose a special challenge, as one hopes the children, at least, are more malleable and responsive to an improving influence.

My daily life continues as usual, though of course absent the pleasant awareness that I may encounter you at a social gathering or around some corner. I viewed the latest exhibition displaying photographs of oddities from far corners, so to speak, of the globe, and pretended to believe the descriptions accurate. I took tea with Mother, and provided her attentive sympathy on the subject of the vulgar indulgence of the business class in luxurious furnishings. I purchased some of the new ready-made doll costumes for my older cousin's rapacious daughters. I then rewarded myself for familial devotion by escaping to the latest vaudeville show. Have they vaudeville in Cowbird Creek?

If so, she had failed to happen on it.

Various acquaintances — I must confess I did not commit all their names to memory — ask about you, having somehow divined that I might be in a position to hear your news, so I hope you will soon oblige them as well as

Your obedient servant,

Charles Sterling Elliott

Susannah folded the letter and tucked it away in her dressing table drawer. The act recalled her to her current surroundings, which seemed newly unfamiliar. Reading the letter had carried her imagination back to St. Louis. She half expected to hear her mother's footsteps, coming to solicit her advice on tonight's supper menu, and to smell the smoke of her father's pipe.

She took a deep breath, then another when the first proved unsteady, and took her volume of *Little Dorritt* to the sitting room, where she might find a few of the other boarders to remind her of her present circumstances and surroundings.

Chapter 8

TWO WEEKS later, Bronka brought the first McGuffey reader to Susannah and confirmed that she had read it through. Bronka's arithmetic skills had been at her age level from the start, but it remained difficult to judge her understanding of other lessons.

Camelia popped over at the dinner hour with another book in her hands, this time the long-awaited Polish history. Susannah, who had been eating a hasty sack dinner at her desk, accepted the book and immediately opened it to the title page, admiring the engraving of a gentleman in a cloak and armor, the name "Jan III" underneath. As with the volume of poetry, the words looked utterly unpronounceable. And yet Bronka could read them without thinking twice about it.

When the students had all returned to the classroom, Susannah opened her mouth to call the oldest students forward, then changed her mind and made her way over to Bronka's seat, the book of history in her arms. Bronka had brought the book of Polish poetry to school, but was dutifully studying McGuffey's second reader. She heard Susannah approach and looked up with apparent relief at the interruption. When she spied Susannah's burden, her face lit up in striking contrast with her resigned expression a moment before.

Susannah laid the book while Bronka burst out with, "Oh, thank you, Miss Teacher! I will take this home and handle it most carefully!" Her hand stole out to touch the cover, but she quickly pulled it again and looked down at her reader.

Susannah cleared her throat to recall Bronka's attention. "You are welcome to do so, of course. But first, I wondered how difficult it would be for you to translate some passage in the book into English, a passage dealing with any momentous — important — episode in Polish history."

Bronka gaped up at her. "You want I should write about Polish history, in English?"

Was the task too difficult? Or only too unexpected? "You do not need to translate every word, or stay especially close to the original." She allowed herself a smile. "After all, I will have no way to do a comparison! But I hope the attempt will not only help you with your English, but might allow me to expand your fellow pupils' history lessons with events of which I know little."

Bronka's eyes went even wider. "You would use what I write to — to teach the others?"

"The older ones, yes. It would be good for them, I believe, to be reminded that their own country is not the only one in which history occurs, or the only place where people face great challenges with matching courage." It was a guess, and perhaps a risky one, but Susannah's vague impression of Poland's place in the world — or should she say Poland's place in Prussia? — supported it.

Bronka picked up the book and clasped it to her breast, despite its weight and bulk. "I will work very hard to do this. When should I begin? I was not yet finished this time reading the McGuffey." She looked over at the reader, and the loathing that briefly crossed her face made Susannah shudder.

"Why not begin right now? The reader can wait. If

you have any questions about how to go about it, you
 may come to my desk and ask me." Though Bronka might
be too shy, after all that had happened, to call attention to
herself in that way. "Or you can just write yourself a note,
in whichever language you please, about what to ask me
the next time I call your class forward."

"Thank you so much! Oh, and may I take this book
home also?"

"Yes, of course. Though if you mean to take the book
of poetry home as well, the two will make for a heavy load
to carry so far." The idea that popped into her head was
surely inappropriate, and yet out it came. "You could leave
them here for now, and send your brother to pick them up
in the morning."

Bronka shook her head. "But then he would have to
take them with him to the mill, and they could get dirty. I
will carry them myself."

Saturday afternoon, as Susannah was about to
dismiss school for the week, Bronka came up to her desk,
with her usual diffidence. "Miss Teacher, I have a request.
I do not know whether what I would ask is allowed."

Susannah stood, rather than sit looking upward. She
regretted it when Bronka took a small step backward. She
hastened to say, "Please tell me, and we'll see whether
there's any difficulty or no."

Bronka swallowed and said, "I would like to come to
the school and work on the history, tomorrow after church,
if Father McCarthy says it would not violate the Sabbath. It
would be quiet here, and without anyone sitting next to
me, there would be plenty of room on the desk to keep the
book open and also to write. I would be very careful, and
leave everything just as I found it."

In St. Louis, there would have been the question of

meeting Bronka to let her in, or giving her a key. But the schoolhouse had been built without lock or key hole. And from what she had seen of members of the Marek family, she could rely on Bronka to keep her word.

She gave Bronka the most reassuring smile she had at her command and said, "There is no need to finish your translation by any particular time. But if you would like to work here on Sunday, you may."

* * * * *

Karol often thought back sadly to how bright-eyed and confident, even bold, Bronka had been back home, and how much she had changed, especially after that first day at school. He had confessed to the sins of wrath, resentment, and holding a grudge, but even as he came to understand Susannah better, he was not sure he had altogether forgiven what she had done to his sister.

He didn't know what to make of Bronka lingering after church that Sunday. He persuaded Mama and Papa to go home in the wagon, not wanting them to stand around in the cold, and waited, pacing back and forth and blowing on his hands. He could probably have waited inside the church, but Bronka might see it as intruding. And he preferred moving while he waited, which he could hardly do inside.

Bronka finally came out and saw him. She apologized before she even reached him. "I'm sorry you felt you had to wait! But at least Mama and Papa went home. It'll be . . . easier, that they aren't here with you."

He stared at her. "What can you mean?"

"Miss Teacher — that is, Miss Shepard has asked me to put some part of the Polish book of history into English, and read it to the class when I finish. I have not got as much done as I would like, with my other work to do and all the things that go on during the day — the talking and the pupils going to the teacher and back again . . . so I asked her if I could work today. And Father McCarthy has given his permission."

Then Susannah was still doing everything she could to help Bronka. If he couldn't forgive her now, fully and freely, he was no sort of Christian.

As for Bronka's plans . . . Karol put aside thoughts of asking the priest whether he could do odd jobs on Sundays. No doubt anyone who had such work to be done, and refrained from doing it, would object to what they would call Sabbath-breaking. But there was something useful he *could* do, if he went home first and told their parents what was happening. "I'll walk with you, and then, after I run home for a little, I could come to the school and help you. Unless your teacher wouldn't like it."

Bronka chewed her lip for what felt like a long time, and then said slowly, "I have no dictionary for putting Polish into English, so I do come to a stop often. I haven't liked to interrupt Miss Shepard too much, to try to explain the Polish and ask for the English. That makes another reason it is taking me a long time."

Karol kissed the top of her head and said, "I'll be there when you need me. And if you wouldn't mind, I'll bring the book of poetry with me. It's been too long since I read anything in our own language." Or in any language, for that matter.

Mama, of course, could think of many more useful things Bronka should be doing instead of spending even more time at school. But on the way home, Karol had thought of an answer for her. "There are so few of us, anywhere in the county or the counties around us, who speak Polish, and Bronka's German is not that good. You care so much that she learn how to be a good wife and mother, but who will she marry? And what man needing a wife will want one who can barely speak English? Bronka had no part in the decision to come to America, but now she must make a life here."

Mama sank down in the nearest chair and put her apron to her eyes. Papa crouched beside her and rubbed her shoulders, almost as if she were one of the children. "Hush now, dear one. Our son is becoming wise, I think. And Bronka will be fine, with all three of us to help and guide her."

Mama nodded, got back up, and went to stir the pot of soup on the stove.

Bronka was hunched over the history book when Karol arrived, muttering to herself as she read the lines. She had spread the book across the two-pupil desk, but made to shove it to one side as Karol walked up. He bent over to pull it back into place. "I can put my book on my lap. Or use another desk, so long as I don't move anything."

A sudden mischievous urge popped into his head. "This one will do." He walked over to Susannah's big desk at the front of the room and plunked down the book between the sheets of blank paper on one side and her slate, showing arithmetic problems for the little children, on the other.

Bronka gasped. "That is —"

"I know." He grinned. "But she won't catch me at it. And there's plenty of room. Besides, this chair is more my size than those little seats."

He set himself to reading, but almost at once, Bronka

asked him how best to translate something. He pushed aside concerns about how crude his wording might be, gave her his answer, and did his poor best to help her with the spelling. Then he returned to the book of poetry.

He had not read many poems back home, but he had always heard about the wonderful Three Bards. Now, when any words of his own language had become precious, the beauty of the poems had him blinking and turning away from where Bronka sat, though she would have understood his tears.

Now my soul is incarnate in my country,
My body has swallowed her soul,
And I and my country are one.
My name is million, for I love and suffer for millions.

By more luck than he deserved, his eyes were dry when he heard the door open behind his back. Bronka jumped out of her seat, jostling the legs of the desk so they squealed against the floor. "Oh, no! Teacher, I am so sorry! I should have made him sit somewhere else, or go home. But, but he said the other desks were too small for him."

Karol had also sprung out of his — or rather, Susannah's — chair and faced Susannah. She wagged a finger at him, though he thought he saw her fighting a smile. He bowed and said, "I am a little big for the other desks, but I could have fit into one. I apologize."

She set the smile free and said, "No need. And Bronka, please don't fret — don't worry. I had wished there were someone I could assign to help you, but none of your other students had the knowledge to do so. Mr. Marek, I will keep your secret, so long as you keep mine. My neighbors, and those at the boarding house, would be shocked that I visited this place on the Sabbath. But I was taking a walk, to enjoy the brisk air and sunshine, and I thought I'd see whether Bronka had been able to come. The priest gave his permission?"

Given how many Protestants felt about priests – as if they were puppeteers and the faithful their puppets – he was glad to hear Susannah speak of the priest and his authority without any sign of dislike or disapproval. Bronka nodded eagerly. "Yes, if I went home and said three *Zdrowaś Maryjo* afterward. I don't know what it is in English."

Bronka hadn't said, before, that Father McCarthy had set that condition. Karol wasn't sure what it meant, but said for Susannah's benefit, "That is the Hail Mary."

"Ah, I see." Karol doubted Susannah did see, quite, but at least she was being polite about this Catholic custom. "Are you done for the day? You could — you both could — join me on my walk."

Bronka looked longingly at the blue sky out the window, but said, "I should work some more, I think."

Before he could be tempted away, Karol said, "Thank you for the offer. I'll stay and help Bronka, if she needs it, and then go home with her."

"Good day, then, and I hope the work goes well! A blessed Sabbath to you both." And she left by the back door, moving quickly, with no sign that she would have liked to stay behind.

Karol sat back down at Susannah's desk, but the poems failed to hold his attention as much as before.

Chapter 9

THE MORNING was by far the coldest since Susannah had arrived. With the cold weather came changes in her classroom. Five of the younger children failed to arrive, while four older boys, none of whom she recalled seeing in town, filed in and stood awkwardly against the wall. The tallest of them gave her an awkward bow and said, "We're here for winter, ma'am, 'til there's more work on the farm again. I'm Bill, and this here's my brother Harry, and Mo and Joe from the place over the hill."

She looked at the row of boys and did her best to smile as if she didn't have to crane upwards. "Welcome, all of you. Amos, you and Billy grab that desk in the corner and move it next to that vacant desk at the end of the row. Mo and Joe— " She fought down a thoroughly inappropriate snicker at the rhyming names. "You may sit in the desk already available."

While the boys got settled, Susannah determined to ask Dr. Gibbs the cause of these changes when next she saw him, and turned her attention to questioning all the new arrivals and giving them their first assignments. By the time she dismissed the class for dinner, she felt reasonably content with how the morning had gone. Thomas, the boy from town who had previously been the oldest boy, had been standoffish at first, or perhaps the farm lads had been the ones to keep their distance – but they had all trooped outside together.

Looking out the door at the end of dinner hour, ready to call the children back inside, she noted with some alarm that not only had it begun to snow, the snow had already begun to form sizable drifts against the walls of the schoolhouse. She clapped her hands to draw the pupils' attention. "The weather promises to make your trips home more difficult if we await the usual hour for dismissal. Please prepare to leave for the day. Get your coats — line up, younger children first, to take them off the hooks. You may leave any unfinished work here for tomorrow." She realized, suddenly, why some of the smaller children had not come to school. They must live far enough from town that traveling to and from school in winter weather could make their trips difficult or even dangerous. How often would this happen? Was there some way she could send work home for them, and have it returned for her review? She would have to give the matter further thought.

And what would the snow do to the other children's shoes? She noticed, now that the problem had occurred to her, that the big boys who had first shown up that morning were wearing boots. Presumably it was their standard winter footwear. As for the others . . . if she had thought of it, she would have tried to acquire galoshes in a range of sizes. She could only hope the shoes the children were wearing were not their only pairs.

With some natural excitement at the break in routine, the children retrieved and donned their coats. When it came Bronka's turn, she looked at the history book on her desk and then at Susannah, uncertainty and worry on her face. "I am afraid what the snow will do to the book. I have nothing to carry it in."

"You may leave it here. Indeed, if you haven't yet finished your translation, it would make more sense to keep the book at school until you finish. It should be quite safe."

Bronka relaxed with relief, took down her coat — the same overlarge winter coat she had worn the first day, finally needed — and left. She was the last pupil to leave, and Susannah, looking after her, saw the many footprints already filling up and disappearing.

Susannah put on her own coat and hat, tidied her desk, and headed out. It was the first heavy snowfall since she came to town, and all the houses and streets looked quite different. In fact, as she came to where she thought her first turn should be, she was not quite sure she had her bearings.

She jumped to hear a male voice to her right. "You dismissed the school, then? Mr. Grint also closed the mill early. Has Bronka already left?"

Susannah collected herself and replied, "Just a few minutes ago. You could catch up with her, I expect."

He shrugged. "It is not so far, and she is, we are, used to snow much deeper than this."

Then why had he come to the school? She pushed the question out of her mind. At any rate, he was now saying, "It all looks different in snow, I think."

She looked around again. "It does. I should keep walking before I manage to lose myself."

He stepped out in the general direction of the boarding house. "I may as well go with you. It would not do for you to wander about in the cold."

Did he think her such a delicate flower? But it would be more pleasant to have a companion, and embarrassing to lose her way and be seen wandering about. And of course, he already knew where the boarding house was.

Her toes were growing chilled. With all she had to arrange, and too much to think about, before leaving St.

Louis, she had neglected to get new boots, or even have these boots mended. She asked Carl, "Do you know where in town I would find a good cobbler?"

"You could try Mr. Finch. We pass his shop on the way, but maybe you will want to wait for better weather to stop in. He is the only cobbler or shoemaker I know of here, but I can't say whether he's a good one."

How careful he was not to say more than he could vouch for. It boded well for his character. She had not always encountered such scruples among her acquaintances in St. Louis. But she must find a topic of conversation, and not about Carl's virtues, to be sure. "So the snow is much deeper where you come from?"

"Often, yes. Up to my father's chest, sometimes, or higher. Sometimes my father and I would work together to make a path, pushing through it, if it was not high enough to bury me. And it snowed more times than I have seen it snow here."

Susannah kicked up some fluffy new snow for the pleasure of watching it float down again. "I always loved snow as a child. My friends and I would make whole families of snow-people, if there was snow enough. I remember one winter when the first snow fell, hardly more than a dusting. My best friend and I made a dirt snowman and plastered snow on it."

They trod on for a few more steps before Carl said, "You must miss those friends. It is hard at first, coming somewhere new. I remember."

"How long ago was it?"

"I lose track, with everything else to do besides remember. But I think a little more than four years since we came this far, and stayed. The boat arrived maybe six months before that."

She could hardly imagine living through so many

changes. To think that her own travels, crossing all of one state line, had loomed large. She asked, hoping the question was not too personal, "Have you made friends here, at least?"

He shrugged his broad, snow-covered shoulders. "A few. Men I worked with, and our neighbors, and one or two others. I am usually busy, and I have much to do at home when not working for pay."

His speech had a pleasing, almost musical rhythm to it. And when had she last walked with a man near her own age? She had given so much attention to studying for her certificate, while girlfriends tempted her with parties and outings. It had not occurred to her before that her new life need not, necessarily, be entirely devoted to her work, so long as she did that work well.

* * * * *

When had Karol last walked through the snow with a girl by his side, let alone such a pretty one?

He could only remember one time, not long before his parents told him they were leaving, going all the way across the sea to the wild and famous country of America. He had been leaving church and had let the rest of his family go on ahead, while he walked beside Elzbieta. He had been too shy to say much, but she had talked enough for them both, as she always did. He had dared to wonder why she walked with him, instead of with the group of girls she spent so much time with, or with his friend Alojzy that all the girls looked at and whispered to each other about.

He and Elzbieta had parted when their paths did, and he had not talked to her again.

But now he walked beside Susannah, close enough

that he could have held her hand. He allowed himself a quick glance at her as she gazed around delighted at the snow covering gates and bushes. Snowflakes were sticking to her hat, a fur hat like his own, and melting in her long dark hair.

They reached the boarding house too soon. Before she could climb the step, he gathered his nerve and said, "Maybe we will see each other at the Christmas market."

She stopped and turned toward him, puzzlement wrinkling her forehead. "What Christmas market is that?"

"Has no one said about it? A few days before Christmas, we bring the tallest tree we can find into the square, and anyone in town who likes can help decorate it. People set up stalls to sell all sorts of things – food, toys, winter clothes, and ornaments for the tree -- and families bring their own special ornaments if those are sturdy enough not to break when people bump against them." He laughed, remembering. "The littlest children hang what they bring or buy on the very lowest branches, sometimes so low the ornaments touch the ground. Those of us who are taller decorate up high, or use a ladder to reach the top. Sometimes I hold the children up to put an ornament where more people will see it."

She smiled up at him as if she approved. He could imagine how she would look at him if she knew he was imagining holding her slim waist and hoisting her up in the air to place a giant wooden snowflake on the tree.

He did his best to ignore that picture and went on, "I have been to this gathering before, three times now. If you plan to buy any ornaments, I could show you which booths have the best ones, if they are there again."

It was the thinnest excuse to spend time with her. There were not so many booths that it would take her long to see all they offer. But she smiled again, showing her dimples, and said, "I would appreciate your advice."

Should he leave it there? Best so. He could leave it for another time to ask, in so many words, whether he could accompany her there. He tipped his hat to her, cold air creeping up the back of his scalp, and headed home, humming "*Bóg się rodzi*." And then, under his breath, in English: "Raise your hand, God Child, Bless the beloved Motherland . . . ."

Chapter 10

AMOS had been less troublesome than Susannah had initially feared, but now that winter was limiting the amount and variety of exercise he could take during the dinner hour, he was more inclined to restlessness. This morning he had progressed to playing tricks on the girls, hiding two of their dinner baskets while Susannah was preoccupied giving the second grade children an arithmetic lesson. When dinnertime came and the baskets were not at hand, one of the girls started to cry, which Amos had apparently not expected; he had scuffed his toe and apologized. But Susannah was not optimistic enough to assume this would be the last time he misbehaved. Of the older boys, one was quiet and reserved enough that he might not be inclined to initiate any misbehavior, but she could well imagine his being led into it by the others.

The schoolroom had not, when she first saw it, contained a switch or ferule for corporal punishment. She had taken that as a sign that Dr. Gibbs did not consider such punishment the obvious or inevitable choice. And Susannah, disinclined by nature to resort to violence, would be glad to do without it. She might, in fact, find that as small and slight as she was, even a boy of Amos's size — let alone one of the bigger boys who had arrived with the winter — would defy her rather than allow himself to be whipped. She imagined a boy towering over her, grabbing the stick away from her and breaking it, brandishing the pieces in front of her face . . . .

She shook her head to dislodge the vision. Alice, copying the map of the continents onto her slate, looked up at her with a quizzical expression. "Does your ear itch, Teacher? Our dog Major does that sometimes, and Daddy says it's because his ear itches."

Susannah's struggle not to laugh distracted her better than shaking her head had done. "No," she said, "my ear is fine. Now how is your map coming along? Oh, that's good — but do remember not to leave out South America."

Bronka asked Susannah if she could stay after school to work on her translation, and Susannah assented, using the time to write up some lesson plans. When a knock came at the schoolhouse back door, she was startled to look out the window and see that darkness had fallen. She opened the door to find Carl, who tipped his hat and said, "I've come to walk Bronka home, if she's still here. She said this morning that she might be staying, if you allowed it."

Bronka looked over at Carl, biting her lip. Susannah came to look at what Bronka was writing, and saw she had paused mid-sentence in her translation. She smiled at Carl and said, "Do come in while Bronka reaches a good stopping place."

Carl lifted one foot and looked at the snow and slush on the bottom of his boot. "I wouldn't want to dirty your floor. I can wait here."

Susannah glanced at the floor and confirmed her impression of it. She stepped back, opening the door wider, and said, "It'll need cleaning tomorrow morning in any case. I'll assign one of the older pupils to do it, and let the others have a few more minutes to socialize outdoors." If the weather was too challenging, she could let the children come in and stand near the wall while she or a pupil did some hasty cleaning near the door.

Carl still hesitated, but scraped his boots on the step as well as he could and then entered. She waved him toward the nearest desk. "Do sit down. You've a long walk ahead of you." And it would be easier to talk to him if he was more at his ease.

He looked at her and replied, "Only if you sit also. You must have been standing most of the day."

She'd been sitting since school let out, but it would be better for her, as a temporary hostess, to make her guest comfortable and keep him company. Seeing him wedge his long legs under the desk led her to notice once again the height of him, and his broad shoulders and muscled arms. Searching for a topic of conversation that would distract her, she fell back on the mundane, "How was your day at work?"

Carl shrugged and looked down at the desk. "Like other days there. I had no special trouble with the miller or the customers. I was busy enough not to have too much time to think, and not too busy to get the work done." He looked up and made a visible effort to look more cheerful. "And you, were your pupils well behaved?"

A sigh escaped her before she could stop it. Of course Carl noticed, and said, "Not all of them, I think."

"It was only one of the boys, bedeviling the girls. The children get restless in this weather." She glanced over at Bronka, who was either too absorbed in her work to listen or pretending to be so. Susannah lowered her voice to just above a whisper. "And I'm not sure what to do about it. I haven't yet had to . . . to discipline any of the children beyond a stern word or two."

Carl's eyebrows went up. "In all this time? You must have done a very good job making them respect you and care for your good opinion."

A cheering way to think about it. "It may be. But

sooner or later, I'll have to do something more, it seems."

Carl had the far-away look of someone remembering the past. "When I was the age of your pupils, I did not often dare to make trouble. My father would whip me for sure."

His words sparked an idea. Could she enlist the boys' fathers? Could she talk to them before any more problems developed? Or would it make her look weak?

But Carl was still talking. "And anyway, by the time I was old enough to make much mischief, I had Bronka to think of. As busy as my parents were, I was the one taking care of her often. She looked up to me, and that made me think of myself — " He laughed. "I thought I was a very big boy, very grown up, and I had my, what is the word, my dignity to look after."

Carl stopped short and looked hard at her, probably because she had sat up as suddenly as if someone had stuck a pin in her. That might just work! If she could combine both elements of what Carl had told her . . . .

Her shoulders lost their tight tension, and breathing was suddenly easier as she said to Carl, "You may not have realized it, but you've given me the idea I needed. Thank you!"

Carl looked a little startled, but stood up and gave one of his little bows. "I'm most glad to hear it. I will always be happy to help you in any way." He stopped short and turned toward Bronka. Was that the trace of a blush on his cheek?

Susannah stood up also and went over to Bronka's desk. Bronka was sitting very still, not writing and (as far as Susannah could tell) not reading either. She must have been eavesdropping, as was only natural. Susannah made no comment and only asked, "Are you ready to leave? You've done plenty of work for today."

Bronka put her papers inside the book and closed it

carefully. "Thank you, Teacher. Yes, I can leave now. I should help with supper, if Mama hasn't done everything by now."

Carl fetched Bronka's coat for her, and then her dinner pail. Susannah opened the door for them, and they went out into the night.

She would probably need to make separate treks to the farms on which the older boys lived, but a little discreet investigation over the next two days revealed that their families knew each other well and that, in fact, the fathers in two of the families were brothers. It was possible that if a meeting with the first of them went well, that father would be willing to speak to the others, if she trusted him not to garble her message.

Susannah spent the following school day studying the demeanor of the older boys, while trying not to let her scrutiny become apparent. By dismissal time, she had at best a tentative assessment, but she feared to wait any longer.

She could think of no way to visit their families without the boys being present, so she made a virtue of necessity and asked one of them, Steven, to escort her to his home. He at once acted the part of a sinner discovered, going pale, dropping his eyes and shifting from one foot to the other — which at least confirmed her guess that she had chosen wisely. Or did he only dread the appearance of guilt, should he arrive home with his teacher on his heels?

"I am not going to your parents with any complaint of you," she said, "but beyond that, your parents can explain my errand to you when they see fit. Shall we go?"

Susannah had wondered whether to expect a stern, taciturn man, or an angry, defensive one. She had somehow not expected a rotund, jovial fellow who, if he was particularly bright, chose not to make that fact obvious. He cocked an eyebrow to see them approach, but said nothing to Steven except, "Get on with your chores, then. I'll call you if we need you." The boy glanced toward Susannah warily, but obeyed.

Meanwhile, Steven's mother had hurried forward, her thin face and furrowed forehead a marked contrast to her husband's appearance and manner. "Come in, Miss Shepard, do," she said, fast enough to echo Susannah's heartbeat, "and I'll get you a little something after your walk. Some coffee, and a biscuit with blackberry preserves?"

Over the refreshments, Susannah explained her errand to both parents, beginning with her request. "I believe it would be good for your son and the others his age, and for the youngest boys, if elder could work with younger — helping them with their work. Your son, for example, could help the little boys with their figuring." He was not, perhaps, as advanced in that area as he might be, but he was enough ahead of the younger pupils for that purpose.

The father beamed at her. "Well, that's a right nice idea, and I'm sure the lad would be glad to do it. Wouldn't he, Mabel?"

The aforementioned Mabel peered at Susannah with some suspicion. "Is that all you've come about, then? How's our boy been behaving himself?"

Susannah took a breath not as deep as she would have liked. "He's adjusting quite well to the school routine. Frankly, I'm hoping this additional duty, with the responsibility it involves, will stave off any tendency to restlessness that might otherwise develop over the next months."

The father sat forward just enough to suggest that he had picked up some intention underneath her words. "We wouldn't, neither of us, want him to get restless like that. But miss, I'd like you to promise that if he does, you'll send word to us somehow, and we'll deal with it. Your coming all this way to help our town, you shouldn't oughta be having trouble from big fellows like him, as should know to behave themselves."

Susannah sent up a silent prayer of thanksgiving, and replied, "I will, if that proves necessary, though most likely it won't. I'll be letting you get back to your duties, and thank you for your time and your hospitality."

As she made her way out, she realized that in her relief, she had failed to ask about their talking to the families of the other boys. Nor would she want to push her luck with that additional request. She would have to visit at least one of the other families as well.

The next morning, the other two boys stared and gaped when Susannah beckoned to their comrade, escorted him to the desk where two little boys were alternately writing on their slates and rubbing out the result, and set him to his new task. The older boys leaned together whispering until Susannah made her way to their desk and did her inadequate best to loom over them. "You know better than to talk instead of work. Does either of you have a question to ask?"

The boys looked at each other, the shyer of the two elbowing the other. The latter cleared his throat and said hoarsely, "Why does he get to work with the little 'uns and not us?"

If she had expected this reaction, she would have congratulated herself on her clever strategy. As it was, she concealed her surprise, or so she hoped, and did a quick mental review of the boys' skills. "Very well, then," she said to the bolder of the boys. "You may review Amos's progress on his history report, and make sure he doesn't exaggerate or invent any of the battles. If you're not sure of the facts, consult me." She hesitated and decided on a gamble. "And if you happen to learn that he's planning to play any tricks on the girls, you could inform him that no gentleman would do such a thing."

The boy stuck his chest out, probably to relieve the pressure as it swelled with pride. "I'll sure do that, Teacher! Should I go talk to him now?"

"Yes, do. Thank you." As he strutted away, she studied the remaining boy shifting impatiently in his seat. How could she best employ him? Even if she had another troublemaker to subdue, this boy might not be well suited for the task.

An image appeared in her mind: Carl, as he might have looked many years ago, walking hand in hand with a much younger Bronka. Or watching over her as she ate her dinner, cleaning up her messes, wiping her face.

She looked at the boy awaiting her decision and said gravely, "I have no wish to assign you a duty that would be beneath your dignity. But if you have no such objection, I would appreciate your help with one or two of the youngest girls. They are unused to spending so much time away from their families, and take any difficulty very much to heart. You could comfort them by your resemblance to their older brothers and their fathers, and reassure them of their ability to master the work before them."

The boy looked at her wide-eyed. Susannah held her

breath as he slowly looked toward where the younger children sat, squared his shoulders, and said firmly, "I would like to try to do that."

She had not thought to wonder how Thomas, the oldest town boy, would react to seeing his peers acquire responsibilities, and she almost missed the hurt expression on his face. She turned toward him, trying (probably without success) to give the impression that she had meant to speak to him all along, and said quietly, "You have done so well in both your studies and your deportment that I would like to let you choose how you will assist one or more of the younger children." It was perhaps an exaggeration, especially as to his studies, but if it made him too complacent, she would deal with that at some future time.

His eyes lit up, and he leaned forward as he said, "I've been wondering whether it might be possible — whether there was room, in the school day, for any attention to drawing. It's always been an interest of mine, and I helped my sisters." He pointed to where they sat in the front and middle rows. "They always enjoyed our little drawing lessons."

Susannah would love to include art instruction as a regular part of her curriculum, but at least until she became more skilled at managing the children, there was hardly enough time. Still . . . . "I could include such lessons as a reward for good performance or good behavior, if the pupil liked the idea. That would ensure that you had only interested and biddable pupils. Shall we give it a try?"

His enthusiastic and repeated nods made him look younger, and more endearing, than usual. "Oh, yes!"

Bronka worked after school again that day, and Carl came again to walk her home, later than the last time. Susannah took the time only to say as Bronka packed up, "Things are going well with the bigger boys, due to the ideas you gave me. Thank you again!"

He shook his head, as if amazed that anything he had said could have been so useful. The pleasure that filled his face warmed her as she made her chilly way back to Miss Wheeler's.

Chapter 11

LOUISA answered Susannah's letter with effusive thanks that Susannah had thought of her, and obvious relief that Susannah's situation and spirits were not worse than described. She had not mentioned repeating any of what Susannah had told her to any of their mutual acquaintances, but given how natural Louisa would have found it to do so, that fact meant little. Of more importance, to Louisa at least, was the position she had obtained with a school not far from her family home. Susannah wrote congratulating her and describing, in general terms, her own increasing comfort with her daily tasks and the confidence that necessarily followed.

She had, of course, answered Charles Elliott's letter, though she had found less to say than she had expected. She thought of sharing anecdotes about her work — her students and their progress and problems — but when she picked up her pen to do so, the idea felt inappropriate. It was not only concern for her pupils' privacy. As she reread his letter, there was a tone — an implicit assumption that her current situation was beneath her, and Charles could best console her by inviting her to find amusement in it — that displeased her, even disappointed her. So she had written a letter she would have to call superficial, lacking in much content beyond pleasantries and descriptions of the countryside.

She opened his latest letter with both curiosity and some trepidation.

Dear Miss Shepard,

What a pleasure it was to receive your letter! If the elegance of your handwriting is not sufficient recompense for the absence of your elegant presence, it is at least some consolation.

Was she truly so elegant in her manner? Or did Charles consider elegance the most important attribute for a woman, and therefore the greatest praise he could bestow? She would not have thought an educated gentleman would put any aspect of appearance and manner quite so high.

I could wish myself to have greater involvement in trade, that I might have a reason to visit your new environs. But I trust you will return to St. Louis from time to time.

The first of those sentences, Susannah guessed, was less an expression of an actual desire than a veiled reminder that he had no need to engage in such activities. As for the second . . . she had given little thought to when she might visit her family and friends, probably because the obstacles were so daunting as to depress her. Neither she nor her parents could afford any travel that was less than urgent. And in whatever amount of time it would require to save up for that expense, President Brecker could be doing as much damage as his prestige would allow and his malice dictate.

She would like for her family to visit her instead. Or at least one of them, her mother or father, to keep the cost down. They could see her school, meet Camelia and Dr. Gibbs . . . meet her other friends, like Carl . . . .

She dragged her attention back to Charles' letter. He'd attended a musicale, at which his aunt had played a piece she had recently mastered. *Do the residents of Cowbird Creek gather for such activities?*

He probably thought not. She had not lived here long enough, nor met sufficient people, to know. But it was pleasant to think that any of the houses she passed, or at least the larger ones, might contain a piano, or someone diligently practicing flute or violin. And she had a faint recollection of having heard piano music as she walked along one of the streets in the town square, though she hadn't noted its source.

Charles had also been to the theatre, and described the production with his usual wit. She could imagine sitting next to him, hearing his whispered comments on the text, the performers, the stage set. Despite the flaws he mentioned, it sounded like a performance she might have enjoyed. She allowed herself one sigh, finished the letter quickly, put it away, and pulled out her notes for her next lesson on American history.

By the middle of the following week, Bronka had come to the end of the passage in the Polish history book on which she had been working. She brought the single sheet of paper, filled with careful writing, to Susannah for correction or critique. Susannah thanked her, promising, "I'll look through it to see how the English reads, and if anything needs a little change here and there, we'll work on it together."

Naturally, the English could have been better, in some places too confusing for her to guess at the meaning. And the spelling! It pained her to leave it uncorrected, but Bronka might well have more trouble reading the piece aloud if the spelling changed. That could wait for afterward.

In winter, more of the children who lived in town brought their dinners to school, and almost all who did so ate inside, which made privacy more of a challenge. The day was, however, relatively mild, which allowed Susannah to invent an errand for Bronka's seatmate to run, replenishing the supply of slate pencils. Her absence meant Susannah could sit down beside Bronka and quietly go through the phrases that needed correction and those that simply baffled her. There was no way to keep Bronka from being crestfallen about her errors, but Susannah did her best to reassure her.

At the end of the dinner hour, Susannah called the class to attention and announced, "We have a special treat today. Bronka, who grew up in Poland and used to read a great deal there, has done us the favor of translating a page from a book about the history of her country." Susannah was glad the King of Prussia was not present to hear her call Poland its own country, but the pride on Bronka's face was fair recompense for ignoring any scruples about accuracy. "Bronka, please come up here with your translation."

Bronka looked around the room, her jerky movements suggesting sudden panic. Before the other pupils could react, Susannah beckoned to her. If she had to, she would go to Bronka and shepherd her to the front. But Bronka gulped and made her way forward, the paper betraying the trembling of her hand.

One of the older boys elbowed his seatmate, and two of the girls in the second youngest group whispered to each other and giggled Susannah rapped her knuckles on the desk. "I require quiet and attention, all of you, when any of you is speaking." And then, inspired, "You may be sure you will all have a turn to recite to the class at some time, and will be glad to have your fellow students treat you with respect when that turn comes."

The children quieted down. Bronka took long enough to begin that Susannah's heart was in her throat, expecting any moment that things would become unruly again and possibly frighten Bronka out of reading at all. But at last, in a voice barely loud enough for the back of the room to hear (and that far only by straining), she said in introduction, "This book is about a great victory the Polish king John had, more than two hundred years ago." And then, she read, her voice growing stronger with every word: "One week had to be enough to get ready. The bravery of the commander, and the soldiers, and the people in the town lasted through nine weeks of battle . . . ."

When she got to the end of the page, she let her arm drop to her side and looked around wide-eyed as if suddenly awakened and finding herself there. And then, slowly, a smile spread across her face.

Susannah swallowed, cleared her throat, and said, "Thank you very much, Bronka. Now, does anyone have any questions for Bronka about what she read, or about her homeland? If you do, raise your hand and wait for me to call on you."

When she saw the smile replaced by wide eyes and sudden pallor, Susannah knew she should have told Bronka what she planned, or even given her the choice whether to take on this new challenge. But it was too late to change course. Instead, she made a point of looking only at the younger children at first. Little Alice obliged her by raising and waving her hand. As soon as Susannah pointed to her, she asked, "Where's Poland? Is it far away?"

Susannah hoped Alice failed to see the melancholy in Bronka's eyes as she replied. "It is far, very far. We traveled by carriage and train from our village, and then by train to the port, and then we spent so long crossing the ocean that I didn't count the days. My father told me that to cross the ocean, we would travel five thousand miles. And then we had to cross this country from where the ship landed."

Alice's mouth and eyes made matching Os. Meanwhile, from the middle row of seats came a boy's voice, asking, "What's so special about Poland, anyway?"

Susannah pivoted to look sternly in that direction. "You are not to interrupt, or to shout out a question before I have called on you." She turned away to look for raised hands, but Bronka had other ideas. Her voice shook, but she spoke out loud and clear.

"Poland is a very old country, much older than this one. We became Christians nine hundred years ago. We had great kings and much wealth, for hundreds of years. We have great forests and many mountains. And we have had great poets, artists, thinkers. I am most proud to be Polish."

The room grew very quiet. Finally, a nine-year-old boy named Rufus raised his hand, and when recognized, asked eagerly, "What do people eat in Poland? Is the food good?"

Laughter, pitched high and lower, came from all corners of the room, but Rufus, undaunted, simply waited for Bronka's answer, and Susannah let the breach in decorum pass without rebuke.

* * * * *

When Bronka came home from school, Karol had a dizzying moment of wondering if they were back in Poland, and everything since had been a dream. She walked almost as she used to, with steps as free and firm as a man's, and carried her head high. And she was whistling! Mama always claimed the habit was unladylike, but now she looked at Karol with happy relief written on her face.

It hardly needed Bronka's account of reading to the

class, and answering their questions, and defending the honor of Poland, for him to know that Susannah had kept her promise.

The next morning, he woke before the sun, grabbed one of yesterday's biscuits, and half ran to the school, to be there when Susannah arrived.

Rather than ambush her in her own classroom, he waited by the woodpile. That gave him the excuse, when she approached and saw him, to offer, "Shall I carry in some of the wood? You must be running low, after all the cold weather."

She smiled politely and said, "Thank you, but the bigger boys have been carrying it in for me."

He could have smacked his forehead in dismay. Now she would group him with her pupils. But he forged ahead. "I would still be happy to help. But I came here, really, to talk to you. About Bronka, and something else."

He opened the door for her and followed her inside. As soon as she hung up her coat and hat, he burst out with, "Thank you. You should have seen my sister, when she came home. But of course you saw her all day, saw her after she spoke to them all. You have helped her so much!"

She put out her hand to interrupt him, or to contradict him. "If I helped Bronka, I only helped her recover from what my mistake did to her spirits. I am glad I managed that, at least."

She seemed still troubled by that memory. Karol looked in her eyes and said slowly, "Was it so much a mistake? You had no Polish books yet. I had not been honest enough to tell you, at the train station, what language your pupil would speak, or who she was to me. And she must learn to read, not only speak. Is there a better way to teach the reading of English?"

He had assumed an answer of "no," but Susannah cocked her head and thought about his question. "McGuffey readers are very useful. I don't know if you looked past the first pages, but they . . . improve as one goes further. Still, they are meant for young children, and are written to catch their interest. Bronka will not be the last, I'm sure, to come here without reading English well, but too old to delight in pictures of animals, or to see themselves in stories about young children. I'll talk to Camelia — to Mrs. Grant, the librarian — about what else could serve." She stopped and sighed. "I hope so much that Bronka can learn to read in English. I fear there will never be many books in Polish available here, and it would be such a loss for a dedicated reader to be deprived of the pleasure and comfort, the — the *nourishment* that books bring."

He could tell she was speaking of herself, and he imagined her at a desk or table or in an armchair, in the evening, with lamplight gleaming in her hair as she bent over a book.

He had never cared about reading as much as Bronka did, and since they came to this country he had given it no thought at all. But now he wondered if books could come to hold the same magic for him. And the picture in his mind grew to show Karol sitting across from Susannah, or even beside her . . . . Susannah bending over him to see what he was reading, her hair brushing his shoulder, her warm breath on his cheek . . . .

He dragged himself back to the present and the schoolroom, hoping she had not noticed his mind wandering. "I hope so also. And I am sure with your help, this will happen."

Susannah glanced toward the door, beyond which he

could hear footsteps and children's voices. "I appreciate your confidence, and will do all I can to justify it. And now I'd better get ready for the children. Thank you for coming by."

Her smile was warm enough to make it more than a polite order that he leave. He bowed to her, made his way out through the crowd of curious children, and walked as fast as he could to the mill.

Chapter 12

SUSANNAH had initially assumed that the younger children from farm families would stay home only on the coldest or snowiest days. But apparently, it was the custom for them to await the spring before returning.

She hadn't appreciated until these children vanished from the schoolroom how much their presence had brightened the day, how their innocent mistakes and earnest efforts had provided its own special relief and reward. And of course the children themselves were missing important instruction. She recalled her earlier resolution to formulate a plan for remedying the problem, and scolded herself for letting more immediate matters distract her from it.

She sought out Camelia one day after school, asking her to serve as a sounding board. Camelia welcomed her with hot green tea, cold tongue, and cheese toast. While Susannah was still helping herself, Camelia grinned and said, "I hope you're here with some new idea or scheme. Tell me all about it!"

Susannah chuckled. "You know me so well already! Yes, I have an idea, and I want you to tell me whether it sounds sensible and whether I'm missing some pitfall. I want to go see the children who don't come to school in the wintertime. I could bring them some lessons to do, or borrow some books and drop them off. I'm guessing they aren't coming to the library either. Could you spare a book or two for each of them? That'd be up to ten books, easy ones, the more pictures the better."

Camelia clapped her hands in glee. "I think it's delightful! I'll pull some books right now, as many as I think you can carry." She paused, tapping her chin, and said, "You might consult any of their older brothers and sisters who are still coming. I'll make you a list of the ones I know about. Ask, if you can ask delicately, how their parents would feel about it." She pondered some more. "And there's one other thing you might do."

Camelia stopped again, and seemed determined not to go on without prompting. Suppressing a bit of irritation, Susannah asked, "And that would be?"

"Winter weather can blow up quickly. You wouldn't want to be stranded, and put the family in an awkward position. Why not ask young Carl Marek to go with you, and help you get home if need be? And he could help you find the various farms."

It was a pleasant notion, but Susannah put it aside. "I'm likely to go right after I dismiss the school, when he'll be working. And I imagine any of the older siblings could act as a guide."

The next morning, she set the students to written work and approached the back row of desks where the older students sat. She already knew that Amos's younger sister was among her absent pupils, but even though Amos had become less troublesome with the passage of time, she did not completely trust him to guide her to various farms without larking about in some detour or teasing her with wrong routes.

So she started by asking the oldest girls whether they had young siblings staying at home, and whether they knew the way to the homes of the others. The first girl had only an older brother and sister, and the second was a relative newcomer, unfamiliar with most of the farm families. Susannah was preparing to resign herself to a male pupil when the third girl, Gertie, eagerly named one of the second grade boys as her brother, and asserted stoutly that she could find the others with no trouble.

Susannah deferred the trip to the next day. That would give the girl time to tell her family she would be late getting home, and to prepare them for the visit. As for the other families, she did not want to burden Gertie with traveling around to alert them. She would simply show up and hope for a friendly reception.

The next afternoon, Susannah dismissed the school an hour early, so as to make as much of the trip to the farms as possible before sunset. She waited for the children to file out of the schoolhouse, breaking into shouts and laughter as they started homeward, and then packed up everything she would need. Gertie shyly held out her arms and said, "May I help you carry things? That bag?"

That would be the bag of books, and given that Camelia had perhaps overestimated Susannah's strength a touch, the aid would be welcome. "Yes, Gertie, and thank you. I'll carry the lantern for later. Why don't you go ahead of me, and I'll close the door behind you."

As they walked, they discussed the locations of the farms where the children lived and the best route for reaching them. Susannah had thought of going to the farthest farm first and then working their way back; but Gertie lived almost as far as the farthest out, and it would be considerate of Susannah to end up at Gertie's home rather than require her to make her way home from elsewhere. They headed first, therefore, to a small farm about a mile from the edge of town, where seven-year-old Timothy lived with two younger sisters not yet old enough for school. The odors of animals and manure and hay lingered despite the cold air. The children's father was at work at a pond off to the side of the house, chopping ice for their ice house. Susannah led Gertie to the side door and knocked.

It took a couple of chilly minutes, and she was about to knock again, but finally a young woman in an apron appeared, at most a couple of years older than Susannah. Her hair was escaping its bun, her expression harried. Susannah quickly explained their errand, and the woman, though obviously surprised and a little taken aback, made them welcome — as did Timothy, running to meet them and almost tripping his mother in his enthusiasm. The mother led them to the kitchen, warm enough to be cozy, and cleared away some piecework lying on the table so Susannah could set the bag of books down and pull out the two she'd brought for Timothy. By now the other children had shown up, overcoming initial shyness and looking at the books with awe. Were these the first books they had seen?

She declined the offer of a cup of coffee, for fear of needing the necessary between farms, but accepted fresh-baked sugar cookies on her own and Gertie's behalf. She left untouched the sheet she had brought of words to copy, guessing that the mother would have little leisure, and possible little capacity, to oversee the exercise. Then it was off to the next farm. It had started to snow.

By the time they reached their next stop, perhaps a mile and a half from the first, it was full twilight, and the snow was halfway up her boots. This time her young pupil was the family's only child, and the mother welcomed them with an eagerness born of isolation. Susannah had come in more thoroughly chilled this time, and she reluctantly accepted a few sips of hot coffee.

The next farm, fortunately not far away, had two of her pupils, a boy and a girl, who both eagerly declared that they would make it to school next winter. Their mother, smiling, gave Susannah a wink suggesting they might be overly optimistic, but gratefully accepted a book for each child and promised to assist them with the arithmetic and spelling lessons Susannah had written out for them.

As they were gathering their things together to leave, the woman looked out the window, tsked, and said, "I do hope you don't have many stops after this, Miss Shepard! The snow is piling up that deep, it'll be hard going soon enough."

"Just my place," Gertie said cheerily. Susannah did her best to show confidence as she followed Gertie out the door, into snow almost over the tops of her boots. Gertie, several inches taller than Susannah and with boots to match, strode out energetically, and Susannah did her best to catch up without sending snow down her hose to chill her feet.

* * * * *

Coming into the kitchen to warm up after his walk home, Karol heard a faint distressed sound from the front room and went to investigate. Bronka stood at the window, her nose to the glass they had bought with his latest wages. The snow drifting down and piling up, made a pretty sight. But Bronka turned toward him with her forehead wrinkled in worry. "I do hope the teacher is not in trouble, out there in this weather."

"Trouble? Out there?" he exclaimed. "Why, what is she doing where the snow will trouble her?"

Bronka wrung her hands. "She is taking books and

lessons to the little ones, the children who won't be back at school until the spring. It's the first time she's doing this, and she may not have known how long it would take. Gertie is showing her the way, but Gertie will assume that Miss Shepard can handle the weather as well as she can."

Karol looked up at the clouds. "It looks like more snow, maybe for hours yet. Pushing through the drifts will wear her out."

Bronka sighed, turned away from the window, and said, "I'm sure Gertie's family will give her shelter, for as long as need be. I should help Mama get supper ready." She headed for the kitchen, leaving Karol to take her place at the window and imagine where Susannah might be. Was she still making her visits? Would Gertie be able to find their path in this weather? And it was getting dark — would Susannah be forced to spend the night with Gertie's family? Would they have a mattress for her, or only a makeshift pile of blankets as her bed?

"She'll be all right. Come have supper." It was Mama, standing in the kitchen doorway, long wooden spoon in her hand.

Karol turned away from the window, dragging his feet as he made his way to the table. He was hungry from splitting shingles and a full day of work before that, but it was not only hunger that made him hurry. As soon as he swallowed the last bite, he shoved his chair back hard enough that it squeaked on the floor and said, "I'm going to see how deep the snow has got." He could feel Mama's stare on his back as he left the room.

It was hard to tell, exactly, from the window. When he opened the front door, he saw a solid bank of snow almost two feet high. He'd have no great trouble flattening a path, but Susannah could never make her way through it all the way from Gertie's to town. Gertie's father might manage, but he was a thin fellow half a foot shorter than Karol.

Susannah might think it forward of him to show up, unasked. The family there would wonder, and might gossip. Or she might have turned back before the snow got too deep, and he would be trudging through the cold and bothering the family for nothing. But he could let such thoughts stop him from helping, if that help was needed, or he could go.

He went back into the kitchen, where Papa had pushed his chair back from the table and was lighting his pipe and Bronka and Mama were clearing the table. He hooked his thumbs on his suspenders and announced, "I'm going to the Johnsons' farm. Su — Miss Shepard may be there, with no way to get back to town. If she's there, I'm going to break a path for her."

Bronka looked at him wide-eyed. He expected Mama to protest, but she just said, "I'll get your warm scarf, and your thickest socks," and left the room.

Papa said nothing, but Karol thought he saw a hint of a smile around Papa's pipe.

* * * * *

Susannah, sitting at table in the Johnson family's cozy kitchen, tried not to look toward the window facing the yard. It would make little difference whether the snow had stopped. She could hardly venture out into the night and try to find her way home, even if she could force her way through the snow, and she would not inconvenience, or possibly endanger, anyone in the family to assist her.

Gertie and her mother had huddled together before supper, whispering, both looking concerned — or was it embarrassed? She had suspected they were trying to figure out the best makeshift manner to accommodate her overnight. She knew some farmhouses were large and had extra rooms for company. The home in which she must now take shelter was not among them.

As they were finishing the bread and potatoes, Mr. Johnson looked at Susannah across the table and said, "You're welcome to stay 'til morning, but if you'd rather, I'll get you to town."

Gertie's little brother, the pupil Susannah had come this far to see, piped up, "I'll help, Daddy! I'm big now! Us men'll do it!"

Before the farmer could tell him otherwise — or, Lord forbid, allow him to come along — Susannah shook her head and said, "That's very kind of you, sir." How to turn down the offer without appearing to spurn it?

As she scrambled for the right words, a resounding knock came at the kitchen door. Gertie hastened to open it, to reveal Carl standing there and brushing snow off his arms and shoulders. He squared his shoulders as they stared at him and said, in an almost challenging tone, "I've come to take Miss Shepard back to town."

Mr. Johnson stood up, putting his hands on his hips and thrusting his chin forward. "I've offered to do it. You needn't have troubled yourself." Behind him, his wife worried her dress with her fingers and bit her lip. Carl looked from one to the other for a few seconds and said more respectfully, "That was good of you, sir. But both of us will make quicker work of it than one of us alone, if you'll let me help you."

Mrs. Johnson relaxed, and then turned to hush the renewed clamoring of the little boy to take part in the adventure. As Gertie hurried to fetch her father's coat, hat, scarf, and boots, Susannah donned her own outerwear and edged closer to Carl, saying quietly amidst the bustle, "Thank you. Are you sure you can make it to town without trouble? I could stay here."

Carl looked in her eyes. "I can get us there, better than the farmer could, and you'll have a more comfortable night at Miss Wheeler's. I also worried the snow might turn into a blizzard, but it won't, not soon anyway."

Susannah was about to ask how he knew, but Carl looked around at Mr. Johnson, now finished dressing for the snow, and edged his way to the door to go first. The farmer grimaced, but fell into line behind him, saying to Susannah, "You stick close, miss, and holler if you slip or have trouble keeping up."

She did have trouble keeping up, though only twice. The first time, both men simply stopped and waited for her. The second time, she slipped on a slick patch of snow where Carl's boots had pressed it down. Before she could fall, he had turned around and grabbed her hand in his. Even through his mitten and her glove, she felt the warmth of his grasp before he let go.

They stopped, briefly, every few minutes to warm their hands in their armpits and catch their breath, or to let Susannah do so. During one of these intervals she asked Carl, "How would you have known if a blizzard was coming?"

Carl stamped his feet, to warm them or to knock off accumulated snow, and replied, "It'd be windier, and the air would be more damp. And sometimes, you can feel the air pressure — your head hurts a little, or here." He pointed to his sinuses. "Or it feels like something pushing on your forehead."

Then it was time to move on again. But at the next halt, she asked him, "What if a blizzard happened during the day, with the children still at school?"

Carl frowned. "You should keep more wood inside. Enough to burn for days, even. Or else just outside the door, where you can get to it without moving even a step away from the building. Some blizzards, they turn everything white, and you can't see your hand if you hold it out, or know where you are, even if you're near shelter. It can happen all of a sudden, so don't try to go for help, or take the children home."

Susannah shivered, not only from the cold. Carl's keen eyes saw it, and said apologetically, "I just want you to be safe, always. And the children, of course."

She mustered up a smile and said, "Let's keep going, if you're ready." The snow and the darkness might not be a blizzard, but they were beginning to frighten her nonetheless.

She was drooping with the fatigue of the journey, both of body and of spirit, when they finally stood before the boarding house door. The door had been locked for the night, but Miss Wheeler answered after a single knock, throwing the door open wide and exclaiming, "How I've worried! I hoped you had holed up someplace, but I see you had an escort of good angels to get home instead. Come in, all of you!" She waved aside the men's reluctance to enter this long after the usual hours for male visitors. "Nonsense, the least I can do is to let you warm up and put your wet things by the stove, and give you something hot."

Several of the boarders had heard the noise and crept out of their rooms, peering inquisitively at the weatherbeaten party. Susannah could have groaned at the questions she would face on the morrow, but she smiled pleasantly at them as if nothing unusual had happened before following the men to the kitchen for whatever succor Miss Wheeler would provide.

* * * * *

Buttered toast had never tasted so good, and Miss Wheeler gave them plenty of it. When they could eat no more, she offered them the small room near the kitchen, used for storage but (she claimed) easily cleared, for them to shelter until morning; but the farmer said no, his family would be watching for him, and Karol, imagining Mama and Bronka fretting late into the night, said the same.

Bundled up again, the two men went out into the night, snow falling but lighter than before. Karol walked with him to the edge of town. When their paths parted, Farmer Johnson stuck out his hand and said, "Thank you, lad, for helping out. I'd have managed, but I'm sure the young lady had an easier time of it due to you."

Karol shook his hand and said the man was welcome, and that he hadn't done that much. Then he took his leave and finally headed for home, thinking of Susannah snuggled warm in her bed at the boarding house, or maybe saying her prayers by her bedside, lamplight gleaming in her dark hair.

By the time he put his cold hand on the kitchen door, the snow had almost stopped, and a few stars glittered in the sky.

Chapter 13

KAROL HAD told himself over and over that he would have to wait for the Christmas market and hope to find Susannah there. That he should not push, should not intrude, should not risk offending Susannah or drawing the unwelcome attention of those who would think him below her station. But when he woke the next morning, that voice had gone silent, and a new one whispered in his ear. Surely, after last night, Susannah would be in charity with him, and not eager to find fault? Even if she refused to meet him, she would do it kindly, and not hold a grudge.

So he apologized to Mama for not sitting down to breakfast, grabbed a muffin and slice of bacon, kissed Mama's cheek, and hurried to the schoolhouse, there to wait for Susannah. It only now occurred to him that the hardships of the night before might keep her from her work. If she failed to appear, he would go to the boarding house to make sure she hadn't fallen ill.

But there she came, moving a little slowly as her boots sank in the snow, but with rosy cheeks from the cold — and a smile for him when she saw him beside the back schoolhouse door. He listened to her thanks for his help the night before, told her it was nothing, and stammered to a halt, leaving her looking at him quizzically and waiting to hear his errand.

Best just get on with it. "I told you about the Christmas market. I hoped, I came to ask, whether we could go there together. Instead of just hoping to find each other in the crowd, when we might be there not at the same time."

If only his accent didn't get thicker when he was nervous!

In the quiet before she answered, he could hear footsteps and talk and laughter coming through the front door. It must be almost time to open the school, and he would have to run again, this time with people in the streets, to get to the mill on time.

At last she said softly, "I would like that. When is the market, and where should we meet?"

He hoped he looked less delighted than he felt. "It happens next Friday. We can meet wherever would be easiest for you, but —" Like a fool, he had failed to plan for success. "You could come to our home." She would meet Mama and Papa sooner or later, and that there was no good reason to delay it. And — "Bronka might come with us." He would rather have only Susannah to think of, but having Bronka there would make everything easier. And for Susannah as well as for him.

He told her where to find the house. She would find it humble compared to Miss Wheeler's, but at least she wouldn't be comparing it to something like the mayor's house. Unless she came from such a house, back in St. Louis.

It would have been easier in many ways if the market had been held on a Sunday, after church. But the Sabbath-breaking that would involve for those selling food and trinkets — and, to those who observed the Sabbath more strictly, those attending — ruled that out. So at two o'clock on the day, by general agreement, shops closed their doors, employers sent their employees on their way, and the teacher of Cowbird Creek's school opened the front door and wished her pupils a merry time of it. Or so Karol imagined as he stood in the doorway of his house, doing his best to ignore the chatter and questions of his family behind him.

Susannah came walking up before he had managed to drive himself wild with expecting her and worrying she might not come after all. She wore the same coat and gray leather gloves he had seen before, but a new knitted hat. Seeing him notice it, she laughed and said, "From my landlady! I'm told I can expect to receive presents from my fellow boarders as well — and I hope I can find gifts today to give in return."

Karol always turned over most of his earnings to Mama for the household, but he kept a little. After Susannah agreed to go with him, he counted those savings, and then counted them again. He had enough, if he spent most or all of it, to buy her some small gift in honor of Christ's birth. Or there was the carving he made on the ship, the girl dancing — it would cost him nothing, but it might not be good enough. He had changed his mind over and over about whether either kind of gift would be proper, and whether he dared.

He'd have liked to greet her in some new way, on this first visit to his home and the first time they would go somewhere together. But instead, struck dumb, he stepped back and let Bronka rush forward crying out, "Welcome, Miss Shepard! Isn't it a lovely day for the market? And I'm so happy we can show it to you!"

He could tell Susannah, too, had been nervous by the way she relaxed and smiled at Bronka. "As am I! I confess I'll be glad to have guides."

Keyed up as he was, he almost jumped at her using the word "confess." For an instant, he thought she might be Catholic after all — but that was nonsense. A good Catholic would not, most likely, use that word so casually.

Meanwhile, Papa had come up and was offering his hand to shake, as Karol had been too cowardly to do. "Welcome! Americans do this, yes? Shake hands, men and women both?"

Whether or not Papa was right, Susannah shook hands with him without hesitating or drawing back. "I'm so glad to meet you. And I want to apologize, to you and your wife, for not knowing how best to help Bronka when she first came to school. I've learned so much from her, and I'm very grateful."

Bronka, now standing near Mama, made a little cry of protest. Mama came to stand next to Papa. "No, please, we wouldn't think of it, a teacher must do as he, as she thinks best. We are only grateful that you let a big girl like Bronka, and with her poor English, come to school at all."

If Mama saw the shadow cross Bronka's face, she gave no sign of it, and Karol could think of nothing helpful to say. Meanwhile, Mama asked Susannah, "Can't I get you something hot to drink, to warm you? I have hot cider, made just as I made it in the old country."

Karol was hard put not to dance about with impatience. "Mama, there will be cider at the market. Not," he hurried to add, "as good as yours, of course."

Bronka had settled the matter, and saved some time, by bringing a mug of cider to Susannah and offering it with a little curtsy. Susannah thanked her, drank it right down, and said, "That was lovely! Now I'm ready to go out in the cold again. Shall we?"

Even if he had not been here with Susannah (and Bronka, of course), Karol would have loved the market.

There were so many different kinds of things that people had made.

There were, of course, the treats, candied fruit and sugar candies and chocolates, some so fancy they looked more like the ornaments for sale all around them. Karol offered to buy one sweet apiece for Susannah and Bronka. He had to persuade Susannah to accept, and then to reassure Bronka that she didn't need to put up a fuss of her own.

For people who decorated their own trees with candles, or used them to light their dinner tables, there were candles of all shapes and colors, some with many colors, straight or in spirals, short and squat or tall and slim. Most of the candle vendors sold bases with hanging counterweights to hold the candle on a tree. And there was every other kind of ornament for a Christmas tree: glass bulbs, clear or colored or sparkling, and tin stars, small and simple or with many stars facing every which way or fastened together; and snowflakes, large and small, tin and glass and copper; and little dolls, with cloth faces or the finest clay ones, with every kind of hair a doll could have. He saw Bronka looking at the dolls and sighing, then turning quickly away to prove that she was too old for such things.

And then Bronka grabbed his hand and pointed. "Look, Karol, carvings like yours!"

She usually remembered to call him Carl in public, but she must be too excited. He bent closer to the carvings, a whole stall with the carvings and nothing else, smelling of wood shavings and polish and paint. There was a set to be sold together, a Nativity, Maria and Jozef and the baby Christ Child in the manger, along with two sheep and a donkey. Then there were other animals, the kind he saw every day, horses and cows and chickens, and even a dog. There were carvings of men and women, girls and boys, some put close together as if in couples, but available to buy one at a time.

Susannah, standing close next to him, clapped her hands. "Oh, how marvelous! It must take so much work and skill."

And Karol, standing there, knew the wooden dancing girl in his pocket was as good as any of the carvings in the stall. Her skirts flew around her as if she twirled in the dance, rippling as cloth would, and her face would have made many a young man fall headlong in love. It would have been better if he had been able to make the skirt and bodice from a different wood than the rest, and glue the pieces together, but he'd had no way to do that aboard ship. He had at least found some red berries, once they reached Nebraska, and rubbed the berries into the skirt so it took on some of their color.

Bronka was so absorbed in looking at the carvings that he thought he could leave her there for a minute or two. He tapped Susannah's hand and gestured for her to follow him a few steps away. She looked puzzled, but she followed him to a clear patch under a nearby tree.

He took a deep breath of frosty air, blew it out in a cloud, and pulled the wooden figure out of his pocket, unwrapping the handkerchief around it. He held it out to Susannah. "I hope you won't take offense if I offer you this small token. For the season, and to tell how much I appreciate all you're doing for Bronka. It's nothing much, just something I made on the voyage to America, but you would make me happy by taking it."

Susan looked at the little dancing girl and reached out her pointer finger to touch the skirt. "She's wonderful. You made this, yourself?"

Bronka had rejoined them while he was thinking only

about Susannah and his gift. She broke in to say, with a pride that reminded Karol of their mother, "He is so clever with his hands! He makes many such things."

Susannah took the dancing girl and its wrapping in her hand, gently. "Then if I would not be depriving you . . . I would love to have it. Thank you so very much." She folded the handkerchief around the carving and placed it carefully in the pocket of her skirt. Then she looked dismayed. "But I have nothing — oh, yes! Please wait here just a moment." And she hurried off, winding her way through the crowd.

She was back, her face bright with excitement, before standing around could make Karol too much colder. She thrust both hands at him and said, "Here!" She was holding a tiny golden trumpet, with a metal scroll of music coming from its bell and a bright red cord to use in hanging it from a tree.

He reached for it, and was able to touch one of her hands in its smooth leather glove as he picked up the ornament. "Thank you. That is not necessary, but kind."

Susannah looked away and then back up at him. "It's silly, I suppose. You've never said anything about playing music. But I can imagine you blowing a trumpet, or singing in a chorus, something bold and — and triumphant." Then she turned away, as if she'd said more than she meant to say.

Bronka filled what could have been an awkward pause. "How did you guess? Carl sings so well, you should hear him! At home, we would go from house to house at this time of year and sing — Carl, what do you call them in English?"

"Carols, I think. We would dress up like people in the Bible and other stories, and sing at people's houses. And sometimes put on little plays. Do you do that here?"

"Caroling, yes, but not dressing up, or putting on plays. What a glad picture you paint for me!"

They had stood under the tree by themselves long enough. Karol shepherded them back toward the crowd, which was clustering around the giant tree in the center of the square. Right away, children came running with decorations in their hands, some of the smaller ones clutching at Susannah's coat skirt and showing her what they had brought or been given to hang on the lower branches. She admired each ornament, no matter how simple or crudely made. He marveled at her sweetness, but had to wonder. Had she praised his dancing girl, and even the other carvings, just to be kind?

But as the children ran back toward the tree, he saw Susannah pat her coat, over her pocket, in an absent-minded but caressing stroke.

Susannah pointed to the tree. "Will you hang the trumpet up?"

Karol clutched the little trumpet tight, the bell digging into his palm. "I think not. I would rather take it home. We will have a tree there, and I will hang the trumpet where it can play its music for us all through the season."

* * * * *

Had she ever had such a day, three hours so thoroughly given to enjoyment and pleasure, since she was a child? The brisk air, not too cold with all the people standing close together, and the sunshine, then the sunset and the gentle dusk; the excited children, many with hats and mittens knitted from bright red or blue or green yarn, and their high voices blending together or standing out with a sudden shout or laugh; the unmistakable scent of the giant fir tree's branches, and their rough tickle when she touched them; the welcome warmth and sweetness of the hot chocolate Carl insisted on buying for them . . . .

And just when they were getting ready to leave, a group of townspeople and farmers, young and old, collected in front of the tree and prepared to sing.

Susannah made bold to push Carl toward the singers. "After what Bronka has told me, I must hear you!"

He shook his head, shaggy with needing a haircut. "After what Bronka said, you would only be disappointed."

Bronka grabbed Carl's arm and tugged him toward the crowd in front of the tree. "No, you must come, we will both sing!"

And as the rest of the people quieted down, and the carolers began with "O Come All Ye Faithful," she soon heard that Bronka had spoken truly. Carl's voice, a warm baritone, rang out with all the joy of the season, rising up with Bronka's sweet high tones, lifting the song into something near sublime.

Carl pulled Bronka away from the singing after three songs. "Mama will be expecting us. She'll have made something hot and hearty," he coaxed as Bronka pouted in protest. "Susannah, I'm sure you would be welcome to join us."

She was not so certain, and reluctant to overstep. "Thank you, but Miss Wheeler likes to know how many will be at table, and would be displeased to have the number change without notice. It's been a wonderful afternoon. Thank you so much for making sure I attended."

Bronka grabbed her hand and squeezed it. "It wouldn't

have been nearly so nice without you."

Carl said nothing, but he nodded with enough energy that the fur on his hat stirred.

Brother and sister escorted her back to the boarding house. After farewells and more thanks, she stood on the step and watched them walk away down the street, Bronka's excited chatter and Carl's quieter replies fading as they reached the corner and were lost to view.

Susannah stepped inside to warm herself, but did not shed her outer garments or prepare for supper. It was, in fact, not quite time for the meal — and she had one more errand, one she would have been embarrassed for her day's companions to witness.

She walked briskly back toward the square, hunched forward against the wind, her gloves deep in her coat pockets. As she had hoped, the wood carver had not yet packed up his booth. He beamed at her, showing two missing teeth. "Back for one of my pretties?"

She smiled back at him and said, "Back for something, yes. For one of the carvings of men. Do you have any that appear to dance?"

"I'm afraid not, but look at this lively fellow! I'd think he might jump up to dance any minute, don't you?" He held up a man about three and a half inches high, dressed in a short jacket with a fur collar, booted feet set broadly and his head thrown back as if in a laugh.

"How much?" She hoped she wouldn't be required to haggle over it, and that she could afford to buy it without doing so.

"Two bits. It would be more, but I'll be leaving soon, and any sale is a good one."

She had two bits and more. She sighed in relief and said, "I'll take it."

Back at the boarding house, she pulled both carvings out of her pocket, the one she had bought and the one Carl had given her. As she had thought, they were almost of a size, the man taller than the woman.

She put both figures on the mantle above her fireplace, side by side. Now the dancing girl would not be alone.

She glanced back at them as she left the room to go down for supper.

Chapter 14

MAMA had indeed made something hot, a hearty stew of chicken and carrots, thickened with corn meal. It only now occurred to Karol that she, and Papa too, might have enjoyed going to the market. He could talk them into going next year, or just make his tale of today so inviting that they would decide for themselves not to miss it.

He took special care to describe all the sights and sounds, tastes and smells (at least the more appealing ones), and to point out the ways in which it had — now that he thought of it — reminded him of home, partly reawakening and partly easing the ache of homesickness. "Some people, especially the children, wore their holiday best, I think. People greeted each other with all best wishes for the holy season. And we had caroling, in front of the big Christmas tree, and some of the songs were songs you would know, though in English of course."

Papa held his bowl out to Mama, who filled it to the brim a second time. He put it down, took a spoonful, and leaned back in his chair, saying, "No one makes so good a stew except my *kochanie*. Such lucky children you are, to grow up with such good food, and plenty of it!"

Karol could only hope his work at the mill, and the odd jobs he and Papa found, and what they grew and raised at home would be enough for Bronka to have good meals and plenty of them until she married and set up a home of her own.

After supper, Bronka washed dishes faster than usual, to the point that Mama scolded her and made her wash the stew pot a second time. He did not have long to wonder why she hurried so. As soon as she had draped the dishcloth over the rod to dry, she took Karol's hand and tugged him toward the sleeping room. Plumping down on the bed, she folded her arms and said, stern as Papa could be, "And now you must tell me about you and Miss Shepard!"

He gawked at her until she broke into giggles and then said, almost breathless with laughing, "You like her, I know you do! Tell me what you've said to her when I wasn't around, and what she said to you!"

He switched over to glaring until she stopped laughing, and answered stiffly, "Enough of your nonsense! We haven't said anything when you weren't around that we wouldn't say in front of you, or her other pupils for that matter."

Back came the giggles. "Then you should! What are you waiting for? She must be almost your age, or even older. She should marry!"

"Bronka! Women in this country do *not* have to marry. And if she wanted to marry . . . ." He couldn't bring himself to say what must be true. She would want a man with more to look forward to, one who could build her a house and hire a servant. Could support her, without her having to work.

Although . . . she loved her work. He could see it in everything she said about her pupils, in the way she had dedicated herself to helping Bronka, in the pride she now took in Bronka's better English and better spirits. He said under his breath, more to himself than to Bronka, "Women who want to work can work after they marry, here. Like Dr. Gibbs' wife, who works as his nurse."

Though it might be different, more acceptable, for a wife to help her husband's work in that way.

But all this was trying to eat Sunday's dinner on Saturday, at best. He had never done so much as hold her hand, except for that moment in the snow. Let alone kissed her, or tried.

* * * * *

Over the boarding house's cold ham and mashed potatoes, there was much discussion of the day's festivities. Miss Wheeler had attended early on before returning to supervise the cook, who had herself worked briefly in her brother's booth selling candied fruits and small jars of preserves. The young women who worked in various shops had found ribbons they planned to use for next spring's bonnet trimmings, or had stocked up on chocolates to eat in their rooms, Miss Wheeler admonishing them not to leave smears of chocolate on the furniture.

As Susannah finished her cider and reached for the pitcher to refill her glass, Miss Wheeler asked her, "I saw you there, didn't I? You were with one of the immigrant children, a girl, and a boy who looked something like her. Her brother?"

Susannah put down the pitcher, her glass still empty. "Yes. Bronka is one of my older pupils, and the two of them are quite close."

The oldest boarder, a widow who never tired of complaining about her late husband's business partners, peered at Susannah through her lorgnette. "I believe many of the immigrants we see nowadays are *Catholics*." The final word fairly dripped with disdain.

Susannah made herself retrieve the pitcher and pour

half a glass of cider. "Yes, many of them. I find it most interesting, learning about the previous experiences of those students who have less familiar backgrounds to share." She took a carefully dainty sip. "It is instructive for those of my pupils who grew up in Cowbird Creek, or similar places, to see what variety of customs exist elsewhere."

"*Customs*." The widow's tone, if possible, conveyed even greater distaste. "That would include *doctrine*, no doubt. And Popish practices of all kinds. I wonder the school board wishes our local children exposed to such things."

Susannah hoped her expression showed none of her dismay. She had congratulated herself on being broadminded about Bronka's — about Carl's — religion, without it occurring to her that other opinions might come into play.

She could hope that Dr. Gibbs, at least, would not share what might be a common prejudice against their Catholic brethren. But it would be prudent to consult him. She could only hope the board was not already discussing the issue, about to take some action that would put Susannah in a difficult position. That might, in fact, require her to take a stand in defense of her Catholic pupils — the pupil she had now, and others she could expect in the future.

If, in that future, she was allowed to have any.

Somehow, Susannah had failed to learn before now just where Dr. Gibbs and his wife Clara had their medical office. She asked about it at the breakfast table, and immediately regretted it as an onslaught of concern and suggestions and opinions followed. "Are you ill, dear Miss Shepard?" "Best take some of my tonic first, I make it just as my mother used to . . . ." "I always say professions are unhealthy for a young woman . . . ." "Immodest, I call it, that so-called nurse working with a doctor and seeing all sorts of half-*naked* men, I don't doubt!"

Miss Wheeler intervened. "Ladies, ladies! I'm sure Miss Shepard is grateful to all of you for your providing so much . . . information. But perhaps we should start by answering her initial question. Miss Shepard, Dr. and Nurse Gibbs have their practice next door to the pharmacist. Mind, if they're called away, you may not find them there. I hope your need isn't urgent."

"Thank you so much, Miss Wheeler." It took some self-control not to emphasize the *you*. "I'm actually quite well. I simply require some information I believe Dr. Gibbs may be able to provide. I'll stop by sometime soon and hope to find him there."

After school, Susannah dropped off her belongings in her room, hiding around corners and listening for footsteps to avoid any more diagnoses or prescriptions for nonexistent ailments. She sat down at her dressing table, inspected her hair, deemed it suitable, and made her way back outside, looking down at her feet to avoid the patches of ice that made the street a dangerous game of hopscotch.

It was thus to be expected that she almost ran right into the butcher in his blood-stained apron. He grabbed her arm, exclaiming, "Steady on there, missy!" — rather as if she were a nervous horse. She apologized, exchanged obvious observations about the state of the streets and the weather generally, and escaped on her errand.

As she approached the office door, she slowed down, uncertain about whether to knock and wait or just enter. A medical office was neither a general store nor a private residence. What rules applied? As she stood questioning herself, a man dressed like a bank clerk passed her and walked right on in. She followed him with a sigh, resigned to waiting her turn.

The clerk had been directed to a stool, and Mrs. Gibbs, her nurse uniform reassuringly cleaner than the butcher's apron, was holding some sort of metal tool in the clerk's mouth and peering down his throat. Dr. Gibbs stood at a counter, writing in a big book rather like a ledger without columns. He looked up at her with polite curiosity. "May we assist you, Miss Shepard? Or one of your young charges?" His smile fell away. "Your visit wouldn't concern Alice? This is one of the days she goes to the library until we finish our hours here, so we've had no opportunity to see her this afternoon."

She should have predicted that worry. "No, no, Alice was as good a student as ever, and appeared to be in fine health and spirits when she left for the day. I'm sorry to have worried you. I actually came to ask your advice on something, in your capacity as a member of the school board."

Back came the inquisitive look, and he said, "Clara, Miss Shepard and I will be in the back if you need to consult me. Miss Shepard, please come this way."

He led her to a room probably intended for more private examinations and treatments, with a long, padded examination table, trays of instruments on shelves, and an odor with elements of liniment and some sort of antiseptic. Fortunately, there was also a chair. As she sat down, she noticed a pair of shiny new boots in black leather peeking out from underneath it. Dr. Gibbs, who had seated himself behind a small desk in the corner, followed her gaze and chuckled. "An anniversary present from Clara, who has had ample opportunity to notice that my vanity attaches itself conspicuously to the condition of my footwear."

Really, just listening to the man's vocabulary was refreshing after a day with pupils whose sophistication barely extended to words of two syllables.

But such observations were only a way of stalling. Susannah forced herself to come to the point. "Dr. Gibbs, I've recently realized that soon or late, I may encounter difficulties as to how to fulfill my obligation to teach religion to my pupils."

Dr. Gibbs leaned forward, elbows on the desk, resting his chin in his hands. "If I may hazard a guess, Carl Marek's sister, and their family's Catholicism, has given rise to this apprehension."

"Some of the other boarders at Miss Wheeler's noticed me attending the Christmas market with Bronka." Honesty compelled her to add, "And her brother. The boarders made . . . comments."

Dr. Gibbs twitched an eyebrow. "I can well imagine. May I ask what you have done, to date, in the way of teaching religion in your classroom?"

"I've set the younger children to reading from the Psalms, as I believe many parents do when undertaking their children's education. But I've used the ones I consider easier to read, or with imagery likely to attract the children, rather than giving priority to the most religiously instructive."

Dr. Gibbs nodded in encouragement. "Indeed, Clara and I read some psalms with Alice in her fifth year, for just those purposes."

"I've also had the children read from the Beatitudes, which do contain more doctrinal content. And just last week, I set Amos — you know him, I expect."

Joshua lifted his chin out of his hands, leaned back in his chair, and laughed. "Oh, yes! One of my livelier patients." His face clouded. "Although I have been hard pressed to answer his questions about my experiences in the War of Rebellion without depressing his high spirits. I could not countenance shaping my answers toward the scenes of bold battle and triumph he would have preferred."

As if drawn by some mysterious marital clairvoyance, Mrs. Gibbs at that moment looked through the open door to the room and studied her husband. "Mr. Quilner has gone, with a bottle of your preparation for catarrh. Can I assist in any way?"

The look of understanding that passed between them, and the softness of Dr. Gibbs' expression, sent a pang through Susannah that she could not have identified and would not have wished to dwell on. "Thank you, my dear. I may in fact have need of your insight."

He gave her a short summary of what had brought Susannah to consult him. Mrs. Gibbs nodded along, then hoisted herself up to sit on the examination table and folded her hands, obviously prepared to listen. Susannah tried to recall where she had been in her account. "I set Amos to reading Judges 7, concerning Gideon and the Midianites. I believe that is all I have done as far as teaching religion specifically. I have also, from the beginning, given lessons in morals, which of course accord with Christian teaching but have a more general application. The later McGuffey readers include much such material, but I have not relied on them only."

Mrs. Gibbs, somehow appearing dignified even with her feet dangling from her perch on the table, asked quietly, "What do you know about Catholic doctrine and how it differs from Protestant?"

It was a question she should already have asked herself, instead of relying on unexamined assumptions. The normal school's instruction in teaching religion had not, as far as she knew, included any elements of Catholicism. She herself had been raised a Methodist, and had found Cowbird largest Creek's congregation to be Methodist as well. Her acquaintances back home included Catholics as well as Lutherans and Episcopalians, but she had not known any of the Catholics well enough to inquire about their religious beliefs. Perhaps Dr. and Mrs. Gibbs could tell her which of her assumptions were correct. "I believe Catholics, unlike Protestants, look to the Pope for guidance, rather than reading God's Word in the Bible." She stopped, struck with a realization. "I suppose, then, that by having the children read from the Bible, I have been in a way teaching Protestant rather than Catholic religion."

"That," said Dr. Gibbs, "may mollify some potential critics, though I don't in fact know whether or to what extent Catholic families do likewise. What else?"

"Don't Catholics pay a great deal of attention to saints? They celebrate their feast days, and even do some sort of worshiping of what they call relics, some of which contain the remains of dead bodies." She shuddered at the thought. "And I've heard they raise our Lord's mother Mary almost above our Lord himself."

Dr. Gibbs pursed his lips. "That might be something of an exaggeration. But from what Catholics have told me, they consider Mary as a loving intercessor, through whom they may approach God in all his persons with their prayers." He smiled. "They may, in fact, consider our more direct approach, bombarding the Father and Son and Holy Spirit with our requests, as a species of rudeness, or at best boorishness."

Susannah sat bolt upright in indignation. "But our

Lord himself instructed us as to how to pray, and made no mention of bringing his blessed mother into the matter!"

Joshua laughed and then covered his mouth. "My apologies, Miss Shepard. That is a more or less accurate, if forthright, statement of one of our doctrinal differences from what we may call our elder brothers in Christ."

Susannah refrained from grinding her teeth. "But what am I to *do*? I would hate to make Bronka feel excluded or unwelcome, much less put her to a choice between her faith and her schooling. And the question is likely to arise again in the future. I doubt those who wish me to act almost as a second minister will refrain from interfering for much longer."

"True enough," said Dr. Gibbs. "You might devote some time to writing down some of the most important Protestant precepts, and then phrasing them in ways as inoffensive to a Catholic point of view as possible. Clara, what do you think?"

Mrs. Gibbs slid down from the table and moved a little toward the door. "Such a plan may be more practical if Miss Shepard is able to consult someone more familiar with Catholicism. You are already acquainted with Bronka's brother. Would you be willing to ask him for guidance?"

Susannah knew she must be revealing her dismay at the thought. Just when he seemed to have forgiven her for her earlier blunders, and their effect on his beloved sister! "I — I don't know . . . ."

Clara's keen gaze seemed to read her every thought and feeling. "He could, at least, introduce you to his priest. You could explain to him, to Carl, the nature of your dilemma, and that you hope the priest might be able to help you navigate between this modern Scylla and

Charybdis."

Dr. Gibbs stood up, prompting Susannah to do the same. "As so often, my wife has offered a solution to a difficult dilemma." Mrs. Gibbs smiled in response, which might have been the first time Susannah had seen her do so. Dr. Gibbs smiled back, then turned back to Susannah and said, "I wish I could make the necessary introduction, but I've had no occasion to learn which priest serves our local Catholic residents or where he is located."

Mrs. Gibbs resumed her progress toward the door. "You must excuse me, Miss Shepard, but I believe I hear the heavy tread of the baker, come with another ailment arising from how freely he partakes of his wares."

Dr. Gibbs hid his face in one hand and groaned dramatically. Susannah thanked them both, and left with more spring in her step than when she had arrived. She almost forgot to watch for ice along her way.

Chapter 15

KAROL wasn't expecting visitors when the knock came on their door late Sunday afternoon. As usual lately, the image of Susannah's face appeared in his mind, but he expected the usual disappointment. He had a hard time not grinning when he opened the door to find Susannah standing there, wearing a knitted hat in a green and white pattern that brought out the color of her eyes.

She shifted from foot to foot — cold, or nervous? In case she was cold, he made haste to invite her in. Then, in case she was nervous, he grabbed his coat and led her into the back yard, before the rest of the family could notice her. He brushed the snow off the biggest tree stump. "We can go back inside, of course. But you could sit here."

Susannah sat, which left Karol to figure out what to do with himself. He leaned against the chicken coop, glad he had strengthened it with stone last summer, and waited for her to tell him what had brought her here.

It took her longer than he would expect for her to come to the point, as her tale wandered from her boarding house to the doctor's office. But she finally said, "I need to learn more about your religion — that is, you and Bronka are Catholic, aren't you?"

He started to bristle, as he always did when their Protestant neighbors came out with their ignorance and their insults, but caught himself. Susannah had just expressed her desire not to stay ignorant, if she was, and he could not imagine her insulting anyone except accidentally. And he was keeping her waiting for an answer. "Yes, we are." And she wanted to learn! For a joyful moment, he imagined that he might be the reason . . . But already she was explaining.

"As a teacher, I am expected to teach morals and religion. But not all my pupils will have the same religion, and I must find a way to fulfill the duties for which the school board hired me without offending pupils or their parents, or leading parents to withdraw their children from the school."

"And you want me to tell you what Catholics believe?" He would be happy to talk to her about almost anything, but where to start with so big a subject? She should really speak to . . . . "You should talk to our priest. He can answer all your questions, I'm sure."

Susannah clasped her hands. "That's just what I wanted to ask you! Is there a way for me to meet him and arrange a time for him to speak to me?"

"He lives in Elk Leg, a few miles from here. We go there every Sunday. For me to introduce you to him, you would need to come with us." An idea suddenly burst like fireworks in Karol's mind and stole his breath. It might make more trouble than Susannah had already described. But the picture in his mind was so beautiful, it could not be shoved aside. "Have you ever heard of a Midnight Mass?"

Susannah shrank back. "That can't be — you don't mean a Black Mass, that witches hold!"

Karol cursed under his breath, and hoped fervently she hadn't heard. "No, nothing like that at all! On Christmas Eve, just when Christmas Eve becomes Christmas Day, we hold a midnight service, a mass. In the still of the night, we welcome our savior with incense, with music and candlelight, with prayers. It is most special." He forced his hands to unclench and his shoulders to loosen. "And when it's over, the priest stands at the door to give everyone his blessing. I could introduce you then. He does go to other towns sometimes, to give the last rites. Maybe he would come here to meet with you, and help you understand what pupils like my sister believe."

Slowly she relaxed, the alarm in her face fading away. Now she looked like someone in a daydream. Maybe even a happy one.

* * * * *

Susannah had never, in all her life, deliberately stayed awake until midnight. If she had ever seen that hour, it must have been tossing in the grip of fever, or during some stumbling visit to the necessary with half-closed eyes.

To stay awake, or sleep briefly and wake again, and at that hour be surrounded by music and light? The prospect was irresistible. And she would be doing it in order to better carry out her duties.

How much more did the prospect attract her, that Carl would be there at her side? She did not, at this moment, need to know the answer to that question. Her hands were cold, and the stump had become a less than comfortable seat. She stood up and brushed off her coat. "If your family won't object, I would indeed like to accompany you."

If his family had any qualms, Carl said nothing of them. They might even hope to make a Catholic of her, though she dearly hoped Carl had not tempted them with any such possibility.

Rather than try to meet at such an unusual hour, she was to go to Carl's and Bronka's house for supper and simply remain there until it was time to leave. There was, it turned out, another Catholic family, from the next county to the west, with a farm not far from the outskirts of Cowbird Creek, and they would all go together in that family's wagon. She had of course had to tell Miss Wheeler that she would be spending the night elsewhere. Coward-like, she left it to her hostess to inform the other boarders and field their innumerable questions and concerns. She would pay the price later, facing an even more fierce onslaught after the delay.

Miss Wheeler herself shook her head and lowered her eyebrows at the news. "This establishment has a reputation and a purpose of providing safe and wholesome protection for ladies without husbands," she said, in a tone not far from that a minister would adopt. "You must promise me, on your honor and with the Lord's name on your lips, that you will not be leaving the protection of this house with any intention or prospect of sinful behavior, nor any risk of danger."

"Indeed not, ma'am. I swear it, on our Lord Jesus's name." Susannah's penchant for precision made her wish to explain that she would be exposed to, but not by any means adopting, religious practices that Miss Wheeler might well consider sinful by nature. But there was such a thing as imprudently courting trouble.

Susannah expected the Mareks to be thinking about the midnight service to come, and to serve up some simple supper to sustain them until it ended. But she arrived to find a notably festive atmosphere, with a pristine white tablecloth spread on a table she doubted saw such dressing often. As she returned the cheerful greetings and took her seat, she noticed that the surface of the tablecloth was oddly uneven. Bronka, eager to instruct her teacher for a change, explained that hay lay underneath. She might have gone on to say why, but fell silent as her father stood up, followed by the rest of the family. Susannah made haste to follow suit.

Mr. Marek raised a thin white wafer with an unmistakable air of ceremony. He looked around the table and then met Susannah's gaze, saying in his heavily accented English, "Welcome, honored guest, to our *Wigilia* celebration! We begin with what we call an *oplatek*. The designs on it come from being pressed between two pieces of metal that we brought from Poland – and we brought little from Poland. We break it and offer it to each other to show love and friendship. And forgiveness – if our worst enemy were here, we would offer it to that enemy also."

With that, he began breaking the cracker and handing the pieces around the table. Rather than eating them, the rest of the family broke their piece into smaller ones and handed them around as well, murmuring something in Polish. Bronka, however, said softly in English, "I thank you and honor you for all you do for me."

Susannah felt herself blush as she broke off a piece to give back to Bronka, saying, "The honor is mine, for being able to watch how hard you work to learn, and how much you are learning. And thank you for forgiving my mistakes when we first met."

Bronka shook her head as if to disagree that forgiveness was necessary, as Susannah went on to give pieces of the cracker to her hosts, murmuring her gratitude for their hospitality. As she struggled to decide what to say to Carl, he handed her a piece and said solemnly, looking in her eyes, "Like Bronka, I thank you for what you have done for her. And also, for the friendship you have shown me."

Susannah took the piece of cracker and handed him the piece she had at the ready, replying, "I thank you for friendship I needed more than you, alone as I was in a new place. For welcoming me as you have."

When all the crackers were distributed, the men and – at Mrs. Marek's insistence – Susannah sat down as her hostess and Bronka brought in a clear red-purple soup and a big bowl of potato salad. Next came herring in cream sauce, fried mushrooms, dumplings filled with more mushrooms, and more fish. Only meat was missing. For dessert, they had apple-filled pancakes and some sort of seedcake. After they had finished and the women had cleared the table, Susannah getting up and helping before anyone could gainsay her, Mr. Marek fetched a bottle of dark red wine from a cupboard and poured glasses for them all. Apparently, it was time for toasts — to the Christ child, to the new year soon upon them, to each other.

Susannah took only the small sips necessary to take part in the toasts. It would never do to fall asleep during the upcoming service — all the more likely when the service would be conducted in a foreign tongue. However, once Carl and Bronka took her aside after supper and explained what would take place, she thought it unlikely she would be able to nod off. Apparently she would be standing and sitting and kneeling and standing again, all the way through.

Still, by the time the wagon wheels sounded in the street outside, it was only her nerves keeping her awake. She usually read or planned lessons for a while after supper, but the lamp in her room was not so bright as to encourage her to work late into the night, and her days started early. Thank goodness the next day was Christmas, and the school would be closed for the children to celebrate the holiday with their families. Of course, if she spent much of the day sleeping, instead of joining the other boarders in whatever festivities Miss Wheeler had planned, she would excite even more comment and speculation.

Someone must have found a way to tell the farm family ahead of time about Susannah's addition to the party. They scrutinized her as they welcomed her, but no one expressed surprise, let alone objected. Bronka, more excited than Susannah had ever seen her, snuggled next to her and made sure Susannah had more than her share of the quilt they had brought. "Isn't it beautiful tonight! Papa says it may snow later, but now we can see every star!"

And indeed, the stars were so bright that Susannah found herself looking at each one, wondering if it was anywhere near as bright as the Star over Bethlehem.

Until they left town, they mostly kept their voices down so as not to disturb the sleeping residents. But once they were rumbling along the road between Cowbird Creek and Elk Leg, Carl broke the silence to say, "Shall we sing 'O Holy Night'? Susannah, is that a carol you know?"

Carl must have been looking at the stars himself. Susannah answered by singing softly, "O holy night, the stars are brightly shining . . . ." The others in the wagon joined in, their accents changing the words but somehow bringing home to her the familiarity of the song itself. Then came songs in Polish, unfamiliar and lovely. Carl looked over at her as if about to apologize, but she smiled, then made so bold as to take his hand and squeeze it gently before letting go.

The wheels rumbled on, and the wagon drew ever closer to the strangeness awaiting her, but it felt less strange a prospect than before.

The feeling of being an outsider returned when they reached the church in Elk Leg and everyone in their party started greeting people Susannah had never seen, let alone met. They mostly looked like people who worked with their hands, and their clothes, probably their best and carefully pressed, were often shiny with wear. Some had the Slavic features of Bronka's family, while others had the dark hair and eyes and browner skin that probably meant they came from Italy, and still others had the red hair of the Irish. She stood there feeling, somehow, both conspicuous and invisible, until Carl returned to her side and began introducing her to one person after another as "Bronka's teacher, who wants to understand more about her pupil."

She had failed to anticipate this sort of introduction, which might well lead to a train of gossip that would reach Cowbird Creek, but it was too late to fret about that possibility. She greeted those who greeted her, and glanced at the door through which she could see glimmers of the candlelight within.

Finally, at some signal she failed to detect, the crowd streamed inside, to light and warmth and the heavy odor of what must be incense. Her mind flew to the Nativity, and the gift of frankincense. Had it smelled like this?

A marble basin with water stood in the front, apparently for people to dip their hands. She followed suit, hoping there was no special significance to the action. She did not, however, do as everyone else was doing and touch her torso on the sides, top, and bottom, in what might be the shape of a cross.

A small organ sat in a corner near the front of the church, and a tall man with gray hair was playing music that, as she got nearer to it, drowned out the conversations of the people around her. Bronka's parents led the way into a pew, and Bronka and Carl made sure she sat between them. Then the priest, a solidly built man of medium height with wavy brown hair, walked to the ornate wooden pulpit in front of the church — carved in America, or brought with effort and expense from someone's home country? — and the crowd grew quiet.

Susannah's eyes drifted upward, and she saw the large carved crucifix hanging above the priest, the almost naked form of the crucified Savior so real it could almost have cried out, "Oh, God, why has Thou forsaken me?" She forced herself to look away from it, to imagine instead the wooden Nativity scene at the market, and the infant Jesus, bundled up and warm in the manger, and the animals around Him, and the Kings coming to worship with their sweet-smelling gifts.

And then the service began, and she had to pay attention to when to rise, or sit, or kneel. She let the rhythm of the Latin wash over her and soothe her. From time to time she looked over at her companions, not only so she could take her cue from them, but to reassure herself with the joy on their faces.

As everyone went down on their knees again, something new began — people were filing out of their seats, up the center aisle, toward a rail set next to the pulpit, and kneeling again there. Carl, nearer to the aisle, gestured urgently for her to stay where she was. "I'm sorry, I forgot to tell you. We go to take Communion, the — I'll explain later what it means, to us. I should have thought of it, and had you sit where we would not have to push by you."

"That's quite all right." Didn't he know that Protestants also took communion, in shared memory of

Christ's sacrifice? But she stood back as far as she could, to let Bronka and the rest of her family and the others in the pew make their way past.

She knelt down again once her pew had emptied, grateful for the narrow straw-stuffed cushion that ran along the floor. Even with that nod to comfort, her legs grew stiff by the time she was able to stand and let everyone file back in. The service, it seemed, was almost over. The final portion involved the congregants passing a painted piece of ivory set in a silver frame from one to the next, each one kissing it as they received it. Bronka whispered, "That is the Kiss of Peace. In the early Church, people kissed each other instead."

Susannah could only be glad the less shocking custom had replaced that one, and passed the ivory icon from Carl to Bronka without imitating either.

Then her companions and everyone else rose to their feet one more time, and it was time to meet the priest.

Close up, he was younger than she had for some reason expected, with wavy brown hair that reminded her of Dr. Gibbs'. The similarity eased her nerves, little as that made sense. When he took her hand and said, with a lilting accent she had not noticed during the service, "The blessing of the season be upon you, child," she allowed herself to say, "Thank you, Father," as the others were doing. She almost forgot her errand. She had moved a foot to take a step toward the door when she hastily remembered and said, "Father, I came today to learn a little about your faith, but I would like to meet with you, somehow, to learn more."

His smile showed teeth so white they shone in his tanned face. "I would be very happy to help you learn. I gather you came with the Mareks. Do you also live in Cowbird Creek?"

"Yes, sir. I'm the schoolteacher there, and Bronka Marek is one of my pupils."

"Ah, I see." He did not exactly seem disappointed, but the information had led him to reassess in some way. Perhaps he had thought himself meeting a potential convert. "I do, from time to time, make my way there. Would it do if I were to inform the Mareks, the next time I come, and ask them to bring word to you? Then, if convenient for you, we could meet, perhaps over a cup of coffee at a restaurant or at the Marek's home, and I can try to answer any questions you have. It could be that more of them will occur to you as you ponder today's service."

"That would be very kind of you. Thank you, sir — Father."

Bronka and Carl and their parents had reached the path in front of the church, and she made haste to catch up with them. Then, she had little to do but stand near the wagon while they exchanged holiday good wishes with those they saw only once a week, if that often. Soon, however, Carl came up to her, the glow of fellowship shifting into something between curiosity and anxiety. He walked a little away from the crowd, and she followed him, allowing him to ask quietly, "I saw you talking to the good Father. Will he come to town? And what did you think of the service? Are you glad you stayed awake to come with us?"

"Yes, he'll come, though he doesn't know when. He'll let you know when he arrives. He may want to talk to me at your house." Better that than in such a visible place as the restaurant. As for Carl's other questions . . . she cast her mind back over all she had seen and heard and smelled, all she had done, all she had marveled at and wondered about and found disconcerting. She would keep that last to herself, at least for now. "And yes, I'm glad I stayed awake. I'd never imagined anything like this, and I wouldn't have missed it."

His face lit up, and he grasped both her hands and whirled around in a circle. "I'm so glad! I so hoped you would feel that way." He brought them to a halt, but kept hold of her hands . . . .

And then he leaned close, closer, and gently touched his lips to hers.

All she could think, at first, was that here was another new experience in a day, or a night, full of them. And all she felt, at first, was the soft warmth of his lips, the surprising sweetness of his breath, and the firm grip of his hands on hers.

Then he let go of one of her hands and reached up to touch her hair. And memory rushed in, the memory of President Brecker's pudgy fingers in her hair, touching it, admiring it, gloating over it.

She pulled her other hand loose and backed up with a gasp. Carl gaped at her in shock, staring and then turning away.

Bronka came to find them at this most awkward moment, studying both their faces. "Is anything wrong? It's time to go home and have our Christmas breakfast. Miss Shepard, I hope you'll join us?"

It would be ungracious and ungrateful to refuse. And if she asked to be let off at Miss Wheeler's, she would have to face all the others with little time to compose herself, or to think. "Yes, thank you." She climbed up into the wagon before Carl could offer to help her, and sat as close to the end of the seat as she could. Carl hung back, leaving Bronka to follow her. But she could still feel his presence, and the turmoil it inspired in her.

* * * * *

Karol had been too excited to eat much at supper. Now, at the long-awaited Christmas breakfast, with its heaps of eggs and glistening fat sausages and mushroom-stuffed pierogis, his stomach was all in knots, and he had to force himself to eat. He couldn't let Mama and Papa see that something was wrong, and Bronka had already started to fret. He could tell that Susannah was also making an effort, her shoulders stiff, her mouthfuls spaced as evenly as clockwork except for when she forgot to eat and stared off at nothing.

What had he done? Had he somehow hurt her? He had been so careful, had treated her as delicately as if she were made of blown glass. But she had felt nothing like glass, warm and soft and . . . and then it had all gone wrong, and he had no idea how, or what to do to make it right.

The food seemed to help, a little. By the time they had all eaten as much as they could, she was chatting with Bronka and their parents, and as he rose to help clear the table, she even sent a brief, faint smile his way.

If he did something, said something, would he only make it worse? But the thought of leaving things as they were, until who knew when, was too much to bear. Better to try, even if he cursed himself for it later. When she stood up and seemed to be getting ready to leave, he said, "Please, let me walk you home."

She went stiff again, and he added, just above a whisper, "I promise I will not try to touch you. I only want to see you home, this early morning. The sun hasn't yet risen. Will you be able to get in the boarding house door?"

The thought of being shut out startled her. "Oh, I hope so. I wouldn't want to have to rouse anyone to be let in."

"Maybe you should wait a little. I could leave you quite alone, at least as far as my company. You could sit somewhere, or talk to my sister or my parents."

She bit her lip — no, chewed it. Finally she said, "Or we could go for a walk, until day breaks."

It was as if the sun had already risen, bringing hope with it. This early, they might even walk without other company and not be noticed.

When the dishes were done, he told the others that he would be out for maybe an hour, if they were willing to wait with exchanging gifts that long. It was hardly fair, given that they had already waited for Christmas morning instead of giving gifts the night before as usual. And it turned out Mama had another objection, one he should have seen coming. "But I have a gift for Bronka's teacher!"

At least that was an easy problem to solve. "You could give it to her now, and I could give my gifts, and receive any, a little later. If it's heavy, I can carry it for her."

Mama brightened. "No, it's not heavy! I'll be right back." She bustled off to the bedroom. Susannah had been close enough to hear all this, and looked both shy and excited. Mama soon came back with a small box tied with green ribbon and held it out to Susannah. Speaking slowly, to get the English right, she said, "For the season, and in thanks. *Wesołych Świąt!* And please don't worry that you should have anything for us. You have already given Bronka hope and courage, about her life in this new land."

Susannah swallowed hard, and her eyes glistened. "That is so kind of you to say, and kind of you to give me this. Shall I open it now?"

Mama bobbed her head yes, and Susannah sat in the nearest chair and put the box in her lap, tugging carefully at the ribbon. She opened the box and pulled out a small tin angel, wings spread wide, with a loop of silver thread to hang it by. Karol recognized it as a trinket Mama had saved from her girlhood. Susannah lifted it up and let it spin at the end of the thread, saying, "Oh, how lovely! Thank you so much."

Mama beamed, and Papa and Bronka gathered around to see and admire. Karol had mixed feelings about the time all this was taking. It would be cold out, and walking until the boarding house opened might leave too much time for Susannah to get chilled; but he was eager to be walking with her, and trying to fix whatever had gone wrong. He went to get Susannah's coat, held it out for her to put on, made sure she put the gift in her pocket, and then brought her hat and gloves. As soon as she dressed for outdoors, he threw on his own winter coat and the rest.

In a few minutes they were outside, walking through the quiet streets where one could see just a hint of coming dawn. He heard from one house they passed the excited voice of a young child, all ready to begin Christmas Day, and the sleepy voices of its parents shushing it. But no rooster yet crowed, nor cat hunted, nor dog barked at them or followed them. Only the sound of their footsteps on snow broke the silence.

He was trying to find the right way to ask his questions when Susannah said, "You must want to know what happened, back at the church."

"What I most want to know is what I might have done to hurt you or make you afraid. Anything else, I will be glad to hear, if you wish to tell me."

She took a deep breath and blew it out in a frosty

cloud. "I most wanted to tell you that it wasn't, isn't, your fault, how I acted. I had wondered, even, whether it would happen — whether," and this in a whisper, "you might kiss me. And when you did . . . I liked it."

She stopped, and said nothing more until he couldn't help prompting her. "And then? What changed?"

She opened her mouth, closed it, and opened it again to say, still in a whisper and forcing even that, "I can't tell you."

She had started shivering, and he guessed it was not, or not only, from the cold.

Watching her, listening to her, he knew only one thing: someone had hurt her. And it was too late to save her from that harm. Could it have been some man in Cowbird Creek? If he ever found out it had been . . . but it was more likely a man back in St. Louis.

It crossed his mind that if not for that villain, Susannah might never have come to town, and he might never have met her. The very thought made his head ache. He should think, instead, of how he could help, whether there was anything he could do to help her now. But he could think of nothing.

No, there was one thing. He could find her some shelter. He spied a familiar barn, in which he knew there was only one easygoing horse. "Shall we go there, and warm up? I know the family. They wouldn't mind."

Susannah said nothing, but she let him lead her into the barn. Molly, the mare, put her head over the stall, nosing Karol's shoulder. He laughed and stroked her muzzle. "Here, come meet a new friend."

Susannah reached out slowly and put her gloved hand on Molly's neck. She sighed in pleasure and said, "Oh, so warm! You're lovely to meet on a cold day, aren't you, sweet girl? Merry Christmas to you!"

He could have kissed Molly — and must he be thinking of kissing? — for being the one to get Susannah talking again. "Yes, she's a good old girl. I'll bring you a carrot later, Molly, for welcoming us so kindly." The homey smell of hay filled his lungs, and he found himself breathing more deeply. He hardly dared look at Susannah, but a quick glance showed her more relaxed, leaning lightly against the edge of Molly's stall.

It seemed best to let the warmth and quiet, and the mare's sweet calm, do what they could. They stood there, sometimes stroking Molly, for maybe ten minutes before he said, "Are you feeling warm enough to walk again?"

Susannah looked squarely at him. "I think you know it wasn't only the cold. But this was just what I needed. Let's go on."

They left Molly and the barn behind. Karol steered them toward the less traveled ways, where they were less likely to be seen together. Their path had the added benefit of taking longer before they would arrive in the middle of town. He should probably find something to talk about, but he had no idea what to say.

They were approaching the more crowded part of town, with voices coming faintly from a few houses and the first sunbeams of a beautiful day lighting roofs and leaves. He finally found his tongue and said, "If I promise not to do anything that might trouble you, may I still see you when you are not at school, sometime?"

She came to a stop and stretched out her hand to touch his sleeve, almost as she had touched the mare's neck. "I would — I would like that better than not to see you. I'm sorry . . . ."

He shook his head so hard his hat flew off, and they both scrambled after it, finally laughing. Susannah picked it up, shook it off, and handed it to him with an exaggerated curtsy. He took it, put it on, and said, "You have nothing to make you sorry. Merry Christmas, Susannah. Thank you for coming with us. I'll tell you when the priest comes."

She looked startled, as if she had forgotten why she had come to the service last night, almost as if what had mattered was his company. That, more than anything else, cheered him as he headed back home, hearing Susannah calling "Merry Christmas!" to someone she met along her way.

Chapter 16

SUSANNAH should go back to the boarding house and brave the ladies' questions, but the thought was so daunting that she let herself amble along the town square, admiring the many decorations that had by now appeared there. She remembered the tin angel and made her way to the tree, taking more time than necessary in finding just the right spot where the angel would show to best advantage. When she had finally hung it up and stepped back to admire it, a farmer's wife came up to her with a tray of hot drinks steaming cheerfully in the morning light. "Some hot chocolate, my dear? Or coffee?"

The thought of coffee, hot and bracing and good for staying awake, was as welcome as manna in the desert. "Coffee, please. How much is it?"

"Only three pennies. And if you catch me before I leave the square, you can have another mug full for just one."

Susannah followed the woman at a discreet distance as she drank the coffee, so quickly she burned her tongue. She took more time with the second cup, and then, allowing herself one sigh, turned her steps toward Miss Wheeler's. She entered just as the boarders were gathering around the dining table, mostly dressed in their best, although the eccentric boarder who had been living there the longest wore her usual dingy black dress and oversized bright yellow shawl. Miss Wheeler welcomed Susannah with thinly disguised relief. "Just in time, dear!

We've volunteered to make gingerbread men for the minister and some of our town ladies to take to the poorer children. Now, would you like red jellybeans for their buttons, or green?"

Was it only good luck, for the ladies to have something keeping them busy when Susannah reappeared? She rather suspected that Miss Wheeler had planned the activity for that purpose. To be sure, the ladies chatted and gossiped as they worked, but it took almost ten minutes for one of them to turn to Susannah and say, "And how was your visit? How is the new family from St. Louis liking Omaha? Did they bring any news of your family?"

Susannah blinked, wondering if she were sleepier than she had realized. After her momentary confusion, she realized, with a mix of gratitude and shame, that Miss Wheeler had decided to take the prudent course of making up a story to render Susannah's absence less controversial. She struggled for an answer with a minimum of falsehood to it. "My family are all well, thank you, though they are sorry not to have me there for Christmas. The family to whom Miss Wheeler refers seem to be settling in well." Before anyone could extend the conversation, she bent her head over her gingerbread man and made a point of taking great care in deciding whether to apply three buttons or four.

In penance for taking liberties with the truth, she volunteered to carry the basket of gingerbread men to the church, and then, when invited, to join the charitable ladies, all better dressed than she had ever been, in making their rounds among the poorer families. She managed to hold back most of the yawns that threatened, so that she could hope to appear no more sleepy than the rest of the party.

When the flock of ladies turned a corner near Carl's

and Bronka's house, the minister's wife tapped Susannah on the shoulder and said, "You have a pupil, don't you, in one of those houses on the edge of town? They're immigrants, aren't they, and I've seen the lad carrying boxes for travelers at the railway station. Should we bring them some gingerbread, do you think?"

Her heart in her throat, Susannah forced a smile and said, "Oh, no, I shouldn't think so. The young man has a steady job at the mill, and there are no young children there. I'm sure there are other families who need treats more."

"Well, my dear, you know best. Now, who else did I have in mind? I should have made a list." And on they went, Susannah silently giving thanks for her narrow escape.

She would, at that, have liked to give some gingerbread to Carl and Bronka, but she had some idea by now of the depth of their pride. If ever she made gingerbread for the family, she would make it with Bronka and Bronka's mother at her side, all sharing the work and its result. If Carl were in an unusually merry mood, she could just see him tossing a pinch of sugar at his sister, or even throwing it in Bronka's hair like snow.

Susannah returned from the morning's charitable rounds just in time for Miss Wheeler's bountiful Christmas dinner. Miss Wheeler did her own cooking, and months of experience had confirmed how good a cook she was — maybe, in fact, better than Susannah's mother. But sitting at the festive table, surrounded by women who were no longer strangers but had not actually become friends, she had to fight back the sudden pressure of tears.

As soon as dinner ended, she went to her room and pulled the letter from her mother, received two days before, from under her pillow. She had saved it for today without knowing whether it would be a Christmas treat or bring more to worry her, but knowing she would need that small contact with family and home. She sat down at her dressing table, opened the letter, and kissed the neat handwritten opening lines.

My darling Susannah,

Merry, merry Christmas! I hope Cowbird Creek is properly festive, and that you've joined in those festivities. We continue to miss you very much, of course, but we hope you're too busy and happy to miss us very badly.

Pa is well, busy at the paper as usual. Business picked up a bit before the holidays, as people came in to place personal ads wishing their friends back east or farther west a merry and blessed Christmas. There were also many obituaries, as the winter always brings with it some departures among the very old and the very young. We have been lucky enough to avoid losing anyone among our close friends, though Mrs. Bayless — you remember, the lady who always showed her vegetables at the State Fair, whether or not they were especially fine that year — died of lung fever at the beginning of December.

Susannah smiled a little at the memory of the ever-hopeful Mrs. Bayless, and sighed at the news of her passing. She would remember the woman in her prayers, and ask that her example help Susannah keep in mind the vanity that might color her own plans and beliefs.

I have sent you a package with all of our gifts for you. If it hasn't arrived, my apologies, but it will give you something to anticipate, and extend your Christmas a little longer.

She would have to ask Miss Wheeler whether anything had come for her, and if not, check at the general store tomorrow. She could only hope her own box, sent home last week, had arrived in time, and that the trinkets from the holiday market would not strike her family as too rustic.

The Lord bless you and keep you, dearest daughter — all our love, Ma

Susannah hugged the letter to her breast, hard enough to make the paper crinkle, before she put it down and went downstairs to ask about her Christmas box.

Miss Wheeler had been happy to produce Susannah's Christmas box. "It came last night, my dear. I had thought to mention it at supper, but then you had your supper elsewhere. I hope it was as good as ours . . . ."

Susannah managed to say how much she regretted missing Miss Wheeler's offering without telling any falsehoods about the alternative she had chosen instead, and carried her box up to her room. Even though it made little sense, she found the omen hopeful — if she had her box on Christmas Day, perhaps the gifts she had sent home had arrived on time as well.

As soon as she had hauled the box to her room, she set it down on the floor, pulled out a fresh piece of paper, sat at her dressing table, and picked up her pen.

Dearest Ma,

I am about to open your box, which arrived providentially on Christmas Eve. It was so good of you to send it! I will continue this letter with my more particular thanks after I have done so.

She put down the pen and knelt on the floor beside her bed to open the box from home. At the top, she found a framed sampler, rich with floral embroidery around cross-stitched text reading PATIENCE, LOVE, FAITH. Kissing the frame, she placed it on her bed and pulled out three books: Mark Twain's *Life on the Mississippi*, Sarah

Jewett's *A Country Doctor*, and a collection of Elizabeth Barrett Browning's poetry. She took deep breaths until thoughts of the Mississippi could fade in immediacy, distracting herself with wondering whether Dr. Gibbs would agree with the observations Miss Jewett had recounted.

Next came a dress in a brown and green plaid, probably her mother's handiwork, neat and appropriate for the classroom. Reaching into the depths of the box, she found the last two items: warm knit socks, and a box of hard candies from her favorite confectioner.

Here was another chance to give a treat to Carl and his family. . . . But just downstairs were the other boarders, with whom she had already failed to socialize on this holiday as much as expected. She put the socks and dresses away, squeezing the socks first to enjoy their thick and yielding texture, and took the box down to share.

Susannah had been delighted to find, at the market, a silver ornament in the shape of a book. The day after Christmas, Susannah bundled up and took a walk before supper in the direction of the library, hoping she might find Camelia at her desk.

When she arrived, the desk stood unoccupied, and Susannah looked around the small space in case Camelia was in some corner reaching for a book or restocking the shelves. She found, instead, Carl and Bronka, apparently engaged in the same search. Carl was holding a carefully wrapped box, big enough to hold something larger than Susannah's tin angel. As Carl bowed to her, Bronka pointed to the box as she greeted Susannah and explained, "Carl made one of his carvings for Mrs. Grant! and the miller let him leave a little early to give it to her."

Carl's mouth twitched in something grimmer than a

grimace. It seemed likely that the miller had extracted some concession in return, perhaps docking Carl's pay. Hoping to restore his good humor, Susannah said brightly, "I'm sure she'll love it. I certainly loved my dancer. What did you make, Carl?"

His smile, welcome after that brief frown, had a hint of mischief. "Stay long enough, and you can watch Mrs. Grant open it and find out. You see her coat is still on the hook, so she should be back soon." He put the box in the center of Camelia's desk.

The door opened just then and Camelia's cheery voice called out, "Fee, fi, fo, fum, I smell visitors! Welcome, and merry Boxing Day! That's a holiday in England the day after Christmas, and we can always use more holidays. Who's run out of things to read?"

With the bounty of books Susannah's mother had sent, she could not claim any such need. Carl, however, raised his hand, waving it about like one of Susannah's youngest pupils. "I finished the last two — I've already put them on the return shelf. I think I'm ready for something harder." What had Carl been asking Camelia to give him, and how long had he been doing it? Susannah saved her questions for after Carl and Bronka left. For now, she would get to see what Carl had made.

By now Camelia had noticed the box. "Gracious me, how did this intriguing object find its way here?" She studied each of them in turn. It must have been easy to find who was responsible, with Bronka standing on tiptoes in eagerness and Carl looking shy. Susannah took a step back to make it clear she deserved none of the credit.

Camelia sat at the desk and opened the box with the greatest of care, explaining cheerfully, "All this wrapping is another present, so why shouldn't I make sure I can use it some time?" When she had the box unwrapped, she opened it and lifted out a carving about ten inches high. Susannah's jaw dropped. She made haste to banish the unladylike expression, but no one was looking at her in any case.

It was a tree with books instead of leaves. The largest books had tiny carved titles, most in English but one in the clusters of consonants Susannah recognized as Polish. Carl had used one sort of wood for the trunk and branches of the tree and another, lighter, for the books. About half the books were open, and two had pages ruffling as if in the breeze.

Camelia set the tree down gently and then thrust out her hand at Carl. "Young man, I must shake hands this instant. You are a great artist, and one day I'll be bragging to library patrons about the days before you were famous, when hardly anyone in town knew how talented you were. It's too much of a gift, but don't you dare try to take it back!"

All four of them laughed, and then turned the discussion to what books Carl had just returned and what he wanted to try next. Susannah had read one of the latter, and could not help but be impressed that Carl planned to attempt it. "A man's reach should exceed his grasp," she murmured quietly, and then stopped in mid-quotation, realizing Carl might mistake her meaning if he heard.

Carl took his books and thanked Camelia, and he and Bronka turned to go, Carl looking solemnly at Susannah as they left, his earlier levity gone without a trace. She could only hope the change came from the memory of their awkward encounter Christmas morning, rather than from his overhearing her ill-advised comment. She waited to be sure brother and sister would not be returning before she asked Camelia, "How did this start, Carl borrowing books regularly?"

Camelia cocked her head and looked thoughtful. "You know, I think he'd have liked to be part of your class, if he weren't too grown and if he had the leisure. He was plenty sharp enough to know that he'd be able to earn better wages, or start a business and run it without being cheated, if his English improved — but he had to earn whatever he could right away instead. So when I got to town, he was on my doorstep the very first morning I opened up, wanting books he could — how did he put it? 'Books I can read, but just barely.' And he's been working his way from easy to more challenging ever since. And now, what can I do for you? Need something challenging?" She laughed at her own joke, though the idea was not actually a bad one.

Susannah pulled the little ornament out of her pocket, acutely aware how much less impressive it was than Carl's creation. "I brought you something also, and while it pales next to what you just received, you might be able to combine the two."

Camelia turned the silver book this way and that to catch the light. "Oh, but it's so pretty! I can hang it on one of the branches of Carl's tree, and watch people do a double-take when they see that one book looks different from the others. If it's anyone I want to tease, I can tell them that of course it's made of wood, just cleverly painted, and can't they see it? Bet I can get one or two people to believe it." She suited her action to her words, hanging the book between two of the wooden ones. She laughed again, Susannah joining in before she made her farewells and headed to the boarding house.

On her way, she found herself thinking about Carl's

industry and determination, and wondering what his neighbors made of it. For that matter, what would Susannah's acquaintances back home think? Would they cheer him on? Or would they think he should be content in his current "station"?

She tried to imagine Charles Elliott expressing admiration for Carl's enterprise and ambition. But she could not make that scene come to life.

Chapter 17

KAROL woke up early from restless sleep, went into the kitchen for one of yesterday's biscuits, dressed in warm layers, and went out back to chop wood. There were times, like this morning, when he could almost reach back and feel what it had been like to be younger, to be a boy with shoulders narrower and arms thinner, and less flesh on him to hold the heat and keep out the cold.

Lifting an axe had been so much harder, in that boy's body. He had done his best, but sometimes he could hardly pull the axe out of the wood and raise it one more time, no matter how little wood remained in the cottage. Now, he rejoiced in the strength of his arms and shoulders, the ax obeying him without a struggle. The exercise warmed him just enough, and he piled up more cut wood than the family would need for a week.

Lifting the axe and chopping wood, breathing in cold air and blowing out frosty clouds to catch the morning light, made it easier to keep other thoughts at bay. Until they forced themselves in, and took up the rhythm of his work.

What now . . . with Susannah? What now . . . at the mill? What now . . . what now?

He cared for Susannah. There was no use in denying it. Not to himself, at least. He was tired of hiding from the truth. From how much he wanted a woman — if it was the right woman — in his life. A woman to hold and protect, a woman to encourage and advise him, a woman

he could trust, the woman whose stove he would supply

with wood, the woman with whom he would be a man complete, the woman who would make him a father, the woman with whom he would grow old.

Now, when he might have met that woman, there was so much that stood in his way. And he knew no axe that could clear that path.

He had finally gotten too warm. He put down the axe and straightened up, stretching his back and arms before filling his arms with wood and going inside. Mama greeted him as he came into the kitchen. "My good son, you bring so much wood! Stack it by the stove and sit down — I have your breakfast almost ready."

At least worry hadn't hurt his appetite this time - not like Christmas morning. It happened more when he got excited, like the day he found out they were leaving Poland for America. He had been so eager — sorry, also, about leaving his friends and everything he knew, but America! The land of gold, of wild Indians with their feather headdresses and bold cowboys, and no kings or nobles, and no one ever telling him what to do, ever again — except Mama and Papa, until he grew up.

He had seen the cowboys now and then, covered in trail dust and smelling of cattle, and the Indians, though never a one wearing a headdress of feathers. But gold was hardly to be had, except for a few of those who went west seeking it. And there might be no king here, nor any nobles who called themselves such, but the miller had plenty to say about what he should and shouldn't do, and so did some people in town, though they said it behind his back.

They might say it to his face, and Susannah's, if he worked up the courage to court her, and if she decided to fight whatever demons haunted her.

Mama slid a plate of eggs and bacon and spiced potatoes in front of him. She poured coffee for them both and sat down across from him. She would wait to eat breakfast until Papa and Bronka ate theirs, in case there wasn't enough to go around.

She watched him shovel in heaping forkfuls, one after another, and said in a knowing voice, "Thinking about the schoolteacher, are you?"

He dropped his fork and gaped at her. She chuckled. "I have four brothers. I know how a young man acts when he's ready to court some girl. You chop enough wood for a castle, you stay out in the cold until you're hungry as a wolf. I know."

He picked up the fork and went back to eating. Mama wouldn't nag him to talk while his mouth was full. But too soon the plate was empty, and she sat there drinking her coffee and then holding the empty mug, waiting.

He sighed and surrendered, if not completely. "I like her, yes. She's smart, and she cares about Bronka and the other pupils. She made a mistake and admitted it and tried to make it right. She works hard."

"We thought you'd find yourself a nice Catholic girl, maybe one of the girls in Elk Leg. When you were ready."

What could he say? "I might have. But then Susannah came to town. And . . . she could become Catholic." Not that he had any reason to think she would do it.

Mama nodded, the look in her eyes like the one he'd often seen when she looked at vegetables and decided if they were good enough for the table. "Living at the boarding house, who knows if she can cook? And her clothes look like they came from a store, or even some fancy tailor." Mama sniffed. "But I could teach her such things. To be a teacher, she must have learned all the things she has to teach. She'll know how to learn something new, if she's willing."

"Mama! Why would she even look at me, a laborer, at a job with no prospects of better?"

Mama scoffed. "A strong handsome man, who works hard and will find his way in the world, here in a country where you can! You won't be under the miller forever. And she likes you already. Any fool — or at least, any mother — could see that."

Karol hadn't told the family about what happened Christmas morning. Whatever had gone wrong, it was no one's business but his and Susannah's. Except . . . Mama would keep pushing him toward Susannah, if he didn't explain. "I thought so too, for a while. But when I . . . she pushed me away."

Mama sighed. "I saw that. When we left the church. But I saw that she kissed you, first."

Karol ground his teeth, made himself stop, and replied, "What does it matter what she did first, with what she did after?"

Mama got up and took her mug to the sink. To his surprise, she grabbed a plate and put eggs on it, though not a big helping and with no bacon beside it. She brought it back to the table and said as she sat down, "I need something in my belly to talk about this."

About what? He waited in suspense as she took a mouthful, then put her fork down again as if she had thought twice about eating. She swallowed the food and said heavily, "When I was a girl, the lord's son caught me alone, when I came to drop off a sack of grain. You know we had to give the lord of the manor part of whatever we grew."

He knew that. Their first months in America, she and Papa repeated that often, to encourage him as they all tried to find their way.

Mama swallowed, though she had taken no more food. "He found me alone, and pushed me up against the wall. He — ran his hands all over me, and pushed his face into my neck. And he did more. I hadn't been with a man, but of course I'd seen the bulls with cows, and the horses. I'd wondered if it was the same with people. That wasn't how I'd wanted to find out."

Karol's hands curled into fists, tighter than ever they had before. He wanted to find a ship and sail all the way back to Poland, so he could find the landlord's son and beat him to a pulp, beat him until he cried for mercy, and then drag him all the way back to cower at Mama's feet. And in this dream of revenge, Karol would somehow not be killed for it.

"When he was through, he let me go and laughed, and he patted my behind as I left. I almost hated that more than everything before. I ran home crying and told my mother. She pulled me to the side of the house away from where my father was mending a chair, and told me to talk quietly so he wouldn't hear. Then she told me that it happened to many girls, but it was best to keep fathers and brothers from finding out, because there was nothing they could do without making things worse. She would tell me, she said, how to make a man think it was the first time, when I came to marry. She didn't say whether she'd had to do the same."

Karol would have got up and hugged Mama — but with that memory filling her thoughts, he wasn't sure she would want any man's touch, even his. And that meant . . . . "Are you saying someone attacked Susannah that way?"

"It might have happened, and she left St. Louis to get away from him. Or she might have fought him off, and he threatened to get revenge somehow. That happened too, sometimes. There was one girl I knew who refused a lord, and he made sure the boy she was supposed to marry was sent away to the war."

The coffee Karol had drunk had gone bitter on his tongue. "And you think it's the same here, as bad here as it was in the old country."

Mama pursed her lips. "Maybe not as bad. I don't know. The rich men here, maybe they have less power, and maybe they worry more what the other rich men think, or what their own wives would say if they found out. But for months afterward, I could hardly bear to have a man come near me, except my father and brothers. My mother took the grain to the landlord after that. She said his son wouldn't bother an old woman like her."

He searched for some light in this darkness. "But you married, after all. You let Papa close enough to court you."

She relaxed and leaned back against the chair. "It had been a year, I think. And he was such a kind boy, and with beautiful eyes. Yes, he does have! You look at them sometime. And I was tired of being afraid. Your Susannah, she's a brave girl, to come here and start over. She'll get tired of it too."

He should have said that Susannah was hardly his Susannah, but he liked too well how it sounded. Still, there were more obstacles to overcome. "She's not Catholic."

"Isn't the priest coming to town, just to talk to her? He must be used to showing people the way to the Church. You can leave that to him."

If Susannah went so far as to convert, would she lose her job? He couldn't imagine the town continuing to employ a Catholic as the teacher who had to teach religion in its school, which is why Susannah would be talking to the priest in the first place.

Meanwhile, however, Mama was still busily planning his life. "But a better job, that would help. The miller has sons, and one of them will probably get the mill when he's too old. Which could be years, anyway." She plucked at her lips with her fingers, the way she always did when she was thinking. "Your carving — there should be a way to make a job out of that. You're so good at it, and you know it."

He did know it, and knew there was no way to make money at it — not in a little town like Cowbird Creek, at any rate. "You want me to sit out in the square every day and be my own holiday market? That should give everyone a good laugh. Susannah would be so proud."

"Don't you get smart with your mother. You need to get to work. I'll ask your father later, see what he thinks. With all the odd jobs he does, he knows what all the shops and businesses do. He might have an idea."

Mama was right about one thing — he would be late if he didn't hurry. He gave her a quick kiss on the cheek and grabbed his coat.

His route took him near the train station. A piece of paper, one he hadn't seen before, fluttered in the morning breeze, and he spared the time to look at it. And then he took a moment more, to read it again.

Strong men wanted to be brakemen on the Union Pacific Railroad. See the West! Good pay. Inquire at the station.

Karol had heard railway men talk about that job. It was far from safe, with brakemen falling off trains — though he'd bet he wouldn't do that — or getting crushed. But because of those dangers, the railroad had to hire new people often, and it had to pay well to get them.

Whatever happened with Susannah – and most likely, nothing ever would -- it might be worth the risk to earn more money. And he could see a little more of the country he must now call his own.

Chapter 18

SUSANNAH had chosen the transition from January to February for the school's two-week winter break. The children could spend as much time as their parents permitted playing in the snow, when there was any, or working off their high spirits in other outdoor activities. Rather than expect them to do much in the way of more taxing schoolwork, she met with Camelia and obtained at least one book for every child to borrow, books she hoped would engage their interest enough that they might actually read them at least partway.

Not until she waved the children goodbye on the day before the break did it occur to her that she had also given herself a period of relative leisure.

What would she do with herself? At home, she had had a greater variety of acquaintances, and far more ways for them all to entertain themselves. Then she had been more productively busy at college. And she had been just as busy teaching school in Cowbird Creek. The industrious habits she had formed over the fall and early winter months now worked against her — she would not have enough to do, preparing for school to resume, to take much more of her time than she usually had available.

Camelia was her closest friend in town, and she could attempt to see more of her than their usual schedules allowed, but she dreaded expecting too much
Of their friendship, putting Camelia in the position of

either enduring or deflecting unwanted overtures. Of the few men whose manner had suggested any interest in furthering an acquaintance, none had inspired a wish that they would pursue such an intention. And while her fellow boarders at Miss Wheeler's could occasionally be good company, particularly if she was in a mood to welcome some substitute mothering, she more often found herself straining to be friendly and polite. There were people in town — Dr. Gibbs and his wife, and no doubt others to whom they could introduce her — that she could look forward to knowing better, but she lacked Camelia's cheerful and undaunted energy, her willingness to put herself forward and assume others would be glad of it.

She began, therefore, by catching up on her correspondence, writing to her parents and to Louisa, and then to other school friends she had not ventured to contact before. She even wrote to her brother, hardly an eager or diligent correspondent in general. When sending missives to those she had left behind threatened to make her melancholy, and even an hour spent reading left her restless, she resolved to imitate her pupils and engage in wholesome exercise outdoors.

Several of the other boarders stared at her as if she were undertaking some reckless adventure as she walked through the front room, encumbered — not to say swallowed — by her coat, hat, gloves, and scarf. She unwound her scarf enough for them to see her attempt a reassuring smile. As soon as she had stepped outside and encountered the crisp morning air and brisk breeze, she wrapped the scarf around her face again and strode forth. At least three inches of fresh snow made her grateful, as often before, for her sturdy if unfashionable boots.

She had hoped taking a walk would lift her spirits, and it was doing so even more than she had hoped. After all, she was still young, in good health, and at liberty. And the snow was powdery and fine, rising up in little puffs from her boots.

Could she make bigger puffs of snow? She glanced around to make sure no one was watching, and then drew back her left foot and kicked. She beamed and clapped her hands at the veritable cloud she produced.

A few more steps and kicks, a few more clouds, and she grew restless again. She needed a destination. Where hadn't she been, in this little town?

Of course! She had lived for months in a town called Cowbird Creek, and had never seen the creek. For that matter, she had only a guess as to where to find it. She set out in what might be the right direction, following a slight downhill slope and now hoping to find someone along the way who could tell her where to go. She allowed herself one more cloud of snow.

Almost immediately, she spotted a man whose coat failed to hide his broad shoulders. His blond hair peeked out from under a well-knitted woolen hat. He looked for all the world like Carl Marek — but what would a laborer be doing, going for a stroll on a Tuesday morning? Or was it? It couldn't be Sunday, could it? Even if she had lost track of the days to that extent, surely the ladies at Miss Wheeler's would have been dressed for church, or already attending?

His approach removed all doubt. It was Carl. Had he seen her childish behavior? If so, she could only hope her bulky coat and scarf hid her identity, not to mention her blush. But that hope survived only moments, as his eyes brightened and he smiled at her. "Good morning, Miss Shepard! How are you enjoying the time out of school?"

Something about his open countenance made her

want to give an honest answer. She unwound her scarf enough to talk and admitted, "I have rather forgotten what to do with this much leisure. And you? It appears you are also at leisure this morning."

Moments later, she realized she should not have pried into his affairs so. But he answered, with no sign of offense, "The miller decided to take his family somewhere warmer for a few days." Now a frown did shadow his face. "And rather than leave me to carry on, he closed the mill until he and his sons return."

She must have allowed herself to look concerned, for he visibly shook off his irritation and asked, "Is there somewhere you are going, or are you only wandering to enjoy the sunshine?"

She hesitated, suddenly embarrassed to admit her ignorance. But what good teacher let herself be afraid to learn something new? "I meant to visit the creek, the one for which the town is named. Though I'm not sure how to find it. Am I heading where I should, or have I already gone astray?"

Carl stood up even taller. "I can show you." Then he slumped down a little. "If . . . unless you would rather have only your own company."

She had all too much of that, even if she enjoyed his company less than she did. "No, please do walk with me and guide me. Do we keep going downhill?"

"Yes, and not far." He chuckled. "As you might have guessed, since nothing is far here."

She had thought the creek might be a mere trickle, a remnant of some more substantial past stream, but it was a creek worthy of the name, if not remotely the width or apparent depth of a river. Not that she had much expertise in judging the depth of such a surface, frozen over into a patchwork of smooth and rippled surfaces, with little waves of ice where the water met roots or rocks in its path.

Susannah was suddenly beset by the memory of another winter, many years ago, and a sheet of ice, stretching almost to the horizon . . . . She had been holding her father's hand . . . .

Carl's voice, gentle and low, brought her back to the present, to find she was blinking away tears. "You are thinking of something? I hope it is not so very sad?"

She would have liked to bring forth a reassuring little laugh, but once again, something about his presence made the idea seem disagreeably dishonest. She cleared her throat and said, hearing the huskiness in her voice, "Not sad at all, really. It only makes me sad to remember it, because it's a memory of home. Did you know that the great Mississippi River can freeze over? It did so in my childhood, more than once, but I only remember the second time."

Did he want to hear about it? It certainly seemed so. He was leaning forward like one of her pupils at story time. It cheered her as she went on. "I was small enough that I could only see out away from the bank, where it looked as smooth as the most placid pond. But so much wider than any pond I had ever seen! And it was frozen hard enough that people were walking on it, and skating. I wanted to join them, but my father would not trust the ice that far. So we walked along, and bought hot cider from someone selling it, and then went home to supper, where I told my mother all about it at least three times."

She could picture it all so clearly, and even feel her father's hand holding hers and the warmth of her mother's hug. And then, the breeze brushed her face, and she was back along this little creek, far from family and home.

But not, after all, far from every friend.

Neither of them had much to say as they walked back into town. Susannah had no insight into Carl's reasons; for herself, she was feeling shy about the emotion she had shown.

No, she was hiding from the truth again, as to why Carl had fallen silent. Her own silence must have been responsible. From small clues she had barely noticed when they fell, she had now pieced together the fact that he considered her above him in position. Given any lack of encouragement from her, he could well be lecturing himself for presumptuousness in speaking to her as an equal.

Not that she knew what to say, that would sound natural and friendly after such a silence.

What would her mother advise? And why must she keep thinking about her parents when she was trying to once again hide her homesickness?

What came out, once again, was what she had only just been thinking. "I wish you could meet my parents. You'd like them, I'm sure."

She had avoided looking toward him as she spoke, but she could feel the change in his walk as he gave a little start. When she did look, he was almost staring at her. "Your parents?"

"Yes, if they ever visit. It would be hard for them to come, but I hope that if I stay here for long, they can find a way."

Silence again. They were almost back at the boardinghouse when he said, almost too quietly to hear, "I hope you will stay so long. And I would be very glad to meet them, if they ever come."

Chapter 19

SO FAR, Bronka was Susannah's only Catholic student. And Bronka would understand that Susannah's duties included teaching religion. But Susannah still found herself stalling.

Her latest compromise was to teach religious history. It wouldn't hurt her pupils to realize that for most of its history, Christianity *was* Catholicism. And it came as quite a shock to some. One little boy jumped out of his seat and declared that she had it all wrong, and that he would have his daddy come and explain it to her. She found it amusing until the boy added that his daddy always said women shouldn't be teachers, because they got everything mixed up anyhow. She should have controlled her temper, rather than snapping back, "And that's what happens when little boys don't listen to their teachers. They grow up not learning properly, and then they can't help saying such things to their children." If she didn't lose her job for failure to teach religion more often, she might lose it for impertinence toward parents.

She made a list of questions for the priest, whenever he should turn up. She made a trip to the library for children's books about Jesus, to read from in class or to inspire her lessons less directly. And she waited.

The Sunday after next, Bronka came to the boarding house in early afternoon, looking around with eager curiosity, and told her that Father McCarthy had arrived at their house and could stay for another hour or more, and could she possibly make the time to come?

When they reached the Mareks' house, Bronka led her to the kitchen, the warmest room. The priest was sitting at the table with a cup of coffee and some sort of filled pastry, chatting pleasantly with Mrs. Marek. He stood up as Susannah approached, which she had not known whether to expect, but did not extend his hand, which would have truly surprised her. Meanwhile, Mrs. Marek bustled forward to welcome her and offer her the same refreshments. She accepted the coffee, tried without success to decline the pastry, and sat at the table across from the priest as the priest returned to his own chair.

Knowing that she was likely to find herself tongue-tied when this moment came, Susannah had written out a list of questions. Now, however, it felt even more awkward to pull it out and consult it. She tried to remember all the items as the priest said, "Welcome, Miss Shepard, if I may be so bold as to welcome you to another's dwelling. I would have liked to come sooner, but my schedule is busier than you might expect. Now that we are both here, how may I be of assistance?"

Susannah cleared her throat. "Thank you so much for coming, Father."

He managed to interrupt without seeming rude, a skill that must be invaluable in his profession. "If it troubles you, you needn't address me as Father. You may just call me Mr. McCarthy." His smile revealed unexpected dimples. "You would then know more about me than some of my congregation who have never heard my last name, let alone used it. Indeed, there are times when I could easily forget it myself."

"If I may, then, I'll call you Mr. McCarthy. Or Sir, if that would be appropriate." At his nod, she asked the first question she could bring to mind. "Do Catholics worship Mary, the mother of Jesus, as if she were divine?"

The priest paused before answering, gazing a little up and to the side as if consulting some remembered text. "That rather depends on how you define divinity. Are you familiar with the concept of saints?"

"I think so, sir. At least, I know Catholics pray to them, and that some churches — at least, in other countries — keep . . . I believe 'relics' is the term?"

"Relics, yes, though you are correct that they are rare in this country, in part due to how reluctant churches in our faithful's countries of origin would have been to part with them. Saints are those whose lives and works, including works made manifest after their deaths — deaths that were often, though not exclusively, those of martyrs — manifest their special closeness to God, and His choice to perform his beneficent wonders through them. Mary is the saint first and most directly chosen by God, to be the instrument of his greatest miracle, the Incarnation of one of His Holy Persons as a mortal man. Because she was our Lord's mother, and experienced His loss as a mother would, Catholics tend to view her as most likely to understand their own sorrows, and to view their sins with the greatest charity." He dimpled again. "We are, in general, less bold in approaching God directly with our various petitions, and prefer to invoke the assistance of those to whom God has already shown special approval. But we do not view any saint, even Mary, as divine, as only the Father, the Son, and the Holy Spirit are divine. You Protestants do acknowledge the Holy Trinity, I believe?"

"Yes, sir. Though there may be some sect, somewhere, that does not."

What next? "Are Catholics forbidden to read the Bible?"

The priest's eyebrows lowered and came together. "By no means, my child — excuse me, Miss Shepard. This misunderstanding arises from the fact that priests do urge caution in interpreting the Bible, as the ultimate meaning of its text is a matter for the Church to determine. There is, perhaps, variation in the extent to which some priests emphasize the caution and others emphasize the blessings to be derived from devotional reading."

Susannah was embarrassed to ask the next question, but presumably the priest would not be ashamed of the answer, whatever it proved to be. "If the Pope, or a priest, tells a Catholic to do something that's against the law, would the person be treated as a sinner if they follow the law instead?"

The priest grimaced as if he had heard this question, or related accusations, all too many times before. "Miss Shepard, the Catholic Church, like other Christian institutions, draws a fundamental distinction between secular and religious law. 'Render unto Caesar,' after all. I can't say that no priest would ever stray into the error of instructing his flock to violate American or Nebraska law, but I will say with some confidence that no higher Catholic authority, and certainly no pope, would do so."

Susannah could not find the priest's certainty as reassuring as he no doubt intended, but there was no point in belaboring the issue. Next came a question she had heard from a veteran of the War of Rebellion, a man whose comrades in arms had included at least one Irish Catholic. "If the Vatican and the United States of America went to war with each other, what would American Catholics do?"

Father McCarthy sighed. "It is, I imagine, an unsatisfactory answer that such a war is inconceivable for practical reasons. Yes, priests do sometimes think in practicalities! . . . The Pope's ability to make war, or to defend the Vatican in case of war, is so severely limited at this stage of history that you and your pupils need fear no such conflict. And diplomatic relations between the Vatican and this country are much improved since their low point in 1867, when one of those involved in President Lincoln's foul murder enlisted in the Pope's army under an alias, and then escaped when the Pope discovered his identity and ordered his arrest." The priest shuddered and made the same gesture the congregation had made at the midnight mass.

Mrs. Marek had left them to their discussion. Susannah, hoping she was not overstepping her position as guest of the house, looked to the stove and saw as she had hoped that the carafe of coffee was there keeping warm. She rose and poured more coffee for the priest and then herself. He smiled up at her. "That is most welcome. My thanks. Now where were we?"

If only she could look at her list! It might have preserved her from blurting out, "Do you believe that I and my pupils and their families are going to Hell?"

Father McCarthy looked at her with what she would have to call compassion. "My dear, I would never pronounce such a doom upon you. Not only is your life, I hope, far from over, but there are — how shall I put it — complexities and subtleties in the doctrines of salvation and redemption that many people, including many Catholics — and, I daresay, some priests — overlook." He chuckled. "Indeed, I sometimes think that Catholics, especially the Jesuits among us, rival the Jews in debating the fine points of doctrine, and looking for what one might irreverently call loopholes." He took a sip of coffee and added, "It is also worth pointing out that the

Catholic belief in Purgatory, a realm between Hell and Heaven in which we may be cleansed of our sins, is really more merciful than the more uncompromising views of some Protestant denominations."

The priest drained the rest of his coffee. "I must leave soon. Do you have any more questions? We could, of course, meet again, if you have many."

Once more she found herself asking a question she had surely not planned to ask. "Can — can Catholics marry Protestants? Would the Protestant have to become a Catholic?"

The priest's gaze become uncomfortably direct. "Yes, Miss Shepard. Catholics must marry within the Church, which welcomes converts, whether brought to it by marriage or some other path." His look became less penetrating as he added, "While we have barely touched on the differences between Catholic and Protestant beliefs, we have said even less about the similarities, which run very deep indeed. And even on the level of day to day religious observances, if you were to travel to England and attend an Anglican service, you might find it far more similar to a Catholic one than to, say, a service held by Methodists or Baptists." He stood up, prompting Susannah to do the same. "The differences in our faiths, while important and profound, matter less to most members of my flock, most Catholics in general, than priests and bishops might like to suppose."

Mrs. Marek came back into the kitchen, probably prompted by the sound of chairs pushed back from the table. She picked up one of the pastries from the basket on the counter, and urged the priest, "Here, Father, take some more of the *kolaczki* with you for later."

Father McCarthy smiled and put out a hand in polite refusal. "I must not, indeed. I have enough difficulty resisting the sin of gluttony without bringing home such temptation. But our young friend need not hold to such exacting scruples."

Mrs. Marek, without giving Susannah a chance to refuse, plucked three of the pastries and wrapped them in a napkin. "Please do take them. I baked too many." Susannah doubted Carl and Bronka were unable to consume the basket's contents, but she had eaten almost none of the pastry Mrs. Marek had already pushed on her, and allowed herself to accept.

Bronka and Carl emerged from wherever they had been keeping themselves and bid the priest farewell. Susannah, though wondering what the minister would think, curtsied to Father McCarthy and said, "Thank you so much, sir, for taking the time to answer my questions. You've given me much to think on — that is, much material for the lessons I'll need to teach."

She had thought that Carl might offer to walk her home, but apparently he was borrowing a buggy to take Father McCarthy back to Elk Leg. Before they left, however, he reached out slowly, leaving her time to retreat, and when she held still, took her hand. "Thank you for coming. Maybe we can talk some time about what Father McCarthy has explained."

Susannah tried to pay more attention to what Carl was saying than to the warm grasp of his hand. "I'll want to think it over, before I talk about it. But — I may well wish to do so. Thank you."

The priest left with a tip of his hat, Carl following after. Susannah thanked Mrs. Marek for the pastries, donned her coat and hat, and left to go back to the boarding house. She let herself extract one of the pastries to eat on the way.

She had barely gone a dozen steps before starting to

lecture herself. How had she forgotten to ask about baptism of infants? And confession, priests taking it on themselves to bestow God's forgiveness? She would have to take the priest up on his offer of another meeting.

* * * * *

Karol rarely got the chance to drive a buggy. He might have been tempted to test what it could do — if he hadn't had a passenger, and his priest at that. He kept the horse to an easy pace and sought out the smoothest parts of the road. When he glanced over at the priest, he saw that the man had sat back and closed his eyes, and he slowed the horse even more.

But soon enough the priest opened his eyes and sat up. "There's nothing like a cat nap to refresh the weary! Though it may be of less interest to the young and strong."

Karol dared to answer, "Father, I would have thought you quite young, still."

The priest laughed and replied, "What a generous fellow you are, to be sure! But I've known that about you for some time. Which reminds me, I'm impressed with your friend, Miss Shepard. She strikes me as an intelligent, curious, and serious young woman."

Karol found that description more intimidating than helpful. He could not argue with any of it, but it left out such qualities as *warm, generous, kind, sweet*, and of course, *pretty*. He supposed priests had to train themselves not to think about pretty girls, and after a while failed even to notice them.

This might be his only chance to find out, from someone other than Susannah, what she was thinking. What she thought of Karol, even. But — "Father, when someone who isn't Catholic talks to you in private, is it like the confessional?"

Father McCarthy cocked his head. "Not exactly like the confessional. With a discussion such as I had with Miss Shepard, my obligations are much like those of any honorable man, to keep confidential what the person with whom I spoke expected me to treat as such."

Carl slumped down over the reins. But Father McCarthy added, "I am, however, free to make very general comments. For example, I found Miss Shepard's questions a mix of the expected and the . . . informative."

And that was all. Just enough to set Carl's head spinning, without any idea of which direction he should be facing when it stopped.

They chatted about the chance of snow, Carl's work at the mill, Bronka's studies, and other such subjects until they were almost at the priest's small house next door to the church. The mention of the mill had set Karol to brooding again, and brought the railroad job to mind. As they pulled up in front of the house, Karol asked, "Father, what do you think about dangerous jobs that pay better than the ordinary kind?"

It might be the first time he'd seen the priest frown. "I would be concerned to hear that you were considering such a job. What would attract you to it?"

Hadn't he just explained? "The wages. A man should earn enough to support a family."

Father McCarthy jumped down from the buggy seat, as spry as any boy, and stood facing Karol. "A man should remain hale and whole, in order to support them throughout his and their lives. And a man's healthy body is a gift from God, to be treated with the respect such a gift merits. We must talk about this again, when I have more time."

Karol kept his expression properly respectful. "Of course, Father. Thank you."

"And thank you for the ride. Until next Sunday, then." He started to turn away and then spun back. "By the way, I neglected to mention — though I would guess I have no need to point out — that Miss Shepard is rather pretty, as well." The priest's eye twitched as though he had almost allowed himself to wink.

Karol just sat there on the buggy seat, staring after the priest, until the horse snorted and tugged at the reins to recall him to his senses.

Chapter 20

SUSANNAH had not talked to Dr. Gibbs in some time, but as she prepared to leave the schoolhouse that Friday afternoon, a knock on the front door announced his arrival. After his first greeting, he remarked, "I saw the children streaming out. They looked and sounded cheerful and happy, and not showing the sort of desperate relief of prisoners escaping confinement. I'm impressed, though not surprised in the least."

Susannah smiled and picked up her books and papers. "Thank you so much, Doctor. Did the sight of contented children lead you to come reassure me, or were you seeking me already?"

He stepped back from the doorway to allow her to exit, then walked beside her. "I come bearing an invitation. Our good friends Freida and Jedidiah Kennedy have just arrived in town, and Clara and I would be pleased if you could join them and us for Sunday dinner. Camelia Grant will be there as well, so we should be quite the merry party."

With Camelia included, it would certainly be a lively one. "I'd be most happy to attend. From where are your friends coming?"

Dr. Gibbs chuckled. "It would be easier to say what town in four or five states they haven't visited on their way here." At her raised eyebrows, he continued, "Jedidiah is a medicine man, with a wagon and a show, traveling from town to town selling his wares. It's a long and strange story, how he and Freida — Freida Blum, then, a Jewish widow — met when she lived here; how he won her heart; and how I came to regard someone in Jedidiah's profession as a friend, rather than a public nuisance and a menace. I'm sure you'll learn more about our shared history at dinner."

Susannah hardly knew which feature of this summary should most arouse her curiosity. "He came through town selling patent medicines, and in some manner wooed and won a respectable widow, and persuaded her to pull up stakes and spend her life in a wagon with no other home to call her own?"

Dr. Gibbs shook his head, but not in negation. "Hearing you recount it, it sounds even more difficult to believe than it did at the time, but that is the plain truth of the matter. In fact, the comfortable home Freida left behind to wander the country with Jedidiah is none other than Clara's and my current dwelling. She made a gift of it before she and Jedidiah rode away, as Clara and I were about to be married and had only my small rooms to share."

They had reached the point where their paths home must diverge, so Susannah said, "They sound like remarkable people. I look forward to meeting them."

Dr. Gibbs smiled broadly. "I must agree that they are. Until Sunday, then."

As Susannah walked the rest of the way, the story of Freida and her unlikely swain played over and over in her mind. Of all the married couples she had known, back home or in Cowbird Creek, she could think of none to compare with the couple she was soon to meet. Compared to the comfortably established Jewish widow and the perpetually traveling hawker of wares, any such union as —

She cut off the thought before she could finish it and hurried inside.

Susannah arrived at the appointed time, but even from the front path, she could hear that the rest of the party had assembled before her. Of course, the Kennedys might be staying at the house — but then where had they stowed the wagon? And Camelia's distinctive contralto stood out occasionally from the rest of the din.

She had no idea how anyone managed to hear her knock, but the door swung all the way open at once, to reveal not Mrs. Gibbs but the broad figure, round face, and curling gray hair of a woman who must be Freida Kennedy. She held little Alice, clinging about her neck, in one sturdy arm, and thrust out the other to take Susannah's hand. "You must be this darling's teacher, I'm so glad Joshua managed to entice you to town, such a bright child needs to go to school, as long as it's a good school, and I hear such wonderful things about you and what you've done! Come in, come in! You'll excuse my acting like a hostess, dear Joshua will have told you all about how I used to live here, not to mention how forward I am, he doesn't even try to reform me. Welcome!"

Susannah pulled off her gloves, shook hands, and squeezed between Mrs. Kennedy's capacious form and the door frame, to be greeted by a large Irish setter wagging his tail and sniffing her shoes. She bent to pet the dog, his warm fur a welcome treat for her cold fingers. The dog withdrew, perhaps to investigate the enticing aromas filling the entry way. But before Susannah could get more than two steps in, Mrs. Kennedy caught up with her and added, "And I'd get so tired of hearing Mrs., Mrs. all afternoon, I've bullied everyone else into calling me

Freida, you must do the same, and Jedidiah would be too polite to insist but you should call him by his first name, what you'd call his Christian name, also, and we'll all be cozy together."

Camelia's voice came from the sitting room. "After all, you call me Camelia, it's only fair!"

Mrs. Gibbs made her way past Mrs. Kennedy — Freida — and took Susannah's hand in turn. "Do come in. We'll have dinner shortly, but Freida and I have a few finishing touches to, well, finish. Let me take your coat and hat. Do sit here near Joshua, who serves as the calm eye of the social storm."

Dr. Gibbs rose from his chair to greet her, dislodging the dog's head from his lap in order to do so. "Thank you for joining us! I heard — naturally — Freida's insistence on the use of Christian names, and am glad for the occasion to ask if you would do Clara and me the favor of addressing us in the same manner."

Her host might be as calm and relaxed as her hostess had promised, but he would evidently not provide a refuge from startling notions. She could only nod, invite him to use her Christian name as well, and save her first attempt at calling him Joshua for later.

And she pondered, in the short moments between outbursts of conversation, the fact that Freida's phrasing when she used the term "Christian name" suggested she might not, upon marrying Jedidiah, have become a Christian.

But of course, there was no reason to assume Jedidiah was a Catholic.

Freida must have deposited Alice somewhere, for she interrupted Susannah's musings by bustling in from the kitchen. "Dinner's ready, everyone come sit while it's hot!"

Camelia jumped out of her easy chair. "Dinner's

ready, and we're ready for it! I would wager, if I had someone disreputable enough to wager with, that it'll be the best I've had in weeks. Where should I plant myself?"

Clara came forward to direct everyone to their places, putting Susannah between Camelia and their host, Alice in a chair with an extra cushion next to Joshua, Freida and Jedidiah (though he had not, himself, invited her to use that name) sitting opposite. Not that Freida had sat down, as she was busily bringing one serving platter after another to the table. Once she had finished that task, a clattering sound from the kitchen suggested a plate put down on the floor for the dog before Freida finally took her place and entered into energetic conversation with Camelia. As Joshua — she *must* get used to the invited informality — carved and served the roast, Freida's husband bent toward her with a genial, even charming, smile. "I hope your time in Cowbird Creek has been agreeable so far. I'm always glad to have an excuse to visit, and to see our hosts, to whom Freida and I owe so much."

Susannah accepted a filled plate from Joshua and put it down in front of her. "I had understood that Joshua and Clara owed a great deal to your wife."

"Indeed we do," Joshua put in. "For example, it would have been quite impossible to host this gathering in my former rooms, or to prepare such a feast. And that reminds me it is time to give thanks. Freida, would you like to begin?"

Freida finished whatever she had been saying to Camelia and beamed at him. "Of course!" She then not only began to speak in some foreign language, but almost to sing the words. Even more astonishing, Joshua and Clara, after a slight hesitation, joined in her recital, while

Alice looked on attentively. Jedidiah made no attempt to echo them, but sat smiling fondly at his wife. When the prayer, as it must have been, concluded, Camelia actually applauded. "You see, Susannah, I have my own students! Joshua and Clara came to me a year ago, when they were last expecting Freida and Jedidiah to visit, and asked me to find the text of the blessing said before eating — a *barucha*, it's called — and any pronunciation guide I could track down. It's Hebrew, of course."

Susannah, hoping her curiosity would not offend, asked Freida, "Might I know the translation?"

Freida nodded vigorously, curls bouncing, and said, "Of course, you should know, you could someday have a Jewish student and they might invite you home! In English, you would say, I think it is, 'Blessed are you, our God, King of the Universe, who brings forth bread from the earth.' Of course, we have so much else here, but if I'd done the barucha for everything else, it would all get cold! Some people say a different barucha that covers everything, but this is what I learned as a child, and here I am a hundred years later, still saying it."

Clara followed the moment of quiet this stream of words left behind to say, "Miss Shepard, might you like to say grace as well?"

"Ah, certainly." But how? At home, it had always been her father's task to say grace, and Miss Wheeler naturally did the honors at the boarding house. Susannah had never before done so, and had no well-honed prayer at the ready. In this exuberant and spontaneous company, she disliked the thought of reciting some overly familiar childhood blessing. Instead, she extemporized. "Lord, thank you for your many gifts to us, including on this holy day the gifts of hospitality, fellowship, and a bountiful repast. May I always remember to cherish such gifts as they deserve. Amen."

The warm looks from everyone at the table gratified and embarrassed her at once, and she looked down at her plate. Camelia dispelled any awkwardness by tapping her plate with her fork. "There we go, all properly thankful. Let's eat!"

When all had eaten as much as Freida could urge on them, and Susannah had helped Camelia, Clara, and Joshua collect the plates (fending off Freida's and Jedidiah's offers to assist), the parents excused themselves briefly to put Alice to bed (with bedtime kisses or hugs or head pats all round). Once the hosts returned, they all settled in the sitting room to digest the meal and sip the delicious fresh coffee Clara provided. As Clara refilled Freida's cup, she asked, "Have you had the chance to do any sewing lately? Susannah, you may not know that Freida is an accomplished seamstress and dress designer. Cowbird Creek lost what claim it may have had to high fashion when Freida left us."

Freida laughed, her ample bosom jostling the coffee cup and making the liquid slop almost to spilling. "Our kind hostess exaggerates, though I must say I did have plenty of ladies asking me to sew for them, I especially loved dressing their daughters. This trip I've done only a little sewing for my friend Madam Mamie's girls, they're even more grateful than the society girls, they almost never have anyone fit a garment to them."

Had Susannah heard her properly, or had she dozed off in an overfed stupor and dreamed it? Freida Kennedy was on friendly terms with, from the sound of it, the owner of a brothel? And her husband, now scratching the dog's ears until the beast practically melted with contentment, and the town doctor and nurse all took this friendship entirely in stride?

Before Susannah could recover from the shock, Freida turned to her and said, "And you, so nicely dressed of course, but I would love to sew for you, sometime, I could do some sketching while I'm here, just looking at you makes the ideas bubble around in my head like a pot of stew boiling!"

Susannah had to clench her teeth together to force back a hysterical giggle. Would she wait in line with some of the local prostitutes for Freida to measure her? And would the eager seamstress confuse the dress intended for her with whatever it was Madam Mamie required her soiled doves to wear?

But it was a generous offer. And Susannah had not had a new tailor-made dress since before she graduated from teacher's college. With a pang, she recalled that her parents had talked of presenting her with one on that occasion, before her future and the family's finances were both thrown into confusion. And she had kept Freida waiting too long for an answer. "That would be very kind of you, if it wouldn't interfere with your spending time with the friends you're here to visit."

A half hour later, after Freida brought out some large chocolate cookies and tried to persuade the guests to find room for them, it was time to go. Camelia suggested that they escort each other home, which only increased Susannah's gratitude for and satisfaction with the evening — the first such occasion, it struck her, that she had had since leaving St. Louis.

When they had said their thank-yous and goodbyes, Camelia took Susannah's arm. "Here I am, walking you home instead of some young gallant. At least I stride out as boldly as a sailor, let alone our tamer local youth."

Susannah laughed, but was surprised to feel a certain pang. Alone with the woman who had become a friend, she found herself saying what she had not said even to herself, though in a last impulse of caution, she avoided any details. "I confess there is one young man whose company would content me even as much as yours."

Camelia's bark of a laugh made her jump. "Carl, you mean. As if I hadn't seen *that*."

Cold air chilled Susannah's teeth as her jaw dropped. "But — I haven't — I didn't — "

Camelia's lope slowed to a more sedate walk, and she patted Susannah's hand. "I do apologize. I shouldn't tease, but I so rarely have the opportunity! But I'm right, aren't I? Or is there something I don't know?"

Camelia didn't know about the kiss and what happened afterward, or why it had happened. And she must know Carl was Catholic, but she might not know how Susannah felt about it. Not that Susannah really knew, herself.

Camelia spoke more soberly than was her wont. "I see matters are more complicated than I would hope — or you would hope, no doubt. I wish you a happy resolution, and won't venture to predict what it might be. And here's Miss Wheeler's. Good night, my dear."

Susannah, grateful for Camelia's tact, forced out a "good night" without a waver in her voice. As she climbed the steps of the boarding house, she gave herself a firm scolding. She had just had a delightful evening, and tomorrow she would return to a job she genuinely loved, one that the perfidy of President Brecker might have prevented her from obtaining. She had made friends, in a town so small she could reasonably have doubted how many she might find. She must not repine at what the future might or might not hold.

That night, as she got ready for bed, Susannah found herself wondering what the priest would make of a woman like Camelia. Or Freida, equally irrepressible, and Jewish to boot. Or Clara Gibbs, working beside her husband and subjected daily to sights that would shock most women, married or no.

What would he think about the kiss? Had he, perhaps, even seen it, and said nothing about it — at least to her?

Had he, likely skilled at the reading of hearts, noticed what Camelia had perceived?

She did her best to let all such thoughts go, to breathe them out with one great sigh, as she knelt to say her prayers.

Susannah couldn't say how she found herself to be standing alone in the empty Catholic church, afternoon sun streaming through its brightly colored windows, waiting to make her confession. She had never done so before, and could only hope the priest would guide her through the procedure. Before she could ask herself more questions, a door she hadn't noticed opened in the wall behind the altar, and the priest called to her from the room beyond. "Come in, my child, and close the door."

She had had a vague idea that confession involved privacy, and there was in fact a structure, a sort of wall, in the middle of the room, but it was only an empty wooden frame with a post in the middle. She could see the priest quite clearly. There was no chair, only one of the cushions on which the congregation had knelt during the Christmas mass. The priest waved her toward it, and said, "You may begin, my child. What are your sins?"

She had expected something more formal, or in Latin. But he might be making allowances for her ignorance. She knelt down, trying not to expose any part of her limbs as she did so, though her nightdress made that difficult. When she had settled herself, she stammered, "I — I've been envious, Father. I have envied the happily married couples I know."

The priest's voice now came from behind her. "That is only natural for a healthy young woman. Mother Church recognizes the needs of the flesh." And she felt hands on her waist. She spun around, only to confront not the priest, but a stranger. The room had grown darker, and it was hard to see his features, but she could see, and recognize, the smirking greed on the stranger's face.

She struck out at him with her hands extended, to scratch the leer off that face, only to awake to the pain of her hand striking the wooden frame of her bed. She sat up and hugged her throbbing hand to her breast.

She lay awake for she knew not how long, trying to remember the dream, to go through it step by step until it lost its horror. The dream faded, but some of the horror still lingered even as sleep overcame her.

Chapter 21

THE FLYER near the railroad station, growing dirtier and more tattered whenever Karol passed by, fluttered as if taunting him. He should be striding out in a more manly fashion — he was not so tired as his walk would suggest. But doing the same tasks day after day, with no change to expect, left him feeling like an ox dragging a wheel round and round, or a prisoner breaking rocks for a wall that would keep him from escaping.

He detoured to the town square, with a vague notion of searching the Christmas tree for the tin angel his family had given Susannah. But all the ornaments had been taken down, to be stored their owners came to collect them.

He turned to go, only to see Susannah sitting on a bench under one of the lanterns, huddled in her coat and hat. He hurried over to her and asked, "May I sit with you?" And when she looked up at him, her eyes haunted, he added, "May I help you, with any trouble you may have?"

Looking at her, he recalled what Bronka had said as he grabbed a hasty breakfast, just before he left for the mill — something about Susannah seeming tired at school the day before. How could he have just walked out the door, without asking for details? He could only hope to make up for it now.

Susannah smiled, a brief glimmer of an expression that vanished by the time he sat down. She glanced at him, looked away, and looked back again. "I had a — a silly dream, two nights ago. It made me curious about something that's really none of my business, but you're someone I can ask, now that you're here — if it isn't something Catholics must keep to themselves."

He could only imagine what ugly tales she might have heard about the secret rituals of Catholics, come to disturb the peace of proper Protestants. "I'll certainly answer if I can, and I doubt you'll be asking about anything I can't."

Her gloved hands clenched and unclenched in her lap. "It's about confession. I wondered how it works. Whether . . . whether you're in a room, by yourself, with the priest."

Was she imagining scandalous goings-on? "You go through a curtain and kneel in a small booth. There's a screen, wood or metal, between the priest and the one confessing. You can't really see the priest, only hear him."

Susannah gave a shuddering sigh, and sat up straighter, but seemed somehow more relaxed at the same time. "I knew it couldn't be like my dream."

He would not ask her about something so private as a dream. He desperately wanted to know why it had troubled her so much, but she had not come to him in her trouble, and he could hardly hope she would confide in him.

And yet, she was speaking again, so softly he could barely hear. "I think I should tell you why . . . why I acted that way on Christmas morning. I already told you it wasn't anything you did. But I need to tell you why it happened."

He should assure her that she owed him no explanation. But instead he listened, barely daring to breathe in case she changed her mind.

"Something happened back in St. Louis. Something I

never expected, something I was too — too innocent to fear. And — and I'm afraid it's changed me.

"The day I graduated from the normal school, the teacher's college . . . ."

The tale she told him, slowly, in halting words, had him so hot with anger he no longer noticed the cold. All he could think of, all he could feel, was how much he wanted to hunt the blackguard down and give him what he deserved.

Mama had been right. Though as Susannah's story came to a close, he knew with relief, mixed with guilt at feeling it, that Susannah's sufferings had not been so great as his mother's.

And Mama had, in the end, been able to bear the touch of a man, or Karol would never have been born. He could only hope Susannah was as strong, and that whenever she was ready to think of a husband . . . but even if the kiss that felt so long ago might give him hope, it was a fool's hope. There were so many obstacles in the way.

It made him angry all over again that she ended with, "I'm sorry."

He moved his hand toward her, slowly so she could pull back, and when she made no such move, put his hand over both of hers. "You must never be sorry that someone, a vile person, hurt you. You should only be sorry when you hurt others, and not always then. And you owe no apology to me. If you had scars on your face, I hope you wouldn't cover your face to hide them. It's much the same. Don't be sorry."

She looked him in the eye, finally, and tried to smile. It hurt to watch her try and fail. And if she meant to speak, she couldn't do that either. He pulled back his hand, stood up, and asked, "May I see you to Miss Wheeler's?"

He thought for a moment that she would need help to

stand. But she made it to her feet, stood close to him, and then put her hand on his arm, so he could take care of her as he walked her home.

* * * * *

It might or might not have helped to give Carl the explanation he deserved, but Susannah slept better that night than she had in weeks, if not months. Miss Wheeler, at breakfast, said with approval, "There's a spring in your step! I'm glad to see it. A good start to a good day, let's hope."

It was easy to smile, without the dragging fatigue. "I'm just as glad, you may well believe."

And indeed, the school day had remarkably few bumps in the road. Alice proved herself ready for the next McGuffey reader, one of the slowest boys made only one mistake in his arithmetic, and the pupils listened with tolerable attention to her explanation of what rhetoric was and how they would soon be practicing it. To Susannah's surprise, Bronka seemed particularly eager to face some of the other students in debate. Her English had improved enough that such a match-up might not be disastrous.

When Susannah stopped by the general store after school, the luck of the day continued, for she found a letter from Charles Elliott waiting. At least, she was used to thinking of such events as fortunate, though the eagerness with which she had formerly awaited his letters had faded over time. He had continued to ask after her welfare, express his regret for losing the opportunity of encountering her in person, and invite her to share any piquant anecdotes about her neighbors. It was hardly his fault that as she came to know those neighbors better, their individual personalities tended to crowd out her awareness of them as quaint rustic characters.

This latest letter, however, differed from its predecessors.

I must confess that I had hoped you would somehow find a way to celebrate Christmas with your family, and that I might see you before you returned to your western environs. I had even, in moments of optimistic fantasy, imagined you announcing to your family that you had decided to return home, that whatever considerations had driven you from them had proven insufficient by comparison. If such a vision ever tempts you, I would be grateful if you saw fit to confide it to me, as one to whom it would be of particular interest. . . .

Had she ever imagined that homecoming? Not without her imagination moving inexorably onward to the evils likely to follow, unless President Brecker had grown less resentful in the meantime. But she had let her mind stray, once or twice, to some scene, its contours hazy enough that she could ignore doleful realities, in which Charles made the declaration at which he might now be hinting.

But she had not entertained such fantasies in some time. She could remember none even as long ago as Christmas, let alone as winter slowly moved toward spring. When her thoughts of school and pupils, boarding house and town, allowed her any room for idle fantasy, fantasy had borne her in quite a different direction.

Neither Charles' dapper dress and fashionable grooming, nor his erudite manner and compliments, continued to cast their enchantment. No, when her mind her to memories of Carl, of his generosity to all within his drifted outside the current of routine and duty, it carried compass, his reliability, his honesty, his earnest concern for her welfare.

Carl would not expect her to uproot herself for his benefit. He might not even object to her continuing to teach, if . . . But now her imagination was running away from her in truth.

Susannah reached into her dressing table drawer and pulled out a clean sheet of paper. She sat at the table, dipped her pen in the inkwell, and wrote, *Dear Mr. Elliott, Thank you for your concern about my well-being, and about the Christmas I passed so far from home. But indeed, I have found Cowbird Creek a congenial community, and have begun to make friends. The town makes Christmas quite festive, and I very much enjoyed its offerings.*

I do miss my family and friends, and hope to visit at some point, unless they are so adventurous as to visit me. But not only do I expect that my reasons for leaving town would await me if I returned, I have surprisingly little desire to do so . . . .

Chapter 22

SUSANNAH had heeded Carl's warning and asked Dr. Gibbs to have the timber merchant provide more wood than had been usual. She thought he would ask why, but he simply told her to expect it within ten days' time. When the wood arrived, she had the older boys move much of it into the schoolhouse, spreading the task over several days so as not to overtask the boys doing the hauling or take too much time from their studies.

She waited a few days before the second phase of the task, moving the remaining outdoor woodpile to sit right against the wall. She had feared to alarm the younger children, but even the youngest could remember a blizzard or two. Indeed, Alice Gibbs spoke knowingly of blizzards in stories her parents had read her; and when all the wood was where it needed to be, Rufus came up to her at the dinner recess, gave her a hug around the knees, and thanked her for keeping them safe. She looked around to see whether any of the other children had noted this lapse in discipline, and seeing them all absorbed in their dinners or their companions, knelt to give him a swift embrace in turn.

And for all that, while they had cold and snow enough, February had ended and March was well along. Most of the younger children had returned to school, and no blizzards followed them. Susannah looked at the melting icicles dripping on the wood pile and heaved a sigh of relief, while wondering whether she should have the bigger boys move the pile again to avoid the effect of damp wood on the schoolhouse wall. But it would be a shame to put them to that trouble, and might inspire some grumbling she would then have to quell appropriately.

And then, at half past two in the afternoon, she heard the wind whistling outside the window. She sidled over as quietly as she could and put a palm against the glass. Surely it was colder than it should be?

She called the room to attention. "I have a question for those of you who sat outside, or went home, for dinner. Did any of you notice a pain here— " She pointed to her sinuses. "Or a feeling as if something was pressing there, or develop a headache?"

The children looked at each other, mostly in confusion, but two girls and a boy raised their hands. Susannah called on the first girl, who stood and said, "My head hurt a little, Teacher."

More hands went up, and Susannah ruefully realized the likelihood that the notion would be contagious, or the other children seek the attention of having experienced these symptoms. She ignored the new volunteers and pointed to the second girl, who blushed and said, "My nose felt funny, and when I used my handkerchief, it didn't help."

To be fair as well as thorough, she pointed to the boy, who mimed something pressing on his forehead and made a face, saying, "Like that, Teacher. What does it mean?"

Susannah glanced at Bronka, who had gone pale. She, at least, knew what these signs could portend.

Susannah assumed her most decisive stance and said, "I need two of the older boys to start bringing in wood, in case a blizzard is on its way. Look for dry wood first. Stack what you bring with the rest here." She should involve the older girls as well. "Bronka, please go outside and close the shutters. Stay very close to the building, close enough to touch it. And when you all come back in, tell us whether it's much colder than it was at midday, and how hard the wind is blowing. I need you all to be good reporters, and not exaggerate — not make anything up for the sake of excitement. Now go on."

The bucket of water from which the children got their drinks was only about half full. Should she ask Bronka to fill it, or do so herself? But the pump was at least three yards from the back door. She would have to ration the water instead, in spite of not knowing how long the blizzard would last. If necessary, they could push open the door just enough to scoop some snow in for melting.

Alice had tears in her eyes. Evidently a possible blizzard outside her very own school was a different matter from blizzards in storybooks. Without Susannah giving her permission to speak, she said, voice quavering, "I want to go home."

It was as if Alice had opened the floodgates. Three more of the younger children started crying, and full half the others talked at once, saying much the same as Alice. Amos looked around the room, puffed out his chest, and said, "I can take the little 'uns home, right enough. Just say the word. I reckon some of the other fellows'd do the same."

Susannah put out a hand to still the resultant clamor of excited would-be heroes. "Thank you, but no. None of you will leave the schoolroom until we know for certain that any danger of a blizzard has passed. Surely some of you have heard about how even the strongest, venturing out into a blizzard or caught there, can lose their way."

Timothy put up his hand, and when called on, said proudly, "My Paw got caught in one of them whiteouts and near froze, but he walked right into the side of somebody's barn and found the door and let the cows warm him up. Maw cried and prayed over him when the neighbor found him after and came to tell us."

Susannah smiled at the boy and said, "Thank you, Timothy. So we will all stay here, together and safe." Should she add more wood to the stove? No, there was no knowing how long they might need to stay inside, and had better hoard the wood rather than use it too freely.

Amos opened his mouth as if to argue further, but the rattle of the shutters on the windows stole his words. The boys sent outside came back in with their arms full of wood and their backs and shoulders encrusted with snow. The wind slammed the door behind them. One of them said, breathless, "It's got so cold out!"

The other added, "The icicles all froze right up again. And I couldn't see the tree out back."

Through the small crack where the shutters met, Susannah saw nothing but white.

It had begun.

If she set the students to any sort of written work, or even doing arithmetic on the blackboard, the whistle and rattle and hiss of the storm would be hard for the children to ignore. And it might be her imagination, but the room felt colder than usual. So she called them to attention once more and announced it was time for a lesson in geography. "I'm going to tell you about the Congo Basin in Africa, where it's very warm except when it's stifling hot. When it rains, steam rises from the leaves of the trees and vines of the forest. . . ."

It made her feel warmer, at least. When she had exhausted the wonders of the Congo Basin, she moved on to Mali, "where it's even hotter. In Mali, you would find the Sahara Desert, one of the hottest places on Earth. Everywhere you look, you would see sand, stretching as far as you could see. And where there's rock instead of sand, it's so hot it would burn your hand to touch it."

Little Timothy wiped his brow as if sweat were dripping down it.

"There is grass in the Sahara, and bushes, but little of either. And in some parts, it may not rain for *years*. But when it does rain, what do you think? There are seeds buried in the sand, the seeds of flowers, waiting all that time, and when it rains, suddenly there are flowers blooming in the desert, all colors, all over."

Alice listened with wide eyes. Then she raised her hand and asked, when called on, "What do all those flowers smell like?"

Susannah had never wondered, and was glad to have this deficit brought to her attention. "Well, let's see. Dry air doesn't hold scent well — but the air would still have moisture for at least a little while, after the rain. So for a few minutes, at least, the desert should not only bloom like a garden, but smell like one."

Alice sighed with delight.

If only the wind hadn't slammed into the windows just then, and brought them all back to the here and now. Most of the children jumped, or twisted around to look at the shuttered windows or at each other. A few of them whimpered.

Susannah hoped she hadn't visibly winced. What distraction next?

"Time for a spelling bee, girls against boys. And you children who are in McGuffey's second reader or a more advanced one will take turns reading the words. Get ready!"

A spelling bee, of course, did not involve every child simultaneously. She could enjoin silence while others made their attempts, but she would not enforce that silence harshly, not when they were all — teacher as well as pupils — struggling to stay calm, to be brave. Now one child would sniffle and wipe a runny nose on a handkerchief or even a sleeve; minutes later, another would whimper, "If only Paw would come!" Even Bronka kept looking at the door — but her look expressed nervousness, even fear, rather than longing. Susannah quietly went to stand at her side and pointed to the nearest corner, leading the way to it. When Bronka had joined her, she asked in a soft whisper, "What is it? Is something troubling you, more than the storm itself?"

Bronka nodded, the whites of her eyes showing, and whispered back, "I'm afraid Papa or Kar — Carl will try to come, and lose the way."

Startled, Susannah answered, "But surely they know better? Carl explained it to me himself, that no one must leave shelter."

"But . . . that was before it happened. Carl has such a warm heart, he can never bear for someone he — cares about to be in danger, in need of him, and not go into that danger for their sake." Bronka looked at her as if hoping for her to understand something else, something unsaid.

The thought of Carl in that storm, trying to see where nothing could be seen, as the wind pounded at him and pushed him out of his way . . . it was if the blizzard reached through the wall to whirl around her heart and chill it. And all the while, some small, treacherous voice wailed within her how small she felt, how unequal to this task, and how much she wanted him to come to her.

Silently she grasped Bronka's hand, squeezed it, and made her way back to her desk, leaving Bronka to do the same.

Susannah had hoped the blizzard would abate in time for the children to go home for supper. As she lit the lantern, she knew she had hoped in vain. Some of the little ones were whining about being hungry, and the biggest boys had started a more ominous grumbling about how they could make it to their homes, if no one kept them prisoner here . . . .

What had she learned about hunger in American history? There was a narrative published anonymously, from a veteran of the War of Independence . . . . "Gentlemen!" she broke in, as sternly as was in her. "You would do well to take as examples the brave soldiers who fought to establish this country. They suffered sorely from hunger for many weary days, with little or nothing to eat, sometimes subsisting on burnt ears of corn from fired fields. And of course, they understood the absolute necessity of obeying those placed in command over them — which, I must remind you, describes myself. Will you be insubordinate deserters, or will you show your younger comrades how to endure and persevere?"

That, for the moment at least, appeared to settle them. She turned to the class as a whole. "If any of you brought dinner and failed to eat it all, or have been keeping morsels of any kind in your desks or among your possessions, now is the time to share. Please bring out anything you have of that kind and put it on your desks."

Slowly, items appeared on a few desks: sticks of candy, beef jerky, a stale dinner roll, a moldy biscuit, a wrinkled apple. Susannah borrowed a knife from Amos, gathered the offerings, and cut them into small pieces, trimming away the mold on the biscuit. The stick of candy did not cut evenly, but she swept together the variously sized shards. Was there anything she could use as a tray? Yes, the broken desk top in the closet, which she had kept around for possible conversion into firewood. She appointed one of the boys who had so recently been rebellious and gave him the task of putting the food on the makeshift tray and carrying it around to each child in turn, accompanying him to prevent any unfair grabbing of extra portions or squabbling over preferred tidbits.

When every child had had a pitiful serving, Susannah thanked her assistant and had him lean the desk top in a corner. They would probably need to put it in the stove before long, and hope nothing in its constituents or varnish would render it unsuitable as fuel.

As the children wolfed down what little she had been able to provide for them, she went to peer through the crack between the shutters of the window farthest from the children. From what little Susannah could see of the sky, it had grown as dark as the blowing snow would allow. But . . . surely there was less snow carried on the wind? Or had the wind become less fierce? She had stopped noticing the sound of it, but now concentrated as hard as she could on hearing it. Fortunately the children were weary enough that their chatter and stirring about were at a minimum.

Yes, the wind had died down. She put her palm flat against the glass: still cold, but that need not signify.

What would occupy the children while she investigated? Song — a round. She picked one of the third grade girls and asked her to stand, saying, "You may now lead the school in singing "Are You Sleeping, Brother John?" Children, I want you to keep the song going as *long* as you can."

Once the song was well underway, she crept to the back door to open it. Something resisted her efforts. There must be a snow drift piled against it. Rather than call upon one of the strongest boys and attract attention, she set her shoulder against the door, as low as she could without losing her balance, and pushed.

Slowly, the door yielded to the pressure: one inch, two inches, three, until it stuck fast at five. But that was enough to let her see that the snow was falling downward, not blown across the yard, and not falling heavily at that.

Did blizzards have a calm in the middle, like the eye of a hurricane? She had never heard so, and Carl had not warned of any. Still, she could hardly be sure. How long should she wait before —

And then, she saw lanterns approaching, more and more coming into view, a dozen or more, heading for the front door. She drew her head back in and clapped her hands, disrupting the song and not caring. "Children! Let us rejoice and praise God, for the blizzard has passed, and help has come. Let us open the door and welcome it!"

As she wrenched the front door open and stood beside it, a ragged but enthusiastic cheer rose from every throat, except for the two children — including one of the oldest boys — who were crying instead.

Now she could see the faces of the men rushing up the path. The minister. Joshua Gibbs. Parents she knew, and others who had never come to meet her.

And in the forefront, almost shoving through the others in his haste, Carl Marek.

Bronka had crowded up behind her, so Carl reached them both at the same moment. He gripped Susannah's hands in his, squeezing them almost tight enough to hurt, and looked in her eyes for a few endless seconds before turning to embrace Bronka. Bronka, so strong through the long, difficult day, even now forbore to shed tears. Susannah turned away and greeted the rest of the men, thanking them, reassuring the fathers that their children were well and had behaved splendidly through the ordeal, watching the reunions. Timothy bragged to his father that he had saved them all by warning them about getting lost in the storm; Amos, starting to complain that he could have come home and led some of the others, received a fierce order not to talk such d— nonsense, and then an equally fierce hug that lifted the boy off his feet.

Joshua Gibbs, Alice clinging to his leg, reached Susannah and said in an unmistakably husky voice, "Clara and I, and every parent with a child in this school, and the whole town owe you an enormous debt of gratitude. We have waited and prayed, hoping and believing that you would have the wisdom to keep the children here, that you would be steadfast in holding to that course. I am not surprised to see our faith justified."

She could find nothing to say, and then realized there was something she must. "It was Carl Marek who told me the warning signs of a blizzard, and how to prepare. You owe him as many thanks and more." Out of the corner of her eye, she saw Carl turn at the mention of his name, realize what she was saying, and look at her with some deep emotion welling in his face.

Whatever Carl might have said or done, or Joshua might have said to answer her, they were interrupted by the minister clearing his throat and saying, in his most ringing tones, "I will now lead us in a prayer of gratitude and thanksgiving."

She had never prayed so fervently, and with such a full heart. And yet, as soon as the prayer was done, she found herself wondering whether Carl and Bronka would have prayed differently, if they could.

Chapter 23

LOUISA'S letters would not have served as examples of rhetorical distinction, but they were usually coherent. Susannah was not sure what to make of her latest.

I do hope that all is well and continues to go well for you, and that you are living a good and Christian life and don't find that difficult so far from home. It's difficult enough for some of us even with friends and families nearby . . . .

Was Louisa in some sort of trouble? Her open, trusting nature might make it all too easy for her to fall victim to a seducer or some other cad, though in their years at school, Louisa's very innocence had seemed to provide an invisible armor. Susannah put the letter aside and attempted to put it out of her mind as well. It would be supper time soon, and she had arithmetic problems to prepare.

* * * * *

Joshua returned from a trip to the general store and found Clara with Alice on her lap, reading Hawthorne's *Tanglewood Tales*. He had planned to confide in Clara as soon as he got home, but the sordid difficulty confronting him made too discordant a contrast to the sweet scene before him. He blew them a kiss and made his way to the necessary to buy time.

When he returned to the sitting room, it was empty. He found mother and daughter in the kitchen, where Clara had turned the table into a makeshift crafts studio complete with ink, paper, clothes pins, fabric scraps, and yarn. Joshua waited, leaning against the doorway, until Alice was fully absorbed in her task and then retreated back to the sitting room, Clara close behind him. She took his arm and led him to the sofa, sitting close beside him and taking his hand. "What trouble clouded your manner when you first came in, and does so still?"

Joshua pulled the letter out of his waistcoat pocket and unfolded it. "This awaited me at the store, addressed generally to the School Board. It appears to be from the President of William Simmons Normal School in St. Louis. I was — by good fortune, perhaps — the first member of the board to come by after it arrived."

He handed it to Clara, who took it but did not immediately read it. Instead she read his face, and said, "Does it explain why Miss Shepard had no references to provide?"

"Yes — but the nature of that explanation depends on whether we believe what the man has to say. I need your opinion. I would rather not believe him, and that may be coloring my reaction to the style in which he expresses himself. Though as splendidly as Miss Shepard has acquitted herself of late, I would hesitate to credit his claims in any case — or at least, to give them the weight he assumes we should."

"Well, then," she replied, with a trace of a smile, "I will read it aloud, and your preference for my voice may in some measure counteract that initial reaction." She squinted at the somewhat ornate handwriting and began.

To the esteemed members of the Board entrusted with the intellectual, moral, and religious education of the precious children of Cowbird Creek:

I have taken some pains to discover where one of our former pupils, a Miss Susannah Shepard, may have taken herself when her conduct and resulting notoriety made her remaining in our fair city untenable. My prayers were answered when another former pupil, who had once been friendly with Miss Shepard, mentioned that the woman in question had written to her from your town, and had obtained a teaching position there.

Clara paused and turned to him with raised eyebrows. "I rather feel that I should have a lawyer looking over my shoulder as I read, advising me to be cautious. This is either unpalatable truth, or gross slander."

Joshua nodded. "The former would explain why Miss Shepard had no reference from the college she attended. But the same would be true if she had reason to expect calumny from that quarter."

"Indeed." Clara cleared her throat and resumed reading.

I regret, and apologize to the members of your Board, that I did not discover the woman's true nature until she had obtained credentials from our institution. But I was soon undeceived, as my own observation and general report revealed her lamentable lack of modesty and good character, and her disregard of truth and public morals. I can only pray that none of your children have been corrupted by her teachings or her example.

With confidence that you will hasten to take appropriate action, I am and remain,

Yours faithfully,

President Samuel Brecker

Clara handed the letter back to Joshua and said, quietly but emphatically, "I'm rather inclined to spit." She gave a small chuckle at Joshua's double-take and then asked, "What will you do next?"

Joshua stroked his beard and said slowly, "I suppose it would cause comment, rather than making it less likely, if I asked the owner of the store not to mention my receiving this letter. But I had better act quickly, in case he does tell anyone about it. I must first speak to Susannah."

Clara knew, of course, how little he relished that prospect. She covered his hand with hers, pressed lightly, and asked, "Should I be there when you do?"

Would meeting with the two of them embarrass Susannah more? But if this man had wronged her in some way, and now lied to cover up the fact, she might find a woman's presence reassuring. And Joshua could use Clara's good instincts and sound judgment. "I'll make sure of it."

* * * * *

When Susannah came down for supper, Miss Wheeler drew her aside and handed her a folded note. "A boy brought it a little while ago. He didn't say who it was from." Her hostess appeared to be restraining her curiosity with some difficulty. Susannah thanked her and put the note in her pocket. She tried to pay attention to the chatter around the table, to ignore the note's presence and suppress her own curiosity about who might have sent it. Camelia? The parent of one of her pupils? Or even . . . Carl?

She declined an invitation to join some of the other ladies for a game of hearts and mounted the stairs with a steady tread. Finally reaching her room, she closed the door, sat at her dressing table, and retrieved the note. Opening it, she glanced first at the signature. It came from Joshua and Clara Gibbs.

Dear Susannah,

There is a matter on which I find I need to consult you. If it would be no trouble, Clara and I would much appreciate your coming by after supper this evening.

What could be so urgent as to prompt Joshua to specify a time, and this very evening? It must concern the school in some way. Did Clara Gibbs play an active role in school affairs? Well, she would find out more this evening. She checked her hair in the mirror, grabbed a light wrap, and headed downstairs.

Miss Wheeler was still in the dining room, making sure everything had been cleared away to her satisfaction. Susannah nodded to her and said, "Dr. Gibbs wishes to see me. I should be back before long. But in case it's later than I expect, I'll bid you good night." She kept walking rather than invite more questions. Besides, she mustn't keep Joshua waiting.

Joshua, opening the door, looked more serious than Susannah had ever seen him. She had been telling herself on the walk over that she had no reason to be anxious, but it seemed she had been wrong. She accepted his quiet invitation to enter and followed him to the sitting room, where Clara was standing rather than sitting, her hand resting on the fireplace mantle. It was Clara who spoke, calm and somehow reassuring. "Please sit anywhere that looks comfortable to you. Would you like some cider? A cordial?"

Susannah selected a chair with a straight back, to help her stay alert, and declined any refreshment. Joshua looked almost disappointed. Had he been hoping to postpone whatever he had called her here to say?

Joshua and Clara both sat down on the sofa, a few inches apart. Joshua cleared his throat and said, looking almost straight at Susannah, "I received a letter today that troubled me, and whose contents I'm not sure how to assess. I would ask you to read it and shed any light on it that you can."

He picked up a paper that had been lying face down on the table near the sofa. As soon as he turned it over, she recognized the handwriting, from seeing the occasional proclamation posted at William Simmons.

Did her heart stop, or only her breathing? She felt frozen, the way one might in a dream, as if she would never move again. The room, by contrast, swam around her. How could she feel so ill when frozen, when dreaming?

* * * * *

Susannah had gone chalk white. She swayed in the chair, and it had no arms to catch her; he and Clara sprang up at the same moment and moved to each side of it, which left Clara the one to catch Susannah as she began to topple.

Between them they half steered, half carried Susannah to the sofa they had just left. Clara left briefly to retrieve the smelling salts from her bag, but did not immediately use them. Instead she said softly to Joshua, "It was my observation that she reacted not to the mention or sight of the letter — nor to the contents, of course, since she had no chance to see them — but to the only visible aspect of the letter as it lay. Namely, the handwriting. Do you think the same?"

He could no longer be surprised by Clara's keen mind and swift analysis, but he still took great pleasure in it, enough to make him smile despite his worry about Susannah and his regret at having contributed to her collapse. "Yes, indeed. The next question is why the sight of this man's handwriting overset her so. Has she been living in fear of what he might reveal?"

Clara tilted her head and gazed toward the ceiling, as she did when thinking hard. "If we credit the letter's allegations, then her supposed notoriety would mean that any of various people could have sent us the same news. And she responded immediately to the handwriting, without even a second to process the fact that her alleged sins had found her out. No, it must be something about the man himself." She paused, and her manner altered, her expression bringing back too many past moments when Clara's own history cast its shadow over her. "And I would hazard the guess that something passed between them that frightened her. Even horrified her."

"You think we're seeing something like the 'soldier's heart' that afflicts some after battle, even long after."

Clara looked grimmer by the second. "You can guess in what sort of battle a woman most often acquires such scars."

Susannah stirred on the sofa and muttered something Joshua couldn't quite hear. Clara took Susannah's wrist, measured her pulse, and said, "I can rouse her any time, or she may regain consciousness without aid. Before that happens, I have one question. Why, if this man attacked her or otherwise mistreated her, would he draw attention to himself and give her reason to speak out and damage his reputation?"

Joshua shrugged. "He may think his reputation impervious to damage. The pomposity in his letter would go well with that attitude. Or he may, rather, expect Susannah to be as spiteful as himself, and spread her story far and wide. In that case, he could hope to anticipate her if she delayed, or contradict her if she has told of him already."

Susannah was moving more now, turning her head from side to side, opening her eyes. Joshua put his arm under her to help her sit, saying to Clara as softly as he could, "And now, to find out the truth of the matter. And as gently as possible, to do as little harm as we can."

* * * * *

Susannah tried to clear her head, to make sense of what had happened and was happening. She was lying on the sofa — how? Something had reminded her, suddenly, shockingly, of President Brecker and his assault. What had it been? And now — a man was touching her, holding her! She cried out and struggled to get free —

But Clara Gibbs was kneeling beside the sofa, reaching out to take her hands, and saying in a voice both firm and kind, "You're quite safe, Susannah. No one will harm you. It's only Joshua behind you, helping you sit up. You had something of a spell, but are recovering nicely."

Recovering from what? Joshua had said something, and showed her something. A letter . . . a letter from Brecker, a letter that had troubled him and that he wanted her to explain.

Susannah forced herself to keep breathing, to fight the panic that tried once again to overwhelm her. She needed to face this moment, this crisis. She reached out a hand, though she couldn't stop it from shaking. "Please let me see the letter."

Clara picked it up from the table and handed it to her, saying, "I must warn you that it makes accusations against you. Accusations I am not, at this point, much inclined to credit, but we must know whether there is any truth to them."

Joshua helped her reposition herself so that she was

sitting upright, and moved the oil lamp closer to her. She took as deep a breath as the tightness in her chest would allow, and began to read.

Out of the corner of her eye, she could see her hosts, now seated in chairs to her left, watching her with concern. As she read the opening of the letter, she herself wondered if she would make it through to the end without collapsing again, or breaking into tears. But as she came to the substance of the letter, the hypocritical falsehoods, the sneering malice behind every line, something else happened.

At first, she wasn't sure what energy was filling her, running through her limbs, her very veins. Then she realized. It was fury.

She forced herself to read every last scurrilous word, welcoming her growing rage, and finally slapped the letter down on the table. "This is false from beginning to end, though it could be rewritten with little trouble to apply to Mr. Brecker's own behavior."

Did they believe her? Clara was looking at her with something of concern and something also of pride, as if approving of her anger. Joshua simply looked grave as he said, "Tell us, please, what actually happened between you."

So she told them.

She had hoped the anger would stay with her to the end. It was a short enough tale, once she came to tell it. But when she came to Brecker's pulling their bodies together and fingering her hair, chills started to run all through her, and she could see her hands tremble.

She made it through and fell silent, waiting for judgment.

That judgment came swiftly, with Clara sitting close beside her and grasping her hand, and Joshua, in startling contrast, muttering something fierce as he made a fist with one hand and slammed it into the other.

Susannah took a deep breath, taking in faint scents of the potatoes and roast beef her hosts must have had for supper. As she blew it out, she realized that she had cleared only one obstacle of possibly many. "Has anyone else in town received such a letter?"

Joshua frowned. "This letter was addressed to the school board, and I was fortunate enough to get to it first. But he may have written someone else, someone whose name he could discover with a little effort. Possibly the mayor."

"Should we ask Mayor Pomfrey, then," asked Clara, "whether he has received such a letter? Miss Shepard, what do you think?"

It almost startled Susannah to be addressed — no, to have her opinion treated as important, after Brecker's slander and her recent incapacity. But she pulled her thoughts together and considered the matter. "It would be hard to frame such a question without arousing his curiosity, if no letter has come to him. And if Joshua felt compelled to explain, Mayor Pomfrey might take him to task for not sharing that information immediately." She stopped short and then made herself go on. "Or for hiring me at all."

Clara stood up. "For now, then, we put this testament to malice out of sight and, as much as feasible, out of mind. And I believe we could all use a restorative cup of tea."

Chapter 24

THE APPROACH of Easter reminded Susannah that she had been remiss: it had been some time since she gave a lesson in religion. In fact, it had been long enough that it might be best to repeat portions of her previous lesson. This time, however, she spoke to the pupils in two groups, younger and older, so she could keep things simpler for the former and explain a few of the less scandalous complexities to the latter.

To the younger children, she said, "There have been Christians for a very long time — almost two thousand years — but not forever. Before our Lord's birth, most people believed there were many gods, who acted much like men and women. Only our Lord's people, the Hebrews, knew there was one God who ruled all the world and everything beyond. Now there are Christians all over the world, though there are still other religions as well. And not all Christians agree on how to worship, but they agree on the most important things."

She could only hope their parents would also agree with that statement.

To the older students, she reminded them that Europe had been almost entirely Catholic until early in the 16th century and then explained how that had changed. "Martin Luther was a priest, but he saw that not all priests acted as our Lord would wish. He disagreed with the leaders of the Church about many things, even the Pope, who was supposed to be closest to God. And as people all over Europe argued about who was right, King Henry the Eighth was becoming more and more upset that he had no heir, especially once his queen was too old to have children. . . ."

By the time she had finished her abbreviated version of England's abandonment of Catholicism, it was time to dismiss the school. She had even managed to explain that Catholics still considered the Pope as the ultimate religious authority, while Protestants did not. Next time, she would try to clarify any confusion about Bible reading.

Bronka lingered as the other children streamed out the door, apparently determined to walk Susannah at least partway home. As Susannah gathered her things, Bronka chattered about the upcoming holiday and the weeks of voluntary deprivation that had apparently preceded it. "We give up things for Lent — meat, butter, sugar, fruit — and eat sour soup, and bread with olive oil, and lots of herring. It makes feasting on Easter that much more exciting! And Mama says I may invite you to join us — please do!"

"That's very gracious of her, and of you. I'd love to."

Bronka rattled on. Apparently Catholics, too, dyed Easter eggs. "Wait until you see them! My mama makes the prettiest ones, though she says I'm getting almost as good. And . . . there's something we do with them, sometimes." She paused, to make sure she had sufficiently engaged Susannah's curiosity. "If there's someone . . . *special*, we give them one of the eggs."

They had reached the turn for the boarding house. Susannah smiled at Bronka and said, "I'll see you tomorrow, then. Thank you again for inviting me."

"Oh, but of course! It wouldn't be the same without

you. Until then!"

As Susannah got ready for bed that night, she spared a somewhat wistful thought for what Carl's and Bronka's family must be doing at that very moment. They would be on their way to another midnight mass, dressed in their finest, all ready for the joyful celebration of Christ's resurrection. The whole family, together, while Susannah sat brushing her hair so far from home.

But she had the loveliness of a sunrise service to look forward to. And she had best get to bed without any more woolgathering or moping, to make sure she wouldn't nod off in the middle of it.

The little church lacked the majestic stained glass of her church back home, but the clear glass let the rosy rays of sunlight shine through. And while the singing had little in common with the chants of a Catholic service, with their flavor of antiquity, she knew all the hymns and joined in with a will.

Miss Wheeler's boarders returned from the sunrise service to a bountiful breakfast, with a lovely ham at its center. Their hostess had even put two Easter chocolates by each plate. Afterward, almost all the boarders gathered to dye their Easter eggs. Miss Wheeler set out the dishes of dye, several each of every color to keep jostling and elbowing and broken eggs to a minimum. "Feel free to combine colors if you wish — but try not to carry one dish's color to another!"

Susannah stayed long enough to dye three single-colored eggs, yellow, red, and green, and one egg combining shades of blue from turquoise to violet. Miss Wheeler had thought of everything — she gave every boarder who took part a white wicker basket to put their eggs in. Susannah thanked her, carried the basket carefully to her room, and examined the eggs to make sure none of them had cracked. Then she packed the blue egg in lilac tissue paper and replaced it in the basket on top of the others.

She left by the back entrance, to avoid questions, and made her way to the Mareks' house. As she approached, she set the basket down gently between two bushes, hidden from the house until she might want it, and went to knock on the door.

Bronka threw the door open, beaming, showing no sign of a sleepless night. She glanced at Susannah's empty hands, and her smile may have dimmed, but so briefly that Susannah could have imagined it. "*Wesolego Alleluja*! That means 'Happy Easter,' I think — at least, it's what we always say on Easter morning. Come in!"

As she entered and exchanged holiday greetings with Bronka's parents, Susannah spied a basket on the table. Unlike the one she had hidden outside, it contained not colored eggs but a variety of foodstuffs, including bread, sausage, plain eggs, and a curiously shaped object. She stepped closer and saw it was a sculpture of a lamb, done in butter. Bronka, following her eyes, pointed to it and said, "You see, Carl isn't the only artist in the family! Mama and I, we made this."

Behind Susannah, the voice she had been waiting to hear said quietly, "We bring such baskets to the Easter service, and the priest blesses them."

Susannah turned around to see Carl standing very still, holding something hidden in his hands. "Bronka and Mama made the butter. And I made this."

He opened his hands to show an egg like a stained glass window, like something of jeweler's make, panes of color intricately patterned and joined. "This was the best one I made. I kept it for you."

She could not tell, from his expression, whether he knew Bronka had told her of the custom. But she was so very glad she had listened. "It's beautiful. As beautiful as everything you make. And — wait here, please. I'll be right back."

She spun on her heel and ran out the door to where she had left the basket, turning back to see Carl standing in the doorway, puzzled but expectant. She stopped to catch her breath and then walked back to him, putting the basket on the step at her feet and lifting the wrapped egg. "I made this too — for you. It's nothing like as fine as what you made, but here it is."

Carl silently reached his cupped hands toward her. She laid the egg in them and peeled back the tissue paper. The delicate shading was nothing like his intricate artwork, but she found it pleasing, and could only hope he would as well.

Carl touched the egg very gently with one forefinger and looked up at her, his eyes shining like morning sun through stained glass.

The moment lingered, neither of them breaking it, until Carl's mother called out from the kitchen, "Come, all of you! It's time to feast!" Carl took the basket in one hand and reached out for her with the other. They joined the family hand in hand.

The next day, Susannah tidied up after school with special pleasure. Duty done, she need not simply return to the boarding house or run some errand. Camelia Grant had invited her to a late tea, along with Freida Kennedy, still in town though due to depart within days. Camelia had even dropped hints of chocolate cake with coconut frosting. Her pupils would have roared with laughter at the thought of the proper Miss Shepard licking her lips.

She had never yet, in all the time since she had met Camelia, seen the inside of her house. Given how comfortably her husband had left her, it was likely to be well furnished. And while Susannah could not have said in honesty that her friend was noted for her refinement, she suspected the visible appointments of her dwelling would reflect good taste. Not that it mattered. Different as Camelia's and Freida's backgrounds were, they were in some essential aspect kindred spirits, steering by their own stars rather than by their neighbors' expectations. Susannah was grateful for this chance to see them together, without the distractions of a larger gathering, before Freida and her peddler husband resumed wandering hither and yon.

Cheerful as the prospect before her, the sky clouding over did little to dampen her mood. But when she knocked on the stout oak door with its polished brass knocker, she heard no clatter of energetic footsteps. After half a minute or so, she knocked again, and this time, Camelia's voice came from some small distance, calling out, "Oh, yes, Susannah! Do come in."

She opened the door, causing a brass bell almost the size of a cowbell to chime, and stepped inside. An anteroom held a highly practical collection of coat racks and umbrella stands, the latter atop what looked very much like the tarp a rider might throw over his shoulders to keep off rain. Just past this entry came a corridor lined with reproductions, unless some were originals, of American and European paintings. She stopped in front of one, Johannes Vermeer's *The Music Lesson*, which she had not seen since the fateful day of her interview with President Brecker. She shook off the memories, and the chill they sent down her spine, and followed the muffled sounds of her hostess and someone else, presumably Freida. What Susannah was hearing must be conversation, and yet something about the sounds added to her uneasiness.

The drawing room she eventually found had somewhat more conventional, and abundant, decoration — white painted walls and cornices, neatly placed wainscoting, a pleasant scattering of knick-knacks, and a most welcoming fire in the oversized fireplace. Camelia and Freida sat in ornately carved chairs at a table that bore, in addition to tea pot and cups, a bountiful spread of tomatoes stuffed with watercress, jellied chicken, toasted crumpets dripping with butter, pots of strawberry jam and marmalade, candied nuts, and slices of the promised cake. Camelia sat forward in her chair, leaning toward Freida, while Freida, rather than eating or drinking, was clutching some small object in her large hands, and — Susannah saw with horror — with tears trickling down her cheeks.

Susannah had not, until this moment, realized how much comfort she had derived from meeting Freida and her husband, a couple so unorthodox as to suggest that any woman with sufficient courage could follow her own path toward happiness. Now, seeing Freida apparently distraught, she quailed, the picture she had constructed of the couple beginning to waver like smoke dissipating in a sudden breeze. She froze in place, afraid either to intrude or to confirm her disillusionment.

Camelia turned toward her, showing no sign of dismay at Freida's state. Freida, following Camelia's gaze, dropped the mysterious object — something made of wood — onto her broad lap, fished out a handkerchief from her pocket, wiped her face, and said, "Look at me, such a spectacle, I must be scaring you silly! But not to worry, I'm fine, better than fine, I was just so moved, even telling

Camelia about it makes me blubber." She beckoned Susannah closer, Camelia nodding encouragement, and Susannah hesitantly approached.

Camelia stood and pulled out a chair, opening her mouth as if to greet Susannah or to explain, but Freida overrode her, exclaiming, "Such a young man, and so clever, and so generous and understanding! Wait until I show you."

Susannah sank into the chair, utterly bewildered, as Freida picked up and held out what proved to be a small wooden cylinder, tapered gracefully at the ends, with an unfamiliar symbol carved into one side. Freida deftly flipped it about to show that rather than a solid cylinder, it had more the shape of a scroll, and that one end was hinged so something could be placed inside.

Camelia, meanwhile, poured out a cup of tea, pushed the pitcher of milk and the sugar pot toward Susannah, and gestured toward the food. Freida laughed. "Yes, please take something — if you wait for me to stop talking, you'll be thirsty and starving! And of course you have no idea what I'm talking about. Camelia, why don't you tell her, you'll be so much clearer than I am."

Susannah added milk to her tea, took a sip, and found it excellent. As she helped herself to a crumpet and a luscious-looking slice of cake, Camelia plucked the object off Freida's palm and held it out for Susannah's inspection. "This is no ordinary carving, but a *mezuzah*. Jews put them up in the doorways of their dwellings. There's a paper — no, parchment, isn't it? — scroll inside, with a Hebrew prayer written on it. Most often, I believe, the prayer is something like the one you heard at Dr. Gibbs' house, when he invited Freida to say a blessing at dinner."

Freida broke in to say, "I somehow never put one up

on my house, when I had a house here, so I could hardly take it with me when there was nothing to take. And I never thought of putting one on the wagon, but whyever not, it's where I live."

Susannah took a bite of her crumpet and tried to make sense of all this. "And Camelia gave it to you?" Except hadn't Freida said something about . . . . Susannah dropped the remains of her crumpet on her plate. Meanwhile, Freida chattered blithely on. "And when that nice young man, Carl Marek, came to see the wagon, because he'd never seen one up close, he and Jedidiah were talking about how much Jedidiah has done to make the wagon as much like a home as ever he could, and then Carl came to Camelia and asked if there was anything special Jews did to make a house a home, and Camelia looked it up in one of her books, and she found out about mezuzahs. And she told Carl, and of course, clever as he is with wood, nothing would do but him making one as a present, for me to put on the wagon, so thoughtful!"

Freida paused to pour herself more tea and take one of the larger slices of cake. As she took a bite, Camelia stroked the polished wood appreciatively. "This symbol he carved, that means 'life,' doesn't it, Freida?"

Freida gulped down a mouthful of cake and nodded enthusiastically. "That's just right, and what better reminder to have where I can see it every day, to live my life while I have it? You should know, Susannah, we Jews don't spend as much time thinking about some afterlife, we try to make this world better as much as we can, and enjoy what God has given us while we're living."

Susannah stared at the tea table and then asked Freida, stupidly, "Then everything's all right? You and your husband?"

Camelia blinked at the abrupt and rather bold

question, but Freida took it in stride. "All right, better, just lovely! Jedidiah is sorry he didn't think of getting a mezuzah, but really, how should he know? *I* didn't know how much better I'd feel seeing it when I hoist myself up into the wagon, I could kiss that young man, but I'd frighten him into the next county, and what a shame that would be!" She startled Susannah into further confusion by winking.

Susannah slumped back in her chair, overwhelmed with relief. The shining image of Freida and her husband solidified in her mind, unsullied, undispelled. And beside it appeared the likeness of Carl as he might have looked when he handed Freida the mezuzah — smiling, a little shy, and then proud to see her delight.

The tea party continued, Camelia and Freida talking about Freida's past travels and where she and Jedidiah might travel next, but Susannah barely heard it. She was roused from her thoughts by Freida getting up to leave. "Thank you so much, what a delightful little feast! And Susannah, I'm so glad you came to Cowbird Creek, the people here are lucky to have you, I'll miss you when we leave. If you get restless, you could come with us on one of our shorter jaunts when there's no school, such fun we'd have!"

Camelia also stood up, and Susannah made haste to do likewise. After the goodbyes had been said, and Freida had made her majestic way out the door, Camelia took Susannah's hand. "My dear, you hardly said a word — though given the way Freida and I go on, you would have had to fight to get a word in edgewise! — and there's more tea. And those crumpets won't improve with sitting overnight. Do come and have some more, and tell me what's been going on with you."

Susannah yielded to her hostess' persuasion, though she was out of practice at eating such bountiful teas, and they returned to the drawing room. She was about to rejoin Camelia at the table when Camelia said behind her, "Should I have asked Carl to join us, do you think?"

Susannah froze in place. Camelia came up, put a hand on her arm, and turned her around. "Now don't let me put you off your feed! Come back and help me finish off this tea. But I'm right, aren't I, that you were thinking of Carl earlier?"

The prospect of confiding in a friend was irresistible. Susannah sat, fortified herself with another crumpet and more tea, and searched for the best way to begin. Finally she said, "I've seen him do everything from rescue my belongings from a thief, to losing his temper and shouting at me, to apologizing most sincerely, to showing himself an admirable son and brother, to guiding me through daunting weather. He's talented, but modest. He's honest and doesn't seem to think twice about it. And what he did for Freida doesn't surprise me. I could never have imagined meeting someone like him, and — and seeing so much to admire when I did."

Camelia listened with bright-eyed attention. When Susannah came to a halt, she said slyly, "And you may not have noticed, but he's quite a handsome fellow, and you can see how strong he is just from looking at those arms and shoulders. I don't suppose you actually mind any of that."

Tea would hardly cool Susannah's flaming cheeks. She took a sip anyway.

Camelia refused to take the blush as a sufficient answer. "Come, now, you may as well say it out loud. I promise I haven't hidden the man in a corner to hear it."

Susannah laughed and then sighed. "I see I must yield. Yes, I have noticed his appearance. And his . . . fitness, which he demonstrated the moment I met him, in chasing after that scoundrel who ran off with my case. I would imagine his work at the mill requires both strength and endurance as well."

Camelia went so far as to grin. "And if you haven't dreamed of those strong arms around you, all I can say is that you need to let go of the reins on your imagination."

But the mention of dreams brought her nightmare rushing back. It was not enough to wipe away the images of Carl, retrieving her case from the thief, guiding her through the snow, giving her the wooden dancer, rushing to the school the moment the blizzard died down . . . working late in the night to make Freida a gift that would bring her comfort on the long roads from one town to another. But she could not answer Camelia's expectant expression.

Camelia divined Susannah's mood and sat patiently in her chair, waiting for Susannah to finish coping with whatever kept her from responding. Determined not to disappoint her friend, Susannah defiantly dragged the dream the rest of the way out of its hiding place. The scars of her encounter with Brecker had plainly not healed, but Carl was not responsible for those scars. Nor was Father McCarthy, or any other priest. Could she resign herself to be ruled by the perfidy of others and her own fears? Neither would make acceptable company for what she hoped would be a long life, one full of better, brighter possibilities.

No, Brecker might well be vindictive enough to wish he could blight all her prospects, but she would not be so weak as to allow it!

Susannah sat up straight and said to Camelia, "You made a suggestion just now, probably in jest, that Carl might have joined us today. In sober truth, do you think he could comfortably accept such an invitation? I find I need an opportunity to speak to him, and it might be better if I — for now, at least — avoided anything so conspicuous as descending on the mill. Nor would I wish to invite myself into his home, though his parents might welcome me or at least feel obliged to act welcoming."

Camelia's eyes went wide for an instant before she lowered her brows in apparent concentration. "If I enlist his assistance in some credible way, that fact and my well-known eccentricity might keep any gossip to a minimum. And if I then let drop that you'll be there as well, I expect he would be much more likely to overcome any embarrassment or other obstacles. When shall we arrange it?"

Susannah smiled ruefully. "Before my courage drains away, I should think. As soon as your duties and engagements permit, unless Carl's schedule requires a longer delay."

Chapter 25

KAROL had been trying for weeks to work up the courage to declare himself. The task was none the easier for his doubts about his likely success. Everything from Susannah's reasons to distrust men, to their so different place in society, to their even more serious difference in religion argued against her accepting him, even if she might have otherwise been tempted. A trace of relief

When Miss Grant — Camelia, he corrected himself, as she had insisted from their first meeting that he call her so — appeared in the mill yard just when he would be leaving for the day, he was mystified, but not so much as when she invited him to join her for tea the following Sunday afternoon. Could she really want to talk to him about books for Polish children younger than Bronka, just in case any should arrive in town? And why would a tea table be a better place than the library, where he could look at the books in English for children that age?

Then, as he enjoyed stretching his legs to match her pace, she added, "Oh, and Susannah will be there. As a teacher, she should know more than a childless old stick like me what sort of stories the youngsters would like. Will you show up? We would both be so disappointed if you don't!"

He would have asked questions if he had known what to ask, and if he expected her answers to shed any light. Neither being the case, he stammered, "Yes, if you,

you and Susannah, you, if you really wish me to come to tea, I'd be happy to."

Camelia clapped him on the shoulder. "Splendid! Sunday, then. Two o'clock." And with that, she spun around and walked just as fast in the other direction.

Karol looked around for a rock or stump or post to support him, but seeing none, he sat on the ground and stared after her. But the ground was damp, and his family was waiting supper for him. He got back to his feet, shook his head in a vain attempt to clear it, and headed for home.

In church that Sunday, it took all Carl's effort to concentrate on the service. At one point, he found himself so distracted that he forgot to get to his feet after the singing of the *Agnus Dei* — which made him think of Susannah at the Christmas mass, and her earnest efforts to keep up with what the congregation was doing around her. His fond smile was ill timed, coming in the middle of the congregation's confession of unworthiness to receive the gift of Holy Communion, and he was lucky none of those around him noticed and scolded him.

Finally it was over, and the people streamed out as always, asking and receiving the priest's blessing on their way. Karol had to make himself meet the priest's eyes, reminding himself to confess his inattention when next he made his confession. The priest, however, spoke even more cheerfully than usual, saying after he gave Karol the usual blessing, "If you and your family, and those you rode with, can wait in the yard for just a moment, there's someone to whom I'd like to introduce you."

The priest's wish was Mama's and the farmer's command, and they waited in the early spring sunshine, Bronka pointing at the crocuses fighting their way out of the warming earth. Soon the priest joined them, along with a tall man whose broad shoulders made even Karol feel like a stripling. "Mr. McIntyre, Carl Marek. Carl, this is Mr. Sean McIntyre, formerly of Chicago, where he was a well regarded maker and seller of home furnishings."

The man thrust his hand out to shake Carl's, his grip strong and his palm tough as saddle leather. "I had a brother pass away too young from a fever, and got to thinking it was high time I saw more of the country while I still could. Then, when I got this far, I met a likely widow, and we suited each other, and looks like here I'll stay." He pointed to a well-dressed woman about Mama's age, chatting with a group of other matrons, and beamed in her direction.

Pulling his attention back to Karol, he said, "Carpentry and the furniture business is what I know, and I figure I should do what I know how to do instead of fumbling around at something else. But this time I'd like to do less of buying and reselling and more of making the furniture in house, like I did when I was young. The problem is, I'm aiming to sell to the more wealthy and particular customer, and while I can put together a chest or bed or chair that'll take the heftiest man and last long enough for him to give his grandson, I've no great skill at fine details and fancy trimmings. I'll need someone good at carving, with what you might call an artist's eye. And Father McCarthy told me he knew a likely young man with just those skills."

Karol glanced at the priest, who gave him an encouraging smile. Karol stood up tall and replied, "I'm not one to brag, but from what people have told me, Father McCarthy has the right of it."

"That's the spirit! I like a man who knows his worth, and doesn't mince around playing at false modesty. Mind you, this is a new venture and could founder. You'd be taking a chance. But I'd pay you a fair wage, since the good father tells me you'd be in no position to invest capital, and if the business thrives you'll have plenty to do, and a share in what you bring in. Of course, you'd have to give up whatever work you're doing now."

Papa had gone serious, and Mama was chewing her lip. He would want to talk to them about Mr. McIntyre's proposal — but he already knew he couldn't turn it down for the sake of safety. He would give his all to make sure the business succeeded — and if it failed, he was still young and strong and known to work hard. If he couldn't return to the mill, there would be some other job for him, whether in Cowbird Creek or elsewhere, even farther west.

Which reminded him of a key question. "Are you planning to set up here in Elk Leg, or somewhere else — like Cowbird Creek?"

Mr. McIntyre's wife had finished her conversation and came to join him as he answered, "Could be here, could be there. You'd rather live near your parents, I'm guessing? I'll have to see what properties I can find there, and here, and in between." He gathered Mrs. McIntyre in beside him, chucking her under the chin, and added, "If need be, I could get you a horse for going back and forth, so you don't waste working time on walking. The missus's people raise horses, and I can get a good deal, easy."

Mrs. McIntyre whispered in her husband's ear. He patted her hand and said, "Well, we're off home. You can think it over, and we'll talk next Sunday."

Karol looked over at his parents and Bronka, and then back at Mr. McIntyre. "I can tell you now, sir, that unless either of us comes up with some reason it couldn't work, I'd like to take your offer, and would be glad and grateful for the chance."

Mr. McIntyre slapped him on the back, hard enough

to rock a less sturdy man. "That's the spirit! Until next Sunday, then. Good day, Mr. Marek, Mrs. Marek, Miss Marek."

Karol watched them walk away, his head in a whirl. Bronka ran up and threw her arms around him. "My brother, the furniture maker, the businessman!"

It was time and past time to go home, with dinner to get through in time for his afternoon appointment. But before he joined his family and the others at the wagon, he found the priest, bidding farewell to the last of the crowd, and thanked him as earnestly as he knew how, and knelt down on the spot for the priest to lead him in a prayer of thanksgiving.

The journey back to Cowbird Creek was too short for all they had to say. But by the time they gathered around the table, he knew that his family would stand behind him. Now, he had only to wonder what Susannah would think of his new prospects. He thought, or hoped, he knew.

Mama always made a special effort over Sunday dinner, and he always looked forward to it, but he'd need to save some room for whatever Camelia might be serving. He had been coward enough not to mention the invitation, but now he must, or Mama would think he'd taken ill — though he kept the chance that Susannah would be there to himself. At least he had no need, then, to explain why he stayed in his Sunday best instead of changing into working clothes and finding some useful job to do.

Bronka cornered him when she was finished with the dishes, tugging him out back and all the way to the chicken coop. Pulling some leftover crumbs out of her apron, she sprinkled them for the chickens and asked him, in a voice too excited to be a whisper, what was *really* going on. "Does Miss Grant want you to carve something for her? Or to start helping her with the library?"

Karol might have his guesses, but he had no intention of sharing them. They might be wrong. Bronka's guesses might even be right. He put his sister off with a promise to tell her later what had happened, and only hoped the tale would be one he could stand to share.

Chapter 26

KAROL had made as finished a carving as he had time for after Camelia had invited him. It was only two children sharing a big book, but it would have to be enough. He found a clean handkerchief, wrapped it, and put it in his pocket. That left him with nothing to do except feel the minutes crawl past. It would be rude to arrive early. He knew that, and Bronka had practically clung to his collar to prevent him from leaving too soon.

But he would only grow more nervous with waiting, and he might get kitchen dirt or worse on his clothes. Camelia would understand. He kissed Bronka on the forehead and Mama on the cheek, waved to Papa where he sat smoking his pipe on the porch, and left.

Camelia welcomed him with a smile even wider than usual, and a hearty handshake that brought Mr. McIntyre, who might soon be his employer, to mind. "Come in, come in! What is this? I'm giddy with anticipation. Oh, how lovely! I can't wait to put it on my desk at the library and show it off to all comers. Now, what shall we do while we wait for Susannah? I'm being very British today — I made tea sandwiches, the little ones with soft fillings and the crusts cut off. Shall I sneak you one, while you have time to brush off any crumbs?"

She had noticed his clothes, then. It ought to make him more nervous, but instead it made them something like conspirators. She only confirmed that notion when she said next, "Once Susannah comes, I thought I might do some dusting upstairs. Terrible the way dust gathers." She grinned. "Especially when I decide to notice."

He was about to say something dignified and grateful when his stomach rumbled. He thought Camelia would laugh, but instead she took his arm, more gently than he expected, and led him to a chair. "Sit down, dear boy, and relax if you're able. Here, try a sandwich."

He would have refused with thanks, but she was offering, and it might keep his stomach quiet when Susannah arrived.

And wasn't it time? Where was she?

* * * * *

Susannah had sat through the Sunday service with her lips shut tight unless she needed to join in prayer, as if her intentions might otherwise pop out. How many more times would she sit in this comfortable company?

When she got back to the boarding house, she went to her room to calm herself before enduring the midday meal. Her efforts must have failed, for when she came down to eat and to tell Miss Wheeler she'd be going out afterward, her hostess eyed her and said, "You're rather flushed. You haven't come down with a fever, have you? May I check your forehead?"

Susannah could do nothing but nod. The gentle touch on her forehead brought back such memories of home that she had to force back tears.

Miss Wheeler shook her head, still unsatisfied. "No fever, then. But I do hope you'll wear a wrap later."

Susannah fled back to her room as soon as she had eaten enough to avoid raising more concern. There, she inspected her outfit as best she could without a larger mirror. Should she change? But Miss Wheeler and the other boarders might notice, and draw who knew what conclusions. She waited, pacing in her little room, until the proper hour, and then jumped to hear a knock on the door a few minutes before she had planned to leave. Miss Wheeler said through the door, "You've a caller, my dear — the minister, with someone I haven't met. A new parent, perhaps? I told them you were going out, but he said he'd only need a minute. I've put them in the sitting room."

She must, absolutely must, act as if the visit was an unexpected pleasure, not an unexpected hindrance. She pasted a smile on her face, grabbed a wrap suitable for the spring weather, and followed Miss Wheeler down the stairs. The reverend stood when she entered the sitting room, as did the stranger who had been sitting next to him. "Miss Shepard, it is my pleasure to introduce Mr. Dell, newly arrived in Cowbird Creek. He has three children of school age."

"Seven, nine, and thirteen. I'm very happy to meet you, Miss Shepard. Their mother and I've done our best, schooling them at home, but we're ready to try some formal teaching, if you have the room for 'em."

"So good to meet you. Yes, I can certainly fit them in." She might have to procure another desk from somewhere, or find someone to repair a broken one. "I'd love to talk longer and hear more about them, but I have an appointment."

"I sure wouldn't want to keep you. My wife always tell me I talk too much. Why, just last week — "

Mercifully, the minister broke in. "We'll all see each other next Sunday, I'm sure, and we can speak at greater length then. Good day, Miss Shepard."

As she said her goodbyes and hurried out the door, she tried not to think about how uncomfortable she had felt in church, and what future Sundays would be like.

She had only made it halfway to Camelia's when the town clock bonged twice. As she scurried through the streets, with each step she pictured the faces, from Cowbird Creek and from home, of those she would shock and disappoint if she did what she was contemplating. Her mother; her father. The minister who had just bid her goodbye with such genial confidence. The minister who had blessed her at her confirmation. The classmates with whom she had shared challenges and successes. Her older brother, if he had lived to know what she might do.

And then, between one stride and the next, an image arose of someone she had never met, someone who had died long before she was born: Johannes Vermeer.

Vermeer, citizen of the Dutch Republic. A painter, dependent on his fellow citizens for his livelihood. Vermeer, who had, at the age of twenty-one — just Susannah's age — turned his back on his upbringing and converted to Catholicism, in part, at least, to marry the woman he wanted . . . the woman, one could hope, that he loved.

In a Europe where to be Catholic could mean arrest and execution — not in the Dutch Republic, perhaps, but all around it — he had chosen to be Catholic.

She had come to a stop, there in the street. She had no more time for thinking, for weighing consequences. She must get to Camelia's, and to Carl.

When she dragged herself from the whirlpool of her thoughts, she saw that she had missed the final turn of the road, and had to hurry back. She knew she must be breathing fast as Camelia opened the door, a rare worry line on her forehead. Susannah looked past Camelia and saw Carl, and a sudden peace came over her.

Was she lacking in reverence, that the phrase that

came to mind was "the peace that passeth all understanding"? It didn't matter, nothing mattered, except Carl standing there, his face pale and his hands gripping each other so tightly that his knuckles had gone white. She walked up to them, gently took his hands in her, and prised them apart. He blinked, and relaxed, and took her hands in his, enveloping them. "Your hands are cold. Is it so cold outside?"

She drank in the sight of him. "No. It's warming up. It begins to truly feel like spring."

Behind her, Camelia said, "Well, I'll be off to my dusting. Susannah, have some tea! Carl's ahead of you by one sandwich. Don't blame him, I made him do it." And away she went. Susannah could just hear a chuckle as their hostess mounted the stairs.

Carl gestured toward a chair. "Please, sit. The sandwiches are good."

She had all in a moment become ravenous. She put out her hand for the teapot, wondering to see it shaking, but Carl was there before her, pouring out, handing her the milk, offering her the sugar. He put two of the sandwiches on a plate — egg salad in one, something that might have been ham salad in the other — and handed it to her. She picked the ham sandwich up and took a large, unladylike bite. She finished it in two more bites and, laughing, took a slice of pound cake and dropped it on her plate.

They had said almost nothing, certainly had settled nothing, and yet it seemed almost unnecessary to speak. She sipped her tea, hot and delicious, the best tea she could remember, and waited to see which of them would break the silence. Carl took and ate a crumpet, wiped his mouth on his napkin, and finally said, "I may have new work."

Susannah listened and ate as Carl explained what Father McCarthy had done for him. He spoke with an energy greater than she had ever seen in him before, an energy and a hope that filled her with joy.

He made sure to tell her that matters were not settled, that he didn't yet know where the business would be located. "But if I take this job, I'll make sure you could still reach the school without a horse or buggy." He stopped abruptly, as both of them listened to the echo of what he had said. He gripped his thighs with his hands and stared at her.

Susannah refilled his teacup, put down the teapot, and looked in his eyes. "I shouldn't say this. But I would like to marry you."

Carl gasped, and tears appeared and shone in his eyes as Susannah blinked away her own. He stood up and shoved his chair backward, so hard the legs rattled and it almost fell over. She could never say, after, which of them moved toward the other first, which of them first reached out to hold the other tight.

It was the ticking of Camelia's grandfather clock that brought Susannah back to their surroundings. She could not bring herself to let go, but said into Carl's chest, "We have so much to decide."

"Yes," Carl answered, his voice low and quiet above her head. "Am I guessing right that you will keep teaching, if they let you?"

She nodded, her cheek rubbing against the freshly pressed linen of his shirt. "For now, at least. If they let me, and if you and your family don't object."

Carl pulled back enough to look at her. "Object, to Bronka and all the other children having such a fine teacher? I would bite my tongue out first."

"But there is so much to do, to keep a house. Cooking,

cleaning, mending . . . ."

He drew her close again. "We'll find a way. We might be able, with what this new work will pay, to hire someone to cook for us or bring us meals. Or if you were willing, I could build another room onto our house, and we could live there. My mother and Bronka would be happy to cook for us all."

Susannah was less certain, but she let it pass for now. "And I could do mending and cleaning in the evenings, whether we live with them or apart. But if I'm not allowed to teach, if I lose my job . . . everything will be harder."

Carl's large hand, gentle for all its callouses, stroked her hair. "It will be harder, yes. But not harder than it was for me, coming to a new country. Or for you, leaving home and making your own way."

The clock ticked on for another minute or so before Susannah said, "I don't know what to do about our religions. Except . . . I'm willing to become a Catholic, if that's what I need to do so we can be together."

She might have had a faint hope that he would protest, say it was unnecessary in spite of what Father McCarthy had told her. But instead, he took her face in his hands and kissed her, not gently but passionately. And she returned the kiss in kind, no fears or nightmares in her way.

They broke apart as footsteps heralded Camelia's return, followed by a hearty laugh. "Well, I don't need to ask what happened, do I? My very best wishes and congratulations to you both!" And then, less boisterously, "And may I say, though I hope it won't frighten you, that I do believe you're two of the braver young people I've met in my time."

Carl looked at Susannah. "Do you feel brave?"

He might be expecting her to deny the praise. But

she took his hand again and said firmly, "I do."

Over the remains of the tea, the three of them talked about the furniture business, about how long it would take if they built a room onto Carl's family house, and finally, about the topic that loomed largest. Susannah bit her lip, released it, and said, in a voice almost as strong as she tried to make it, "I'll have to talk to Father McCarthy about some things. When I spoke to him — at your house, Carl — much of what he said . . . reassured me. About reading the Bible, and about Mary and the saints — though I need to ask him if one can be a Catholic without praying to saints, or if not, just what one would have to say in those prayers." She took a breath, swallowed, and went on," As for any conflict between civil law and Catholic doctrine, I'll hope that never happens. And if it does, I'll do what my conscience tells me, with all the considerations that exist by that time."

Carl muttered a prayer under his breath and visibly shook off worry. "What about confession?"

Susannah hesitated and blurted out, "It seems too easy! I confess my sins, no matter how awful they might be, and I'm forgiven, just like that?"

Carl smiled a little. "Not quite 'just like that,' depending on the penance the priest gives you. But it does seem too easy, sometimes. Which only means that we have a hard time believing in the great grace and mercy of God."

A silence fell, followed by Camelia saying in a more lighthearted tone, "Well, I do like that way of looking at it!"

The clock's rich tones signaled the third quarter hour. Susannah looked up at it and said, reluctantly, "We really should be going. Camelia, I can't thank you enough for what you've done for us today."

Carl interrupted her don't-mention-it wave. "Before we go, there's something you should know. Something I haven't told either of you."

Susannah had just time enough for her stomach to sink and her breath to catch before he said, slowly, "My name is not really Carl."

She and Camelia both goggled at him, and Camelia demanded, "Then good gracious, what is it? Ezekiel? Ebenezer? Or something too strange for me to even guess at?"

Carl remained serious. "Nothing of which I needed to be ashamed. But I was. When we came here, when we got off the ship and were herded into the shack with the immigration officers, they asked my name. And when I told them, they laughed."

Susannah, already indignant on his behalf, opened her mouth to protest, but Carl kept on. "My name is Karol." It sounded almost like Carol, but with more emphasis on the second syllable. "When I told the officers my name, they laughed, and asked me whether my father had wanted a girl instead of a boy, or was I a girl after all? They could see I was angry, and one of them said, 'Oh, I beg your pardon, *miss!*" Carl's — no, Karol's — fists clenched. Susannah seized his nearest hand and massaged it until it relaxed.

She said, softly, "So you became Carl."

"One of them, the only one who hadn't laughed, told me that Carl was the closest English name. He looked around at the others, and didn't have to say more. I nodded, and he took the ledger, scratched out whatever one of the others had written, and wrote Carl. And Carl I have been, ever since, except in confession, and at home when no one outside the family, or other Polish people, are around."

Susannah said softly, "Karol. Is that right? When do you want me to use it?"

He looked at her as if they were the only two people in the room, in the town, in the world. "I would like you to call me Karol when we stand before the priest to be made one flesh."

The words made her heart race and her nerves tingle. It took close to half a minute before she could collect herself and say, "I could speak of my intended, and then my husband, Karol, in town, with those I know and those I meet. They'd get used to it, and then you could stop using Carl so often, if you wished."

Karol stared at her, plainly stunned. He said, slowly, "I hadn't thought I could use my name in this town, ever. I will . . . talk to Father McCarthy, next Sunday, about what Mr. McIntyre might say, if I am to work for him."

Next Sunday. Susannah's heart beat faster. "I'd like to go with you again, on Sunday." She smiled faintly. "I believe I, even more than you, need to talk to Father McCarthy."

Karol straightened up. "We'll talk to him together. Camelia, I — we — owe you our deepest thanks. Susannah, I'll walk you home."

Susannah let her eyebrow twitch upward. "Yes, Karol. Of course you may walk me home." She emphasized the "may" just enough to make her point, and went on, "Camelia, let me add my profoundest thanks to Karol's."

Karol had rocked back just a little on his heels. Camelia laughed. "Don't you mind, Karol, if Susannah has a mind of her own, even as a wife. All the best wives do. And it was my very great pleasure."

Had she spoken too tartly, and in front of Camelia at

that? Should she apologize? Did she have anything to apologize for? And what was Karol thinking, walking beside her, saying nothing?

She heaved a sigh of relief when he started whistling. And when he grabbed her hand and began swinging their joined hands in time to the tune, she knew that, whatever was to come, all was well between them.

Whatever was to come.

Susannah did not expect to see Camelia the very next morning, let alone waiting near the schoolhouse door. But there Camelia stood, with the look of a woman with a secret or good news or both. As soon as they'd exchanged greetings, Camelia followed on Susannah's heels as Susannah entered the schoolroom. Without waiting for Susannah to find a way to ask her business, Camelia said, "I'm just guessing, mind you, but I'd wager you haven't thought too far ahead. As in months or years from now, when you find you've started a family."

Susannah's chest went tight. She had not so much failed to think about this likelihood as refused to think about it. She had always known that if she found a man she wanted to marry, a man worth marrying, that fact might mean the end of her life as a teacher, even before she had children. When she started her studies, the possibility had felt remote . . . which told her, now, that she had never really seen Charles Elliott in that light, whatever her fancies might have been.

And once she became fully engaged in those studies, the goals of doing well, graduating, attaining a prized position, had allowed her to continue hiding from that still-distant future. But now, Camelia was forcing the issue. She could hide no longer.

serve you well."

nt of the added weeks,
ould be tested by the
ing her mind. But she
t is only fitting. As a
w hard my pupils have
studying with you will

nd you, my son, must
ed, as she prepares to
er life, but two."
d his lip. "I'm worried
about how they'll treat
whether they'll let her

My child, how did you
?"

"Dr. Gibbs put an
as going to place one
ave town, and I wanted
nswered Dr. Gibbs, and
nd the rest of the school
do. Karol's right, si —
to keep doing it as long
Karol doesn't mind."
t the next step is for me
e time in a day or two.
t back to town. Karol, is

't know how long we'd
some dinner for

Camelia caught her arm and steered her toward the big chair behind Susannah's desk. "You're looking shaky. So sit down and let me tell you I've found — well, perhaps not a complete solution, but something better than no solution at all. No time to tell you about it right now — I just wanted you to know. Now you put the matter aside and enjoy thinking about your engagement, and we'll talk it all out soon. Say, a week from Wednesday? I'd ask you to come sooner, but I'm leaving town to visit a friend, everything's scheduled."

Susannah swallowed and was about to answer, but Camelia patted her shoulder and said, "No, that's not good enough. I can see the wheels whirring around in your head, still. Stop worrying this instant, or I'll be standing here pestering you when those children come in, and they'll worry along with you. Can't have that, can we?"

At least she could spend the next week feeling curious as well as apprehensive. Camelia read her expression and patted her shoulder in approval. "That's better! Now we'll both be about our days. Until next week!" In moments, she had gone through the back door and closed it behind her. Susannah stood up, made sure she was steady on her feet, and went to welcome her pupils.

Chapter 27

SUSANNAH had expected more of the Cath
congregation to be surprised when she turned up ag
and so obviously with Karol. She had feared hostility at
second intrusion from an outsider. But quite a few peo
seemed to have somehow heard the news; and rather t
any resentment at Karol's choice, most of them seer
either grateful or smug that one of the Protestants
closely surrounding them had accepted the Faith.

The service had less magic to it than the midni
Christmas mass, and knowing that she would soon hav
participate more fully made it seem more alien. But
ignored her nerves and paid close attention. When
service ended, Karol sought out a near giant of a man v
must be his prospective employer. Rather than eit
interrupt or join their conversation, she wandered the fr
yard of the church, admiring the few remaining crocu
and finding two daffodils and a tulip.

Just as she thought of going back inside to sit dov
Karol came up to her, beaming. "All is settled! He l
found a site for the business, on the edge of Elk Leg near
Cowbird Creek, and bought a horse for me to use getti
to and from work. If the business grows as he hopes,
might even open a workshop nearer our home. Also
think Father McCarthy is ready for us."

There was no use asking herself whether she w
ready for him. Remembering an expression used by a

the most important virtues, and will

Susannah quailed at the thoug
or longer, in which her courage w
possibility of turning back, of chang
squared her shoulders and said, "
teacher, I must always remember ho
to work to learn what I teach them.
be a very useful reminder."

The priest looked at Karol. "A
be the helpmeet Susannah will ne
make not just one great change in h

"I will! But . . . ." Karol chewe
about the people in Cowbird Creek,
her. Whether they'll shun her. And
keep teaching, as she wants to do."

The priest nodded gravely. "
come to be Cowbird Creek's teache

It seemed so long ago.
advertisement in the paper. I wa
myself, because I . . . I needed to lea
to teach as I'd been trained to do. I a
we wrote back and forth until he, a
board I suppose, decided I would
Father. I love teaching, and I want
as . . . as I can, if they'll let me. And

"Well, then. It seems to me tha
to speak to Dr. Gibbs. I should hav
Meanwhile, you'll be wanting to ge
your family waiting for you?"

"No, Father. I told them I did
be. We can walk, and they'll keep

me."

Father McCarthy stroked his chin. "You could do that, certainly — but how would you like to join me and share my dinner? I won't claim that my housekeeper's cooking rivals your mother's, but hunger makes the best sauce, as they say. And after, I can drive you back in the buggy, and let you off close to town. Word will get around soon enough, if it hasn't already, but there's no need to stir it up sooner by my driving the two of you to either of your doors."

Karol looked at her for an answer, and she said, "Thank you very much, Father. I'd be glad and grateful to join you." And added, suddenly light of heart, "You can teach me the proper grace to say. It's none too soon to learn."

* * * * *

As more people moved into Cowbird Creek and surrounding communities, Joshua was a little more likely to meet a stranger, though it still happened rarely enough to be refreshing. The man who appeared at the office that Tuesday, with brown wavy hair not unlike Joshua's own, was familiar only by report — or at least, his clerical collar so suggested. The man confirmed Joshua's guess when he introduced himself as "Father McCarthy" from Elk Leg.

Noting Joshua's scrutiny, he smiled and said, "I am here to consult you not as a doctor, though I may well do so in the future, but in your capacity as a member of the school board. If any patients come in, I'll defer to their need and come back later or another day."

Joshua said to Clara, listening with bright-eyed interest, "The father and I will be in the private examination room. Please let me know if I'm needed up here." Without further ado, he led the priest to the room in back.

The priest tilted his head and lifted an eyebrow. "Rather like our confessional, though roomier. I'd hazard a guess that it sometimes serves a similar function."

An astute deduction. "There are certainly times when the state of the mind affects that of the body. I imagine you've found the same, though coming at it from a different direction. Now, please sit down, and you can tell me what you need from the Cowbird Creek school board."

The priest, so instructed, took the single chair, holding his hat in his lap. "My errand concerns Miss Susannah Shepard, your teacher. I'm told — to speak plainly, Miss Shepard has told me — that you were instrumental in bringing her to town."

A picture began to form in Joshua's mind, stitched together from almost unnoticed fragments of gossip and observation, now framed by the priest's words. "I was, and I consider it one of my better decisions. She has fulfilled not only my expectations but my hopes. I'd be most sorry to lose her."

A trace of relief crossed the priest's face. "From what she's said, she would be most sorry to be lost. But she has made plans which might raise some concerns on the school board and among her pupils' families. Do you know Carl Marek?"

Of course. "I've treated him and his family for the occasional injury or illness, though they tend to take such matters in stride where possible. Carl and Susannah met the moment she arrived in town, when he retrieved some of her luggage from a thief. He's one of your flock, I gather."

"He is. And now, he and Miss Shepard plan to

Camelia caught her arm and steered her toward the big chair behind Susannah's desk. "You're looking shaky. So sit down and let me tell you I've found — well, perhaps not a complete solution, but something better than no solution at all. No time to tell you about it right now — I just wanted you to know. Now you put the matter aside and enjoy thinking about your engagement, and we'll talk it all out soon. Say, a week from Wednesday? I'd ask you to come sooner, but I'm leaving town to visit a friend, everything's scheduled."

Susannah swallowed and was about to answer, but Camelia patted her shoulder and said, "No, that's not good enough. I can see the wheels whirring around in your head, still. Stop worrying this instant, or I'll be standing here pestering you when those children come in, and they'll worry along with you. Can't have that, can we?"

At least she could spend the next week feeling curious as well as apprehensive. Camelia read her expression and patted her shoulder in approval. "That's better! Now we'll both be about our days. Until next week!" In moments, she had gone through the back door and closed it behind her. Susannah stood up, made sure she was steady on her feet, and went to welcome her pupils.

Chapter 27

SUSANNAH had expected more of the Catholic congregation to be surprised when she turned up again, and so obviously with Karol. She had feared hostility at this second intrusion from an outsider. But quite a few people seemed to have somehow heard the news; and rather than any resentment at Karol's choice, most of them seemed either grateful or smug that one of the Protestants so closely surrounding them had accepted the Faith.

The service had less magic to it than the midnight Christmas mass, and knowing that she would soon have to participate more fully made it seem more alien. But she ignored her nerves and paid close attention. When the service ended, Karol sought out a near giant of a man who must be his prospective employer. Rather than either interrupt or join their conversation, she wandered the front yard of the church, admiring the few remaining crocuses and finding two daffodils and a tulip.

Just as she thought of going back inside to sit down, Karol came up to her, beaming. "All is settled! He has found a site for the business, on the edge of Elk Leg nearest Cowbird Creek, and bought a horse for me to use getting to and from work. If the business grows as he hopes, he might even open a workshop nearer our home. Also, I think Father McCarthy is ready for us."

There was no use asking herself whether she was ready for him. Remembering an expression used by a shopkeeper back in St. Louis, she murmured, "In for a penny, in for a pound." Karol looked toward her, forehead wrinkled with confusion or worry. She took his hand and squeezed it in apology, and asked, "Where is he?"

"He's probably in his little office in the back of the church. We can look there, and if we don't find him, we could go to his house, nearby."

But the priest found them, popping up from the side yard where, he told them, he'd been admiring a new baby. "Such a sweet little boy, with his mother's bright red hair, though not much of it. I've suggested the mother go into Cowbird Creek to see the doctor — she's still weak from the birth, and I'm hoping Dr. Gibbs can give her a tonic of some kind. But now, what can I do for you two?"

Karol started to speak and then looked at Susannah instead. He must have taken her implicit rebuke at Camelia's to heart. She stepped as close to Karol as she could and said, "Father, we want to be married. And — and I know, I remember, what that means. I'm ready to convert."

The priest's warm smile bathed them like sunshine. "I will pray for your great happiness, and I believe that prayer will be answered, so long as you cherish each other all the days of your lives as you plainly cherish each other now. But what makes you think, my dear, that you're ready to become part of our flock?"

She stared at him in bewilderment and turned to Karol, who only nodded. Father McCarthy said more seriously, "You have barely begun to learn what it means to join the Church. And I will baptize you only when you know more fully what that means, to what you will be committing yourself." At her look of dismay, he smiled again and said, "It will not be so very long. Even that delay may try your patience, both of you, but patience is one of the most important virtues, and will serve you well."

Susannah quailed at the thought of the added weeks, or longer, in which her courage would be tested by the possibility of turning back, of changing her mind. But she squared her shoulders and said, "It is only fitting. As a teacher, I must always remember how hard my pupils have to work to learn what I teach them. Studying with you will be a very useful reminder."

The priest looked at Karol. "And you, my son, must be the helpmeet Susannah will need, as she prepares to make not just one great change in her life, but two."

"I will! But . . . ." Karol chewed his lip. "I'm worried about the people in Cowbird Creek, about how they'll treat her. Whether they'll shun her. And whether they'll let her keep teaching, as she wants to do."

The priest nodded gravely. "My child, how did you come to be Cowbird Creek's teacher?"

It seemed so long ago. "Dr. Gibbs put an advertisement in the paper. I was going to place one myself, because I . . . I needed to leave town, and I wanted to teach as I'd been trained to do. I answered Dr. Gibbs, and we wrote back and forth until he, and the rest of the school board I suppose, decided I would do. Karol's right, si — Father. I love teaching, and I want to keep doing it as long as . . . as I can, if they'll let me. And Karol doesn't mind."

"Well, then. It seems to me that the next step is for me to speak to Dr. Gibbs. I should have time in a day or two. Meanwhile, you'll be wanting to get back to town. Karol, is your family waiting for you?"

"No, Father. I told them I didn't know how long we'd be. We can walk, and they'll keep some dinner for me."

Father McCarthy stroked his chin. "You could do that, certainly — but how would you like to join me and share my dinner? I won't claim that my housekeeper's cooking rivals your mother's, but hunger makes the best sauce, as they say. And after, I can drive you back in the buggy, and let you off close to town. Word will get around soon enough, if it hasn't already, but there's no need to stir it up sooner by my driving the two of you to either of your doors."

Karol looked at her for an answer, and she said, "Thank you very much, Father. I'd be glad and grateful to join you." And added, suddenly light of heart, "You can teach me the proper grace to say. It's none too soon to learn."

* * * * *

As more people moved into Cowbird Creek and surrounding communities, Joshua was a little more likely to meet a stranger, though it still happened rarely enough to be refreshing. The man who appeared at the office that Tuesday, with brown wavy hair not unlike Joshua's own, was familiar only by report — or at least, his clerical collar so suggested. The man confirmed Joshua's guess when he introduced himself as "Father McCarthy" from Elk Leg.

Noting Joshua's scrutiny, he smiled and said, "I am here to consult you not as a doctor, though I may well do so in the future, but in your capacity as a member of the school board. If any patients come in, I'll defer to their need and come back later or another day."

Joshua said to Clara, listening with bright-eyed interest, "The father and I will be in the private examination room. Please let me know if I'm needed up here." Without further ado, he led the priest to the room in back.

The priest tilted his head and lifted an eyebrow. "Rather like our confessional, though roomier. I'd hazard a guess that it sometimes serves a similar function."

An astute deduction. "There are certainly times when the state of the mind affects that of the body. I imagine you've found the same, though coming at it from a different direction. Now, please sit down, and you can tell me what you need from the Cowbird Creek school board."

The priest, so instructed, took the single chair, holding his hat in his lap. "My errand concerns Miss Susannah Shepard, your teacher. I'm told — to speak plainly, Miss Shepard has told me — that you were instrumental in bringing her to town."

A picture began to form in Joshua's mind, stitched together from almost unnoticed fragments of gossip and observation, now framed by the priest's words. "I was, and I consider it one of my better decisions. She has fulfilled not only my expectations but my hopes. I'd be most sorry to lose her."

A trace of relief crossed the priest's face. "From what she's said, she would be most sorry to be lost. But she has made plans which might raise some concerns on the school board and among her pupils' families. Do you know Carl Marek?"

Of course. "I've treated him and his family for the occasional injury or illness, though they tend to take such matters in stride where possible. Carl and Susannah met the moment she arrived in town, when he retrieved some of her luggage from a thief. He's one of your flock, I gather."

"He is. And now, he and Miss Shepard plan to

marry, which means that she will be as well. And therein lies the problem, if there is one."

Joshua considered his fellow school board members one at a time, and suppressed a groan but not a frown. "I'm afraid there may well be — or rather, a problem in addition to the common belief that being married should be a woman's all-consuming occupation, precluding any other. I can hope that this town will take a somewhat less restrictive view on the general question of married teachers. It would then be my task to persuade those who would treat Susannah's conversion as a breach of contract, or a danger to the proper education of the children, or both."

The priest relaxed perceptibly against the back of his chair. "I had hoped as much, and I thank you. I would ask whether you think the couple should delay making their intentions known in town, but I fear that will be impractical. In fact, I would hazard a guess that gossip, more accurate than gossip often is, may have already begun."

Joshua thought it likely, which made the matter urgent. "How shall I report to you as to my success or failure?"

The priest considered for a few seconds and said, "It will probably be easiest, and excite the least comment, if you keep Miss Shepard informed. I will not only be seeing her on Sundays, but will be giving her classes once a week."

The priest stood up, and Joshua followed his lead. As they both returned to the front room, one of the town matrons was just coming through the door. She saw the priest, sniffed, and moved to the corner farthest from him rather than sitting in the closer chair. The woman might be habitually distrustful of Catholics in general or priests in particular, but her manner could indicate that the priest had been right about the prevalence of gossip. Father McCarthy's smile had a wry edge to it as he donned his hat, tipped it to the woman, and walked out the door.

Clara left the office an hour early to do some shopping, so Joshua walked home alone. As he exchanged greetings with various familiar residents of town and of nearby farms, he saw in his imagination those who had left, and in particular those who had found it necessary to leave Cowbird Creek behind in order to lead the lives they wished to lead. What he would give to have Freida still here, to be able to care for her in her final years and extend those years as long as possible! To see Jenny flourish, gain confidence, overcome her past!

Susannah had lived here only a few months, but she had already done a great deal for many of the town's inhabitants. After she had been forced to uproot herself once, and had become part of a community supplying at least some of the sense of belonging she had left behind, was she now to be ostracized by her neighbors, or driven away entirely?

As he approached their home, he was already planning the meeting he would convene, not only of the school board but of several other influential citizens. It would be tricky, including all those who might otherwise take offense if such decisions were discussed without their invaluable input, while still maintaining control of the meeting's direction.

In the end, though, this was a decision affecting not just the school, but the town as a whole. It might not be for him to try to impose his views . . . .

He had done his duty before, despite the cost and

against far more deadly opposition. He would do so again. He would speak out, and do his best to call upon the better angels of their natures. And he would pray for less costly success than had been granted their martyred president, who had so eloquently expressed his hope for the same.

Chapter 28

SUSANNAH was back at Camelia's again, after school and thus later in the afternoon, but Camelia still treated the occasion as afternoon tea. In spite of how long it had been since dinnertime, Susannah was far too nervous to touch the rolled ham or cheese straws. She did accept some tea, but only because her throat had gone so dry.

Camelia sipped her own tea, set it down, and looked Susannah in the eye. "My dear, we must start by facing an unwelcome fact. It's quite impossible for you to keep teaching once you're visibly expecting. Parents, irrational creatures that they are, get terribly squeamish about it — even though many of them live on farms and their children see not just the life cycles of the animals, but even how the calves and foals and such get started. And even those children who haven't absorbed the notion that they should be horrified will be just brimming over with questions you won't want to answer, especially when they're supposed to be *answering* questions about arithmetic or the largest cities in Peru."

Susannah could picture those parents, and those children, all too easily. She even knew which parents would be the most absurd about it, and which children would ask the most embarrassing questions — some of them on purpose.

"Quite apart from all that — and you'd do as well handling it as anyone could — there's the discomfort and inconvenience you'd go through. Well, you'll be going through it anyway, but not in a schoolroom with no comfortable chairs, let alone a bed, and the necessary too far away. While I've never had the experience, I've seen many a friend and acquaintance go through it, and of course I've read about it." (Of course.) "I'll be happy to regale you with all the details, but you can wait for everyone else you know to do that once they know you're expecting. For now, I'll just say that when the time comes, you may have fewer regrets about *not* teaching for those months."

Camelia could well be right. She *sounded* right. But after all, Susannah wouldn't be expecting all the time. What about all the months or years in between?

Susannah bit her lip until she could speak. Before she was ready to try, Camelia barreled on.

"And when you've got an infant, and later a toddler running you ragged and maybe another infant too — well, at least you'll have Karol's family here to help, but you'll be busy and weary enough. Not that it's all going to be weary and dreary! There are great joys ahead of you, and not just from that handsome husband's company." Her gaze had gone pensive, but now she looked directly at Susannah again. "I fully expect to envy you."

That admission echoed in Susannah's heart, and she gave it the time it deserved. But she was still at an impasse, and Camelia had promised some measure of hope. Time to prompt her. "What of the school, then? Does it close, so soon after opening? Who can fill my place?"

She was startled, even offended, when Camelia winked at her. "Can't you guess?" At Susannah's blank look, she went on, "Who in this town may know almost as much as you about the subjects you teach — or at least, is in a good position to fill in any gaps in her knowledge? You ponder that question while I pour us some more tea — and

I'm going to leave the food out, because in a couple of minutes your appetite might come out of wherever it's hiding." She suited the action to the words and then sat back in her chair. "Figured it out yet?"

Susannah stared at her hostess. "You must be describing yourself — at least, I know of no one else in town you could mean. Would you actually take on the post of teacher?"

Camelia popped a cheese straw in her mouth, chewed vigorously, swallowed, and said, "Why not? I like youngsters, and plenty of them hereabouts — and their parents — know me. And the library doesn't come close to using me up. I could leave school for the library, then maybe keep it open later. I'm ready to be tired at the end of the day for a change — I'll probably sleep better."

Susannah was slowly coming to believe that Camelia was serious, and in fact genuinely interested. But she could hardly neglect to mention another obstacle. "You've never taught, have you, beyond explaining things to people now and then? It's not . . . there are methods, techniques. The time I spent preparing wasn't all, or even mostly, studying the subjects. It was studying how to help children learn."

Camelia laughed. "Exactly! Or almost exactly, as I'm no child. But I'm sure you have the skills to help me learn what you learned. Don't you?"

The idea took root in her, and blossomed. She, on her own, to take the place of the entire college in which she had trained. The college run by her nemesis. Even if Brecker never knew of it, the idea had a satisfaction akin to revenge.

But Camelia wasn't done. "You can invite me in to give some lessons while you're still in charge, in case anyone on the school board wants me to have more direct experience. And the lessons you give me won't end when I take your place. I'll bring my problems and confusions to you for whatever advice you can give me — or for commiseration, if you've got no advice to give. Not that I'll need an excuse to spend time with my friend!"

Susannah hadn't quite realized that she had feared losing touch with Camelia — more than that, feared losing that part of herself that had existed before she and Karol grew close, before she ever contemplated marriage and a family as anything other than a hazy expectation. The banishing of that fear felt like a precious gift.

She breathed deeply. The sandwiches — ham, chicken, egg salad — smelled good. How had she failed to notice? And when had the light, gold with afternoon, begun dancing on the wall between the shadows of young leaves?

But the moment of elation insisted on fading, slipping through her fingers. Even as they talked about ideas Susannah had for the school's future — Friday evening "literaries" with recitations and debates, public spelling bees, school plays — she had to confront the fact that she would not be the one making such plans happen. Instead, she was left with the sadness of that future, not so distant now, when she would have to leave her career behind. Of course she was getting Karol, the life they would share, in exchange. And she would have her own children to cherish and teach . . . but the variety of challenges she faced in the schoolroom, the children of different ages and different backgrounds, the growth of trust between her pupils and herself . . . .

Camelia stopped chattering in mid-sentence and looked at her with sympathy. "I know it's a loss, still. But you'll just have to make sure Karol reminds you why it's worth it. I'm confident he will."

Susannah sighed. "I know he will. It's ungrateful of me to repine."

Camelia waved the words away. "Nonsense. We none of us like to give up what we value, even though we none of us get everything we want in this life. . . . Still, I think I can cheer you up a little. There's no reason in the world you couldn't pop into the schoolroom now and then, fairly often in fact, and give some lesson you particularly enjoy. The children still there from when you were in charge will be thrilled to see you."

The weight in Susannah's chest lifted a little.

Camelia nodded in satisfaction and went on. "And we can arrange it more often as your children get older. Then, when I'm getting too creaky and cranky to cope with children's antics, you'll be all ready to come back full time. Why shouldn't you?"

That future was too far off for Susannah to grasp. She had little conception of how that Susannah, so much older, many years married and mother of who knows how many children, would weigh alternatives, what she would long for most. But just to know that she need not abandon her profession and know it was forever! She gazed at Camelia, heart too full for speech. Camelia beamed, polished off a sandwich, and said briskly, "Why don't you go tell Joshua what we've cooked up between us. Dear man, he's probably been fretting, discreetly, about this very problem."

She would tell Joshua, right away. And then, she would go for a long walk in the sunshine until she could tell Karol.

* * * * *

Susannah had not wanted to tell him why she was meeting with Camelia, though she said so little about it that he knew more was going on than two friends having a late tea. Her failure to explain was all of a piece with the way her moods had swung this way and that in the past days, from an almost wild happiness to warm affection to brooding on her own.

Karol took a minute to walk out to the yard and look up at the sky: clear after the morning's rain, with a ray of sunlight slanting toward the door and showing the arrival of evening. His workday was almost done. Would Susannah still be at Camelia's? When she was through, would she come to find him, or leave it to him to seek her out at Miss Wheeler's?

The miller's younger son walked over and elbowed him in the side, saying with a grin, "There's your intended, looking purty as a picture, you lucky dog! Go on over, or you'll just be looking over your shoulder and likely walk into the hopper and get yourself ground up."

He had never found it easy to act friendly around the man, but with Susannah pledged to him and the prospect of leaving the mill behind, he could at least make himself smile as he hurried over to where Susannah stood waiting.

She looked different. She even stood differently — not shifting from foot to foot, or looking at the ground with shoulders slumped, or eyes darting every which way. She looked peaceful.

As soon as he moved toward her, she moved toward him, not running but walking with a spring in her step, holding out her hands. He grabbed them and held them tight, looking in her eyes for an answer to whatever questions had been plaguing her. She let go of his left hand to reach up with her right and rest it against his cheek.

"It's all right, Karol," she said softly. "I see the way forward, now. For me, and for us."

He swallowed and answered, "Didn't you before?"

"I knew which way I'd decided to go. But I didn't know quite how, or how stony the road would be. Now, I think it's a path I can walk, even if it isn't altogether smooth, and be glad to walk it. Now I can be glad about all the wonderful things along our way."

There was still a faint shadow over her, even with the brightness in her eyes. He would walk her home and get her to tell him all about what Camelia had said and what had happened. If she needed comforting, he would try to comfort her. And if, as it seemed now, she was more glad than sorry, he would be glad with her, joyful to see her happiness and to share it.

Chapter 29

JOSHUA'S first move in dealing with Susannah's engagement was, he acknowledged to Clara, a risky one. "And with Susannah having most at stake, I felt it right to consult her. She not only approved, she asked to go with me."

Clara, sitting on their bed, brushed her hair as she listened. "So the two of you bearded the minister in his den?"

Joshua finished polishing his boots and put away the supplies while Clara finished with the last few strokes. "We did. Susannah appreciated having someone to support her — someone other than her young man, who might be viewed as precipitating the crisis. And she acknowledged the tactical disadvantages of leaving the minister to hear the news from others, and likely growing more indignant with each serving of gossip."

Clara stood up and turned down the bedclothes, an invitation to him to keep his account short. He admired the way the lamplight silhouetted her tall slim form in her spring nightdress, and summed up by saying, "He was, naturally, dismayed, and spoke seriously to Susannah about her decision. I admired the courage with which she answered him. I believe he intends to meet with Father McCarthy, if the priest is willing."

Clara got into bed. "Then you've done a good day's work, and must leave the next steps to be taken by others. And now, I intend to claim your attention."

Joshua spoke to Susannah again one more time before the meeting, at the end of the school day, to discuss whether she or Karol or both should be present. He recommended against it. "Of course you are very much interested in what is said and by whom. But if the ultimate goal is to reach a decision as satisfactory as possible to as many people as possible, it would be best if those in attendance feel free to speak their minds. Your presence, in particular, might lead some participants to restrain themselves, while at the same time resenting the need for such restraint."

Susannah stood beside her desk and tapped the fingers of one hand against the blotter. She bit her lip, released it, and said, "But they may have questions for me. What if the absence of an answer to such a question proves crucial to whoever would have asked it?" Her fingers stilled, and she laid her palm flat on the desk, with an energy just short of a slap. "I should, at least, be near at hand, so that you can summon me in such a case. I could leave immediately afterward."

It was an eminently sensible suggestion, and accordingly, Susannah was to wait in the back room of Joshua's and Clara's office, a block away from the meeting hall. Her state, when she arrived there, might have inspired him to give her a short medical examination under other circumstances: she was breathing in quick shallow pants, and her face was pale. She had brought a book with her, a history of the Thirty Years' War, but he doubted she would read as much as a single page. He escorted her to the back, moved a more comfortable chair there, and spared a few minutes to make meaningless conversation in the hope of calming her. She at least could conjure a smile for him when he hurried off to arrange the chairs for the meeting.

The members of the school board arrived just as he finished, all except the eldest in the group, who moved slowly when he bestirred himself at all. Soon after, Mayor Pomfrey bustled in, giving his usual impression of being so much sought after that he must keep to a minimum the time spent in such activities as walking. However, his smile and hail-fellow-well-met manner faded away as he approached Joshua and said, "We need to talk before this meeting of yours gets going." He beckoned Joshua toward the corner farthest from the door, and Joshua followed with an unpleasant premonition of what was to come.

As soon as both men had reached the spot the mayor evidently preferred, that worthy peered at Joshua and said in a stage whisper, "I received a communication some little while ago, and now wish I had paid more heed to it. Did you by any chance receive a letter from a President Brecker?"

Joshua drew himself up straight and said, "I did, sir, and investigated its floridly worded allegations. I am confident they have no foundation."

The mayor pursed his lips. "Well, well, I'd certainly like to believe that. In fact, I don't mind admitting that was my first reaction. This Brecker seemed a prating, self-satisfied sort of fellow, if you don't mind my saying so. But since then, the way our schoolmarm has been walking about with that young Polack, and now I hear she aims to marry him! It gives me to wonder, Doctor, indeed it does."

Joshua suppressed his reaction to the vulgar slur and replied mildly, "Surely her intention to marry suggests Brecker's accusations of loose morals are unfounded."

The mayor harrumphed and said, "Well, that's as may be. Now it's time I said hello to a few folks." And off he went, already reaching out his hand for a handshake.

Meanwhile, the miller and the owner of the general store had arrived, guffawing together about some story the one had been telling the other. Not long after, Camelia appeared and shook Joshua's hand. He had had his qualms about including her, given that at least two or three of those present might regard the very presence of a woman as a provocation, and then chastised himself for cowardice. He had asked her to let a few others speak first so that her comments might be better tailored (and less likely to provoke those who preferred a woman to be softspoken and conventional). She appeared to receive the request without resenting it, understanding it was intended to serve the goal they shared.

By only a few minutes past the appointed hour, all those invited had assembled, except one.

Joshua moved back to the lectern and was about to call the meeting to order when the minister appeared in the doorway. Joshua stepped to one side and stood silently while the minister made his way forward and took Joshua's place. The various conversations yielded to attentive silence, more quickly than Joshua could have made them. The minister stood facing the assembly, looking slowly around the room, and then said, "I am here not to urge you to one or another course. In fact, I am still undecided about what I think would be best for our town, both those in my congregation and the rest. I intend to listen carefully to these proceedings, and ask you all to listen to each other, and weigh what you hear against whatever ideas you have brought here today. Dr. Gibbs, you have the floor." He made his way to an empty chair and sat down.

Joshua went back up front, wishing he could fetch a chair for himself instead of having to hold himself tall, and that Clara was with him, and that he knew his efforts this day would bear good fruit. He had not done much public speaking, and could only hope he was speaking loudly enough to be heard without bellowing and looking the fool. "Some of you know what we are gathered to decide. It is, on the surface, merely the question of whether one schoolteacher, living and working in Cowbird Creek these past few months, shall continue to do both or either. But it is my view, and the reason I have asked for this public discussion, that the decision we make about Susannah Shepard will play a significant, even a crucial role in what this town becomes, what it decides to be, in the months and years ahead."

He took a sip of the water on the lectern, saying a short prayer of thanks that he had remembered to put it there, and went on. "I considered explaining my meaning before opening the floor to comments, but upon reflection, I decided it would be best if I hold my comments for later. If you wish to speak to the question posed, please stand, one at a time." He stepped back, only one step so he could exert some control if chaos ensued, and held his breath until he realized he was being absurd. It would take far longer than he could hold his breath for those assembled to run out of wind.

A school board member, also a member of the city council, stood up and said, "My boy likes her. Says she tells a corker of a story about battles and such. And he's reading and figuring better than before she came. What's the problem with her?"

The miller popped up and growled, "The problem is she's marrying that Catholic fellow Carl Marek as works for me, except he might be quitting and going to work with some furniture peddler from Chicago. A troublemaker, I might call that young man." And then, grudgingly, "Though he's a hard worker, I'll say that for him. He'll likely be able to support the schoolmarm, if she stays home and does for him like a — " He shut his mouth in mid-sentence, no doubt remembering that Clara, whose services he might need at some future time, did not confine herself to hearth and home. He sat down, tugging at his beard.

"A Catholic and a troublemaker, you say?" The general store owner did not trouble himself to stand, but sat back in his chair. Joshua was probably imagining that the chair creaked in protest. "We've had Catholics hereabouts for a while now, if not many of 'em. I worried they'd bring in all those big families they have, but they haven't. And so far, none of them have been layabouts or busybodies, so it wouldn't be so bad if we did get a few more like 'em. What trouble has this Marek made, aside from finding someone to work for as is willing to pay him better?"

The miller made no reply beyond muttering to himself. Joshua stepped forward and spoke before anyone else could comment. "Indeed, this is no longer an entirely Protestant community. Nor do we have only Protestant children in our school. So far, I'm aware of only one Catholic pupil, and I don't know when we will have more, but sooner or later, more there will be."

And, Joshua reflected, under the Nebraska constitution passed not so many years ago, every one of the male pupils would, when of age, be voters.

"See here, Doc," piped up another school board member, not going so far as to stand up, but pulling his feet down from the back of the chair in front of him. "Weren't our common schools established to teach morals and religion to our young people? How can a gal who's throwing her religion away teach it to her pupils? As for morals, I'm not acquainted with the morals of Catholic folks one way or another, but I'd hate to find out too late that they ain't what anyone should teach in our school."

Camelia rose from her chair, quite at her ease, and said, "As it happens, gentlemen, I have known quite a few Catholic citizens in my time. I have also read several learned accounts of typical Catholic beliefs, concerning morality as well as religious doctrine. I believe you need fear no scandalous or unsatisfactory teaching on the subject. As for teaching religion, Miss Shepard has, until now, been a Protestant all her life, and is unlikely to forget everything she knows about her religion upon marrying."

"I should add," said Joshua, "that Miss Shepard is available to answer any questions you would care to put to her. By that I mean I can bring her here within minutes."

"Good idea," the mayor said, pulling out a cigar. He looked over at Camelia, hesitating, but her benign smile apparently reassured him, and he went on, "We can all have a quick smoke while you fetch her."

* * * * *

Hurrying behind Joshua, Susannah thought wildly that she should have worn more and brighter colors. Nuns wore black and white, didn't they? She needed to look as little like an anti-Catholic cartoon as possible. At least the cartoons usually featured men, and priests or bishops at that.

Joshua granted Susannah a moment to straighten her clothing and compose herself, then opened the door for her and followed her into the hall. The gathering was at least relatively small, though the men were sufficient in number and social standing to intimidate her if she allowed them to do so. But not men only, she saw as she made her way to the lectern — Camelia's purple dress and bonnet stood out among the men's less colorful costumes. The amount of smoke in the air suggested how the men had passed the time waiting for her, and she struggled not to cough. As she passed Camelia's seat, Camelia gave her a very visible wink. She drew comfort from it, at least until she espied the minister sitting off to one side.

The stirring in the audience suggested that some of them had thought of standing, but that no one had gone so far in that direction as to inspire imitation. This might be the first time they had confronted the question of the proper etiquette for welcoming a female speaker. She put aside all such musings as she reached the lectern, stood behind it, and gripped its sides. "Gentlemen, and Mrs. Grant, I understand some of you have questions for me. I fully understand that you do, and will be happy to answer as best I can."

The oldest man present, who she believed was a member of the school board, stood up, winced, and sat down again. "Well, I've got a question. When we talked about whether Cowbird Creek had found its teacher, we discussed — " This with a significant look at Joshua. " — Whether we should hire an older woman, a widow or spinster, or a young lady such as yourself, who would sooner or later give up teaching for a husband. We decided to take that chance, and keep our ears open for word of an older candidate in the meantime." Some movement among the others suggested they had not intended one of their number to speak so candidly, but he ignored it and continued. "What I mean to say is, are you really planning to get married and keep teaching all the same? Just how long do you think that'll last, and shouldn't we be ginning up our search for someone else?"

Susannah found it easier than she'd expected to smile as she said, "Thank you, sir, for raising a concern I'm sure some of your fellows share." A couple of chuckles acknowledged that she had hit the mark. "I intend to keep teaching, with my husband's full consent. I admit I would not have put myself forward for the position of teacher, particularly at such a delicate time as the opening of the school, if I had not intended to remain in that position for years to come. I had little thought of courting or marriage, young though I am. But I suppose that's what happens to many people. They think they know where their lives are going, and then life surprises them."

The man grunted as if unimpressed, but she thought she saw some softening in his manner, perhaps a memory of his own youth. He nonetheless continued questioning her. "And when you have a family? Surely you don't expect to keep teaching then!"

Susannah tried to maintain what she hoped was the appearance of calm confidence. "I have thought about how to ensure that when that time comes, the school will be provided for and will not suffer any interruption. I have suggested a plan for Dr. Gibbs to lay before the school board." And Joshua had assured her that he would work with the town's midwife, arrived in town three years before, to keep her and her babies safe . . . but she must not distract herself thinking about such things now.

The man who had raised the matter gave Joshua a look suggesting that this supposed plan should have been mentioned earlier, but he sat down. The minister then rose to his feet, all shuffling and muttering giving way to silence as he did so. "Miss Shepard, your partisans have assured us that you will still be able to teach the tenets of our religion -- even after, as your marriage would require, you abandon that religion for the older creed from which it arose, a creed many of those present may find problematic or even unwholesome. Can you tell us, in all honesty and as you value your immortal soul, that you will be able to do this?"

Susannah hoped the lectern hid the trembling of her knees. She waited for several seconds in the hope that when she spoke, her voice would not tremble as well. But she could not wait any longer, and spoke in a voice not altogether steady. "Reverend, and all this distinguished company — if I were not confident that I can, without cavil, continue to teach Protestant pupils the principles of their faith, I would have already tendered my resignation. The one assurance I can't in conscience give you is that I will attempt to convert Catholics, or children from families of any other religion, to Protestantism. But you, Reverend, will be on hand to undertake that task."

She realized too late that she might have sounded pert, but the minister's mouth twitched in a smile, and he sat down. If anyone else had questions, they chose not to ask them. Joshua came to take her arm and escort her out the door. He steered her toward the town square and a bench therein, which puzzled her until she realized she was shaking again. He looked down at her with obvious concern. "I should get back to the meeting, and attempt to move proceedings along efficiently. Will you be able to make your way to Miss Wheeler's unassisted?"

"Yes, of course. Thank you for being so attentive, but I'll be fine." And she would be. It would have been lovely if Karol could be here, to escort her and reassure her. But he would still be at the mill, and she was well able to take care of herself.

* * * * *

Joshua returned to the hall to find clusters of men standing, or in one instance sitting, all around the room, debating with varying degrees of civility, and Camelia circling from one group to the next. He made his way through to the lectern and rapped on it. "Your attention, please!"

They turned toward him, but none of those standing made any move to sit back down. Clearly he could not demand their attention for long.

"I will briefly remind all of you that not only has Miss Shepard proved most able as a teacher, but that her calm courage and presence of mind may have been crucial in saving the lives of the children in her charge, during the blizzard that afflicted us only last March. I would hope our gratitude for that inestimable service has not faded so soon. But I have something of a more far-reaching nature to address.

"I wish to share with you now a concern of mine to which I alluded earlier in general terms. I care about your decision not only because I consider Miss Shepard an excellent teacher, very well suited to provide the foundation from which our school may grow and thrive. I care at least as much — more, I would say — about what Cowbird Creek will become. We are at a crossroads, gentlemen." He caught himself and was about to add some mention of Camelia, but she gave him a broad wink as if to excuse him. "I came here many years ago, one of many who returned from war victorious, but sorely troubled in mind if not in body. You all have healed me, gentlemen. Though not without the crucial assistance of my wife!"

He paused to let them chuckle, or in two cases hoot, before continuing. "This is a welcoming town. It is a town where not a few strangers have been accepted, and have become valued members of our community. It is a town which has rejected the narrow-minded insistence that every citizen be just like every other. We do not all think alike, and never have. Some of us disapprove of the beliefs held by others. Some of us even consider the morals of others to be less than exemplary. But we have not made it a common practice to turn on each other." Briefly, he wondered whether Madam Mamie would agree. But then, the continued presence of her establishment in a central part of town exemplified what he was saying.

"I hope we will continue to be such a town. I hope that as we grow, and we surely shall, we will not, as it were, grow backwards, requiring all new arrivals to be more like some cookie-cutter model that many of us hardly resemble. I am proud to live in this town!" he almost shouted. "And please do not mistake me — I expect to live and work here for many years to come, whatever you decide. I am not threatening to abandon my patients or my practice. But I will be gratified, and very thankful, if you choose to rise to the occasion and remain, in spirit, in essence, the town which has justified that pride."

Suddenly exhausted, he slumped toward the lectern before he caught himself and moved to step away. A voice halted him, the querulous tones of the oldest school board member, who had arrived at some point before Susannah spoke. "That's all very fine, but she's about to turn Catholic!"

Joshua had hoped he would not need to play the lawyer, but now he stood up straight again and said, "When I first learned of Miss Shepard's intentions, I set myself to do some studying." He would not mention

Camelia's guidance, not in the face of this man's hostility. "I had paid little attention, too little, to the discussions and deliberations that led to our state's adoption of its constitution a few years ago. But in that constitution, there is an entire article devoted to the education of our children. And that article explicitly forbids subjecting any pupil, *or any teacher*, to any religious test. It would not only, in my view, be wrong — even un-Christian — to dismiss Miss Shepard on the grounds of her religion, it would be illegal to do so."

Out of the corner of his eye, Joshua saw the minister's eyes go wide. The previous speaker sputtered, turned his head this way and that, and finally said, "Well, there must be something else wrong with her! If she's ready to turn her back on her church, she can't have fit morals. We can explain it some kind of way."

Joshua looked slowly around the room. No one — not even the mayor, he was relieved to see — seconded the man's suggestion. Joshua broke the profound silence to say, "There we have it, gentlemen. The choice before you has now become plain. I will leave you to discuss the matter, and will return shortly. I find I need some fresh air." And he strode away from the lectern and out of the room.

Chapter 30

SUSANNAH returned to the boarding house once she was through being interrogated. As soon as she had reached her room, she realized that she desperately needed something to do, some busywork to occupy at least some of her thoughts. She put away her light wrap and bonnet and went in search of Miss Wheeler, saying once she found her, "There must be something for which you could use my help. What may I do?"

She thought Miss Wheeler might question her, or simply decline her help, but after a moment's hesitation and scrutiny, Miss Wheeler replied, "Would you rather mend linens, or pick through fruit for preserves? Either would be helpful, but the latter is really the cook's job, though she doesn't care for it. The mending usually falls to me, and I would welcome having the chore go more quickly and having company as I attend to it."

With that very broad hint, Susannah chose the mending, and the two of them were soon seated at a table in the laundry room with a tablecloth spread between them, hems on two sides needing repair. Miss Wheeler gave Susannah an ample supply of thread and needles, and they set to work. At first, they chatted about other boarders, the frequency with which women in different walks of life wore holes in their stockings, and even the weather, constantly threatening rain for the last several days without actually delivering it. Susannah was therefore taken off guard when Miss Wheeler asked,

"How would you say the meeting went?"

Susannah pricked her finger and yanked it away from the tablecloth before any blood could spill on the fabric. "The meeting? You mean the meeting this afternoon." What a silly question. But it gave her time to retrieve her wits.

Miss Wheeler smiled. "Yes, dear. Unless other interesting meetings have taken place lately. Not that I mean to inquire about any . . . private encounters."

Susannah picked up her needle and set it down again, not wishing to court any more punctures. How had it gone? "I don't know. I really don't. No one said everything would be fine, and no one hissed at me or called me a Catholic-loving harlot. But whether they'll allow me to remain at the school, I couldn't say. I don't even know how long it will take for the school board to decide." The school board, after all, were the people who mattered to Susannah's immediate future. But a sudden qualm hit her. She and Karol might not be the only ones who could suffer the effects of Susannah's choice. "Miss Wheeler, will it cause problems with your other boarders, or in town, if I remain here until — Carl and I marry?" She had to stop to let a blush subside. She had spoken so rarely, in spite of everything, about wedding Karol. And she was far from sure how broadly he wanted the fact of his true name to spread.

Miss Wheeler reached out with the hand not holding a needle and patted Susannah's arm. "I shouldn't think it'll cause trouble. If anyone complains, it'll blow over soon enough. Ah . . . when do you think the wedding will take place?" She chuckled. "I expect neither of you young people wants much of a delay."

"I don't know exactly when. There's a great deal I still have to do." Lessons with Father McCarthy, and she was still woefully inexperienced at homemaking, and they had to find a home or build on to Karol's, and she had yet to learn how to cook even one Polish dish!

Her face must have shown her dismay at the number of tasks ahead. Miss Wheeler put down her needle and said, more soberly than Susannah had ever heard her speak, "Susannah, if you have doubts, this is the time to listen to them. It might seem shameful to go back on your word, or embarrassing to change your mind after all the fuss and bother, but it would be worse for both of you if you were to marry and then wish you hadn't. Or even before you marry, if you lose your job and then realize you aren't ready to give up your faith, or to spend your life with this man."

Miss Wheeler's intensity made it impossible simply to dismiss the idea. Did she have any real doubts? Susannah made herself imagine telling the priest she could not, after all, abandon the ideas with which she had been raised; telling Joshua that all his efforts had been unnecessary, but that now, he would have to persuade the school board that she was not too flighty and immature to teach the town's children. Telling Karol . . . telling Karol . . . .

Saying goodbye to Karol, seeing his pain, watching him walk away, walk away without her —

"No!"

Miss Wheeler jumped, almost pricking her own finger. "Are you all right? You're white as this tablecloth."

"I'm so sorry." Susannah tried to catch her breath. "I was just thinking about everything you said. And I'm sure. I . . . I have fears, not doubts. Just as I did when I left everyone I knew to come here. But I'm so glad I did, and I'm so grateful, forever grateful, that I met Carl."

Miss Wheeler stared down at the tablecloth. Susannah

could barely hear her as she said, "Can one man make so much difference?"

Susannah let her mind wander back through all the events of her life in Cowbird Creek, from the meeting whose result she awaited, through the March blizzard, back into winter and Christmas, to the day she opened the school, all the way back to the train pulling into the station. "I'll never truly know that. He was there from the start, turning what would have been a woeful setback into a great relief. Though he hasn't always made things easy for me!" She could laugh, now, at his fiery reproaches after hearing about her mishandling of Bronka's needs. "But my time here has been so much more than simply meeting and growing closer to Carl. Meeting all of you, and making a place for myself, and standing on my own for the first time — I couldn't regret any of it, no matter which way my path turns next."

Neither of them found anything else to say, and they slowly returned to their task. But they had each made only a few more stitches when the doorbell sounded and Joshua's voice called from outside the front door. Susannah couldn't quite hear his words, but the pleasure in his voice rang clear. She ran to the door, heedless of decorum, and flung it open so she could savor the relief on his face. Before she could ask, he grinned like a young lad and said, "Am I addressing the schoolteacher here in Cowbird Creek?"

Susannah clasped her hands to her breast. "Are you? Am I, still?"

He reached out as if to take her hands, and she gladly met him halfway. "Indeed I am! And indeed you are. You have given such proof of your worth, these past months, that the school board was nearly unanimous in approving your retention."

Nearly unanimous. She would not ask who had been

in the minority. No doubt someone would insist on telling her, sooner or later.

Joshua went on. "As for the plan you and Camelia have worked, a few were disgruntled not to have been asked to devise one of their own." He chuckled. "However, even they were relieved not to have so difficult a task before them."

What next? "Does Karol know?"

Joshua's eyes twinkled as he answered, "Not unless someone else has brought him the news. Would you care to be the first, if you can?"

Miss Wheeler ran up, seized Susannah in a hug, and shoved her toward the door, saying, "Go on, girl! Go tell your fellow the good news."

Susannah ran upstairs, grabbed her wrap and bonnet, and ran back down, jumping from the second stair to the floor. Joshua, now laughing, opened the door to let her run straight out.

* * * * *

Karol had had just about enough of the mill. It wasn't really the miller's fault. As bosses went, the man could have been a lot worse. But not knowing what would happen, whether the furniture job would fall through, whether Susannah would keep her job, whether she would after all change her mind, had him so restless he could hardly stand still to take an order, let alone to follow one.

Good thing he knew his job, and didn't have to do much listening in order to do it. But leaving the mill every day felt like getting leave from the army and knowing it would be over too soon.

Busy brooding, he didn't see Susannah running toward him, running right there in the street, until she was only a couple of steps away. He barely had time to worry before her face, brimming with happiness, chased the worry away so fast it made his head spin. Dr. Gibbs came trotting right after her, but stood back beaming as Susannah threw her arms around his neck. He hugged her back, lifting her off the ground, and then set her down to kiss her. After all, almost everyone in town must know by now, or very soon would, that they were to be married.

When he finally let her go, she only moved far enough away to take his arm as he headed for home. They would tell the good news together.

Later, after Dr. Gibbs had carried Susannah's message to the boarding house that she would be away for supper, after Mama had cried and Papa had wrung Karol's hand and kissed Susannah's cheek, and Bronka had danced around them both clapping her hands and madly waving a dishcloth, they sat down to as festive a supper as they could put together on short notice. Mama's fretting about how she would have liked to do more gave way to question after question. "When will you be married? We have so much to plan, so much to do! Of course you have your lessons with Father McCarthy, Susannah, and we need to invite as many of the Elk Leg people as we'll be able to fit. If only Karol's and Bronka's cousins in Winona could come! But maybe there'd be time — your family, they aren't coming from so far, but they'll need time to get ready and to travel. They can come, can't they?"

When Susannah didn't answer right away, Karol glanced over, and then looked harder. Susannah was looking down, fidgeting in her chair and twisting her napkin. Were her parents refusing to come to the wedding?

But that would make her look sad, not . . . embarrassed? His supper felt suddenly like a lump of cold earth in his belly. "You haven't told them. Not about marrying me, or about converting, not any of it."

Tears came to her eyes, and she nodded.

He must not be angry — or at least, he must not show it. As gently as he could, he asked, "Do they know about me at all?"

She looked up at him with wide wet eyes. "Oh, yes! I told them about you from the very first, when you chased the thief and got my case back. And when I wrote about Bronka, I told them about you and what a good brother you were."

Papa spoke then, almost as sternly as if Susannah were his daughter. "You wrote about how my son was good to your luggage and to his sister. But did you write about how good he is to you, and that you plan to spend your life with him, and embrace his faith?"

* * * * *

Susannah was too ashamed even to blush. She thought she would sink through the floor in shame. Why had she not told her parents how her feelings had grown, and later, when she had promised herself to Karol? Was it because she knew they hoped that someday, somehow, she would return and marry someone like Charles?

She should run home and write to them. But she didn't want to leave Karol, so soon after disappointing him. She said, very quietly, "Might I borrow pen and paper? I'll write them right now."

The pen moved so fast across the page that some of the words were barely legible, and she had to strike them out and write them again. Whatever weight had, without her realizing it, slowed her hand in her last few letters home had now lifted.

Dear Ma and Pa,

I have something very important and wonderful to tell you. You'll see at once that it's important, and I very much hope that once you've finished reading, you'll know how wonderful it is as well. . . .

Chapter 31

SUSANNAH had been haunting the general store since she wrote to her parents about her engagement, veering unpredictably between hope and dread of their reaction. One day would find her almost confident that they would trust her judgment, and the next leave her gloomily certain that they would consider her grossly misled and in mortal moral danger.

When the letter finally arrived, she forced herself to pick it up from the counter without letting her hand tremble, but her frozen demeanor must betray her as much as any trembling would have done. She hurried out of the store and took the less traveled route back to the boarding house, creeping in the kitchen door and pathetically glad she had returned at a time when no meal preparation was in progress. She mounted the stairs with her eyes on the worn floral carpet to avoid meeting anyone's gaze. Once she reached her room, she turned the lock, stiff from lack of use, and fell more than sat on the bed, ripping the envelope open and pulling out a single close-written sheet. A glance showed only her mother's handwriting.

My dearest Susannah,

I can understand why you told us so little about the Catholic boy you met, and how you became not only friends, but more. As you say, you may not have been acknowledging your feelings even to yourself for much of that time. And of course you feared upsetting us, when it might not prove necessary. But it has turned out to be necessary, hasn't it?

I'm not sure where to turn for advice. I could ask the minister to tell me more about what Catholics believe, if he knows. I would probably feel compelled to explain my sudden curiosity. Would you object to his knowing what you contemplate?

Oh, my dear, we are deeply concerned. If only you were not so far away, from us and all those here who care about you! I can only urge you to remember your upbringing and your values, and guard against letting the emotions and excitements of the moment lead you to such a drastic change in your life, with consequences I tremble to imagine.

Your loving mother

Susannah dropped the letter on the bed as if it had burned her, and then hugged herself in a futile attempt to combat the chills sweeping through her body. If only she had some hot tea, this minute — or Karol's warm arms around her!

Karol knew she'd been waiting to hear from her parents. Should she show him the letter, as discouraging as it was? What would he think if she withheld it, and then he found out? Which he would. He knew she had written. He, too, would have been waiting for the reply, even if he had not added to her worries by sharing his own.

The two of them were still working out their customs as a couple. The first day after their engagement, they had agreed she would linger after school until Karol could come join her. They had gone to the general store together, only to find it closed for the day. The next day, she had stopped by the store first and gone to the mill to greet him when he got off work — only to regret it when the miller's younger son called out flirtatious remarks, Karol glowering at him in response. She had been late for supper at the boarding house both days. Now, they sometimes met briefly before the supper hour, and sometimes went for a walk after it.

Today was one of the former days. She had spent enough time rereading the letter, and fretting over it, that she had lost track of time when Miss Wheeler knocked on the door. "Your young man is here. Also, it's almost suppertime."

Susannah grabbed the letter, thrust it deep in her skirt pocket, and followed Miss Wheeler down the stairs, parting from her to head into the sitting room. Karol had been sitting in the largest armchair and sprang up with a smile, holding out his hands to her. But in the seconds it took for her to reach him and take his hands, he had already read her mood, and gathered her close for a gentle embrace before escorting her to a chair near his. As soon as she'd settled there, he sat back down, hands between his knees, and asked, "What troubles you, *kochanie*?"

Susannah fished the letter, now slightly crumpled, out of her pocket and handed it to him. "I got this today."

Karol ran his eyes down it, almost too quickly to have actually read it, and looked up with his brow furrowed. "Why is it your mother who writes, and not your father? It is his place, surely, to give his consent to the marriage or to forbid it?"

Out of some self-protective instinct, it had not even occurred to Susannah that her parents might order her not to marry Karol. Perhaps it was that same instinct that had kept her, in her letter, from actually asking for their permission. She had been assuming Pa was angry enough that Ma had maneuvered to write instead. But if so, wouldn't he have forbidden her to marry Karol, even though she hadn't asked him whether she might?

Karol looked up from staring at his hands, with an

air of decision. "I will write to him now, if you give me the address. I will ask for his blessing. And I will explain to him my prospects, and my love for you, and how well I intend to take care of you."

Karol writing to Pa might help, and it was unlikely to make things worse. "I'll give you the address. And I'll write again, answering my mother at least." She would need more time to decide whether to address her father as well.

They had left the door open, of course, and now Miss Wheeler appeared in the doorway, holding up her pocket watch. Karol sighed and got up, giving Susannah his hand as polite if unnecessary assistance for her to do the same. Or maybe he just knew how much she needed to feel his hand clasp hers.

Susannah fully intended to answer her mother's letter after supper. But somehow, she found herself working on a lesson plan until she was too sleepy to concentrate on either that task or any other.

She stopped by the general store the next day, even though she had no particular reason to expect mail. To her surprise, there were three letters waiting for her. There was just enough time, if she didn't stand about looking at the addresses, for her to return to her room before supper and read them. She did not think she could greet Karol and give him proper attention while the knowledge of these letters burned in the back of her mind.

She walked to the boarding house as fast as she could without attracting attention, or perhaps a little faster, and hurried upstairs without stopping for greetings, let alone conversation. As soon as she reached her room, she closed and locked the door and spread the letters out on her dressing table.

One from her minister back in St. Louis. One from

Charles Elliott. And one from —

The nerve of the man! The unmitigated gall! The return address, so ornate as to be almost illegible, began with *Samuel Brecker, President, William Simmons Normal School, St. Louis, MO*. She shoved it away from her and picked up the letter from Charles.

My dear Miss Shepard,

I have no right to wish you had confided in me as to the relationship that was developing between you and the Catholic boy. If I had been less cautious, and had made my feelings known to you earlier, I might have been able to prevent this misfortune .
. . .

It was a reasonably delicate way to say that if he had proposed to her before she left, she wouldn't have left at all. Or would at least have been secure from forming any other attachments. Of course he would assume as much. Refined and courteous as his manners had always been, she had never assumed him to lack self-assurance.

And he might be right to think she would have come at his call, knowing so little of the deeper feelings she could have for another.

I have not wanted to believe the rumors in town since you left, that you had a nature too passionate for virtue and decorum. Indeed, I do not believe it, even now. But I am at a loss, otherwise, to explain what can have driven you to abandon your principles and upbringing.

If you repent of this course, and if you return home, I and all those who care about you will gladly forget this interlude . . .
.

It was a generous offer, if an impossible one. And because it was both generous and impossible, because she had grown beyond the girl whom Charles had charmed and impressed. the girl whose dreams this letter would have crushed had she still existed, Susannah paid that girl the tribute of a few tears before she laid the letter gently aside, patted her cheeks with her handkerchief, and looked at the other two.

She picked up the envelope with Brecker's address and ripped open the envelope, destroying it, quite intentionally, in the process. The scoundrel's letter began just as Charles Elliott's had.

My dear Miss Shepard,

I hope that appellation remains correct, and that you have not taken the disastrous step which Reverend Homell informs me you are contemplating.

I expect that your shocking intentions are the result of the shame you must feel at your highly inappropriate conduct in our last meeting —

Susannah crumpled the paper in her hand and relieved her feelings with a word she had never before allowed to leave her lips. Had the man absolutely no shame? Or had he managed to delude himself into believing his own slanders?

She started to spread the letter flat enough to finish reading it, then tossed it in the wastepaper basket. She forced herself to take three deep breaths before she opened the letter from Reverend Homell.

Dear Susannah,

I address you by your Christian name because I regard myself, still, as your spiritual guide, and because I remember you as an earnest, wide-eyed little girl, eager to learn the tenets and requirements of her faith, and yet awed by that responsibility.

Susannah remembered that little girl. And in a way, she felt more like that child than she had in many years, as she contemplated learning what Karol's faith would require of her.

I fear you have not sufficiently comprehended what you would be undertaking, and to what you would be committing yourself, should you put yourself under the authority of the Pope and his bishops. I grieve, as others will, at the prospect that you will leave the brotherhood and sisterhood of those who have accepted the burden and blessing of facing our Lord without intermediaries.

How interesting, that he and the priest saw Catholicism in much the same light, at least in part.

I know you are not, as a few malicious tongues would have it, given to such unruly passions as to overwhelm your intelligence and moral sense. I know you must have thought deeply about this intention . . .

Was she crying again already? But she had not expected this gift of trust and understanding, and it shook her as criticism might not have done.

. . . However, we fallen creatures all struggle with the influence of passions, and I believe you would agree that you would not have contemplated such a step had you and the young man not developed strong feelings for each other. I urge you to give the matter yet more sober thought, and to consult any minister available to you.

Which she had already done.

Please know, however you proceed, that I will keep you in my prayers, and will always wish the best for you. Please feel free to write to me, now and in the future.

Sincerely, Reverend Homell

Susannah carefully folded up the letter and put it back in its envelope. She might show it to Karol someday, when he knew beyond question that she had stayed true to her course.

The next day, after supper, Susannah read her mother's letter again, started to read it one more time, realized she was stalling, and took up pen and paper for her reply.

Dear Ma and Pa,

I'm not sure how to ease your fears. In your position, and before I met Carl and his family and community, I would have been startled and worried if a friend of mine had followed a similar course.

Please know I appreciate that you raised me well, and provided me with an excellent education, however unfortunate its conclusion. I am studious by nature, or I would not have chosen a teaching career or done well in my training for it. I promise you, I have not abandoned my lifelong habits of mind. Nor have I been swept off my feet, all in a rush.

She had used the name Carl in her letter, to avoid having to explain how that Karol was a perfectly good name for a man. But now it felt almost dishonest to do so.

I met Carl — whose name in Polish is actually Karol — almost the moment I stepped off the train, as I told you in my first letter from Cowbird Creek. From that good beginning, we have moved, over much time, through misunderstanding and acrimony, to friendship and mutual respect, to the tender attachment we now share. I have never known a man of my generation who so combines goodness of heart, natural nobility, industry, determination, humility, generosity, and consideration.

I hope I never find myself in Ruth's position, deciding after her husband's death whether to continue to cleave to his people. But I believe there is a lesson in the Book of Ruth beyond that context: that we should not enter into a marriage without the type and degree of devotion that she demonstrated even after her marriage ended. It would, to be sure, be easier to marry someone within my prior experience and social circle, but I believe coming to know and love Karol has given me a deeper understanding of what marriage should mean.

I would be very happy, and humbly grateful, were you to accept Karol as your son, to the point of traveling here to witness and take part in our wedding. And while that possibility exists, I will be patient, waiting for you to reflect on a situation so unlike what you must have hoped and expected for my future. I hope you will come to believe, as I do, that my future lies with Karol, and that he may safely be entrusted with it; and that the change in religious affiliation that accompanies my choice will leave me still

your devoted and loving daughter,

Susannah

She put down the pen with a hand that trembled, letting a drop of ink fall next to her signature. Forcing her hand steady, she put the pen back in the inkwell and leaned back in the chair. It was early yet, by her usual standards, but she had no strength left for work or even reading. She changed into her nightdress, said the shortest of the prayers Father McCarthy had taught her, and slipped into bed.

* * * * *

Karol had always thought himself able to write English as well as he needed to. But until now, what had he needed to write in English? Not much, and not often. Receipts, when a mill customer wanted one and the owner and clerk were somewhere else. Reminders for himself, if he thought of something new to carve later, and chose to write in English to keep in practice.

And now he had to write the most important letter of his life, and it must be clear, with no clumsy errors in words or spelling.

Dear Mr. Shepard,

I write to introduce myself to you, as I should have done before and wish I could do in person. And to ask your blessing for me and your daughter. I must tell you how I very much love and respect her.

There was no point in asking his permission to marry Susannah unless he would give up marrying her without it. And that he would not do, not unless she wished it.

I have good prospects with a maker of fine furniture. I have much skill at carving.

He disliked boasting, but this was no time for false modesty.

And we can build a room onto my family house. Susannah will not be lonely when only one of us is working. My family is already fond of Susannah and waits to welcome her.

Mr. Shepard might be too proud to be pleased at the thought of that welcome. But could a proud, arrogant father have raised Susannah?

Now he needed to face the biggest obstacle, the reason even a kind and loving father might object to this marriage.

Susannah has told me her family worries about her accepting my family's faith, and that was no surprise. I can only tell you Susannah made this decision after much thought. She asked our priest many questions, and he was happy to answer them.

And what a relief it had been, that the priest would answer her questions, and that those answers let her see her way clear to becoming Catholic. Because if not . . . .

If his answers had not satisfied her, I would never have forced her to change her religion.

Meaning what? What would he have done? What would he have been willing to do, rather than lose her? He didn't know. He couldn't know, without that hard choice actually before him.

I would have let her go, if I was not willing to give up my religion to be with her. I am very grateful to her that she did not ask that of me. I will be thanking her for that, all our lives.

But I know it must be hard for her. And it will be very much harder if you cannot give us your blessing. So I ask again that you do so, if you can bring yourself to it. And I will be, if you allow,

Your loving son, Karol (also called Carl)

Karol realized that at some point while he was writing, he had started holding his breath. He gasped for air, took a few deep breaths, and read the letter over. He could see no mistakes, and while he could have put this or that differently, any changes weren't likely to improve what he'd written.

He let the ink dry, folded the letter up, and laid it aside to give Susannah for mailing. She could read it if she chose, or not. He had done what he could.

Chapter 32

THIS time, when Camelia invited Susannah to tea, she made a point of saying that she was inviting no one else. As she awaited the appointed day, Susannah came up with a few different explanations. By the time she knocked on Camelia's door, her already jangled nerves were further frayed from the suspense.

Her hostess kept to unimportant subjects as they sipped their tea and ate fruit tarts and crumpets with blackberry preserves. Only when their plates bore nothing but crumbs did Camelia lean forward and say, in a more cautious tone than typical for her, "My dear, I've been wondering whether, as a widow, I might have a useful perspective to share with you. I don't know how much you and your mother discussed the nature of marriage, and how best to get on in one. But I hope you'll consider me as a local mother substitute, and might even find it easier to ask me any questions you have."

Susannah had given up hope of being able to ask such questions. She set down her empty teacup and said, hesitant, "I would like that very much, if . . . if . . . ." Why was she unable to explain her hesitation? Indeed, why was she hesitating?

Because she felt as if President Brecker had somehow tainted her, with his wandering hands, with his lust. Or that she had somehow brought his attentions upon herself, been too free in her manner or too careless in her dress, for so respected a man to so forget himself.

Still, Karol had not seemed to think anything of the kind. That recollection comforted her enough to let her move forward, though she began with something less fraught. "My mother did tell me something of what goes on between men and women, but what I could not quite gather, from her description, is whether women sometimes enjoy it — not for the satisfaction of duty, or from looking forward to children, but for its own sake, as men do."

Camelia's eyes had a faraway look as she replied, "Oh, what memories you recall for me . . . ." She came back to herself and said emphatically, "Yes, women can — and should, in my opinion! — enjoy marital relations. I would go so far as to say that after the first time, which is likely to involve some brief discomfort, if a husband's lovemaking leaves a woman cold or even repels her, he must be a bumbler, or ignorant, or inconsiderate, or all three. And if that isn't shocking enough, I'll tell you my guess that once Carl — excuse me, Karol, of course! — learns what he's about, which men aren't born knowing, he'll be none of those."

A phrase Freida Blum had uttered at dinner, weeks before, popped into Susannah's head: *From your mouth to God's ear.* Camelia's daring inspired her own. "Are there any . . . *techniques* you could share with me that a man, that Karol, would find particularly pleasing?"

"Hmmm." Camelia pursed her lips and fingered her chin. "I can think of a couple right off, but as for whether they'd shock that tender virgin you're planning to marry . . . . Let me just give you a general hint. The body parts you'll both be using are very sensitive, and if handled carefully, can give quite intense pleasure. And you should not confine your experiments to simple touching." She studied Susannah's face, which no doubt looked puzzled, and twitched an eyebrow. "I see that's too vague, so let me explain. You like it when Karol kisses you? On the lips?"

Susannah nodded fervently.

"Well, then. Once you and Karol are a little used to each other, and not wanting to hide under the covers, you might see where else the idea of kissing, or of touching with the lips, takes you."

Susannah had neither eaten nor drunk anything in at least five minutes, but she brought her napkin up to her face as if patting it dry, hoping it hid her blush. Camelia's sly smile made plain how little the ploy had succeeded as she went on, "What other questions do you have? Not that this is the only chance you'll have to ask me."

It felt so good to let Camelia tease her, give her hope and comfort. But she must not leave that one question unasked. "If a man — not Karol, and no one here, but before — took liberties and tried to take more, seemed to expect more . . . . If you heard of such a thing, and the man was regarded by all who knew him as a gentleman, what would you think of the lady?"

Camelia thumped her fists on the table, and her eyes flashed. "I would think it highly likely that many a woman had had the misfortune to know him better, and to learn he was no gentleman. I would think the lady in question was only the latest to encounter a well-respected scoundrel. And if she walloped him across the face, I would applaud her — but no matter what she did, whether she resisted or whether she was too bewildered or too much overpowered to do so, I would think her my sister in all but blood, and do what I could for her."

Susannah had not expected, and certainly had not wanted, to cry. Up came the napkin again, but not, this time, for concealment. And to her relief, at this moment she felt no need to hide her face, not from this kind counselor and defender.

Camelia came over and put an arm around her shoulder, held her tight, and then bustled away to make more tea, calling out as she went, "After that, we need sustenance! More crumpets, at once! and cake!"

A week passed, all too slowly, before Susannah received another letter from her parents. Karol had shown her his letter to them before sending it. She could only hope her parents, reading it with much different eyes than her own, would be softened by it, and at least partially reassured. She had tried not to think too much or too often about how they would reply.

And now that she held their latest letter in her hands, she was afraid to read it.

She made herself march steadily up the stairs to her room, close the door firmly, sit down at her dressing table, and open the letter . . . and finally, read it, without opening the window in search of a breeze, or checking her hair in the mirror, or any of the other ways she could put off the moment of revelation.

Like the last, it began with her mother's handwriting.

My darling girl,
My heart is full of both hopes and cares. I know little of the creed you will need to embrace, but I do know what a fine, honorable woman you have become, and I am glad and proud to see it.

Susannah took a deep breath and pulled her handkerchief out of her pocket, balling it up in one hand. She was going to need it.

Your young man has written to us, and we are impressed with his mode of expression and with his devotion to you. I will pray daily that Carl, or Karol, is worthy of your trust, and of any sacrifices that marrying him will entail, and that you will enjoy all the happiness you deserve. We could not, in the end, attempt to stand in the way of you pursuing the path you have chosen after such thoughtful consideration.

I look forward with all my heart to seeing you again, to embracing you and being present on your wedding day.

All my love, Your Mother

Then, written underneath, came a longer passage from her father. The first words made the hand holding the letter start shaking. She dabbed her eyes with the handkerchief, put the letter on the table, and kept reading.

My little shining star,

Of course we will come west, to meet the man who intends to claim you and to see you married. Your intended wrote and asked my blessing, but I doubt he would have given you up if I'd refused it. He writes a good letter, and not as some smooth-talking cheat might do. I could not help concluding that he is sincere, and will do his utmost to provide for you and make you happy. I will still subject him to a rigorous inspection, but I know I would not be able to break your heart by interfering. You must know that as well, from all the years of bending me to your desires.

Susannah smiled fondly, remembering a few of those moments, times she ardently desired a stick of candy or a ride on his back – and later, when she set her heart on attending the normal school. Not that he had been such an overindulgent father as he now painted himself.

I naturally expected you to marry within the faith in which you were reared — but I also raised you to be open to new ideas, to learn the facts for yourself and reach your own conclusions. If what I have taught you has taken you in a direction I had never imagined, it is rather too late to wish I had tried to make you conventional or narrow-minded.

If only she could run to him, this minute and embrace him, and tell him how grateful she would always be for how he had raised her, how much he had taught her!

Every father, I believe, goes through much the same thing when his little girl comes to him (in person or on paper), her heart in her eyes (or her lines), to tell him that she has found the man who will take the first place in her heart. We struggle between what we know is right and the selfish desires of our own hearts. It is right and proper for a girl to leave her parents' home to make her own, to have her own family, to take on the cares and fears and, above all, the joys of having her own children. But it is hard, so hard, to let go and watch your own daughter walk away, even if she has gone far away already. . . .

And now, all she could do was turn away so her tears, flowing too fast for her handkerchief to catch them all, would pose no danger to those precious words. She would read the last lines later, and read the whole again, and then, as soon as she could, show it to Karol so he could share in her relief, and respect and admire her parents as they deserved.

Chapter 33

THE TIME had come, Father McCarthy had told her, to make her first confession. She could remain after services, if it wouldn't interfere with her ride back to Cowbird Creek, or he could come to the Marek home, as he'd been doing for her lessons.

She should use the same confessional as the rest of the congregation. It was childish to let the memory of her nightmare give her pause. But the priest would be coming back to Cowbird Creek in any event, for one final lesson. Embarrassed but grateful, she asked to make her confession then.

The closer she came to the crucial moment, the more nervous she became. Even though forgetting to confess a mortal sin was apparently not a separate mortal sin, there would still be the first one, lurking in her soul and making mischief. But examining her conduct, her thoughts, her feelings as honestly as she could, she could find no mortal sin among them. Unless she had told a lie, at some time? She must have told half-truths, at least. She must make sure to confess the fact.

That left the other kind, the venial sins. One leapt all too easily to mind: trying to control outcomes, rather than trusting in God's will. Vanity, too, as to intellect if not as to her face and form. Pride — that would be a mortal sin if she encouraged the feeling, but it crept into her soul without her knowing . . . moments of wrath, again unwelcome, when a pupil persisted in misbehavior, or worse, simply proved unable to understand or make progress . . . and there was the sin Father McCarthy had mentioned, with his usual acute insight: embarrassment at being Catholic. . . .

She would ask the priest, during their lesson, to suggest some more.

"An interesting request. Which hardly surprises me." Father McCarthy smiled in apparent approval. "Let me ask you: have you been putting Karol first in your heart, before God?"

Susannah found herself wanting to say, at the same time, "Of course not!" and "Of course!" The way Karol filled her thoughts might be a manifestation of original sin, or a dangerous habit. But her spirit rose up against that notion. She looked the priest in the eye, hoping he would not read her expression as disrespectful, and asked, "I may be misremembering, but isn't it nuns who become the bride of Christ when they take their vows?"

The priest cocked his head. "There are some who view them in that light, though it's more often the Church as a whole that we speak of as Christ's bride."

Susannah bit her lip and forged ahead. "I'm not becoming a nun, and it's Karol whose bride I'll be. Must it be a sin to keep some place in my heart for my husband, a place in which he comes first of all?"

The priest leaned forward and lowered his eyebrows, and she feared she had angered him — until he relaxed and chuckled. "Ah, Susannah, I should deal with converts more often, to keep my wits lively. Let us postpone further debate on the topic until a future time. For now, I will not require you to treat your feelings for young Karol as requiring penitence and forgiveness." He paused, his face returning to sobriety. "Are you ready, my child?"

Susannah's breath came short. "I think so. I . . . won't become more ready by waiting. How do we proceed, with no confessional?"

"I gave that some thought on my way here." Father McCarthy looked around the spare room in which they held their lessons. "I believe it will suit if we face our chairs in opposite directions, and put them a foot apart. You can speak softly and yet I'll hear you. And we'll close the door almost all the way."

Not all the way. The spectre of her nightmare moved closer and receded again. She got up and moved her chair while the priest moved his, then sat back down while he carefully leaned the door so that it just touched the jamb. She closed her eyes and listened to his footfalls, and then the creak of his chair. She took a deep breath just as he said gently, "You may begin."

She was really going to do this. She took another breath, shakier than the first, and said, "Bless me, Father, for I have sinned . . . ."

"And now for your penance, my child. You will give service to a neighbor — or rather, a neighbor of mine, a widow who would very much like to learn to read so she can send and receive letters from her son out west. I will arrange a way for you to meet with her and teach her."

Susannah bowed her head. It felt wrong to receive a penance so much to her taste, but then it might be more difficult to teach an old woman, even a willing one. "Yes, Father."

And now it was time for her Act of Contrition. She had written it down when Father McCarthy first taught it to her, and rehearsed it every day of the last week in order to get it right.

It was easy to say and mean, "O My God, I am heartily sorry for having offended Thee." And she did detest her sins, or at least, sincerely regret them. Indeed, she would rather not claim to detest them because she dreaded the pains of hell — as if she had no more moral reason and only feared punishment, like a child afraid of a whipping. Perhaps some day, she would be so bold as to ask the priest about some change in the words. But not today. She had tried the good father's patience enough. And the prayer did go on to say that after all, she cared more about offending God, who deserved from her so much better.

She finished with the solemn resolve to amend her life, and hoped the priest could hear her sincerity.

All this time, they had been facing away from each other. But now the priest stood up and carried his chair so that it faced hers. He took his seat again and said slowly, emphasizing every word, "God, the Father of mercies through the death and resurrection of his Son has reconciled the world to himself and sent the Holy Spirit among us for the forgiveness of sins; through the ministry of the Church may God give you pardon and peace, and I absolve you from your sins in the name of the Father, and of the Son, and of the Holy Spirit."

Did she truly believe, as yet, that another human being could relieve her soul of the burden of sin? Whatever she believed, she felt lighter, and as if the light slanting through the window made its way into her soul with less to hinder it. She breathed a great sigh of relief, rose, and escorted Father McCarthy to the door. He opened it, gave her another almost paternal smile, and left.

Susannah stood in the doorway, looking down the

narrow hallway. It was at most half a minute before Karol came looking for her, the anticipation in his face only lightly touched with concern. She looked up at him, and saw the happiness within her reflected in his eyes as he took her in his warm strong arms.

Susannah saw little of Karol over the next few days, as he and his father cleared the land behind the family home and moved the chicken coop out of the way. Where brush and weeds and wildflowers had grown, there was now bare yellow-brown earth, land from which their rooms would grow instead.

Now, as the rays of the sun stretched long and red across the cleared space, the two of them stood side by side, arms around each other's waists, and dreamed.

Karol took a deep breath of the earth-scented air, and she could feel his chest expand. She closed her eyes to relish the feeling, then opened them in time to see him point east and say, "Our window could face this way. Some of the year, the morning sun might wake us."

Susannah leaned her head against his shoulder. "I like to wake to sunlight. Though I imagine your mother will often be up and about before us, and we'll hear her in the kitchen."

"We may. But see this space here, between our bedroom and the rest of the house? It will be a place to store things, until we can afford to make it a bathroom with plumbing, hot and cold. And next to it, a little room . . ." He turned toward her whispered the rest. "For babies."

An increasingly familiar thrill rippled up and down Susannah's spine as Karol added, "So we will not be so very close to the rest of the family."

She pulled away enough to look at Karol's face. "But I don't want them to think I seek to keep my distance from them, after they've welcomed me so warmly."

Karol turned fully toward her and took her hands. "We will be close enough. But maybe not so close that we hear every sound the others make . . . and they hear every sound that we make."

It was heat, not chill, running through her. The feeling was definitely heat, and it was spreading throughout her body. And then Karol had pulled her up against him, and they were kissing, more passionately than ever before. And still it was not enough.

But it would have to be enough. She drew back, laid her cheek against his chest, and murmured, "Remember we have confession this Sunday."

His laughter shook his chest.

* * * * *

Karol and his father had decided to build the new rooms onto the house before the wedding — or at least, to get as far along as they could. Mr. McIntyre had confirmed Karol's future in the furniture business, so he could leave the mill and have the days to work, with Papa helping on fair evenings while the light held.

It should be easy enough, quitting his job. He should have done it weeks ago, and given proper notice. But he'd best not wait any longer, or he'd feel like a coward — more of one — for putting it off.

He lingered after work the next day, hoping Susannah wouldn't worry at his showing up later than usual at the boarding house. Mama and Bronka, at least, knew what kept him. It didn't help that the general store manager had stopped by near closing time to pick up his flour and was in a chatty mood. Karol waited as long as he could stand to, and then walked up and cleared his throat. "I'm sorry to interrupt, gentlemen, but there's something I need to discuss with Mr. Grint."

The manager narrowed his eyes and muttered something, but the miller actually smiled and said to the manager, "I'll be seeing what's on this young fellow's mind, then. Always glad to see you, and grateful for your custom. Carl, you take a seat in my office while I see this gentleman off."

In about five minutes, just long enough for Karol to wish he had something in his pocket to carve on, the miller ambled in and plopped down in his large and sturdy chair. Karol stood up, too nervous to stay sitting even if the miller might not mind. He forced himself not to pace, but faced the miller and said straight out, "Sir, I'll be needing to quit."

"Yes, yes, I know all about that. Running out on me to go do Lord knows what with furniture or some such. Thought you'd be giving notice before now, in fact."

He had nothing much to say to that, given how embarrassing it would be to admit he'd had no good reason. "I'm sorry, sir. I'll . . . I'll understand if you don't see fit to give me my final pay, with my leaving you short-handed like this."

The miller glared at him — though it looked like how a villain in a play might glare, more than an everyday expression you'd expect to see across the room. "I'd understand it too, and I've got every right to do just that. Running out on me with no notice." Then, to Karol's amazement, he leaned back in his chair and laughed. "I'll bet you think I was never your age, or if I was, I don't remember a thing about it. You just ask Mrs. Grint if I was ever chompin' at the bit. Sure, I've kept you busy while you was here, and I'm sorry to lose a good worker, but I've got a farm lad ready and eager to learn your job once you let go of it. So off with you, and good luck to you." He opened a desk drawer and fished out an envelope full of bills, fatter than usual. "And you'll find a little something extra. A wedding present. Buy that pretty gal of yours something nice. A new dress, maybe."

In the state Karol was in, thinking about Susannah in a dress led quickly to him thinking about taking the dress off her, just as a start . . . but he pulled himself together to say thank you, twice. He was wondering whether to offer his hand when the miller put out his own. They shook hands, and he left the mill, possibly forever, and walked home as fast as he could without running. He had building to do.

Chapter 34

KAROL and his father had worked as fast as they could without carelessness, getting the floor more than halfway laid and trimming planks for the walls, but time was growing short. If they were to finish the rooms before the wedding, they needed help.

And help had been promised. Mr. McIntyre had said he would bring some of the Catholics who lived in Elk Leg, on the next day with no rain in the offing, and might himself help raise and fasten the walls and beams. How many men would come depended on who was willing, and — for those who worked for others — who could leave work with several hours of daylight left. Between those men and Papa and himself, they might hope — or at least, try — to get the rooms enclosed before dark. And if not . . . then they would have to try again another day, though likely fewer would come a second time.

Mama and Bronka and Susannah had made what had seemed like an endless supply of lemonade and haymaker's punch. Now they brought the first pitchers out to the table next to the piles of lumber and nails and slate, before going back to the kitchen to make sandwiches for the first pause in the work.

Karol was listening for the wagon when he heard, coming from the center of town, the tramp of feet and the sound of men's voices. As the sounds came closer and grew louder, Susannah and Bronka ran out and stood

beside him, craning to see. When Mr. Grint and his sons
turned the corner and marched toward them, followed by
six other men from town and a passel of boys, Protestants
all, Bronka started jumping up and down. Karol could feel
Susannah trembling at his side.

Karol met them in the street and shook every one of
them by the hand, even the youngest boys, before leading
them behind the house where the work waited. One of the
men assigned the older boys to the job of fetching parts and
tools for the builders. The younger boys grumbled, and a
few slumped homeward, but the rest lingered to watch.

Before nightfall, the new floors stretched out to cover
all the ground Karol and his father had cleared, and the
new walls stretched up to meet the timbers of the new roof.
All that remained was the roof itself. As the workers
wolfed down refreshments and Karol stammered his
thanks, the miller clapped him on the back and said,
"When d'you want us back for the roof? Better hurry — my
brother's back says rain's coming." The miller picked up
another sandwich, bit, chewed, and then added, "Come to
think of it, we should get a tarp tacked on before we leave.
Back to work, boys!"

When all those from Cowbird Creek had left, and Mr.
McIntyre's wagons had rumbled away, Karol and
Susannah and his family gathered at the kitchen table.
They bowed their heads, and Papa led them in a prayer of
thanksgiving. Karol hadn't seen Mama cry since their first
month in this new country, but now she did, and smiled
through her tears.

Five days later, their house, made new for their new
and larger family, stood complete. And when it rained the

next day, he and Susannah stood under their own roof, dry, listening to the rain on the slate roof, watching raindrops run down their own window.

Next Sunday was their wedding day.

* * * * *

Thursday, just before dinner hour, Susannah called the class to attention and dismissed them early. She had received a telegram the evening before saying her parents would be arriving Thursday afternoon. "And tomorrow and the next day, I will be busy catching up with my parents and preparing for my wedding — "

The cheer that interrupted her was so good-natured that she couldn't force herself to reprimand them. There were, she saw, a few of the children, not only the youngest, who didn't join in it, looking glumly at her or at their desks. She made haste to go on. "And then taking the next day to rest from all the excitement, so Mrs. Grant, the librarian, will be here in my stead. But I will be here Tuesday morning as usual, and I hope to see signs that you spent some of this holiday on your studies."

The girl next to Bronka stood up and, when Susannah nodded to her, said doubtfully, with a glance at her neighbor, "You're really coming back? Your husband'll let you?"

Susannah reined in her temper and said, "Yes, of course. My husband understands that I love teaching. And for now, nothing else stands in the way of my doing so." One of the oldest boys poked his deskmate with an elbow and said something Susannah could almost hear. His deskmate, who could, promptly turned and gave him such a glare that he subsided.

"You may eat your dinners here, or carry them home with you. And I will see you all here Tuesday morning. Class dismissed."

To her surprise, the only children to stand were Alice and, at a fiercely whispered reminder, the small boy sitting opposite her. Alice led the way as the two walked up to Susannah, each holding something behind his or her back. Alice, first again, whipped out a rolled piece of cloth and handed it to Susannah, face bright with expectation. "It's from the girls. We took turns working on it at dinner time, or taking it home."

Susannah swallowed the lump in her throat and said, "Thank you, all of you. Shall I look at it now?"

A chorus of "yes!" and "please!" arose from around the room. Susannah held up the scroll and unrolled it downward, revealing a sampler in mixed embroidery styles, some crude, some more expert than Susannah could have produced. The text, surrounded by flowers on all sides and wedding bells in the corners, read, *Congratulations to the best teacher, who will be the best bride.* Susannah wished she could be as confident.

The boy, without further prompting, pulled out what had once been a segment of a log. It had been flattened on one side for a base, and on top was a sculpture that, with a little squinting, she could tell was meant to represent the classroom, complete with desks, pupils sitting at them, and Susannah standing and holding a book.

Susannah made a point of turning it this way and that to admire all the details. She set it down on her desk and said, "And thank you, boys, for such a lovely keepsake. My husband-to-be makes wood carvings, and he'll especially appreciate it."

One of the older boys scuffed his foot on the ground.

"Likely he won't think much of it, then."

Susannah made haste to reply, "On the contrary! He'll know just how much work was involved."

The boy who had brought her the sculpture said earnestly, "It's so you don't forget us, when you end up quitting after all."

She would not, just now, think about the future, nor wonder how far along in it the prediction would come true. "Many thanks again to all of you. You may go — and I *will* see you Tuesday morning."

She found it difficult to maintain a ladylike pace as she headed to the station. After all this time, she would finally see her parents!

They were coming without her brother, who was staying behind to run the paper. She would miss him more than ever on her wedding day, but it was a profound relief to know him so responsible. When the moment was right, she would reassure her parents that Karol's work would provide enough income that she could continue sending money home, even after she had to stop teaching. But that could wait.

Standing near the railway ticket office awaiting the train, Susannah pulled out her parents' letter to stave off her impatience. This time, she skipped through to her father's final words.

. . . *But it is a father's solemn duty, and at least in part a joyful one, to step aside once she finds that man. And as a father who cherishes one son and looks forward to a heavenly reunion with another, I will gladly make room in my heart for the son I will soon be able to call mine.*

God bless you and keep you, my beloved daughter, and know me always

Your Loving Pa

Susannah folded the letter with shaking hands and

fled into the necessary. She was still there when she heard the shriek and whistle of the approaching train. She wiped her eyes and her face and hurried out to meet it.

*****

Karol had told Susannah he would leave her to greet her parents without him, so as not to intrude on their reunion. But he would have to include in his next confession that this was partly a lie. When he imagined what they might be going through, and what they might think of him, he quailed at the thought of meeting them — especially Susannah's father. Stalling wouldn't make the meeting any easier, but at least it would be later . . . .

They were staying at Camelia's, because she had plenty of room and because she wouldn't take "no" for an answer. So once Karol heard the whistle of the train that was bringing the Shepards, he left the house, with his mother's and Bronka's encouraging words ringing in his ears, and walked to Camelia's, wanting to drag slowly along and walking quickly instead.

Camelia threw the door open wide as he marched up her front steps. "It's Karol! Come in!" she called out, and then whispered to him, "They're lovely people, and they won't eat you up, I promise." He forced what was probably a sickly smile and followed her to her drawing room. An older man with brown eyes, Susannah's black hair, and a bushy beard stood up as they entered, while an elegant woman of similar years, with light brown hair going gray, remained seated but turned in his direction.

Susannah jumped out of her chair and hurried to his side. Grabbing his arm and turning him to face her parents, she announced, "Ma, Pa, I'm pleased and proud to introduce my fiancé Karol Marek."

Her father put out a hand to shake his. "I'm very glad to meet you, Mr. Marek." Karol studied the older man's face, trying to see how much the man meant what he said, and was left unsure.

Susannah's mother now stood and walked right up to him. "Yes, so very glad! I hope you'll indulge me in welcoming you to our family as a son." She faltered and caught her breath before opening her arms for a hug. He moved closer to allow it, and her thin arms held him tight before she let go and moved back toward her chair.

Camelia bustled up and said cheerfully, "I was just about to bring in some tea. Sit yourself down!"

"I thank you," said Mr. Shepard, "but if it wouldn't keep you waiting too long, I thought I'd step out back for a smoke. Come with me, Mr. Marek? I've a cigar for you as well." His expression made plain enough that Karol would do well to accept. He had barely taken off his hat, but he put it back on and followed the man outside.

Camelia had a sturdy wooden bench in her back yard, and they settled on it. Mr. Shepard took out two cigars and handed him one. Karol waited for the other man to light his own before accepting a light from him. He expected questioning about his religion, and could only hope he would have good enough answers.

He had time for only one puff on the cigar before his future father-in-law said, "I knew the day would come when she'd find a man she could see herself marrying, or at least I profoundly hoped it would. But it's come sooner than I expected. Susannah — she might not want me to tell you this, but I must. My daughter has reason not to trust men too easily."

"She's told me, sir. And I pledge to you, I would rather die than betray her trust."

Mr. Shepard lowered his eyebrows. "She told you, did

she? I will have to hope that she sensed you were particularly trustworthy, rather than that she's failed to learn from her painful experience." Puff, puff. "I'm sure I needn't tell you what I'd do if it turns out she was mistaken."

"No," Karol said earnestly, "No need at all. And there are plenty of men here in town who would lay hold of me before you could arrive to do it. Your daughter has earned many friends in Cowbird Creek."

"I could see that from our welcome here today. But I knew she would. My daughter, as you've discovered, is very easy to love." Mr. Shepard stood up. Was the man biting his lip as he turned toward the door? "Let's not keep everyone waiting any longer."

* * * * *

Both Camelia and Miss Wheeler had wanted to help Susannah and her mother on the morning of the wedding. Ma had graciously asked them both to assist. They had to start before dawn to be ready before morning mass. Susannah gave private thanks that the wedding to come would, at least to some extent, distract her parents from the fact that they would be not only attending, but involved in a Catholic service.

Not knowing for certain that her parents would arrive in time, Susannah had made her own arrangements for her wedding dress — assisted by an unexpected gift. Freida Blum had sent a package of the most lovely fabric, a delicate pale green print with tiny pale pink flowers and just a few bits of white lace, along with a letter lamenting in the most dramatic terms that Freida would not be able to fit and sew the dress herself. She naturally ended on the upbeat note, *But you'll be such a beautiful bride, all I could do would be gilding the lily, at least I can imagine what you'll look like!*

Now, her mother helped ease the dress over her head, taking care not to disarrange the loops and twists of the hair style they had chosen. When she was fully dressed, she looked to Ma and Camelia for their verdict, only to see them fall into each other's arms, both sniffling. Then Ma turned to her, laughing through her tears, and said, "I'm almost afraid to hold you, so beautiful as you look!"

Susannah lunged at her mother and hugged her tight, heedless of dress and hair. They stood clasped in each other's arms for a long time. When Susannah looked up, Camelia had disappeared.

Ma took Susannah's hands, her own trembling. "Are you ready? Are you sure?"

Susannah kissed Ma's cheek and said, her voice as steady as she could make it, "I'm altogether ready. And more certain than I've ever been."

Karol had planned to pay for the livery stable buggy so they could arrive early enough for her to make her confession. But as he helped her inside and they took the road to Elk Leg, he told her that Jacob, the stable owner, had refused his money. "He says he's proud of us for not letting anyone tell us who we could marry. He would know about that, with taking Madam Mamie to wife."

Susannah had yet to actually meet the town madam, but she made up her mind then and there to do so. And the decision felt so right that she had no need, she thought, to treat it as a sin to be confessed.

They went in the side door of the church, its entrance tucked between two large buttonbush shrubs for the greater privacy of parishioners, but she could see the crowd already gathering out front. She clutched Karol's hand tighter as they went inside.

She emerged from the confessional to see Karol standing near, unusually pale and fidgeting with the lay of his best waistcoat. He almost leaped forward to take her hand, and said, "Your parents are waiting with mine in the little room just behind the sanctuary."

Susannah opened the door to see the two pairs of parents talking quietly, but could not quite hear what they were saying. All four of them turned at the sound of the door opening. Karol's mother, with her broad face and broad shoulders and her hair tightly covered in an embroidered scarf, looked nothing like her own mother, thin and well tailored. And her mother looked at something of a loss, gripping her father's hand tightly, while Bronka's mother's face shone with joy and pride. But the eyes of both mothers glimmered with tears.

Karol's father spoke solemnly. "Now for the blessing."

Bride and groom knelt side by side. Karol's parents stepped forward first, reciting something Polish in unison while his father made the sign of the cross. They stepped back, and it was her parents' turn. Karol helped Susannah to her feet, and she might not have needed the help, but she welcomed the firm grasp of his hand on her arm.

Her father spoke first. "Karol is a good man. I don't know what your future holds, where once I thought I could predict it. But I have confidence in what the two of you will make of it."

Her mother swallowed what must have been tears. "Oh, my dear daughter. You are starting on such a journey! I remember it well, how much I thought I knew, how much I still had to learn. But I will do everything I can to help you learn it, and I know Karol's mother will do the same."

One more embrace for Susannah from both her parents, a handshake from her father for Karol, her mother's kiss on Karol's cheek, hearty embraces and kisses on both Karol's cheeks from both his parents . . . and they joined hands and walked out of the room, out the side door of the church, to wait for their cue. The door had barely closed behind them when it opened again, as the priest came to fetch them. "It's time, my children. Come and see your welcome!"

The little church had seemed full on most of the previous Sundays, but today it was packed so full it could almost have burst open into the morning sunshine. Susannah and Karol would join the congregation as worshipers before they stood before it to be wed. Bronka was there waiting as Susannah's maid of honor. And there in the front row sat Joshua and Clara and Camelia. Susannah could only hope her face conveyed her gratitude for their presence and their support.

She had thought the service might seem to last forever. But it seemed mere moments later when the usual order of the mass came to an end, and the congregation, instead of rising to leave, rustled and murmured in expectation. The priest beckoned to Karol and Susannah where they sat.

As she stood before Father McCarthy, waiting to make her vows, she had a sudden fleeting thought of President Brecker. But instead of recoiling, instead of having to fight her way back to anticipation and joy, what she found in her heart was pity for how little he understood, pity and the beginning of forgiveness.

And then she was a wife. And Karol was a husband, and hers.

After all the handshakes and hugs and congratulations, it was time to go home. To their home, for the first time. Some of the women in the congregation had left early, to help Karol's mother and Bronka prepare the large festive dinner.

If the church had been crowded, the Marek main room truly overflowed, with some guests retreating into the kitchen or taking their plates outside. The guests made an interesting mixture of familiar from town, familiar (if barely) from the Elk Leg congregation, and family old and new. The social and emotional complexities would have been daunting if she had not had so potent a distraction in Karol by her side, and in thoughts of what still lay ahead.

Karol had of course pulled her veil back from her face at the church, but had whispered to her not to remove it. "You'll see why." And she had worn it all through the party, with helpful women straightening it and repinning it when it threatened to come loose. At the stroke of midnight, as if answering some unheard signal, the crowd quieted down and gathered, all who could fit, in a circle in the main room. Karol steered Susannah into the middle and then joined the others as Karol's mother and Bronka came forward, the former holding a small white cap embroidered in golden thread. Bronka, her eyes sparkling, began to pull the pins away from the veil one by one, putting them in her pocket, and then made way for her mother. Susannah's new mother-in-law, whom she had already begun to call Mama, placed the cap gently on Susannah's head, saying, "Bronka and I made this for you. Now begins your first day as my son's wife, and my daughter."

She and Bronka took Susannah's hands and turned her to face the crowd. Everyone cheered, and Bronka handed Susannah the veil, saying, "Throw it! To the single girls!" Susannah looked around to find that the young unmarried women had conveniently clustered together. She launched the veil up high, and clapped along with the crowd to see it float downward to the eager hands waiting below.

It was not far from dawn when the last of the Elk Leg guests departed. Camelia had left an hour before, one of the men from town walking her home. Susannah knew she should be exhausted, but the energy of the crowd had been carrying her. Now she could feel fatigue trying to claim her. To beat it back, she began carrying dishes to the kitchen, only to be shooed away, Mama and Bronka refusing any help from either her or Karol. Mama whispered, as she shoved her gently out of the kitchen, "Go tell your parents goodbye. And then . . . ." She winked. "Then you and my son, you figure out what to do next!"

Susannah's parents were already standing near the front door. Joshua and Clara, somehow alerted to how late the party would go, had rented the buggy to drive them back to Camelia's. Susannah bit down on her trembling lip as she walked, then ran toward them. They were not leaving town for another two days, or she would have cried outright. Pa lingered, drinking in the sight of her, shaking Karol's hand one more time, until Ma pulled him away. "It's time to get out of their way." And again, more softly: "It's their time."

Their bed had been made up with clean, soft linens.

Ma had already been in, some time during the party, to unpack Susannah's bags. There on the bed lay the nightdress Ma had embroidered. Susannah picked it up and kissed the embroidery, then turned to Karol.

He approached her slowly, as if she might be a deer to be frightened back into the woods, and reached out to touch her shoulder. "Are you afraid?"

She put a hand over his, pressing it against her, and said, "Not very much. Are you?"

He grinned suddenly. "Terrified. But for you, I can face any fears." And then, very soft, "For you, I can do anything. And I will."

She opened her arms to him, along with her heart and her life.

THE END

Author's Note

My mother Bronislawa Zarkowerovna, called Bronia (one of several common diminutives for her name) by family and friends, emigrated from Poland to Canada at the age of fifteen. A brilliant young woman, she had dreamed of being the next Marie Curie. She lived in a village called Maxymuvka, but took the train to the city of Tarnopol to attend high school and then got an apartment there with her younger sister. The mud at the train station was knee deep or more, but my grandfather carried her to keep her from having to wade through it herself.

He was a grain merchant, but was able to get out of Poland, months ahead of the Nazis, by promising to farm land in western Canada. Their destination proved to be Sundance, Alberta. Sundance had a one-room schoolhouse, with a teacher little older than Bronia. My mother spoke more English than most of the family, but that wasn't saying much. Nonplussed by the challenge of this new pupil, the teacher handed her a book of fairy tales and told her to read from it. Unimpressed with the result, she had my mother begin with the work of the first graders and go on from there. It took a year, and the humiliation of that year sank deep, but my mother's English improved substantially. She eventually finished high school elsewhere, but for a range of reasons, she did not attend college until her daughter Karen was thirteen years old.

By the way, her last name is an example of how Polish last names are inflected. Her father Lonyo's last name was Zarkower; my mother's reflected her status as his daughter. I chose not to deal with that complexity in this book, aside from mentioning it here.

The brief mention of classmate Louisa's innocence, and its apparent effect as some sort of protection, is based on my mother's sister Erika, who was very pretty and somehow sold magazines to sailors fresh off sea voyages without being harassed.

The little girl so eager to build a snowman that she constructed one mostly out of dirt was none other than Your Author.

The William Simmons normal school in St. Louis never, as far as I know, existed, though the city did have at least one other. Nor did any normal school I've discovered have a principal or president named Brecker — and if any was led by a similarly nefarious individual, I have found no historical record of the fact. However, I found it all too plausible that a man in such a position of authority might take advantage of the opportunities available to him and the power differential involved. As for Susannah's father's newspaper, I invented that as well, but St. Louis had at least three newspapers during this period (not counting special interest and foreign language papers), including the one mentioned as a rival.

The town of Elk Leg is, like Cowbird Creek, fictional, with the name inspired by the town of Elkhorn.

The school board might not have been called a school board. Some such groups bore names like "Prudential Committee" or "Superintending Committee."

Cowbird Creek's school might, like many rural schools, have started in November rather than September, with a first term running through April and a second from May through August. This custom was not universal, with school calendars varying according to the needs of the particular community — or in this case, the needs of the particular story.

There were many schoolhouse routines and activities I could have included, for verisimilitude and/or for their intrinsic interest, but for better or worse, this book is a historical romance, and I didn't think I should absolutely *drown* the romance in historical detail. The same goes for issues that might have arisen, such as, e.g., a student's being left-handed (actively and indeed brutally suppressed in many schools).

"The Vagabonds," the poem Joshua Gibbs reads to his daughter Alice early on, uses the British spelling "travellers." I modified it so as not to distract readers more used to the American spelling.

The book of Polish history from which Bronka translates a passage is Franciszek Ksawery Kluczycki's *The Vienna Expedition of 1683: A Historical Story*, published in Polish in 1883. That's cutting it a bit fine, with my story starting in 1883, but it was the only Polish book about the Second Siege of Vienna whose publication date worked and whose text I could find and translate.

Scylla and Charybdis, mentioned in Chapter 14, are featured in *The Odyssey*, a six-headed sea monster and a whirlpool respectively. Navigating between them was, to say the least, tricky.

In recounting the Marek family's Wigilia celebration (Chapter 15), I decided not to deal with one custom that would have been inconvenient. Families commonly avoided having an uneven number of guests, but four Mareks plus Susannah makes five. Rather than complicating the group dynamics by importing a Catholic guest from Elk Leg or elsewhere, I assumed that this family either didn't follow that custom or ignored it in order to host Susannah.

The blizzard that strikes Cowbird Creek in late March of 1884 (Chapter 22) is inspired by the Schoolhouse Blizzard of 1888, also called the Children's Blizzard. This tragic event is so called because hundreds of children in the Great Plains states died trying to get home. One contributing factor was unseasonably warm weather that morning, leading to many children coming to school without their winter coats. Nor were all the teachers as determined as Susannah to keep the children indoors, nor as well prepared to keep their schoolhouses at least minimally heated.

In the late 1800s, many communities, either by explicit or by unwritten rules, forbade female teachers to marry, considering the duties of a teacher to be inconsistent with the duties of a wife. This was not necessarily the universal American custom. (In mid-century Utah, at least one community searched eagerly for applicants to teaching positions, be they male or female, married or unmarried.) Nebraska's approach to married women's rights was improving at the time: legislation passed in 1881 accorded married women the rights to hold trade licenses and control their earnings. I have posited that Cowbird Creek, already established as less rigid in its outlook than some towns, would accept (if reluctantly) that the teacher who had proved herself so valuable might be able to perform both functions, and that if not, it was her future husband's lookout. With at least equal reluctance, I decided I could not, however, diverge so far from the views and customs of the time as to have Susannah continue teaching while pregnant or with young children to care for. I doubt the compromise I found will satisfy all contemporary readers, but I hope it will mollify some.

In the previous three books in this series, it did not

occur to me to include a "shivaree" — a raucous form of wedding celebration that amounted to hazing both bride and groom during their wedding night. A shivaree could range from noisemaking outside the couple's home, to demanding entrance and refreshments, to invading the home without permission and playing various pranks (such as mixing up the labels on foods), to abducting the couple and parading them through town in their nightclothes. As alarming as this custom might be in its more extreme forms, it was based on a potentially more dangerous European custom in which the community showed its disapproval of a marriage or other liaison.

So why didn't I include a scene that could have provided drama, comedy, and/or insight into Karol's and Susannah's relationship? Principally because it would have been too disruptive of the narrative flow. I thought of having the possibility of a shivaree discussed, with Susannah shocked and Karol protective, but that seemed like a compromise likely to please no one (including me), both distracting and incomplete. If you disagree, I invite you to write the scene yourself, as fan fiction, and send it to me!

I usually list in my Acknowledgments section the websites, articles, newspaper archives, et cetera that I used in my research. But this time around, I consulted so many that listing them all would make this book even longer than it is, and at least a little more expensive. I am therefore listing only the topics I researched, and only where that research made it into the book or otherwise had a significant impact (e.g., by dissuading me from including some detail or taking the plot in some direction). Here, in no particular order, and broken up for readability, are those topics:

-- the fabric used in men's shirts of the time; the earliest translations of Shakespeare into Polish; Polish and other endearments; Polish curse words; Polish family customs; Polish Christmas eve (Wigilia) customs, Polish wedding customs; Polish culture; Polish contributions to the sciences; the transition to Christianity in Poland; Polish and Irish surnames; Polish girl's and boy's names; Polish literature; Polish historians and historical works; children's literature; novels of the period; one room schoolhouse calendars; rounds people sang; craft supplies available and used; games ladies played; games played on streets; history of rock-paper-scissors; popular amusements;

-- roofing materials; availability of public benches; the history of paste and other adhesives; types of pens used; dates when immigrants came to the U.S. from various countries; the nature of Jesuit education; celebration of Boxing Day; the histories of various bookstores and book catalogs; early American use of fireworks; which carols were sung when and by whom; styles of railroad depots;

-- St. Louis history and culture; St. Louis neighborhoods, parks, and architecture; the degree to which different religious communities in St. Louis mingled; times the Mississippi River froze; jobs on steam locomotives; sounds of steam locomotives; train speeds; the history of separate bedrooms for family members; uses of door locks; the operation of mills;

-- curricula in one room schoolhouses and in elementary schools; establishment of schools in various towns in Nebraska; acceptance of girls in common schools; architecture of one room schoolhouses; blackboards and chalkboards; desks in one room schoolhouses; operation and routines of one room schoolhouses; school boards and the equivalent; history of teaching certificates; higher education in Prussia;

-- Biblical battles; origin of the Oxford (aka serial) comma; common surnames of the time; geographical knowledge and exploration; world's hottest countries; afternoon tea menus in America; hunger in the Revolutionary War; farm chores by season; availability of glass in windows; signs of a blizzard; spring blizzards; school prayer; Christmas traditions; how to hang candles on a Christmas tree; Lent and Easter observances; Hebrew blessings; availability of coconuts; availability of olive oil; details of Catholic mass; midnight mass; extent of prohibition of married female teachers; birth control;

-- contents of the Nebraska Constitution; Catholic settlement in Nebraska; railroad lines in Nebraska; flowers growing in Poland and in Nebraska and comparable climates; soil types in southeastern Nebraska; the typical size of farms in Nebraska; shrubs common in eastern Nebraska; which meal was eaten at midday; the history of beef jerky; history of closets; observance of the Sabbath; Catholic versus secular law; Catholic beliefs and practices, including similarities and differences between Protestant and Catholic beliefs; Catholic teaching concerning marriage;

-- where bonnets were worn and when removed; who wore lorgnettes; handshake customs; child employment; letter writing etiquette; teacher training; "normal schools" (teacher's colleges) in various cities; newspapers in various cities; 19th century obituaries in newspapers; spelling of "theatre" versus "theater"; availability of indoor plumbing; and the 19th century precursor to electrolyte drinks (haymaker's punch).

If any reader would like to see the sources on which I relied for how I handled these topics, please email me at kawyle@att.net and ask me!

Acknowledgments

As always, I made extensive use of Wikipedia, and made innumerable searches on Google Ngram Viewer to avoid anachronistic word usage, also occasionally consulting the Online Etymology Dictionary. I consulted Goodreads lists for some of the books various characters read or were given.

Cheryl Adams, Reference Specialist, Researcher and Reference Services Division of the Library of Congress, helped me gauge the likelihood of a barn raising or its equivalent (adding a room to a house) taking place on a Sunday, and provided information about the restrictions on married and/or pregnant female teachers. Meg Metcalf and Regina Frackowiak, Reference Librarians from the Library of Congress, provided me a wealth of detail about the availability and acquisition of Polish and other foreign language books. So did Wookjin Cheun, Librarian for Slavic and East European Studies, and Scott Phillip Libson, Assistant Librarian for Arts & Humanities, from Indiana University's Herman B. Wells Library, as well as personnel at The Polish Institute for Arts and Sciences of America in New York City. I also owe thanks to various participants on National Novel Writing Month's Reference Desk (one of the NaNoWriMo forums).

Blytha Ellis of the Adair County Historical Society disabused me of the incorrect assumption that Kirksville, MO residents would have been likely to have indoor plumbing in the 1870s. Jeff Kappeler, Director, Dodge County Historical Society/May Museum, and Jerry Kneifel and Cheri Schrader of the Platte County Museum did the same in reference to Fremont, NE and Columbus, NE respectively.

Indiana University reference librarian Anna Marie helped me find cities in the region with normal schools.

My uncle Arian Zarkower reminded me of the name of the town where the family arrived after moving to Canada from Poland (for use in the Author's Note).

My husband Paul Hager, always a fount of knowledge on matters historical, reminded me that the "common school" movement included an emphasis on teaching specifically Protestant values in schools. He also reassured me that I would find a solution to the corner in which I appeared to have painted myself, and reminded me of artist Johannes Vermeer's conversion to Catholicism, which gave me the key to that solution. And he made the suggestion that led me to discover Nebraska's constitutional prohibition on religious exclusions for teachers and students.

And last, but *very* far from least, I thank my invaluable beta readers: Maggie Scheck Geene, Danusha Goska, Steven Karel, Glenda Morris, and Wendy Teller.

About the Author

Karen A. Wyle was born a Connecticut Yankee, but eventually settled in Bloomington, Indiana, home of Indiana University. She now considers herself a Hoosier. She and her husband have two wildly creative adult offspring.

In addition to writing fiction (science fiction, fantasy, and historical romance), Wyle is an appellate attorney, photographer, and politics junkie. Her voice is the product of almost five decades of reading both literary and genre fiction. It is no doubt also influenced, although she hopes not fatally tainted, by her years of law practice. Her personal history has led her to focus on often-intertwined themes of family, communication, personal identity, the impossibility of controlling events, and the persistence of unfinished business.

Connect with the Author

Learn more about Karen A. Wyle by looking her up on her author website (http://www.KarenAWyle.com), Twitter (@KarenAWyle), Facebook (https://www.facebook.com/KarenAWyle), Goodreads (https://www.goodreads.com/kawyle), or her (rarely updated) blog, Looking Around (http://looking-around.blogspot.com/).

Like the book? Please tell readers! Online book reviews are enormously helpful — and old-fashioned word of mouth is terrific as well!

You can sign up for Wyle's monthly newsletter, which includes information about upcoming releases, insights into her writing process, and occasional extras (e.g. cover reveals, character art), and other book news at the newsletter sign-up link on Wyle's author website (see above).

www.ingramcontent.com/pod-product-compliance
Lightning Source LLC
Chambersburg PA
CBHW060934120726
47910CB00002B/326